Cry of Silence

ALSO BY DANIELLE THOMAS

Children of Darkness
Voices in the Wind

Danielle Thomas

Cry of Silence

MACMILLAN

First published 1995 by Macmillan

an imprint of Macmillan General Books
25 Eccleston Place London SW1W 9NF
and Basingstoke

Associated companies throughout the world

ISBN 0-333-59253-0

1 3 5 7 9 8 6 4 2

A CIP catalogue record for this book is available from the British Library

Typeset by CentraCet Limited, Cambridge
Printed by Mackays of Chatham PLC, Chatham, Kent

For my husband, Wilbur Smith, with love
which will last all the days of my life

and

For two new loves who have recently entered and
enriched my life, my daughter-in-law Debbie Schmidt
and my grandson, Cameron.

Acknowledgements

I wish to thank Dr Roger Melvill for his expertise and patience in guiding me through the intricacies of brain surgery, also his wife, Merle, who offered me the hospitality of their home in which to view videos of craniotomies.

Long ago in a place far away
The sky was as blue as the sea
And the sea was as blue as the sky
And the earth was green
And in love with them both.

KATMAI; THE MEANING of the word has been lost. Perhaps when the last glaciers of the Pleistocene epoch retreated, and the first Inuit came to hunt and fish in this area, the name meant the home of great brown bears. The place where the earth trembles. The land where mountains burst and weep fire.

The Alaskan Peninsula is one of the most seismically alive areas in the world. Here nature shows her terrible power as she pushes the Pacific plate northward under the North American continent, cracking the land and spewing up volcanoes.

Today, the six-letter word Katmai means peace and pristine snow-capped mountains, silence lying like mist over milky blue glacial lakes. It means a land webbed with the tracks of huge hunch-shouldered grizzlies. It means time to wonder at a sunset, to shiver to the howl of a wolf. Time to listen to your soul's cry of silence.

Katmai is the world when it was young and man was innocent.

Chapter One

THE CLAWS, sharp and curved as butcher's hooks, were pitted and stained to the colour of old ivory. They dug deep into the still writhing salmon. Rivulets of blood stained the silver sockeye to the rich red it would have become had it spawned.

Swiftly the grizzly bear peeled back and swallowed the oil-rich skin. It ripped out the roe and brains, both delicacies. It turned the twenty-pound salmon over to fillet it, then it paused and lifted its long snout into the wind. Its eyes, brown and close-set, stared into the tall grass and tangled elder shrubs lining the river-bank, but excellent eyesight was not one of the animal's attributes. It relied on its superb sense of sound and smell. Once again it lifted its snout into the wind and sniffed. It shook its massive head in annoyance and dropped the half-eaten salmon. Within moments, one and a half thousand pounds of bear slid silently into the dense undergrowth leaving only a mist of rising insects to mark its passing.

The grizzly was old and dominant. He had clawed his way through many a bloody fight over the years for the right to mount a female. During the long daylight hours of the short Alaskan summer his claws dug deep into the tundra and stony river banks grubbing for roots and berries to supplement his rich diet of fish. It was always a race to fill his huge frame and put on the fat he needed to withstand the long Alaskan winter, when the ground was frozen and blanketed in snow and winds of up to fifty miles per hour added a chill factor to the temperatures trembling at −30°.

The bear stopped in an elder thicket and stood as still as a held breath, listening and again testing the wind for the sour smell of humans. An eddy rustled the silver-green leaves. Again he swayed his huge head from side to side in anger. He wanted to eat his salmon, stretch out on his day-bed of trampled grass beside the river and sleep until the rumbling of his stomach reminded him to once again wade into the icy water below the rapids. There he would stand for hours to catch the salmon, glistening as if plastered with silver sequins, as they twisted and turned in the air in their desperate attempt to jump the falls and continue their hazardous journey from the sea upstream.

'Whoa, bear.' A voice deep and authoritative rang out and echoed through the riverine thickets. The bear resisted the urge to move deeper into the brush, further away from the hated sound. His salmon lay on a rotting heap of discarded fish bones. It was now black with insects, delicately sipping the blood and fresh juices. The grizzly would not move far. He would guard his food. His bulk blended and faded into the dark shadows of the brush. He stood motionless as the people he had smelled approached.

Hank Butler folded his hefty six-foot frame in half as he shouldered his way through the stunted branches of willow, opening a path for the fishing clients stumbling behind him. He swatted ineffectually at the dense clouds of 'no-see-ums' which rose up and swirled dark as storm clouds from the grass as he flattened the tufts beneath his heavy wading boots. The pale sun stood high in the bleached autumn sky.

He was uncomfortable in the thick thermal waders he wore. They protected him from the numbing waters tumbling down from the glaciers and snowfields in the high mountains, but they rapidly became as hot as a sweatsuit when he left the water to avoid the rapids and struggled along the overgrown bear paths lining the banks.

Perspiration ran from beneath his black fishing cap and trickled into his beard. It was the deep amber red of tundra lichens at the end of summer. His eyes were the ever changing green and browns of the Alaskan rivers he loved so passionately. They were set deep into skin creased by squinting into the clear Alaskan rivers searching for fish. A thin white scar cradled his right eye, a reminder of an encounter with a yearling grizzly, when he had been an eager but inexperienced apprentice fishing guide. The accident happened when, attracted, like many young American kids, to one of the last great wildernesses on earth, he was working his first summer in America's forty-ninth state. Even though the confrontation had taken place twenty years before, he still rubbed the scar when he was worried.

Hank changed his fishing rod over to his left hand and wiped the palm of the free hand across his chest, smearing insects into streaks on the deep blue thermal waders. He stopped in the middle of the track, which had been pounded into mud by bears patrolling the river-banks on constant watch for salmon.

Hank had since developed both respect and fear for the grizzlies which roamed the hills and rivers of the three-million acre Katmai Wilderness Bear Reserve. The other three guides at Black Legs Fishing Lodge swore that during the fight with the young grizzly Hank's blood had mingled with that of the bear and it had made him half-bear. He seemed to sense the presence of the dangerous creatures long before they were visible.

As Hank waited for the stragglers in his fishing party to catch up, he readied himself to warn them yet again that they must keep close together when walking along the banks. He took off his cap and ran his fingers through his thick hair which now curled damply on his scalp. Within minutes he was slapping at his head and cursing as black sox and white legs homed in and stung his exposed damp skin. Reaching into the pouch set up high on his waders, he pulled out a spray can of Deet. Screwing his eyes tightly closed he sprayed his head. He coughed and wiped his mouth with the back of his hand as the fumes scraped his nostrils and throat.

Sorry about the ozone layer, he apologized silently as he sprayed his neck, but these Alaskan bugs need tough treatment.

He waited a few seconds for the fumes to clear, jammed his cap back onto his head and cautiously opened his eyes. The two fishermen in the party were now standing close to him, waving their arms and fishing-rods like semaphore flags in a hopeless attempt to ward off the insects. But the girl was nowhere to be seen.

'Where's Kit?' asked Hank.

'She was behind us, way back,' answered Leroy.

During the few days they had spent together Hank had learned that Leroy Sullivan, a West Coast American, was as quick to anger as he was to laugh. He was short and dark and boasted of Irish ancestry going back to the days of the devastating potato crop failure in Ireland when millions of starving Irish fled to the United States. Many were to prosper and reach the highest positions of authority in the country. Leroy was rich and had substituted money for manners and politeness. Hank found it difficult to like him, but he reminded himself he was not employed to like the clients, only to ensure that they caught fish and enjoyed the experience.

The two men stood swatting insects, looking back along the empty path.

'When fishing in bear territory you must all keep close together,' warned Hank wearily. 'I've told you guys before that these grizzlies may be big, but when they settle down to sleep in the brush you'll walk on top of them before you see them. A grizzly who is suddenly awakened is ugly and mean, worse than a drunk with a three-day hangover. One swipe of that arm will take your head off.' Seeing their faces set with annoyance at being reprimanded and remembering that they paid a large portion of his salary, Hank smiled to soften his lecture.

'Kit!' he bellowed and his voice echoed her name across the water.

'Women,' he muttered softly. Leroy smiled and immediately the three men were once again in accord.

The cracking of elder branches and a string of un-ladylike oaths heralded the approach of Kit. She was almost as tall as Hank with the slim muscular body of a young boy. Her brown waders hung around her slim hips in folds and were belted tightly into her waist. Where the California sun had kissed her face she wore brown badges of freckles. Her bobbed hair was tied in a thick pony-tail and hung out of the back of her fishing cap. Her eyes were so pale a blue that at times they seemed as silver as the salmon. Now they were flashing and annoyed.

'Damn river-bank,' she said as she strode up to the men. 'One needs to be a grizzly to push through this stuff.' She scratched at the red lumps on her neck where the white sox had settled and sucked. 'Much easier to wade the river. No bugs there,' she taunted, looking at Hank.

'Yeah,' agreed Earl, looking up at Kit appreciatively. 'Those river stones, round and unstable as balls, are bad but they certainly sound a better deal than this.' He slapped at his neck, leaving red weals on his skin. The insects merely did a quick circuit and landed back on his skin.

Hank glared at Kit and bit down on his lower lip in annoyance. As the cook at the lodge she had heard the guides discuss the inadvisability of bringing clients back from the first day's fishing aching and irritable. She knew that they must slowly ease the fishermen, many of them desk-bound wealthy businessmen from the States, into the rigours and routine of fishing, making it easy and pleasant for them, ensuring they would return the following season.

She knew Hank never made fishermen who had recently arrived at the lodge spend the day wading in the glacial waters. It was exhausting work stumbling over slippery rocks. Thighs trembled and calves cramped, as unused muscles had to stand firm against the buffeting of the currents.

'Kit!' he warned, before reassuring the men that the path they were on was far easier to manage than that particular stretch of the river, above the falls, where the rocks were rounded over the centuries by the river. They rolled smooth and slippery as giant eggs beneath felt-soled wading boots. The current had gouged out man-traps where it split into fans of white foam to by-pass the huge black rocks which fenced off the rapids.

'Let's hit the trail,' said Hank, 'and remember, we keep close together. All of us,' he added, looking at Kit. The men chuckled, suddenly close as brothers in the eternal battle against women.

'You'd probably find it easier if you carried your rod with the tip pointing backwards,' Leroy advised Kit. The small bear bell he wore on the peak of his fishing cap rang out thinly as he swung to face her. 'It doesn't hook up in the branches as much.' There was a long pause. Watching Kit's fingers tighten on her rod, Hank waited for it to break.

'Thank you,' she said finally, her words icy as the water tumbling over the rocks beside them. Hank turned away and walked along the track before he allowed himself to smile.

Kit was the fifth daughter in a family whose father owned a chain of fishing lodges. He was an avid fisherman and travelled across the country fishing both summers and winters. He was determined that if nature denied him a son then his last-born would out-fish any man in the country.

Kit satisfied all his dreams. Not only did she win most of the fishing contests she entered but she had inherited her father's passion for the rivers and fish. She was extremely knowledgeable on all fresh-water fish.

She had discovered Alaska eight years previously. She now worked as a cook in the Black Legs Lodge for the thrill on her days off of fishing the waters of the world's last great wilderness to catch the legendary trout.

They were deep bellied, from the diet of salmon eggs found in the rich salmon-spawning beds. Strong as salmon, due to fanning into the powerful currents, and amazingly large, as Katmai Reserve practised a catch and release programme.

Kit seldom went out to fish when the guides had clients but as they were still waiting for the arrival of another couple from England she had persuaded Hank to include her in the day's outing.

Hank found it difficult to deny Kit anything when she lay beside him on his narrow bunk in the early hours of the morning, waiting for the alarm clock to tear them apart and send her rushing into the kitchen to whip up a breakfast of syrup waffles and sausages with crumbling blueberry muffins for the fishermen.

Their early platonic friendship was based on a respect for each other's extensive knowledge of fishing and had drifted easily into a sexual one. Both had healthy appetites and, thrown into each other's company for six months of the year in a lodge set deep in the isolation of the enormous reserve, it was inevitable that they would explore each other's bodies as well as their minds.

Hank had made it clear that he had no desire for a permanent relationship. He wanted complete freedom to fish the rivers of the world. At first Kit agreed, she certainly did not wish to sit at home waiting for a husband who spent twelve months of the year fishing, but recently, surrounded by photographs of her sister's children, the thought of a baby Hank or a little Kit had become attractive.

Leroy's advice on the correct way to carry a fishing rod still rankled. She was silently composing cutting retorts to embarrass him when Hank stopped abruptly. As Leroy and Earl bumped into each other, Kit smiled.

They would make a good comedy act, for Earl was as large and heavy as Leroy was small and light, as pallid as Leroy was dark. His bullet head was bald and Leroy's black curls hung down to his collar. Earl seemed to find joy in almost everything and his deep-bellied laugh rumbled and echoed across the water whether he hooked or lost a trout, whereas Leroy's humour went back to his ancestors. He seemed to trail his coat behind him, waiting for someone to step on it so that he could start an argument or a fight.

Kit stepped out of the track as the tip of Leroy's rod swung past her face. The fly had been loosely hooked into the fishing eyelet and flashed past her eyes, bright and light as a dragonfly.

She was about to give advice on fishing etiquette when she saw Hank's shoulders stiffen as the track opened into a large patch of trampled grass. Hank stared down at a footprint larger than his wading boot imprinted into the mud. The sharp claw marks pierced deep into the path had not yet filled with water.

'What is it?' wavered Leroy.

Hank was silent, listening and staring into the brush.

'Ssh,' said Earl, then broke off as Kit joined them.

'What except the Abominable Snowman has that sort of footprint?' asked Earl as he looked at the huge fresh spoor in the path.

'A big one,' said Hank soberly, staring into the brush. He realized that even allowing for the spread in the soft mud due to the bear's weight, it was still a very large bear.

'Ah, a grizzly's day-bed,' said Kit, looking at the circle of flattened grass hoping to scare Leroy.

Leroy whistled to show unconcern about the unseen bear.

'Whistles and bells often attract bears,' said Kit. 'They think it may be some kind of prey.'

Leroy swallowed and was silent. Kit watched happily as he unclipped the tinkling bear bell from his hat and tucked it into his fishing vest.

'See the salmon he was eating.' She kicked at it with her boot and stepped back as a black cloud of buzzing insects netted her face.

'Don't,' said Hank sharply. Kit looked at Hank's set face. His fingers nervously pinched the scar. She stepped back rapidly from the salmon and away from the day-bed. 'We've interrupted its meal,' said Hank as he rubbed the scar under his eye. 'I can feel and smell it. The bear is very close. Don't interfere with its food.'

The grizzly watched them. His eyes seemed to cross as he saw Kit move away. Muscles bunched and rippled his coat. Dark as the shadows in the deep thicket, he readied himself to tear into the intruders and defend his catch.

Hank turned and his boots sank deep into a pile of bear scat, dark and nobbled with undigested berries.

'Come,' he commanded as he brushed through the tangled grass. He had no need to warn them to stay close.

'Whoa, bear,' Hank called once again. They were silent and pale as they walked quickly away. The mud made obscene sucking sounds as it clung to and then released their boots.

The grizzly waited for the last muddy squeak to fade before he lumbered slowly to his day-bed. Once he was certain they had gone he checked the trampled grass and sniffed the ground. For a while he stood over his fish indecisively, listening to the crack of branches and soft oaths as the party hurried away down the bear track.

Kit looked back over her shoulder. The grass fronds had woven together again on the light breeze. Fear tickled an icy finger down her spine as she imagined the grizzly, huge and silent, following them, invisible except for the movement of the seed heads in the grass.

The tempting smell of flesh and blood eventually overcame the bear's desire to follow the intruders and he hunched down over his salmon. He ripped into the remaining fillet and swallowed it, as quickly as a dose of bitter medicine, still peering suspiciously from time to time down the river path. Finally he turned round and round on the flattened grass looking for a comfortable place to lie down, but he was restless and irritable. The near encounter with the humans had upset him. He growled softly to himself as he forwent the pleasure of a few hours' sleep out of the wind.

He followed the track taken by the fishing party for a while, testing the wind and sniffing at the tall grasses which had brushed their legs. Finally satisfied that they had left the area he turned back down the path and suddenly swung his huge body into a concealed creek. It had once been a bear track leading to the water. Over the years the swirling current and the weight of the bears had worn the path down to the level of the river. It was now one of the many muddy traps into which unwary fishermen floundered.

The heavy heads of the river grass garlanded the old bear. He looked soft and cuddly as a child's fluffy toy as he waded into the water. The river opened on either side of him leaving a wake of churning white water. He stood firm and dark as a rock as he tested the current before plodding downstream to the rapids.

The dominant old bear was an impressive sight as he waded in the icy waters pausing occasionally to swat at an elusive trout or salmon. He had gorged on fish all summer and his coat, which in spring hung as loosely on his frame as a reject fur at a jumble sale, now shone rich as mink in the sunlight and stretched tightly across his huge sloping shoulders.

The waters deep and clear belied the strength of the current as it raced to tumble over the rapids.

The old bear cut across the undertow and clambered back up onto the river bank. His wet fur hung beneath his belly and combed the mud, but he looked no smaller with his fur plastered to his body than he had when it was dry. He shook himself and the delicate grass heads bent low beneath the shower. His hair, brown with grizzled white tips, haloed him like an Afro wig. He lifted his head. His snout seemed very long as he raised it to the sky. Suddenly his dignified amble gave way to a shambling run. Like most large animals he covered a tremendous distance whilst appearing to be doing a clumsy trot.

Hank stopped as they reached the rapids and surveyed his subdued group. Kit had stopped telling the two men terrifying and totally untrue stories about bears and man-eating moose and now stood tall and still, as obedient as a schoolgirl called before the headmaster.

'We'll fish below the rapids,' said Hank, raising his voice to be heard. 'Keep on the look out for grizzlies, as they love fishing on the falls. If we are lucky we may see Submarine,' he added as he turned away.

'Submarine?' queried Earl, showing the first signs of interest he had displayed in anything since discovering the day-bed.

'He's a dominant old male,' Hank explained, 'probably twenty years old now and he's fished these rapids for the past ten years.'

'They call the brute Submarine,' broke in Kit, ignoring Hank's head shake to remain silent, 'because of all bears he's the only one who actually dives under water for his fish. The others pounce on the fish or swat at them.'

'Submarine has become a legend. He is the most successful bear fishing the rapids,' Hank went on.

'That's why he is so huge,' said Kit, rolling her eyes and puffing out her cheeks.

The fishermen laughed and Hank swallowed the admonishment he was about to give her. She had managed to lighten the mood.

Nevertheless he had no desire to return to the lodge with two men set on hiring the nearest float-plane to charter them away from grizzlies, to the safety of King Salmon, a cluster of fishing chalets and trailer homes on the Naknek River.

'Let's get on in there, then,' said Earl, suddenly eager to fish for the legendary Alaskan trout.

'Yeah, let's rip their lips out,' laughed Leroy.

Kit winced and Hank prayed that she would not allow her love of fishing the extraordinary trout to cloud her good sense.

'Oh, look,' she said in a sweet little girl voice. Hank breathed a sigh of relief as she changed the subject. 'Look at that lovely sow and cub at the top of the rapids.'

Hank snapped around and squinted up at the falls.

A blonde mother grizzly, the hairs of her pale honey coat tipped with silver, had edged her way across the granite outcrop and was standing hindquarters high on one of the water-washed rocks peering down the falls waiting for a salmon to leap up high enough for her to hook.

She did not have a good fishing spot. The choice sites were at the foot of the falls where the weaving sockeye milled like pools of spilled mercury before attempting again and yet again to thrust themselves up the river above the rapids. The blonde bear knew that the dominant males commanded the rocks bridging the foot of the falls and she kept well away.

Hank never enjoyed fishing the wide stretch of river below the falls when bears were on the rapids. He had nightmares of one of his clients not giving way to a bear quickly enough or inadvertently moving between a sow and her cubs.

It was difficult to explain to fishing clients that in the Katmai Reserve bears were royalty. One gave way to them. One broke off expensive fishing line and left the river speedily if bears became interested in the trout being played. Grizzlies were safe and protected. No firearms were allowed, though some guides now carried rifles with cracker rounds. Hank was convinced that the bears abused their privileged position and arrogantly chased fishermen out of the river merely to prove their dominance.

The men looked up at the falls, which had been devoid of animals a few minutes before, and they instinctively moved closer to Hank. The tumbling waters were now dotted with the blonde mother grizzly and her yearling cubs, plus two three-year-old cubs probably just weaned by the mother to fend for themselves.

'Whew, they're huge,' exclaimed Leroy, pointing to the three-year-olds.

'Must weigh all of ninety pounds,' said Kit, grinning impishly at Hank.

If these youngsters impress them, wait until they see a big one like Submarine, Hank thought to himself. They'll be up on top of that wooden viewing platform on the bank faster than I can cast a fly. He glanced up at the platform built high above the falls for tourists who visited the area to take photographs of the huge bears fishing.

'He sure is cute,' said Earl, pointing out the yearling cub, pale and fluffy as a dandelion head, standing on the bank mewing piteously to its mother. It longed to join her, but was too afraid to cross the stones, glassy and smooth as black and green marbles. The mother turned her head to look at her cub. She missed a salmon which flew past her like a thrown dart and sped upstream. She growled at her cub warning it to remain where it was and then turned her attention back to the falls.

'Yeah, cute,' said Hank, 'but make sure you never get within one hundred yards of a sow and her cubs. She'll accept you at that distance, any closer . . .'

'And you're dog's meat,' added Kit.

'She probably won't make it through the winter,' said Hank, studying the loose skin hanging from the blonde bear's shoulders.

'Poor girl has been trying to fish for herself and her cubs. She has been kicked out of all the decent fishing spots by the males,' said Kit.

'Now, no feminist speeches, thank you,' admonished Hank.

'See, even free speech is now a male prerogative.'

'And with good reason,' said Leroy, 'we have all the important things to say.'

Kit swatted viciously at some black legs which had found the soft skin beneath her pony-tail. Ugly red finger-marks stained her neck and Hank knew that they were meant for Leroy. She unclipped and retightened her belt while her breathing slowed and then she turned her attention back to the falls, ignoring Leroy.

The cub still sitting on the bank dangled its paw in the water. It felt the strength of the current and sat back in the grass mewing to its mother that it was alone and hungry.

The roar of the rapids drowned the huge grizzly's dash along the river-bank, but the two three-year-old cubs sensed him and quickly left the rapids to wade in the shallows below the falls. Their sudden departure alerted Hank and he looked around for the reason. Just then the old grizzly broke through the laced thickets and padded out towards his special platform beneath the first rapid.

The old bear saw Hank and the fishing group, recognized their smell and growled deep in his throat. But there were more pressing matters demanding his attention. Another bear, almost large and old enough to challenge him, was on his rock. Unlike the others he had not run away. Instead, as the big grizzly approached he bared his teeth.

'Oh no,' breathed Kit, 'the idiot is challenging Submarine.'

'So that's the famous Submarine,' said Leroy, feeling safe as he stood up on the bank looking down at the bears. He was quite unaware of the power and fury which would be unleashed if the large bears fought, or the danger they would be in. Two angry grizzlies would attack anything in the vicinity.

The great grizzly, Submarine, shouldered aside the force and weight of falling water as if it were no more than a summer shower. Thick creamy foam flew in streamers from his mouth as he rushed at the intruder. The challenger stood firm on the flat, slippery rock, his black lips pulled back high, exposing his long, yellowed teeth. The growling of the two bears rose deep and chilling above the thunder of the rapids.

There was a roar which prickled the hair on Hank's arms. Leroy and Earl, despite their thermal waders, were suddenly cold.

Hank glanced away from the two bears for a moment to judge how quickly he could get his group across to the ladder leading up to the viewing platform.

He missed the initial onslaught as Submarine cannoned into the intruder. The challenger's back legs slipped off the rock with the force of the charge. He hung on the rock with his front legs desperately trying to scramble back. But the great grizzly gave him no chance.

He threw himself onto the hapless bear. Teeth which had recently delicately filleted a salmon tore into the challenger's neck ripping out a chunk of flesh. The flesh tumbled down the falls and the challenger followed it. He had lost all desire to fight. He waded across the river and into the swampland leaving the coveted rock to the victor.

Submarine watched his erstwhile adversary shamble away leaving a trail of pink blood to mark his passage. He roared his defiance and victory. His small eyes were mean and dark as he studied the falls but there was no one he could chase. All the bears had vanished except the young mother who still sat at the head of the falls trying to impale a salmon for her cub.

The battle between the two huge male grizzlies alarmed her. She barked soft instructions for her cub to remain where it was. Her instincts told her to leave the area and get her offspring well away from the angry males, but termination dust already lay lightly on the mountains, the soft snowfall warning all that winter was approaching. She knew that both she and her cub needed more food if they were to survive the sub-zero temperatures. Hunger overrode her fear and desire to flee to safety as she teetered on the polished rocks waiting for a salmon to succeed in jumping the rapids and come within reach of her claws.

Submarine glanced up at her but she was well out of his territorial domain and posed no threat.

'Up,' said Hank, shepherding Leroy and Earl towards the ladder.

'But . . .' started Leroy.

'Move it,' snapped Kit, clipping him across the shoulders with the butt of her rod, 'unless you'd like to meet up with that wounded bear, who'll be going mad once the bugs get onto his raw neck and start sucking the blood.'

Leroy swallowed back his retort about staff striking guests and his short legs took the wooden steps two at a time.

Hank squeezed Kit's hand and he mouthed her a kiss as he bent down to help her up the ladder and onto the platform.

'He's still not happy,' said Hank, looking across to where Submarine paced the flat rock growling and swaying his head.

'Take him some time to settle down now that his blood's up. We'll stay here for a while.'

'Our lunch?' queried Earl.

'It's up in the cache near the fish-cleaning hut,' said Kit. She looked at Earl's stomach stretching the seams of his waders.

'You can't be hungry yet. Those honey waffles and sausages I made for breakfast must still be in your belly.'

'Don't count on it. It's taken years to grow this belly and it needs constant refuelling to keep it going,' guffawed Earl, patting his stomach.

'You could always climb down and walk along the river bank,' said Kit, 'but you will be well within view and reach of Submarine. I must warn you in his present mood he'll probably chase and kill anything that moves.'

'What do you do if a bear chases you?' queried Leroy, suddenly interested at the thought of an encounter between Earl and the grizzly.

'Don't run,' said Hank. 'Like most predators they'll chase anything that runs.'

'You mean you stand and watch that thing coming for you and you don't do anything?'

'Curl up into a ball, hands crossed behind your neck to protect your head, and pretend you're dead.'

'And pray hard,' said Kit. 'With luck he'll give you a bite or two and then leave you.'

'You'd be OK,' said Earl to Leroy. 'Curled up into a ball the bear would think you're a small lump of scat and walk over you.'

He bellowed at his joke and his eyes closed into slits in his broad fleshy face.

Hank and Kit couldn't resist laughing. Leroy scowled and they waited for his outburst but unexpectedly he smiled as he saw the humour of being mistaken for a lump of bear dung.

'You wouldn't be that lucky,' he retaliated. 'Submarine could stop fishing for a week if he had you in his belly. Probably enough fat to see him through two winters.'

'Wouldn't mind something in my belly,' said Earl again, watching Submarine pace up and down the rock slab.

'In this area we don't carry rucksacks with us. Those bears can smell a wrapped candy bar tucked into a back pocket at a hundred yards,' said Hank. 'We always stack our rucksacks and food in high caches well out of reach of the bears.'

'When everything has quietened down here we'll probably be able to go and have lunch at the cache,' said Kit, comforting Earl.

'She's not having any luck,' said Leroy, looking up at the blonde sow.

The cub, waiting for its mother to return to the bank with a salmon, gnawed at the grass then mewed again, but louder. He was hungry and had not yet learned to catch the fast salmon. They had lived for most of the summer on sockeye which had already spawned, turned red and were dying, their bodies leprous and obscene as they wallowed helplessly in the river.

Suddenly the blonde bear shot out her paw and her claws impaled and held fast a salmon. She sat down on a rock with the spray washing over her and tore off and swallowed a piece of the rich flesh before turning to carry the rest back to her cub. When the cub saw its mother eating the fish it begged piteously for a share.

Just as she turned to head back to the bank with the salmon dripping like a silver moustache down either side of her mouth, the cub launched itself from the bank onto the first rock. It misjudged the distance. As the mother dropped the salmon and rushed to drag her cub from the water the current caught and tumbled the small bear down the rapids. The mother screamed her fear at the top of the falls and lumbered through the water from one rock to another, frantic to reach her cub, but unable to get down the rapids.

The great grizzly looked up at the blonde sow rushing backwards and forwards across the rocks then turned his attention to the cub being swept down towards him. He launched himself from his fishing platform, vanished beneath the swirling waters and emerged a few minutes later with a small sodden brown body held firmly in his mouth.

'Oh, let the cub have drowned,' breathed Kit as the fishing party, still as waxwork figures, watched the bear.

'Great guy that Submarine, he saved the little chap,' said Earl with a smile. The smile faded as the cub screamed in terror for its mother. Then all was silent as the grizzly sank his teeth deep into the cub's skull.

Submarine squatted on his rock and slowly disembowelled the cub, savouring the flesh as he would a firm salmon. He discarded the tiny paws and the bony section of the skull but carefully stripped all the meat from the body. He let the skin float away down into the shallows. Only the tumbling of the waters and the call of gulls eager for the scraps of meat broke the silence.

The sow, too young to confront a dominant male, howled out her anger and anguish. She fled across the falls and into the thick brush on the opposite bank tearing and ripping at everything in her way.

Hank listened to the roars and crack of breaking branches then turned to his party still staring in horror at the bloodstained waters where the small brown skin floated slowly downstream.

'While the mother is still on the bank and Submarine is on his rock let's get out of here.'

'But we're safe up on the platform,' quavered Leroy, his tanned skin now pale and grey.

'Not when she comes over to this side,' said Hank. 'Remember, we have to be at the lake for the float-plane to collect us at six.

'We'll radio from the lodge and see if they can come in earlier. There will be no fishing here for days. They'll probably close the place down until the blonde bear comes to terms with her grief and the loss of her cub.'

'But what about our fishing?' said Leroy.

Hank sighed and looked at Kit, who raised her dark eyebrows. He could hear her mocking him as she said, 'This is not the end of the season, bud. You still have another five weeks to go and new clients to deal with.'

'Well,' said Hank, 'we could fish this stretch of the river right now, Leroy, and have the mother cross the shallows onto our side, desperate to punish someone for the loss of her cub. We could also have Submarine come down to tackle the mother. She is young, thin and poses no threat to him. If he killed her as well he wouldn't have to fish for days.'

'We would probably end up as the cub did,' added Kit, pointing her rod to where the cub's skin had caught in a clump of reeds.

The current had turned it over and it wallowed mottled pink and white in the shallows, shining obscenely in the pale sun, attracting the gulls who fought raucously as they stripped off the pieces of fat and flesh left by Submarine.

Leroy swallowed and turned away from the feasting gulls.

'I'll take up the rear,' offered Kit.

'Great girl,' said Hank, thanking her for taking up the dangerous and isolated position at the end of the line.

Quickly they scrambled down the ladder looped together as closely as the segments of a centipede. As they hurried along the bear track they all called 'Whoa, bear,' in various tones of fear. They were eager to alert any bears made nervous by the roaring fight and the distraught screams of the blonde sow that they were merely fishermen and harmless.

The path seemed endless and the wading boots were more cumbersome than usual as they hooked under moss-covered roots and sank into mud holes hidden beneath the trampled grass.

The great grizzly, dark and ugly as death, sat hunched on his fishing platform. His stomach was pleasantly full and he was enjoying the sunshine. Occasionally he swatted idly at a salmon, not really interested in diving for them. Suddenly he stiffened and stretched his long nose up high into the wind towards the track winding along the river-bank.

A low growl rumbled up from his belly as he smelt the rank odour of Hank's party. He shook out his coat and the water circled his body in spinning hoops of diamond drops.

Kit looked back at the falls to make sure that no bear was on the trail behind them. She saw Submarine backlit by water which the sun had cut into a million facets of sparkling brilliance. Suddenly the monster bear became a magnificent wild creature, adhering only to the laws of nature.

She realized that he was part of this great harsh natural wilderness. This small section of the planet not yet tamed and desecrated by man. She knew that they should not judge and condemn him. This subdued her feelings of abhorrence, but did not dispel her fear.

She watched Submarine pad over the rocks spanning the rapids and climb out onto the bear track. As he walked upstream back to his day-bed and away from them, she hurried to catch up with Earl.

The old grizzly yawned as he shouldered his way through the tangled elder bushes and thick tall grass. His lips were still stained dark red. He found his old day-bed, circled it suspiciously, then finally relaxed and lay down, his bulk merging and vanishing into the thicket like a shadow at midday.

Kit breathed a sigh of relief as the track opened out and she saw the river pouring into the huge soft blue lake. 'We turn right to collect our lunch from the cache or left for the lodge and the game wardens,' she said. 'What's it to be?'

'Left,' answered Leroy and Earl with the perfect unison of practised actors.

Hank took her arm as they reached the pebbled shoreline. The lake lay spread between the hills like a sheet of watered silk. Earl and Leroy hurried on ahead to the huts and the safety offered by civilization. She's a great companion, a gutsy girl and does not want any permanent ties. I'm lucky to have her, thought Hank as the small pebbles on the shore crunched beneath the felt soles of his boots.

Looking up at Hank striding beside her and comparing him with the two city men ahead, Kit knew that she now definitely wanted more from him than friendship and a casual sexual relationship. She was determined to get it.

Chapter Two

THE BOEING, smart in its new coat of grey, navy and burgundy, flew on towards the polar ice-cap. The 747-235 had been built to carry and cosset three hundred and seventy-three passengers. This flight was routed to fly over the North Pole itself, to check all inertial navigation systems. Four seats had been removed to fit in a polar pack with extra survival equipment in case the plane had to make a forced landing on the ice cap. The crew took great pleasure in informing the passengers that in almost twenty-four years they had never had to use the emergency polar pack equipment.

It was a long nine-hour flight from Heathrow to Anchorage over the Pole. The passengers found it boring, as at thirty-five thousand feet there was little to see from the windows.

The flight attendant in first class had been on duty for eight hours and was longing to slip out of her uniform and relax in a hot bath in a hotel in Anchorage. She hoped it would help her to adjust to having an early lunch when her body told her it was dinner time. Flying from east to west was the route most of them hated as it took days for the body's internal time clock to adjust to a time difference of almost nine hours. She shifted her weight onto her right foot and carefully eased her sensible court shoe from her left. She wriggled her toes in relief and then hurriedly slipped her foot back into the shoe, smoothed down her red and navy striped dress and tucked a stray blonde ringlet back into her French plait.

'Imperious young one, isn't she?' the senior male cabin attendant remarked, looking at the passenger who was snapping her arm backwards and forwards in the air.

'Paid a first-class fare and is probably getting her money's worth,' answered his colleague.

She smiled ruefully at the chief cabin attendant and walked down the aisle to where the young woman was still holding her arm up.

'Yes, ma'am?' she queried.

'What?' said the young woman, looking away from the tiny television screen, set in the armrest of her reclining chair.

'You beckoned, madam. Is there anything I can do for you?'

Catherine Ticasuk Chargot, known to her friends in London as Casey because her parents could not decide whether to spell Catherine with K or a C when they registered her birth, dropped her arm hurriedly and a deep pink flushed her throat and cheeks.

'Oh, I'm sorry,' she said, pushing down the off button on the television control set. 'I was practising casting. Fly casting,' she added, seeing the look of incomprehension on the woman's face.

'You see,' she tried to explain, 'he makes it look so easy and beautiful.' Casey pointed to the now blank television screen. 'Fishing,' she added lamely, conscious of the amused stares from the couple across the aisle. 'We're going fishing and I was just practising.'

'Of course, madam,' said the attendant.

'She's fishing,' she said in reply to the cabin steward's mute query. He raised his eyebrows and pushed back the starched white cuff of his shirt.

'Almost six o'clock London time. We ought to feed them, take their minds off the next hour or so before we touch down in Anchorage.'

'I'm pleased it's not winter there yet,' said the attendant as they prepared the trolley. 'They say you die a thousand deaths coming in to land. The winds throw this 747 around like a scrap of paper in a gale. A friend of mine swears she'll resign rather than fly this route again in winter.'

She rolled out one of the trolleys, neat as a filing cabinet, with plates of sandwiches and canapés for the passengers.

'Let's see if the pretty passenger will settle for a smoked salmon sandwich and give fly casting a rest,' the cabin steward mused.

'Pretty?' echoed the blonde attendant. 'Do you really find her pretty?'

'Marvellous eyes,' he answered. 'Waking up with them beside you would be better than a holiday at the seaside. To say nothing of her superb superstructure?'

'You men,' answered the attendant, pretending to be angry. 'You seldom get your thoughts above your belts.'

He grinned as they fixed the required smiles on their faces and manoeuvred the trolley down the aisle.

'Casey Chargot,' said her companion with a smile as he carefully folded up the pink pages of the *Financial Times* and leaned forward to tuck it into the seat pocket in front of him.

'You have now confused the entire staff of British Airways. They will think I have a "funny bunny" with me, not an intelligent, attractive young lady whom I hope to marry at the end of the year.'

'Dursley,' said Casey, her neck still washed pink with humiliation, 'I am sorry. I wasn't thinking. I forgot we were in a plane. This film is tremendous and I was carried away. I am truly sorry if I embarrassed you.'

Dursley Carrington put his hand over hers. His long tapered fingers soothed her, as he stroked her hand and arm.

'I haven't seen the film but I read the book before we left London and thoroughly enjoyed it. A gentle story of a man's love of fishing. You have nothing to worry about, Bubbles. I have been assured by Stewart Saunders who owns the lodge that Hank Butler will be our guide. "Old Bob" swears the man is more fish than human. He thinks like a fish. His clients always catch the largest rainbows in the area.'

'Will we be the only two with him?' asked Casey, praying that there would be no other fishermen in the party to watch and mock her as she struggled with tangled lines.

'No, we will be fishing in a party of four.'

'Oh,' said Casey despondently.

'It's going to be all right, Casey. Patience is one of Hank Butler's great virtues. You'll be a great fisher-lady at the end of the trip.'

'Can we offer you something to eat, sir?' asked the attendant, bending over Dursley with a bright smile. Dursley kept his hand over Casey's as he felt her stiffen with embarrassment.

'Why not?' he answered. 'You seem to have fed us constantly since we left Heathrow. I suppose even Strasbourg geese eventually enjoy being force-fed.' The hostess laughed and filled a plate with an assortment of canapés for him.

She had liked the tall, dishevelled Englishman when he first boarded the plane and had given a small sigh of resignation when the girl took up the seat beside him. The sparkle of the square diamond covering the fourth finger of her hand left no doubt about their relationship.

'Why do all the good-looking ones get hooked so fast?' the attendant whispered to her friend as they smiled and mouthed a welcome to the boarding passengers.

'And usually by the short plain Janes,' her friend had answered, studying Casey as she stood waiting for Dursley to remove his jacket before sitting down.

'Plain Jane' is not how Dursley Carrington would have described his fiancée. Casey barely tipped five foot two inches. Her over-ample breasts would have been more suited to someone with a six-foot frame, and her waist seemed tiny in comparison. Her rounded but shapely hips completed the hour-glass figure. She gave the impression of firmness and strength and carried her small body with the grace of a ballet dancer. It was only when you looked into her eyes, brown and gold as a tiger-eye gem, and watched her mouth tilted up at the corners in a perpetual half smile, that her charm and attraction became apparent.

Dursley had never seen eyes so gentle yet sparkling with fun and the joy of living. He nicknamed her 'Bubbles', for whether he was tired, angry or sad, once his lips had tasted her smiling ones and he had looked into the constant laughter in her eyes he felt his troubles melt away.

He could laugh with her. She was like a bubbling mountain stream. She was refreshment for the weary, he once told her at a polo-match in Windsor Great Park, shortly after they met. 'You make me sound like a bordello in some small Mid-western town,' she had replied, her eyes scanning the players as they cantered off-field to change ponies.

As the eldest son, Dursley had inherited the earldom on the death of his father. He was unaccustomed to attractive ladies ignoring him. Usually well primed by their mothers, they were over-attentive and all too easily available to the tousle-haired man in his early thirties. Casey's obvious love for her older brother who was a four-goal player for the opposing team, her love of horses and her knowledge of the game impressed Dursley. He pursued and courted this girl ten years his junior with the single-minded purpose he usually gave to polo.

Casey was not interested in marriage, nor in becoming a countess. Her family were wealthy but not titled and she was very happy working in the Antiquities section of Sotheby's. Dursley, however, was an attractive and strong-willed young man.

Thus, eight months after meeting him, she found herself preparing to become the sixth Countess of Edbury at a large society wedding in London at the end of the year. To escape the strain and tedium of the thousand and one things which had to be organized in advance to make the wedding memorable, and with the help of Sir Bob Franshaw, 'Old Bob', an ex-suitor of his mother, Dursley arranged a fishing trip to Alaska.

'Let them find us at a fishing lodge with all their questions and damn decisions to be made,' he laughed as he told Casey of his plans. Swallowing her dismay, she smiled bleakly at the thought of being cooped up for two weeks in some remote fishing lodge which could be reached only by float-plane. Fishing from dawn to dusk in the all-male company of experts alarmed her.

Dursley had laughed away her fears when she suggested a course of fly-casting lessons before the trip. 'You'll stun them all, Bubbles. It's easy. After all, they only use one-handed fly rods, not the big two-handed ones we use in Scotland.'

Casey wanted to remind him that he had fished the salmon rivers on the ancestral estate from the time he was out of nappies. What was easy to him was terrifying to her. Instead she lifted her face to be kissed and tucked away her fears. Watching the film on the plane had reawakened her doubts and anxiety. She knew that she would find it impossible to make the fly-line cry in the silence as it cut through the air forming perfect loops high behind, then swing forward in tight loops to rest the fly softly and perfectly near the trout. As she munched her smoked salmon, she wished that Dursley had chosen to hide in Bali or Tahiti where all she would have to do was swim and sleep in the sun.

'Penny for them,' said Dursley, watching Casey crumble the sandwich crusts and push them round the plate.

Casey thought quickly. 'I was thinking of the wedding,' she lied, to please him.

'It won't be long now, my little one, and you will be my wife, the Countess of Carrington. Then we can start work on producing a new generation to carry on the family name and traditions.'

He leaned across and kissed her lightly on the cheek, brushing aside a thick curtain of straight hair, black as her doubts and striking as her diamond ring. Casey smiled at him as he ran his fingers through the deep fringe which touched her straight, dark eyebrows. As he took his hand away the weight of her hair swung the fringe back and it looked as if it had been combed by the expert fingers of a hairdresser.

Her hair was the envy of her friends who longed for hair which swung from side to side like a short pendulum. But Casey longed for a head of soft red curls which would tumble round her shoulders and tickle her neck.

As she twirled the engagement ring on her finger, the diamond caught and held the cabin lights. It flashed a kaleidoscope of colours on the seat in front of her. She sighed and turned to Dursley, but he had relaxed the back of his chair, tucked a pillow under his head and closed his eyes.

She studied the man lying beside her as if he was a stranger. His sandy lashes were too long for a man; they shadowed his cheeks. His hair looked as if it had never been combed. Suddenly she wanted to cradle him in her arms, smooth down his wavy hair and kiss him softly on his eyelids, as her father had done to her when she was a child. She wanted to mother the man who was shortly to be her husband. There had been no *coup de foudre* when they met. Lightning had not streaked the sky. Instead there was an easy friendship which somehow ended with a proposal of marriage.

The thought of fitting into the lifestyle led by Dursley roused the same anxiety in Casey as did fly fishing. All his friends knew each other's family genealogies so well. They knew the correct way to dress, without rushing into Purdeys to ask whether breeks were in order if one was not actually shooting grouse. They joked about holidays shared and were rude about 'Old Bob' or James or Christopher, names Casey naïvely believed appertained to chums at Eton or Oxford. She soon realized to her embarrassment that they were earls, dukes and marquesses.

She had much to learn: whose families were traditional nobility and who were the 'nouveau riche'. Who had the names but no money and who had both names and money.

She had whispered the fears to Dursley early one morning but he had only mumbled, 'It really doesn't matter, Bubbles. What matters is that you are to be the new Countess of Carrington and we are really "old".' He had then buried his head in her warm breasts. The rest of his words were lost to her.

She had been swept into the vortex of excitement created by her friends when they heard she was to be a countess and she finally found the prospect of marrying into English nobility exciting.

It was only now in moments of silence, studying his face

closely, that she wondered what had happened to the knight on the white charger, who, as a young girl, she had believed would suddenly appear to sweep her off her feet in a whirlwind of passion, to live happily for ever.

Those were a child's dreams, she admonished herself. You are a very lucky woman. Dursley will make a wonderful husband. Your life will be filled with new and exciting experiences. And you do love him. Even if it's the sort of love that wants to mother and protect him, not tear his clothes off and keep him in bed beside you for a week.

Casey reached out and ran her fingertips softly over his closed eyelids. Dursley smiled but did not open his eyes. He was content. He had found the woman he wanted to marry and bear his children.

Pressure from his family for him to marry and settle down had relaxed, although his mother still made the occasional remark about Samantha, Lady Ogilvy's daughter, or Rebecca, Lady Freemantle's niece. She still felt the necessity of being able to trace blood lines back for hundreds of years, and remembered with horror the story of how great-grandfather Albert almost tainted the family blood line by bringing 'native' blood into the family, when at the age of seventy-four he announced that he was about to marry the Indian daughter of one of his Ghurkas. Fortunately the old man died before he could defile their pure stock. The dowager countess constantly reminded her children not to allow their tumbling hormones to overlook the blood line of the person they wished to bring into the family.

When Dursley first introduced Casey to the family, his mother had studied her round face and thick, straight black hair with some suspicion. 'Some oriental strain in there, Dursley,' she cautioned. But he assured her that Casey's family were as English as muffins and tea, that he had personally checked her antecedents. He breathed a sigh of relief when she nodded and dropped the subject.

*

Casey leaned over and kissed Dursley lightly on the mouth. Switching on the television set again, she was soon lost in the beauty and intricacy of fly fishing. She started as the screen suddenly went blank and a voice boomed in her earphones making her wince.

'Ladies and gentlemen, this is your captain speaking. Would you adjust your watches to Alaskan time. It is now five minutes past ten in the morning in Anchorage. We will be landing in twenty minutes. As we circle you will have a good view of Cook Inlet which was, of course, discovered by our own Captain Cook in his search for the elusive North-West Passage.

'Those of you who are familiar with the history of Alaska will know that he sailed on through the Bering Straits before being turned back by the polar pack ice. The British Admiralty prize for finding the North-West Passage went to Robert M'Clure, an unpopular decision at the time.'

'Garrulous, isn't he?' yawned Dursley as he ran his fingers through his hair and pressed the button in the armrest to raise the back of his seat. 'Probably bored. He's been stuck up there for nine hours and now faces the prospect of more boredom in Anchorage.' He grinned. 'The place jumped when the Exxon Company was flying in thousands to clean up the oil spill from the *Exxon Valdez*.'

'I read somewhere that they have now finally cleaned up all the oil and repaired the ecological damage,' said Casey.

'Surface oil has been mopped up, but the rest has crept under the rocks on the seabed. "What can't be seen, must be clean", seems to be the motto,' said Dursley cynically. 'The gangs have gone and Anchorage is left with empty hotels and shops with no customers. Our captain will be lucky if he finds any form of entertainment apart from fishing and hunting.' He yawned and stretched. '"Old Bob" visited the Great Alaskan Bush Company when he was here last year. Said it was good raw stuff with plenty of dirty local colour. But we know that Sir Bob Franshaw is becoming a dirty old man.'

'Great Alaskan Bush Company?' Casey smiled, once again

moving her engagement ring up and down in the shaft of sunlight to flash rainbow pinpricks of red, green and blue on the grey seats in front of her.

'It's a strip-club cum bar, rather rough but fun, according to Bob,' he answered. 'Not your sort of place at all, Bubbles.' He grinned.

'Yours?' she asked.

'I have you,' answered Dursley, neatly side-stepping the pitfall.

He lifted Casey's hand and kissed her fingertips. She smiled at him, a happy trusting smile. She looked back at her television screen but it was still blank so she closed her eyes and listened to the captain. He was either bored, as Dursley had suggested, or had visited Alaska often, loved it and wanted to share his knowledge of the huge land mass with his passengers. It lay as far north as any American could go and still stand on United States soil. Any American wishing to go further north would have to plunge into the Arctic Ocean and swim under the polar ice-pack to the North Pole.

'The Russians considered Alaska a worthless piece of wilderness, merely a continuation of Siberia. They sold it to America in 1867 for seven million dollars,' explained Dursley as he idly listened to the captain's voice. 'William Seward, the Secretary of State, had to work hard to persuade the Senate to purchase the place. For ages the public called it "Seward's Ice Box".'

'Why America?' asked Casey, her eyes still closed. 'I thought the Russians and Americans hated each other.'

'It was a strange set up,' answered Dursley. 'During the Crimean War, America for some strange reason backed Russia. In fact I think she was her only friend.

'In return, when the Yanks were killing each other off during the Civil War, the Russians sent fleets of warships to stand by. Russia was ready to help if Britain or France tried to move in and grab what was left of the country.'

Casey opened her eyes. 'Crazy world,' she said. 'Russia sold Alaska because she was certain it was worthless and had no minerals. They knew the fur trade was minimal as their traders had killed almost all the sea otters for their pelts. And anything else worth having. America buys the country then does a roaring trade in furs and to top it all at the end of the '60s finds the richest North American oilfields up at the top of Alaska.'

'So you do know some Alaskan history,' teased Dursley.

'I can also read,' retorted Casey. She listened with interest as Dursley continued talking about Alaska.

'Until the Berlin Wall came down and half the Eastern bloc with it. The Yanks had an early warning system and airbase up near Barrow. They needed to pick up any early signals of a possible nuclear strike against the States, by their erstwhile buddies the Russians,' continued Dursley. He yawned again.

'Anyway, we're here to fish and enjoy ourselves, not to worry about politics. Those trout had better be as good and large as "Old Bob" says they are. This is a damn long flight, I think my legs have gone to sleep.'

He stood up, moved into the aisle and stretched his arms up to the ceiling of the aircraft, then smoothly moved into a series of knee bends.

He caught the air hostess watching him as he bounced up from his sixth knee bend, and he smiled at her.

Casey lifted the grey window blind as Dursley sat down in response to the instructions to fasten their seat-belts. They were due to land in fifteen minutes.

'Oh, look,' she breathed. The plane was nearing Anchorage. The tide was going out and the flat wet sands of the shore reflected the steel-grey sky. They stretched in a wide shimmering rainbow of metallic greys and ivory. In the far distance rivers laced the green land, soft grey and gleaming white in the cold light of an Alaskan autumn day.

'Looks damn cold,' said Dursley, leaning across and peering over Casey's shoulder.

Casey did not respond. She was lost in the beauty of her first glimpse of Alaska. It was wild and desolate but somehow seemed familiar to her.

'It seems so untamed,' she said.

'Yes, they probably have more reserves here than we have land on our little island,' answered Dursley ruefully. 'An extra million acres was added to Katmai with the passage of ANILCA under the presidency of Jimmy Carter. Three and a half million acres were declared a wilderness area.'

'Imagine having all that land to give away as a reserve,' said Casey, impressed with the figures.

'Probably done to prevent the natives claiming all the land as being theirs traditionally,' he added cynically. 'It's the only good thing I can think of that came out of that Carter period.'

Casey did not answer. She had heard Dursley complain many times about the Native Land Claims Settlement passed in 1971 which gave natives in Alaska the right to claim back four million acres of land plus a lump sum of nine million dollars. As the owner of vast sporting estates which had been in his family for centuries, he was unimpressed with the new laws which allowed natives worldwide to reclaim traditional hunting rights and land.

'Put them in a plane and fly them over the country saying "Do you recognize this place?" Of course the native is going to say that great-grandpa killed a musk ox there when he was a young man.' Dursley snorted. 'And there goes another piece of prime land.'

Casey kept her nose pressed to the pane. Secretly, she favoured the natives' claims. They were the only ones who seemed able to live with the land. Unlike the Europeans they did not fight with the wilderness nor did they try to tame it.

She wanted to walk along these winding streams, peer into pools pock-marked into the land in an age when rocks embedded in the ponderous bodies of ice gouged out holes as they moved slowly towards the sea. This alien land called to her. It was a cry too strong to be ignored. This was a land tormented and formed by intense cold and cataclysmic volcanic eruptions. The gentle green fields of England seemed far away. She shivered, not only because of the harsh landscape unfolding far beneath the plane. She knew that the time was coming when she would have to tell Dursley the truth about her Eskimo blood.

This was a harsh and unforgiving land with soaring snow-covered mountains and icy winter winds which flayed the body as swiftly and keenly as a bear hunter's knife; a great silent land which tolerated only the strong and the brave. The weak soon learned that the land allowed only the cry of silence from those who lived in it. Those who survived the wild winters learned to live with the elements. They quickly lost any desire to impose their will or city ways on the terrifying forces of nature.

'Ugh,' said Casey, her face still pressed to the glass pane as the plane touched down and slowly taxied to the airport buildings. 'What's all that dirty grey muck piled near the runway?'

'Volcanic ash, madam,' answered the flight attendant as he steadied himself in the aisle with Casey's jacket over his arm. 'Mount Spurr erupted unexpectedly about three weeks ago and the ash covered Anchorage. The city and airport were still in a dreadful mess when we flew in two weeks ago. They have had rain which has settled the worst of the ashfall. They seem to have cleaned up this section pretty well.'

Casey wrinkled up her nose then turned to accept her jacket. She smiled her thanks and suddenly the blonde hostess saw what men found attractive. Casey's mouth turned up in a gentle smile whilst the sparkle in her eyes promised untasted delights.

'We only have to overnight at the Captain Cook so we shouldn't breathe in too much of the ashfall,' said Dursley as he thrust his arms into his dark green anorak and pulled up the zip. He and Casey hurried through the airport formalities. They paused only at a glass case housing a stuffed grizzly bear. Staring up at the huge animal towering nine foot over her, shining in the electric light, with claws long enough to cover a man's hand, Casey shuddered. She realized that the twisting streams she had admired from the plane ran through untamed countryside inhabited by these fearsome creatures. Suddenly the trout streams in England seemed infinitely more attractive.

Chapter Three

THE HUDDLED cluster of buildings serving as an airport at King Salmon, a small muddy town strung along the banks of the Naknek River, famous for its salmon fishing, was crowded with men, burly and masculine in their stained anoraks, thick sweaters and hunting boots. The air was heavy with the smell of unwashed bodies and clothes and loud with male voices laughing and boasting of their prowess in hunting and fishing.

The cement floor in front of the check-in counter was an obstacle course of moose and caribou racks, boxes of frozen and smoked salmon, rifles, bows and fishing gear. There was a palpable feeling of excitement and satisfaction.

These were men engaged in the centuries-old tradition of hunting and fishing. Like Early Man they pitted their skills against the strength and wiles of wild animals and the unforgiving faces of nature. They, too, were taking home meat and fish, the spoils of the chase, to their families. The nine-foot-wide moose racks, heavy as sculptured stone, would hang from the walls of their studies alongside the more delicate, fernlike tracery of the caribou racks. Their city friends would envy the huge soft bear pelts stretched out on the floor and listen with awe and envy to the stories about the wilderness. Alaska was essentially a man's world, understood and loved by men and the few women who ventured into this harsh world of killing.

Kit loved the look and the smell of the men who had camped

out for days, backpacking only the essentials to keep alive. She had spent her childhood with men like them in her father's lodges. She understood and admired them. These were not the African Safari types, with whisky and ice waiting for them in camp at the end of a day's hunt. These men accepted life on nature's terms. They understood that death lay in wait in the silence of the animals they hunted.

'He'll be boasting about this moose for ever,' said Kit, tripping over a widespread rack of horns on the floor.

Hank put out his hand to steady her. His eyes followed her as she headed for the little gift shop tucked away in a corner of the concourse. She may look like one of the boys in her old blue jeans, muddy boots and navy anorak, he thought, but show her a shop and she is all woman. He knew the jewellery crafted from the beautiful emerald green and midnight blue of the Arctic opal and the volcanic black haematite attracted her.

He noticed a few of the men studying Kit as she strode easily and unselfconsciously into the store. A prickle of passion warmed him. Just as he was about to check his watch a disembodied voice announced the arrival of the Dan Air plane from Anchorage. He breathed a sigh of relief.

Stewart Saunders was waiting at the wooden jetty down on the Naknek where they moored the float-plane. Hank knew Stewart was eager to leave to gain clearance for Nonvianuk Lake and the Black Legs Lodge before the predicted bad weather closed in. He glanced through the open door at the concourse to make certain that the couple from England had not yet disembarked, then shouldered his way through the crowd and reached the relative quietness of the store.

'Come on,' he ordered Kit, 'the plane has landed.'

'Which do you prefer, the silver trout or the bears?' asked Kit, dangling two pairs of earrings in front of him.

'Fish,' he answered, having learned from experience that her questions required an answer. He knew he would not persuade her to leave the gift shop until he gave his full attention to the object she was buying.

'Be right there,' she called happily as Hank cleared a path to where passengers were milling round waiting for the luggage. He saw Dursley and Casey as they walked into the building. Hank immediately liked the easy way Dursley carried himself.

An outdoors man, he thought to himself. According to Sir Bob Franshaw, the man is a superb shot and an excellent fisherman. The guides at the lodge were always pleased when a committed fisherman arrived. It meant a break in the tedious task of untying wind knots and retying lures.

'Good-looking guy,' whispered Kit, coming up behind him.

A puzzled line creased Hank's forehead. He did not understand why women found these tousle-haired, boyish men attractive.

'She's a bit of a dumpling,' continued Kit, then changed her mind as Casey looked up at Dursley and laughed at something he said.

'She looks fun to me,' countered Hank, as he walked forward to greet them.

Dursley was a little surprised when he heard that Kit was to be their guide with Hank. 'Old Bob' had specified that Hank Butler and Bill Dawkins would guide them. 'Two of the best in the country,' he had assured Dursley.

'Bill fractured his ankle whilst trying to walk on water to help a client who lost his footing,' explained Hank. He guessed what Dursley was thinking about having a woman as a fishing guide. 'He won't be guiding for the rest of the season. Kit is a wonderful fisherwoman. She knows these waters well. She has fished them for the past eight years,' he added, making it seem that she had also guided for that time.

'And she holds IGFA world records for rainbow trout, Arctic grayling and salmon,' added Kit with a smile as she stepped forward to shake hands. 'Though not all at the same time.'

Kit liked Bill Dawkins but she had been secretly delighted when he fractured his ankle. She had been trying to overcome the male prejudice against woman guides for years.

Stewart Saunders had been unable to find an experienced guide before Dursley and Casey's arrival and in desperation had turned to her. Hiding her euphoria, she had agreed, but on condition that she was given a written contract for two years. Stewart had no option but to agree. He had always admired her knowledge and fishing ability, now he added business acumen to the list.

The second cook, Angela, had taken Kit's place, but she needed help. Once the new clients had settled into the routine Hank, who had a free weekend due to him, planned to fly with Stewart to Anchorage and pick up another cook to ease the workload until the lodge closed for winter at the beginning of November.

Casey was completely cowed by the tall, slim, competent woman who looked so much a part of the masculine scene.

'We'll have to see if we can get some sort of record for you, Miss Chargot,' comforted Hank, sensing Casey's anxiety.

'Casey,' she said, 'please call me Casey, and thank you.'

She smiled at Hank. Hank returned it with a grin and a bond of friendship was struck. Suddenly Casey Chargot was no stranger to him.

'Let's get your luggage into the truck,' he said to cover his confusion at the sudden warmth he felt for this new visitor. He tried not to stare at Casey as he sifted through his memories. But he could remember neither a time nor a situation where he could possibly have met her. Casey Ticasuk Chargot *was* a complete stranger to him, yet he felt an instantaneous deep liking for her and a familiarity with her.

Years before he became a fishing guide Hank had trapped and hunted with Trapper Jack, an Inuit Eskimo, up at Barrow. Once, when crouched behind a snow wall near an aglu, a seal's breath hole in the ice, waiting patiently for the seal to come up for air, the talk had turned to women.

'You will know the woman for you when you feel your heart rhythmed to hers,' Jack had whispered. 'There is one woman whose heart beats to that of a man's. Only one. Take her, don't lose her. You will never find a rhythm to match yours again. Never.'

Hank could feel Kit watching him. He shook away the memory and words of Trapper Jack.

'Let's move, Hank,' Kit urged. 'Stewart is waiting at the jetty. We want to get over the pass before the weather closes in on us.'

Casey paled at the thought of flying in thick mist. She had never been in a float-plane and instinctively distrusted anything that landed on water instead of ground.

All fears of flying vanished as they clambered out of the station-wagon at the jetty and she soon had no time to worry about planes. The sun chose to make a brief humid and watery appearance. It awakened every insect in the area. She was busy slapping the flying things which settled, soft as a lover's kiss, on her throat then flew away and left her nursing red burning weals and spots.

She eyed the safety of the float-plane hopefully. Seeing her distress Hank pulled a spray can of Deet from his back pocket, told Casey to close her eyes and soon had her choking on the noxious fumes, but free of insects.

'Here, keep this with you,' he said. 'It's the only stuff that scares the bugs, they seem to thrive on the other bug juices.'

Kit observed his concern and care for the new client with amazement. Hank usually said that the quicker they learned to accept the hardships of the country the easier they would find the fishing trip. Part of the hardships were certainly the infamous Alaskan insects. The largest in the variety of twenty-seven were laughingly referred to as Alaska's state bird.

'Thank you,' said Casey gratefully as a haze of insects circled the Deet layer, not daring to penetrate it. 'I brought some spike lavender and citronella oil with me. It works wonders on the streams back home but I don't think these things would even notice the smell.' She rubbed the bites behind her ears and at the base of her neck.

'Sourdoughs say that it only takes two mosquitoes to lift you up and carry you away,' laughed Stewart.

Casey smiled broadly, more at ease now that the insects were held at bay. 'Sourdoughs?' she questioned.

'They are old-timers, people who were born up here,' he answered. 'They are really tough and pride themselves on living off the land even in winter.' Seeing her interest he continued. 'When you consider that places like Fairbanks can have forty-five degrees below zero for days on end, it's not surprising that they have to be tough.'

'Come on,' interjected Kit, irritated at the unusual attention Hank and Stewart were paying Casey. She hurried Dursley down the gangplank and onto the jetty, leaving Hank to shepherd Casey into the plane.

The two guides strapped the clients into their narrow seats then climbed in themselves. They sat quietly as they waited for Stewart to complete his checks and warm up the engines.

Stewart turned round and smiled at Dursley and Casey. He asked if they had tightened their seat-belts, then clamped his headphones firmly over his ears. This meant he could fly in peace without the bother of social chitchat. He had long since tired of answering the same inane questions from clients. To protect himself, he devised ruses to avoid their constant chatter.

Hank and Kit, sitting huddled in the narrow middle seats, smiled at each other as they watched him wriggle the rounded caps firmly over his ears. The Black Legs Lodge was an excellent camp and Stewart enjoyed a justifiable reputation of hosting the best lodge in the area.

He was a hard task-master, but attracted the best guides and camp staff in Alaska. Fishermen had now cast his reputation wide and his lodge attracted those who sought the wildest and strongest of the rainbows. They returned year after year to pit their skills against the strength and cunning of the Katmai trout.

Chapter Four

THE BRIGHT green and yellow float-plane bearing the legend *Black Legs Lodge* and a caricature of the insect painted high on the tail circled the wooden chalets strung along the edge of the Nonvianuk Lake to alert the staff that the new clients had arrived.

'Here they come,' said Earl, washing down a handful of chocolate-chip cookies with a can of Budweiser.

'What's the betting he has a valet, or is it a footman? All these Limeys with titles have to be looked after like sick cats,' groused Leroy. He had enjoyed the full attention of the two guides and disliked the thought of fishing with another couple, especially outsiders. 'American rivers should be only for Americans,' was one of his well-worn and annoying sayings.

Earl ignored Leroy and reached for another cookie. Kit had warned Angela, the second cook, that Earl needed refuelling before and after each meal so Angela had placed a table between the two men on the wooden deck overlooking the pastel-blue waters of the lake. She kept replenishing the bowls of cookies and popcorn.

'Bet she's a looker,' mused Earl. 'Those English broads are really something. Tall and slim enough to break in two when you get your arms around them. And they are goers, guess it must be all those horses they ride,' he said.

'Humph,' grunted Leroy. 'This one is sure to have a can of

hair spray in one pocket and lipstick in another. We'll have to fish and walk where her designer waders don't get dirty or wet. Snobs, that's what the moneyed ones are. Just snobs. Think the Good Lord created the world for their benefit. Think they are too good for the likes of us.'

'But you are also moneyed, Leroy,' drawled Earl. 'What was it your grandfather did? Bootlegging during the Prohibition, wasn't it?'

Earl was saved from one of Leroy's explosive replies by the arrival of Dursley and Casey. Dursley matched Hank's long stride easily. Kit kept pace with Casey who was stumbling a little on the newly laid gravel.

'Tall and slim?' jeered Leroy quietly as they watched the foursome approach.

'Ignore that superstructure out front,' retaliated Earl. 'You'll see she has lovely slim legs and a waist you want to measure with your hands. She's kinda neat,' he said as he hefted his bulk out of the sagging deck-chair to greet the new arrivals. 'Earl's the name,' he said, thrusting out his hand, still sticky with melted chocolate.

'Pleased to meet you,' smiled Dursley. 'I'm Dursley Carrington and this is my fiancée, Catherine Ticasuk Chargot. But she answers to Casey.'

'Snobs?' mouthed Earl. Leroy, despite his sneering remarks about the British aristocracy, stood with an ingratiating smile eagerly waiting to shake hands with Dursley.

Dursley flung himself into one of the deck-chairs and dug into the bowl of popcorn, endearing himself to Earl. Any limey who likes popcorn can't be all bad, he thought as he pushed the bowl close to Dursley. Soon the men were involved in a deep discussion on rainbows, mice, glow-bugs, polar shrimp lures and the rivers they would be fishing, Earl pretending to a knowledge he did not possess.

Seeing Casey's eyes glaze over, Kit took her off to find her cabin.

'It's lovely,' said Casey in surprise as she looked around the wooden cabin with its two neatly made single beds. A black stove was belching in a corner warming the small room and the wind rattled the chimney pipe as it danced across the cabin roofs.

'This cabin has a great view,' said Kit, pleased by Casey's reaction. She drew back the beige-striped curtains. Casey peered out through the wire mosquito netting at the seemingly endless expanse of the washed-silk waters of the lake.

In the distance the tell-tale sun highlighted the snow which dusted the mountain peaks, letting all know that soon the land would lie dead, buried beneath its white shroud. Alaska would sing again its lonely yet lovely winter song of silence. Man and animal would cry for the sun in the heavy quietness and darkness.

'I had no idea that the country was so indescribably beautiful,' said Casey, moving away reluctantly as Kit closed the curtains.

'There can be no place like it on earth,' said Kit. 'The severity of the winters here guards its beauty and purity. That keeps out most of the polluted human race.'

Casey nodded. She too felt that over-population was the main reason for the planet's terminal illness.

'How cold can it get?' asked Casey, intrigued at the thought of winters cold enough to make people migrate and return only in the spring.

'The coldest recorded day was minus eighty degrees Fahrenheit at Prospect Creek,' said Kit. She grinned at the expression on Casey's face. 'Don't worry, that was about twenty years ago. All you have to think about is going to bed after supper and getting some sleep. It stays light until about midnight. It lulls you into thinking it's early evening. Your five a.m. cup of wake-up coffee is then most unwelcome.'

Five o'clock in the morning, thought Casey, and this is supposed to be a holiday! She smiled bravely at Kit. 'That sounds wonderful. I'll certainly remember not to be duped by the twilight. Thanks.'

Hank studied the two women as they strolled back to the main cabin for dinner. Kit, slim and strong as the lovely wild rainbows they fished, made Hank feel that he had breathed in deep lungfuls of bracing sea air. She had the clean-cut freshness found in youngsters who surfed the tumbling waves of the California coast. She also promised the languor and heat of the West Coast sun. Once again he admired the assurance with which she had moved into his masculine world.

Looking away from Kit to Casey he was fascinated with the way her breasts, warm in a raspberry polo-neck sweater, swayed as she hurried to keep pace with Kit. She had left her tweed jacket in the cabin and for the first time he was subjected to the full glory of her figure.

'A pocket-size Venus,' he mumbled softly to himself.

'Wouldn't mind getting between those earmuffs on a winter's night,' sniggered Leroy.

Hank compressed his lips into a thin, straight line to avoid replying. He found to his amazement that he wanted to put his arms around Casey and protect her from people like Leroy.

'Pray,' scoffed Earl. 'That one's a lady. She's not your class, bud.'

'Doesn't look English to me,' mused Leroy. 'Looks oriental with that thick straight hair and round face. Chinese maybe or Russian.'

'What would you know? You are about fourth-generation American now. Anyway your people hate the English. You've been blowing them up for years.'

'We have damn good reason to hate the . . .' retaliated Leroy.

Hank ignored them. He had become accustomed to their bitching. He had relaxed once he realized that the insults were both given and accepted in a friendly fashion. Earl and Leroy had fished together in the States and understood one another. Leroy was proud of his Irish ancestry. He had lost none of the famed bite of Irish humour, but being American had mellowed him. He only flew in with flying fists when religion or politics were the subject of discussion. Earl soon learned to stay away from both.

The two men shared a cabin and it had been a wise choice. Insults bounced off Earl's large frame and his booming laughter drowned out Leroy's complaints about bears, fish and food.

'Casey,' called Hank as he pushed back his chair and crunched down the gravel path to greet them, 'is your cabin satisfactory? Please tell us if there is anything you need.'

Kit prepared to meet Hank's eyes over Casey's head and exchange mocking glances, but was confounded when she realized that he was genuinely concerned about Casey's comfort. I had better watch this little pudding, she cautioned herself silently. Not only has she hooked an earl but she has my man running around her as well. Stretching her mouth into a broad smile, she strode ahead of Hank and Casey and ushered the men into the main cabin for dinner. Earl led the way smoothing down his shirt front in anticipation.

It took another ten minutes to get the newcomers to the table as Dursley stopped to examine all the trophy fish and photographs on the log walls. He and Hank collided as they both moved to pull out a chair for Casey and seat her.

'Sorry,' said Hank as he gave way to Dursley. Dursley smiled. He had seen the effect Casey had on men before. She seemed to arouse the protective instinct in the hardest of them. She smiled up to thank him and he knew that he too wanted to love and guard this woman.

Chapter Five

THE SUN teased the fishing party. It flashed into the float-plane promising warmth and brightness, then retreated behind wind-torn clouds leaving behind the threat of a grey sullen day.

Casey tucked her hands into the pockets of her fishing jacket. She wore fishing gloves and her exposed fingertips were turning pink with cold. Even if I knew how to tie on a nymph or a mouse I would never manage with these frozen fingers, she moaned silently.

'Fun, isn't it?' Dursley mouthed at her over the noise of the engines. She braced her boots against the back of the chair in front of her as the wind flipped the plane's wings, threatening to invert the aircraft, and nodded. Just then Stewart banked the plane sharply to the right. Her stomach lurched. She swallowed back the bitterness which filled her mouth, terrified of being sick in front of everyone.

'Look,' said Hank, turning her shoulders to the window on her side. She forced herself to look down as Stewart eased the plane into a tight spiralling turn. It seemed to stop with one wing pointing to heaven and the other down to earth. She was crucified in the air.

Stewart slowly circled a group of caribou lying in the middle of pockets of snow and ice on the high hills. The animals lifted their delicately carved antlers and looked up at the plane as it circled them. They stirred anxiously and some stood up but none would leave the safety of the snow patches. They had fled to the hills in a frenzy of madness to escape the merciless biting and blood sucking of the mosquitoes, botflies and black flies which plagued them incessantly through the summer months. They would not leave their icy refuge until hunger drove them down.

Casey stared at the beautiful dark animals outlined starkly against the snow. In the pure clear light of the Arctic they seemed like creatures from a world long forgotten and she wanted to cry.

'Sourdoughs say,' said Stewart, removing his headphones and turning round, 'that the caribou do their incredible trek hundreds of miles north each year to the traditional calving grounds on the tundra just to escape the bugs.'

'Makes sense,' said Leroy, patting his fishing vest to make certain that his tube of Deet cream was in place.

'It's also a safe area,' Hank broke in. 'Not even the wolves want to go up to that place. Melt pools, frozen ground, iced-up rivers, howling winds. Only crazy pregnant caribou would choose it as a maternity home.'

'They look like reindeer waiting for Christmas and their sleds,' said Casey softly, her nose pressed to the glass pane, her nausea forgotten for the moment.

Dursley tucked a chunk of her hair behind her ear so that he could see her face. 'Bambi complex,' he teased.

'She'll love those huggy brown grizzly bears then,' said Leroy. He winced as Earl hit him across the kneecaps to silence him.

The sight of the tormented caribou had softened Stewart for a short while, but he now replaced his headphones and concentrated on his flying.

As the plane straightened Casey felt her stomach lurch. She ignored the queasy feeling and stared out at the tundra. It rolled beneath the plane like a bolt of grey velvet patterned with luminous white and yellow lichens, now stained in patches to the deep red of autumn. The land would blaze in one last glorious burst of colour before the terrible stillness of winter bleached the country as white as caribou bones left after a wolves' kill.

As the plane dropped lower a vivid stretch of green snaked down the valley. The twists and turns marked a river tumbling down from the mountains. Hank and Kit sat up straight in their seats and studied the foaming water as if able to count the trout.

'Looks good,' said Hank.

'No bears on the water,' said Kit.

'No,' said Leroy, 'the beasts are all lying waiting for us in their stinking day-beds.'

Earl glanced at Casey and hit Leroy on his already tender kneecaps.

'Thanks, bud,' said Leroy. 'Now that you've crippled me, I can go home with Stewart and to hell with the bears.'

Earl started giggling at the thought of Leroy explaining to Stewart why he wanted to return to the lodge. His waders strained at the seams as his stomach shook and tears ran down his cheeks. Leroy stopped rubbing his knees and stared at Earl. Then he slapped Earl on the back and they choked and spluttered every time they looked at each other.

The rest of the fishing party looked bemused. Stewart fortunately could hear nothing, so was unaware of the comedy act. Dursley secretly hoped that they were not going to spoil the day's fishing by acting like two pubescent boys telling dirty jokes.

The plane sank lower and Casey clutched Dursley's hand. She hoped that Stewart was not going to land on the river. It seemed far too narrow and rocky, but she was not going to be first to voice her fears.

Suddenly Stewart lifted the plane over a ridge and before them, like pools of molten lead, lay three small lakes. Stewart circled the largest of the three and Dursley was about to object when the plane dropped onto one float and sliced into the silver water to stop just short of the muddy bank.

'Don't worry,' said Kit, seeing their unease. 'Stewart hasn't ever lost a plane or a guest.'

Casey opened her eyes as Hank eased himself out of his safety straps. The wind cut into the aircraft as he opened the door and stepped carefully onto the float. He then stepped down into the lake, and as the water rose around his thighs Casey realized to her horror that she was expected to do the same.

Kit joined Hank to tug the tail of the plane around to the bank. She ducked swiftly as the wind swung the tail over her head.

'One day that thing will guillotine me,' she muttered. She grabbed the swinging stay-rope and held the plane steady while Hank climbed back onto the float and unpacked the fishing gear from the hold. He heaved the heavy blue nylon backpack over his shoulder, jumped into the shallows and waded ashore.

'All ashore,' ordered Stewart, eager to leave.

He had to fly to King Salmon to offload the camp's refuse, a ruse he had discovered which was most effective in discouraging bears from prowling round the cabins. Angela had also asked him to buy extra blocks of chocolate to counter Earl's appetite for cookies.

'Sit down on the float then slide into the water,' said Hank to Casey. 'It's easier that way.' Casey hung onto the steel steps unwilling to let go and balance on the rocking float.

'Here,' Hank called out to Kit, 'hold this,' and he slung the backpack over her head. She sagged beneath the weight but before she could protest he handed her a fistful of rods and waded back to the plane.

'Turn round and put your arms around my neck,' he said to Casey, 'and I'll help you into the water.'

Kit bristled in silence as Hank eased Casey off the float and helped her scramble ashore.

'Careful!' Kit shouted, her attention suddenly diverted to Earl, who looked as if he was preparing to dive into the lake. Her warning was too late. He jumped into the water with all the grace of a grizzly pouncing on a salmon.

A wave of water shot up and showered Leroy who had taken Hank's advice and was sitting on the float easing himself into the lake.

'You dumb, clumsy Yank!' yelled Leroy as he took off his

knitted cap and wrung out the water. 'You can give me your cap. I'm damned if I'm going to freeze because you're a dummy.'

'I have an extra one,' soothed Kit. 'But you had better get off the float or you'll be on a windy ride to King Salmon.'

Stewart shook his head and climbed back into the plane as Hank pushed it out into the lake. The fishermen stood and watched the plane until it was lost in the smoky sky then they turned and followed Kit and Hank.

The vast emptiness of the rolling country and its brooding stillness silenced them. Even Leroy stopped hurling epithets at Earl and glanced anxiously over his shoulder as he brought up the rear of the group.

As they approached the river and the vegetation thickened, with stubby branches from elder and willow shrubs pulling at their waders, Kit moved back to walk behind Leroy.

Never thought I'd be grateful to have a woman guard my butt, he thought. His step was lighter and more confident now as he hurried to catch up with Earl.

The curtains of wispy cloud parted as the fishing party broke out of the dark riverine shrub. Sunbeams sprayed the tumbling waters with gold dust. Down in the crystal depths the sockeye salmon glowed rich as crimson rubies, as they defended their redds. The trout, dark as shadows, wily as thieves, darted between them gulping down the pink globular eggs which floated out of the redds. Many of the trout were badly scarred or one-eyed, bearing testimony to the ferocity of the attacks by the sockeye.

'We will dump our haversack and any unwanted gear here,' said Hank, pointing to a grey pebbled spit of land edging into the river.

'Is our lunch in there?' queried Earl, unhappy at the thought of not finding the spit of land again.

'Yeah,' grinned Hank. 'We don't usually carry food with us because of the grizzlies,' he explained for Dursley and Casey's benefit. 'These things have radar sensors for noses. But we don't come across them here. We'll be fishing that stretch where the river loops back on itself, so we will be able to watch our food.'

'No bears? Good,' said Leroy. 'Now let's get at the fish and rip their lips good.'

'Get your lines ready here,' said Kit, 'and take everything you need in your vests.'

Soon the air was loud with queries about six or eight weight rods, ten or twenty foot fast sink-tip line and two or six pound leaders.

Casey found a boulder polished smooth by the water and weather. She sat down quietly watching the river, wishing she was back in the familiarity of London.

'Come on, Bubbles,' called Dursley, his rod under his arm and ready to go. 'What's wrong? Haven't you sorted out your line yet? Hank suggested we use . . .'

Casey let the jargon float over her. Wanting to please Dursley she had pretended that she had fished in England. Now the awful time had arrived when she had to admit that she was a complete novice.

'I've got Casey's rod,' she heard Hank say. She stared at him and he winked back.

'I changed the leader. It was a little long for these conditions. Come on, Casey, I'll put you into a good spot and then find second best for the men.'

Everyone laughed, though Kit's eyes did not reflect what her mouth was doing.

'Kit, won't you set the men up at Sore Leg Bend and I'll join you in a minute.'

Kit moved off through the scrub with the three men close behind her. She stayed with them, watching their first few casts. Dursley was throwing beautifully tight loops. She nodded out of respect for a good fisherman and moved on to stand beside Earl.

'Earl,' she said, 'hurling your weight forward will not make that line travel out. Use your arm and let the line sing, that's what it's designed to do.'

'Caught fish all over the States like this,' he answered with a laugh.

'OK,' she answered, moving downstream to where Leroy was untangling his line from a clump of grass-seed heads. 'I'll have you both casting correctly before the end of the fortnight,' she vowed as she hurried to help Leroy before he cut his line in exasperation.

'Whoa, bear.' Hank's voice rang out clearly across the water and Leroy froze. There were not supposed to be any bears in this area. 'Whoa, bear. Bear, whoa. Whoa, there.' Hank's voice became louder and more authoritative.

'Reel in,' Kit shouted, 'and follow me.' The three men obeyed promptly. Leroy lost his leader and egg-pattern lure as his pocket knife nipped through the nylon. Earl needed no urging to short-stick the fish on his line and join Kit.

'Call "Whoa, bear", as we walk, in case it has heard Hank and turned back into the scrub,' ordered Kit.

Leroy pushed through the scrub regardless of the branches tearing at his waders. He wanted to be out of the thicket and onto the river where a man could see what was coming. Dursley walked quickly making certain that his waders were not torn by the stubby shrubs. He had no wish to feel the glacier-fed waters oozing into his underwear. Earl's voice boomed out at every step he took, alerting the bear that there were humans and in the vicinity. He didn't want to surprise anything that made him look like a midget.

As they approached the stony spit Kit slowed down. Their haversack lay on the pebbles and if anything had attracted a bear it would be the smell of food.

'Turn round,' she whispered. 'I think it will go for our lunch pack. Let's cut back to Hank and Casey.' Earl had to lift Leroy to persuade him to go back into the scrub. The sun crept into the thickets and the wet ground steamed. Perspiration soon greased their bodies and dripped into their neoprene waders. Soon they were all scratching their faces and arms and cursing the insects. Finally they saw Hank standing on the river-bank peering at the pebbled piece of dry land. Casey was behind him, her face drained of colour as she stared at the brown bear stalking purposefully towards the blue haversack. It seemed to fill the sky as it drew nearer and Casey shivered.

'Do you have a gun?' she whispered to Hank.

'No. This is a bear reserve, no firearms are allowed.' He smiled to reassure her, as Kit and the three men walked quickly along the river-bank to join them.

'They have right of way and they certainly abuse the privilege,' he joked, hoping to calm Casey.

'Looks like it's wearing my grandma's old fur coat,' said Earl, realizing what Hank was trying to do.

'She must have been your size then,' giggled Leroy, trying to keep the tremor from his voice.

Kit moved across to Hank. The party watched them anxiously as they conferred. The bear smelled the tantalizing odours of ham and pasta salad and walnut cake. He shook himself in anticipation and Casey gasped as his grizzled hair rippled over his body. He squatted down beside the nylon haversack, glanced briefly at the party standing across the river and proceeded to rip the heavy-duty nylon apart with all the ease of tearing pieces of paper from a toilet roll.

'Look at that,' breathed Dursley, now holding Casey close to his side. 'I couldn't cut through that new nylon stuff with my pocket knife.'

The bear scattered pieces of the haversack over the pebbles and ripped open the plastic containers full of ham and salad.

'He's actually swalllowing plastic and paper with the food,' said Casey, staring transfixed at the bear as it finished the food, then ate the plastic packets of ketchup and mustard.

'Hope that gives the brute the worst kind of indigestion possible,' said Earl, watching the bear hurl the empty boxes away.

'It won't,' answered Kit, leaving Hank and walking across to the group. 'Those bears are worse than goats. They have incinerators for stomachs. You wouldn't believe the things they stuff down their throats.'

'Like my lunch,' said Earl. The group laughed nervously.

'Stewart had one at our camp in the early days,' said Kit. 'It broke into the store room, drank the paint, petrol and Avgas. It ended off its meal with a few black garbage bags. We saw it days later walking across the tundra trailing a piece of the black bag under its tail.'

The group laughed, but dutifully.

'Drinking Avgas would kill most things,' said Dursley, impressed with what the grizzlies were able to ingest.

'Listen carefully,' said Hank, joining Kit and placing their rods carefully in the crook of a willow. 'Kit and I are going to cross the river and try to chase him off the food.'

'He's eaten almost all of it. Why not leave him and let him go away?' queried Leroy.

'Because the chances are pretty good that he won't just go away. That's why you break your line when fishing and a bear approaches. You never let them take food away from you,' explained Hank patiently. 'Then they realize that they are dominant.'

'Do you mean that these things are unsure of the pecking order in this reserve?' said Dursley, worried at how pale Casey was.

Hank grinned at him, but it was a mirthless grimace.

'Once they associate humans with food, they'll start bullying all the fishermen in the park, expecting food,' continued Kit.

'And we know how nasty these brutes can get,' said Leroy, ready to elaborate on the bear kill at the falls for Dursley and Casey.

Earl coughed. Leroy caught his eye and instinctively bent his knees to protect them.

'We want the four of you to stay here. Don't move. Don't come to try and help us and above all don't run,' cautioned Hank as he stepped down into the river and held out his hand for Kit.

The three men instinctively closed around Casey, though Earl had to pinch Leroy's neck to pull him away from her and make him form part of the protective circle.

'Whoa, bear!' Kit and Hank shouted in unison as they waded across the river to the pebbled spit.

The bear looked up, then ignored them as he twisted the aluminium frame of the pack into a Chinese puzzle in his effort to wrest food from it.

'Whoa, you damn bear!' bellowed Earl from the bank as the bear found Earl's Patagonia jacket in the bottom of the bag. The grizzly circled it like a flag over its head, trying to free his claws from the matted, fleecy fabric.

'I've just paid three hundred bucks for that jacket. Leave it alone!'

As if on cue the bear's claws ripped through the material and the jacket flew free, to land in the river and be washed downstream.

'Damn, bear, you'll pay for that,' threatened Earl, incensed at the loss of his prized jacket.

Just then the bear growled. Hank and Kit were too close. It was going to defend any food which might be left in the shreds of the haversack.

Kit stopped at Hank's command. He moved in closer to the gravel spit still calling and talking to the bear, hoping that when it recognized the human voice it would leave and go fishing upstream. He was well aware that the Katmai bears were becoming too familiar with humans, losing their instinctive fear and becoming aggressive. It could mean some ugly confrontations in the future.

The grizzly, still too young to challenge a dominant male, but old enough to chase cubs and sows away from the river, growled again and stood up on its hind legs.

'Oh no,' said Casey and buried her face in Dursley's shoulder.

'Look at it grow,' said Earl, in awe as the grizzly unfolded itself to its full height. 'He must be almost twice my height, and I'm just on six foot.'

'It's like looking up at the Empire State Building,' said Leroy, slowly edging to the back of the circle where he would be further away from the creature.

Hank walked backwards very slowly and Kit prayed that he

wouldn't miss his footing on the rocks and fall, scaring the bear into action. As he neared her, Kit held out her hand and they retreated to join the group huddled on the bank.

'Why is he still standing?' asked Casey.

'Hoping to scare us,' answered Kit shortly.

'Well, he sure has succeeded. Someone tell him that he can get down now,' said Leroy, twisting Kit's cap round on his head nervously.

The bear watched them leave and, satisfied with his victory, he dropped to all fours again. He sniffed the shreds of blue nylon garlanding the pebbles, then, with a final glance at the fishing party, he growled and like night giving way to dawn vanished into the scrub.

'We'll give him half an hour and then we'll go and clean up the mess,' said Hank.

'What,' squeaked Leroy, 'go across the river?'

'Katmai is a reserve. We must make a fire and burn the bits of plastic and paper,' explained Hank.

'Then we'll fish,' added Kit with a smile to defuse the tension. 'After all, that's what we're here for.'

'Yeah, tell me about it,' said Leroy. 'I reckon the only way to get trout out of these rivers is to hire a helicopter and fish from that. Then the bears can have the place.'

'You get used to them,' soothed Kit. 'By the end of the week they won't worry you. You'll not even notice them.'

Casey shivered in Dursley's arms. She could not imagine ever becoming used to bears.

Reluctantly they all crossed the river to clear up the mess left by the bear. Where the water was waist high for Kit and the men, it came up to Casey's armpits. It seeped into her waders and down into her boots, and once they reached the pebbled beach Kit persuaded Casey to strip them off. Turned inside out, they dried in the sun and the wind. Casey sat perched on a log.

She silently thanked Sir Bob Franshaw for recommending thermal underwear made from the new fabric which drew perspiration away from the skin leaving the body dry.

Earl forcibly walked Leroy to the end of the pebble spit to save Casey the embarrassment of Leroy's hungry glances at her legs, clad only in thick blue long johns.

The small fire fed with bits of paper and plastic and fanned by the wind burned brightly. Her waders were almost dry and Casey was thinking of the excitement the 'bear story' would cause among her friends back in London when Kit suddenly turned away from it and shouted at Casey sharply. 'Get your waders on, quickly!'

She looked up, ready to protest that the inside of the boots would still be damp, when at the far end of the spit a dark shadow appeared. As she stared, it developed legs and a head. The grizzly was back.

'He has probably seen us and thinks that there is more food,' said Hank, helping Kit and Dursley fit Casey back into her waders.

'Cross the river back to where we were,' he shouted at Earl and Leroy who were still standing with their backs to the fire and Casey. 'Walk slowly and carefully. The bear is back.'

Within minutes the two men were on the opposite bank.

As it approached the group the bear quickened its pace. Hank kicked sand over the fire, picked up what was left of the aluminium frame and herded Dursley and Casey into the river.

'Great day's fishing,' said Kit quietly. 'An excellent advert for the lodge.'

Hank looked at her in amazement as he followed her into the water. She really isn't afraid, he said to himself, and he felt a prick of envy.

The rush of adrenalin and the responsibility of keeping the party safe for another four hours until the plane returned left him feeling queasy. He rubbed the scar beneath his eye until the skin around it was red and tender.

He was wary of half-grown bears. Like adolescents, they were cocky, unafraid and behaved irrationally. He wished he had Kit's ability to recognize the dangers involved with the creatures who roamed this wild frontier, yet not fear them.

Dursley leaned down and offered them a hand to pull them up the slippery bank. 'What will it do when it finds there is no more food?' he said softly, so the others would not hear.

'Either leave and go fishing, or follow us believing that we must have more food.'

Dursley nodded soberly. He had read widely on Alaska before the trip. One of the books listing and describing bear attacks now entered his memory with awful clarity.

'We'll walk upstream a short way,' said Hank as he, Kit and Dursley joined Leroy and Earl. 'But we'll keep a careful watch on the bear,' he continued, forestalling Leroy's objection.

The bear sniffed around the sand covering the dead fire and trailed his nose along the log where Casey had been sitting.

'See, he loves you, Casey,' said Earl as the bear stopped and smelt the log carefully.

Casey gave a small, unhappy smile to please Earl and shivered. She studied the stitching on Dursley's fishing vest. She forced herself to remember the fun they had had, deciding whether Dursley would have time to pull the ripcord and inflate the jacket, if he lost his footing in one of the fast rivers and was washed downstream. The safety of Hardy's in London now seemed so far away.

Hank took off his Polaroid glasses and polished them. When he looked up it was to see the bear, nose held high as he absorbed their scent, wading into the river.

'Here it comes,' squealed Leroy.

'The book says climb higher than forty foot up a tree. Contrary to all beliefs, bears can climb from twenty to thirty,' said Earl. 'Trouble is, I can see nothing higher than three to four feet here,' he said with a forced laugh, eyeing the stunted elders and willows.

For the first time Dursley looked at Earl with something like respect. He had ignored him as one of life's 'fat boys turned joker'. But he now saw a strength and calmness which was reassuring and admirable.

The bear waded across the river as if walking on dry land.

'Move,' said Hank.

The group set off along one of the ancient bear tracks alongside the river at a brisk pace. Looking back over his shoulder Hank saw the bear clamber up the bank. He used his curved claws as gripons, shook himself, tested the air, then turned onto the same track.

'Kit,' he called. 'Cross the river onto the other side. He's behind us.'

Kit didn't even turn around. She immediately put her arm around Casey. Together they slid down the bank into the water. Kit set off for the opposite bank supporting Casey as easily as if she was a child, leaving Hank to remove the men from the bear's path.

'Into the scrub,' said Hank as the men joined the girls. 'Sit down and keep quiet.'

They all squatted. As they did the shrubs closed over their heads and they were at the mercy of the insects.

Casey sat with her head on her knees praying that the bear would not find them. The thicket muted the tumble and splash of the water as it played with the rocks. The silence was oppressive, broken only by her ragged breathing. She started as she felt a hand on the back of her neck. She grasped Dursley's warm hand gratefully. Immediately her breathing slowed. She became calmer and her fingers stopped trembling. Slowly the colour returned to her face.

Watching them, Hank forgot the bear for a few moments. He thought of Trapper Jack. His words rang in his head as clearly as if he was in hiding with them.

'Be it a woman or an animal, if afraid, they need the warmth of a man's hand on their body. It's the loneliness of fear that's bad, not fear itself. No one should have to face fear alone. Damned is he who turns away and does not help. Remember that,' he admonished as he sat carving one of his beautiful knives.

Hank shook himself mentally and crawled to the edge of the thicket. He peered out.

'He's still on the path, sniffing madly. The wind is in our favour. It's blowing upstream so he can't smell us. With his eyesight he'd fall over us before he saw us,' he said as he sat back on his heels.

There was a general sigh of relief and grins all round as Earl's stomach rumbled.

'Sshh,' said Leroy, 'that'll call the bear. He also has a rumbling stomach. Hungry for us,' he added and quickly crossed his arms over his knees protecting them from Earl's heavy hand.

'And you would just about fill it,' retorted Earl.

Suddenly Hank stiffened and Kit crawled across to join him. They looked out of the bushes.

'He has changed direction, the dog,' said Hank. 'He'll cut across our scent if he continues on that track.'

Prophetically the bear froze. It lifted its nose high, boxing the compass. As it caught their scent it broke into a shambling trot towards the river once more.

'It's found us,' said Hank, soberly turning back to the group.

'What does one do to outwit those things?' asked Dursley, stroking Casey's fingers.

'Yeah, what?' echoed Earl. 'They out-run, out-swim and out-climb one. So unless anyone here knows how to fly, we've had it.'

'Not at all,' said Hank and Kit in unison.

'We'll keep walking ahead of it and criss-crossing the river. But we'll make our way towards the lake,' decided Hank.

'Only a little while now until Stewart gets here,' consoled Kit.

'We'll cross to the other bank right now,' said Hank.

They were in the middle of the river when a deep drone filled the air.

'Stewart!' yelled Leroy and a cheer rang out from the fishing party.

'No,' said Hank, studying the float-plane high overhead. 'Wrong colours. It's probably the Lucky Lodge checking up on us. Snooping to see if we've discovered any new fishing spots.'

'Would they do that?' asked Dursley, a little shocked at such unprofessional behaviour.

'They do it all the time,' answered Hank.

'This is a cut-throat business,' explained Kit as they stumbled over the wet rocks. 'All the lodge owners pretend to be co-operative and friendly, but success is measured by the size and quantity of fish hooked during the day, so the lodges steal each other's lures, guides and clients. They also—' She broke off as she saw the bear clamber up the bank they had just left and disappear into the thicket where they had hidden.

'Do all wild animals act in a similar manner?' Dursley asked Hank quietly, leaving Kit to guide Casey through the tall, tangled grass and stunted elder bushes.

'What do you mean?'

'The only wild animals I've been close to have been in Africa. My father used to take us there on an annual hunting safari.'

Hank was silent. Dursley looked ahead and made certain the girls were out of earshot before he continued.

'There, when an animal is about to attack it circles closer and closer until it decides to make the final rush.'

Hank nodded, sensing what Dursley was about to say.

'This bear,' said Dursley, his voice low and serious, 'has closed the distance behind us by more than half. He was a good way behind, only keeping us in sight. Now, one can almost smell him.'

Hank looked at the river again before answering. He was relieved to see that the bear had not yet reappeared. The grizzly was still absorbing their smell in the thicket and almost certainly picking up the pheromones of fear they had left behind.

Probably tearing the bushes apart looking for more haversacks, he thought as he debated what to say to Dursley. Eventually he decided that if they were attacked, Dursley, though he looked like an unkempt schoolboy, would be a good man to rely on.

'He is coming closer,' Hank admitted, 'but we have a few things in our favour. Firstly, there are six of us. He would be hesitant to attack a large group. Secondly, he is not one of the really dominant animals. Hopefully that makes him still a little unsure of himself and his powers. Thirdly, it's autumn and their main concern is to stuff as much food into themselves as possible before they find a hollow in a hillside and go into semi-hibernation for winter.

'Food is his priority, not a confrontation with us. I am hoping that when he explores our hiding place and finds nothing to eat, he'll lost interest in us and amble off.'

'No such luck,' said Dursley, hearing loud splashing in the river.

'No,' agreed Hank, 'he seems to be hooked on Angela's cookies.'

He stopped for a moment to untangle the tip of his fishing-line from a willow. The river seemed to open up for the bear. The rolling rocks became a cobbled street, helping him catch up with the fishing party.

'He's moving much faster now,' observed Dursley. Fear caught and squeezed his vocal cords.

The grizzly's initial fear of the party had almost gone. When they abandoned their food and retreated from his towering stance they proved they were subservient to him. As they continued to give way to him, he became even more confident and quickened his pace. His large head swung as he padded behind them and his nose quested for their smell constantly.

'Let's catch up with the rest,' said Hank. 'We'll cross the river once more and then head up to the lake.'

He glanced at his watch, hoping that Stewart would be early. If not, they had another half an hour of 'hide and seek' with the bear and the grizzly was palling of the game.

Casey gritted her teeth and slid down the steep bank on her bottom. Her boots landed in the sickening softness of a drift pile of rotting salmon heaped against the bank by the current and she gagged as the sickly sweet smell of decayed flesh plugged her nose and thickened her throat. The water clouded and shreds of salmon swirled in the murk. She shuddered as fish slime hung in greasy strings from her waders.

'Awful, isn't it?' sympathized Kit as Casey squelched out of the sewerage of dead fish and back into the clean river. 'I can't understand why nature allows thousands of these salmon to come in from the sea, silver and beautiful, then battle up to the area where they were spawned, turn red and ugly and continue to guard their nests while the flesh slowly rots from their bodies.'

Casey shuddered as a few of the salmon from the top of the heap floated free and swirled around her in the current. The empty eye sockets stared up at her and the pale grey, pink and white of dead flesh gleamed in the washed light of the sun.

She suppressed a second shiver as one of the leprous salmon struggled in vain against the current to return to its nest in the gravel bed. But it no longer had the strength to resist the water. It hit Casey's thigh as it tumbled downstream to die.

'This is one thing I'll never forget,' said Casey. 'The stench and sight of these dying salmon.'

She stumbled into a trench between two rocks and would have fallen if Kit had not steadied her with a grip like iron.

'If Dad could see me now,' said Casey, relieved to talk and not think of the bear for a few minutes. 'He always boasts about his daughter who out-walks the beaters on the grouse moors. He bores his friends with stories about his girl, who skis all day and dances all night. I wonder if he would be as proud of me now, stumbling over these rocks with trembling thighs and aching ankles.'

'Even my legs are wobbly,' lied Kit, suddenly liking Casey.

She is not bad for a rich limey, thought Kit. She hasn't moaned once today and running away from a grizzly is no fun. Anyway, she assured herself, she is definitely not Hank's sort of woman. I am.

She put out her arm for Casey to lean on.

'Here, hang on,' she said. 'Let my legs break the force of the current for you. I'm paid to do it.'

Casey smiled her thanks.

'You two need a man, someone large, to break the current. Use me,' said Earl. He waded back to join the girls in the middle of the river. Leroy stood on the bank looking downriver nervously. The threesome joined arms and stumbled through the water like a badly rehearsed chorus line.

'Earl,' whispered Kit, 'if the bear comes, keep an eye on Leroy. Don't let him run, or make any crazy dashes for thickets. It'll endanger all of us.'

'Sure thing,' he answered and swung Casey up onto the bank beside Leroy.

'Our bear seems to have lost himself,' said Hank as he and Dursley joined the party.

'No lie? Perhaps a salmon tempted him and he couldn't resist it,' said Leroy hopefully.

'Whatever it is that's keeping him away, we'll use the time to climb up the hill. Perhaps once we're down the other side at the lake he'll lose our scent completely,' said Hank. 'You lead, Kit, then Casey,' he continued, 'I'll bring up the rear.'

As they left the sparkling sounds of the river behind them, silence rose to meet and smother them. Casey climbed with her mouth open, gulping in great lungfuls of thick air, determined not to slow down the party.

She welcomed the sound of Earl's ragged breathing and Leroy wheezing asthmatically behind her. The silence of the vast country, which had originally stunned and enchanted her, had now become oppressive. It seemed to stalk her as ominously as the bear. She wanted to scream. She needed to shatter the stillness.

'Those are your cigars, ruining your lungs,' she said, looking back over her shoulder at Leroy as he kicked at the roots lacing the footpath.

'If they had some decent Irish whiskey at the lodge I'd be all right,' he grunted. 'It's drinking all this watery Yankee stuff that's ruining my lungs.'

'Haven't noticed you holding back,' beamed Earl. 'You tear into it like Submarine—' he said, stopping in mid-sentence hoping that Casey or Dursley would not want to know about Submarine. This was not the time to recount the story. But Casey was concentrating on the path and Dursley was scanning the low scrub for any sign of movement. Neither of them picked up the reference.

Dursley was worried that the bear might have abandoned the

futile game of following them, and, like the African buffalo, circled ahead to lie in ambush for them before they reached the lake.

'This is like trying to walk across a giant-size water bed dressed in a fur coat and wellington boots,' said Casey as they broke out onto the open tundra.

Kit grinned. The spongy ground pockmarked with depressions and ridges certainly made walking difficult.

Casey was wearing boots bonded to her thick waders. They were warm and ideal for standing in the cold river but not for hiking. Her heels rubbed up and down on the boots as she walked and the double pair of fishing socks had long since stopped protecting her heels. She welcomed the pain. It stopped her cogitating on the whereabouts of the grizzly.

The fishing group stopped for a moment at the top of the hill, feeling the cold wind with pleasure.

'Keep moving,' said Hank. 'We are now upwind of the bear and there's the lake. Don't scatter your gear around when we reach the lakeside. Be ready to climb on board as soon as Stewart lands.'

Kit looked at him soberly. They both knew that if the bear appeared on the ridge they would be attacked. The grizzly would have made its decision.

They reached the pebbled shore of the lake and Casey sank onto the cold rounded stones in relief. Leroy watched her wriggle around until she found a suitable spot. He walked to the bank where the winter ice had cut armchairs into the mud. He settled back, rested his head on a patch of sundew plants and closed his eyes.

'Damn,' he swore and jumped up. The sudden movement electrified the group. Casey felt the sick prickle of hairs standing upright on her arms.

Leroy's arms danced a semaphore code as he swatted at a cloud of white sox which he had disturbed.

'Walk into the lake,' said Hank. 'They tend to hang around the land not the water.'

Leroy waded waist deep into the freezing water and cursed himself for not having spent the extra dollars and ordered heavier-weight waders.

'Never thought the water would be this cold in autumn,' he called to Hank.

'We may fish in a snowstorm before you leave,' comforted Hank.

Leroy was about to reply when Hank held up a hand to silence him. He shaded his eyes and stared ahead into the translucent purity of the Alaskan skies.

'Stewart,' he said.

'Bear,' said Dursley.

They all spun around and looked up to where Dursley was pointing. High on the ridge, outlined against the sky, its coat blown into waves by the wind, stood the grizzly. It peered short-sightedly across the water.

Leroy's nerves, tattered by the two experiences with bears, broke like an overstretched elastic band. He was certain that the bear was staring straight at him. He waded ashore and ran down the pebbled beach towards the far side of the lake wanting only to put as much distance as possible between himself and the bear.

'Stop!' screamed Kit and Hank together.

Earl launched himself at Leroy to bring him down in a tackle, but age and easy living had slowed his reflexes and Leroy's boots raked his chin leaving him sore and bleeding. 'Don't run! Stay with us! You're safe here!' yelled Hank.

But fear had plugged Leroy's ears and lent speed to his short legs. His boots flew over driftwood, rotting fish and stones.

The bear stood still. It seemed to lengthen its snout as it smelled for what it could not see. Suddenly Leroy cut across the wind as he rounded the far side of the lake.

The bear stiffened as it picked up his scent. It immediately set off after him. It seemed to lower its neck into its hunched shoulders as it loped down the hillside. Horror froze the party. They stood cold and motionless as the granite rocks lining the ridge. The bear flew over the tundra. It seemed to Hank that its feet did not touch ground.

'Whoa, bear!' he yelled, windmilling his arms as he raced down the beach, hoping to distract the bear and draw his attention away from Leroy.

'Oh no,' breathed Kit silently. 'Not again, Hank. Keep away from the bear. You can't help. It'll only kill both of you. I need you. We have a future together.'

Casey saw Kit's lips moving but could not hear what she was saying. She walked across to the edge of the lake, stretched up on tiptoe and put her arms around Kit's shoulder.

'It'll be all right,' she murmured, but Kit neither saw nor heard her.

The bear heard and ignored the shouts. At last he had a single figure to deal with. That figure was showing fear by running away. His hours of hesitation and frustration were at an end. The running figure was his. He was determined not to be thwarted. Foam flew from the grizzly's mouth and flecked the bushes as he ran. The deep silence was shattered by his roars.

Leroy heard the roaring. He looked back over his shoulder. He saw Hank racing along the beach and realized that the bear, its head held low and its ears laid back, flat as a cat, would reach him well before Hank even rounded the bend.

'Hail Mary, full of grace,' he intoned. 'The Lord is with thee.'

His voice was high and shaky as he recited the prayer of his childhood. He found comfort in words he had discarded along with his youth and innocence. He grasped frantically for the faith he had mocked with his hard-drinking, high-living friends. In his terror he sought what he had long abandoned.

'Holy Mary, Mother of God, pray for us sinners now and at the hour of our death.'

Tears streamed down the little Irishman's face and his white lips trembled.

The roaring became deafening. He felt his body vibrate. It seemed to centre over his head. He screamed. No sound came from his wide, gaping mouth. He fell to his knees and clawed at the pebbles, ripping them from the cold wet earth. He found comfort in the pain. The tears fell into his open mouth and down his cheeks. He screwed up his eyes. He did not want to see the bear.

In his imagination, he once again saw the cub tumble down the waterfall. He felt the grizzly's curved claws rip into his body and its teeth sink into his skull, killing him as it had the cub.

He lay on the pebbles, as if nailed to a cross, dribbling supplications to the Virgin Mary. 'Blessed art thou among women . . .'

In his terror he did not notice the plane circle once more over him and then fly suicidally low towards the bank.

The grizzly heard the roar of the propellers. He saw the great bird descending on him. He turned and ran, his legs brushing his ears. He did not stop until he reached the river and could no longer see or hear Stewart in the float-plane.

Satisfied that the bear would not return, Stewart flew back to the lake. He circled it tightly and landed, delicately as a dragonfly, on the surface.

Kit waded out, caught the stay-rope with shaking hands and dragged the plane towards the bank. Earl hurried to help her, but she shook her head. He picked up the fishing gear instead, trying to take over Hank's duties.

Stewart climbed down from the cockpit, balanced carefully on the float and unlocked the storage hold. In silence they stored their rods and the twisted haversack frame and boarded the plane.

Then Stewart, still mute and angry, taxied the plane across the lake to where Leroy lay on the pebbles with Hank kneeling behind him. As he cut the motors Kit opened the cabin door, scrambled down the steps and jumped into the water.

'Leroy, it's all over,' she murmured as she and Hank kneeled beside him.

'Holy Mary . . .' Leroy continued to mumble the prayer, oblivious of their presence.

'And blessed is the fruit of thy womb Jesus,' Kit's voice joined in. Finally Leroy opened his eyes.

'I didn't know you were a Catholic,' he said weakly.

'I'm not. But one of my boyfriends was a choirboy. I listened to the service so often while waiting for him that I suppose I learned and remembered the Hail Mary.'

'Come,' said Hank. 'Into the plane and we'll be home in twenty minutes.'

Kit had moved away from the two men to allow Leroy time to compose himself without the embarrassment of a woman watching him. She stood legs astride, hands hooked deep into her padded fishing vest, staring out at the lake.

She knew that she and Hank would be blamed for the state Leroy was in. Stewart expected his guides to avoid bears and not allow his clients to be terrified or placed in danger. She was not looking forward to the general meeting he would call of all the guides. The thought of being belittled in front of all the men did not worry her. Her father had trained her well and she was able to defend herself and explain her actions in any situation.

Her only fear was that she would be demoted back to the stove. After a taste of the freedom of guiding and being outdoors on the river all day, she knew that she would then resign.

That would mean losing Hank. She felt nauseous at the thought. While she had enjoyed many a 'fishing-season liaison', they usually lasted only for a few months as it was tacitly understood between the partners that once they returned home to the Lower Forty-Eight, the love affair ended. But Hank was different. Taming him into marriage would be like attempting to tickle one of the giant rainbows and catch it by hand, an almost impossible task. But given enough time Kit was determined to try it.

She turned as she heard boots scrunch on the pebbles.

'Well done, Leroy,' she said with a smile.

Hank and Leroy looked stunned.

'You did exactly what you were supposed to do. Lay flat and didn't move. We're proud of you.'

Leroy smiled and threw back his narrow shoulders.

'It's not easy to frighten an Irishman,' he said. He clapped her across the shoulders as he strode confidently to the plane.

Hank gave Kit the thumbs-up sign to congratulate her on turning a humiliated and terrified client back into a braggart.

Stewart used the back of his glove to clear a larger patch on the windscreen. He watched the three in amazement. He couldn't hear what was being said, but there was no mistaking Leroy's body language as he strutted back to the float.

Good girl, good guide, he congratulated Kit silently. When he smiled at her and Hank as they strapped themselves into the narrow seats, she knew that there would be no general meeting and Angela would continue to bake cookies.

Chapter Six

PEG-LEG PETE, the owner of Lucky Lodge, in the same area as Black Legs Lodge and thus the only fishing complex in competition with it, was in a foul mood. Last night's whisky lay heavy and sour in his belly and his head threatened to split every time the gulls screeched or the bald eagles called. His staff had learned to whisper to him when he was on a one-day drunk and to avoid him completely when he was on a two-day drunk. Today was a three-day one and even the cook had found an excuse to leave for King Salmon.

He crashed through the riverine bush slashing at the weathered scrubs with an axe he had picked up from the woodshed. He paused as the sound of laughter bounced through the willows.

Dursley was telling Earl and Leroy a story about partridge shooting in England. He was explaining how a Spaniard 'swinging through', following the bird, as it sped behind the line of guns shot an earl on his left and then repeated the mistake by peppering the cheek of a duke on his right.

The Americans had no knowledge of the traditions of English bird shooting, but found the story hilarious. Casey wriggled like a hooked trout trying to find a comfortable place on the pebbled spit of land. Her eyes shone with laughter. She grinned even though she had heard the story a dozen times.

She and Hank had just arrived by boat which they had

beached further down the shore of the Rainbow River. Dursley stuffed a sandwich into his mouth. At Leroy's insistence he stood up to demonstrate the Spaniard's lack of expertise, when Peg-leg Pete broke through the elders and staggered onto the beach.

'Off my land! Off my river! Away from my fish!' he yelled, peppering the orders with colourful oaths and swinging the axe around his balding head. Dursley swallowed the sandwich and stared at Pete in amazement. Hank stood up quickly.

'Pete,' he said, 'it's Hank.'

'I know you. You weasel. Left me for that glitzy place across the lake. Lucky Lodge wasn't good enough for you.'

Hank chose not to remind him that he had the highest turnover of staff in the area and a filthy reputation, which was well deserved.

Pete swung away from Hank and suddenly saw the boat. It bristled like a porcupine with fishing-rods.

'No!' shouted Hank and Kit, as they realized his intention. Hank caught up with Pete just before he reached the boat, but ducked as the axe whistled across his fishing cap.

'You don't really want to do this,' reasoned Kit, as the axe descended and tore a hole in the side of the boat.

Pete's only answer was to continue swinging wildly at the boat. Fortunately he was seeing three boats. Most of the strokes were wild and missed the actual boat.

'If it's not grizzly bears then it's madmen,' said Dursley, sitting down. He wisely decided that this was a personal matter and best left to the guides.

'I presume Hank and I swim home,' said Casey, eyeing the vast blue lake with apprehension. The float-plane had dropped off another group of fishermen before them, making it necessary for two of their party to go by boat. Casey had volunteered to do the trip in the open boat with Hank. There was an eagle's nest she wanted to see high on a rock rising from the middle of the lake. Hank had whetted her curiosity with tales of the bald eagle which nested on the bare granite rock every spring. When she heard the guides discussing who was to go to Rainbow River in the boat and who would go by plane she immediately begged for a seat in the boat.

Kit had to go in the plane to help offload the fishermen, a task she did reluctantly. She hoped that Casey would be seasick and a burden to Hank. But Casey had sailed the wind-whipped waters off the west coast of Scotland with her brothers from the time she could run fast enough to keep up with them. Casey Chargot was a hardened seaman.

The journey across Lake Nonvianuk was not pleasant. The wind sprang up. Within minutes the curdled blue waters were flecked with foam. Hank watched Casey as she braced herself and tried to focus his binoculars on the eagle's nest. He held the rocking boat in a tight circle around the base of the rock. He expected her to feel ill and ask him to continue the trip to Rainbow River, but she laughed in delight as she caught sight of the eagle resting on the nest of twigs. She handed him the binoculars. As their fingers touched, the boat lurched and she cannoned into Hank. He had held her lightly. Her breasts pressed hard against his chest and her hair, smelling of seasalt and soap, swung into his face.

He laughed with her, but his hands burned and he longed to hold her to him. The violence of his desire frightened him. He was not yet ready to let any woman into his life. He sensed that a commitment to Casey would last a lifetime.

The wife he had always envisaged was an outdoors girl from the States. Someone like Kit, one who thrilled to the lonely call of a loon on a dark lake and to the sight of a wild trout jumping high to take a fly. He had no wish to become involved with a wealthy English girl who would be afraid of the wilderness and blind to its beauty.

'How do we get to the upper reaches of this river to fish without the boat?' queried Leroy, wincing every time the axe rang true and split the boat open.

'Walk,' answered Hank. 'The banks are criss-crossed with bear tracks. It'll take longer, but we'll reach the big fish.' Earl immediately unscrewed the top of the flask and poured himself another cup of hot soup.

'Soup after walnut cake?' said Casey, and grinned.

'All goes into the same old mincing machine,' said Earl.

They had become good friends in the eight days they had fished together. Even Leroy now smiled more often than he snarled. It was difficult not to like Casey.

Kit too had warmed towards her, but she still watched carefully when Hank spent time teaching Casey to cast. He still held her in his arms at night, but at times Kit felt that he was performing a duty, albeit a pleasant one. She sensed that his mind was elsewhere and she was afraid that Casey was the distraction. Her intuition told her that a close bond was forming between Dursley's fiancée and the man she had chosen as her own.

As the days passed in the translucent light and pure air of Katmai, Casey had found to her surprise that catching rainbows was addictive. Each time she prised the barbless hook from the side of the trout's mouth and held its deep-shouldered body into the current, running her fingers lightly down the rosy line beneath its dark green back, she thrilled to the wonder of having a wild creature in her hands.

She knew it was only hers until its gills absorbed sufficient oxygen and it became orientated after the mad whirling and spinning dance it devised to throw the hook. The speed with which it angled out of her hands when it recovered always surprised her. Within seconds it was lost in the pine green water.

She now looked forward to each day's fishing and the hours she spent at Hank's side. He was a patient teacher and she was an apt pupil.

Kit walked back to join the group leaving Hank to reason with Peg-leg and duck his wild swings. The fishing party turned their backs on the demolition job taking place behind them and lied to each other about the fish they had hooked and lost.

As Casey sat and smiled at the fishing stories she let her mind wander to the log cabin, where often at night she lay listening to the warm burble of the black stove and fantasized about Hank.

As the wind rattled the windows it carried with it the lonely, beautiful call of the loon. Her heart now sang the song of silence found only in a true wilderness. England seemed very far away. She had no overwhelming desire to return to the little island. Then, hearing Dursley's gentle snore, she would guiltily think of her future and wonder whether she could live up to the standards set by her future mother-in-law.

'Crazy man,' said Hank, breathing heavily as he dropped onto the pebbles beside her.

Casey dragged her thoughts back to the present. She blinked as she listened to the silence and realized that Peg-leg had stopped wrecking their boat.

'Where has he gone?' she asked, wanting to go and see what damage had been caused, but afraid that Pete would return.

'Probably to the Barabara sites,' answered Hank. 'He usually tramps over the remains of the old subterranean Inuit homes when he has a hangover. He knows it infuriates the people concerned with the preservation of ancient cultures and artifacts. There are some fine examples of Barabaras close to his lodge. Everyone lives in fear that one day he will destroy the remains. He's an old devil.'

'It's that Aleut blood in him,' said Kit scathingly. 'Once they have native blood in their veins they always behave irrationally. It's like trying to make a pet of a wolf and being surprised when it eats you!'

'Native?' queried Leroy.

'Sourdoughs often refer to the early inhabitants of Alaska, the Inuit, Athapaskans and Aleuts as natives,' explained Hank.

'Then I have native blood in me,' said Casey.

Dursley laughed. 'You, my Bubbles, are as pure-blood as I am, English all the way through.'

Casey studied Dursley carefully before answering. She remembered his mother extolling the virtues and necessity of having pure blood lines. Her words rang clearly in Casey's mind. *Nowadays we take more care with the blood lines of our stud horses than we do with our children's choice of partners. Well, that will not happen in this family. I will not have tainted blood staining our family tree.* 'Not if my family history is to be believed,' Casey replied quietly. The moment she had been dreading had arrived.

Dursley stopped laughing and listened intently.

Casey took a deep breath. She was not certain how Dursley would react to her story.

For a moment she hesitated and watched a merganser steer her flotilla of fish-eating ducklings across the river to the safety of shrubs and reeds on the opposite bank. Within seconds they had vanished, their black and yellow markings blending perfectly into the shadows and sun-dappled water.

The party was silent waiting for her to speak. Dursley sat up straight and crossed his legs as if waiting for a court sentence, his half-eaten sandwich forgotten on his knee. Casey coughed and smiled tremulously in response to Hank's broad grin. She knew she must tell Dursley.

Sitting on a pebbled spit of land watching trout flee from the angry attacks by sockeye which lay thick and red as a Persian carpet on the river bed, Casey suddenly knew that she wanted to be part of the strength and silence of this land. It had called to her when from the plane to Anchorage she looked down at the silver rivers floating and twisting like streamers in a breeze. The call had become stronger as she knelt in the glacier-fed waters holding dazed trout in her hands. She needed to be where she could taste the sweetness of the air. Like the blind given sight, she could for the first time appreciate the purity of the light and the air.

Dursley pulled off his fishing cap and as his hair tumbled across his forehead Casey had an overwhelming urge to take him in her arms, smooth his hair and see him smile at her again.

Why dredge up old stories? she thought. Dursley is right. I am English and we will make a good couple. Keep quiet and let history remain where it belongs, in the past.

While those thoughts chased through her mind, she heard Kit say: 'How could you possibly have native blood, Casey? I thought your family had been in England for hundreds of years?'

'They have,' answered Casey, not looking at Dursley, 'but if old family stories are to be believed one of my ancestors made the hazardous journey to Alaska when the trading in sea-otter pelts was at its height.'

'They were so easy to kill,' broke in Kit.

Casey winced, but was happy that the conversation had turned away from her native ancestry if only for a short while. She felt a burning deep down in the pit of her stomach as she wondered how Dursley would accept her 'tainted' ancestry. She felt guilty for not having told him sooner. She knew that he trusted her and believed that there were no secrets between them. Casey hoped that Kit would expound further on sea otters but she was silent.

'I thought sea otters were hunted to near extinction,' said Earl, opening the white plastic container to scrounge for left-overs.

'They were.'

Leroy joined in the conversation for the first time. 'The English have always been a nation of shopkeepers with an eye open for the main chance. The trading class, I mean,' he corrected quickly, looking at Dursley. 'Money made from furs would have pulled them in.'

'That's an unbiased opinion, of course,' said Dursley softly. He disliked having anyone mock his island home or its inhabitants.

Dursley debated the advisability of telling Leroy that the Russians had been the first to exploit the rich fur trade in Alaska. Two Siberian merchants had started the wildly lucrative trade in pelts and put together the Russian American company. The Czar of Russia had given them the monopoly in Alaska at the end of the seventeen-hundreds.

Dursley was tempted to explain to the Americanized Irishman that the English had been granted the right by Charles II to trade in pelts in all land drained by rivers emptying into the Hudson Bay. But he decided not to defend the English. The explanation would be knowledge thrown away on the wind.

He was more interested in what Casey had to say, though part of him dreaded hearing it.

He, too, had noticed her and Hank's friendship deepening. He was proud that another man found his woman attractive. Now, it made him realize that he wanted Casey Chargot as his wife, and not available to others.

'It was about that time,' Casey said, pushing a plastic bag of cookies across to Earl, 'when my great, or was it great-great-grandfather, sailed out to Alaska on one of the many voyages to try to find the fabled North-West Passage. They were side-tracked into buying furs. The rich waterproof pelts of the sea otter were extremely valuable. They spent too much time trading and did not listen to local warnings about the "Big Ice" coming down. Their ship was trapped.

'They thought they would be held in the ice for two or three months but as they learned to understand and talk the language of the local Eskimos, they realized to their horror that it would be at least nine frozen months before they saw the sun again or could hope to repair their boat and sail for England.

'A family of Eskimos took pity on the ignorant Englishmen and built a house of whale bones covered with seal skins. They showed them how to hunt moose, caribou, seals and bears and how to fish in the ice.

'Great-grandpa fell in love with one of the daughters.'

'Whew!' broke in Leroy. 'He must have liked the smell of dried fish and blubber.'

'So would you if you were starving,' said Earl angrily, seeing Casey redden.

'The ship's captain was a little appalled that one of his officers wanted to marry a native, but eventually when Great-grandpa took to leaving his shipmates and spending nights with the Eskimos—'

'They don't like to be called Eskimos,' broke in Kit.

'Inuit or Yupiks. The "real people",' said Hank gently.

Casey smiled her thanks and Dursley felt his heart ache at what he thought he might lose.

'The captain married them and Great-grandpa spent most of

the rest of his life in Alaska. Ticasuk visited England to show the family their three children, but she was unhappy away from her great land of ice and snow.'

Dursley started as Casey said Ticasuk. He remembered that she had said that all girls in the family were given the name Ticasuk because of a promise made to her great-grandfather that all females would carry the name of the wife he adored.

'I bet his parents made her damn unwelcome,' said Leroy who had been sitting crosslegged on the pebbles listening to Casey in fascination.

'My family were probably stunned and horrified,' Casey admitted. 'In those days you did not marry natives. I remember as a little girl the uproar my uncle caused when he went to Bulgaria and married a very beautiful Bulgarian. That was not so long ago,' she added. 'My family considered her "not quite right", though we already had Inuit blood.'

For the first time since starting the story Casey glanced across the red-checked tablecloth which had been spread on the pebbles, but Dursley did not look up.

Dursley had taken the fly box from his fishing vest. He was carefully rearranging the nymphs and mice and sorting the egg patterns into correct colour grading. His long eyelashes shielded his downcast eyes and Casey could read nothing in his face. She felt cold with apprehension that his family and friends would be shocked at her story. Dursley would have to admit that Casey Chargot did not have the 'pure' blood his family deemed necessary to marry into the Carrington family. For the first time she faced the very real possibility of losing Dursley and her stomach twisted as it had when her boots sank deep into the rotting salmon.

Hank watched the two lovers and, sensing their distress, he stood up quickly, knocking over Earl's mug of soup.

'Sorry, Earl,' said Hank, 'but it's time to test the river. Come on, everyone.'

Earl drained the dregs from the mug and helped Kit pack the remains of the picnic lunch into plastic bags and stuff them deep into a haversack.

'Casey, you come with me,' said Hank. 'We need to work on your nymphing technique and I want to find one of the Lucky Lodge's guides and borrow one of their boats. Stewart can talk to Peg-leg tomorrow about ours, or what's left of it,' he said, looking at their battered boat.

Kit walked quietly to the boat and breathed a sigh of relief. Peg-leg had concentrated on smashing in the sides of the boat and their rods seemed to be undamaged.

'Here is your rod,' she called to Dursley. 'I'll set you up on a good stretch of the river and take Earl and Leroy away with me.'

The fishing party gathered round the boat and sorted out their tackle. Dursley stroked his rod tenderly and inspected his reel carefully, then satisfied he picked up his light rainproof jacket and stuffed it into the pocket on the back of his fishing vest. Earl kicked the boat as they turned to wade into the river and it rocked over, exposing the gaping holes made by the axe.

'They take this "last great frontier" business seriously here, don't they?' he said as he hurried to catch up with Kit.

'It's a country which attracts the tough kids and those who want to experience a true wilderness,' defended Kit. 'Peg-leg is a legend in this area. He lost his leg on the polar ice-pack whilst tracking a polar bear.'

'Lucky he only lost a leg,' said Leroy, 'I hear those things actually hunt you. If they set out after you, then you're cat's meat.'

'The bear didn't get him, the ice did,' said Hank.

'Ice?' queried Dursley, his interest aroused.

'The ice-packs are more terrifying than the polar bears,' said Hank. Dursley stopped to listen. He had considered returning to Alaska to hunt a polar bear.

'Hunting a polar bear is dangerous enough,' said Hank. 'It is a clever killer, but the polar ice you have to hunt on is murderous.'

'I didn't realize that,' said Dursley. Leroy and Earl stood close to listen. Casey joined them, hoping that Dursley would put his arm around her shoulders, but he kept his eyes on Hank and his hands caressed only his graphite fishing-rod.

'Sea currents and wind form the polar ice into gigantic pressure ridges. Twenty to forty feet high. Leads open in what looks like endless unbroken ice. As soon as your boat enters the open water channel the wind can change and the lead close and you're trapped.'

'Trapped with the bears,' said Leroy.

'And you had better hope that the huge ice field he is on doesn't break away from the main body of ice or you could end up drifting on the black sea for months, with only the bear for company,' said Kit, enjoying the look of horror on Leroy's face.

'That's when you wish you were an Inuit,' said Kit, smiling at Casey. 'They seem to be the only ones who know how to exist on ice.'

'Enough of your stories, Kit,' said Hank. 'Let's see how many trout we can get in Peg-leg's river.'

'I thought this was the Rainbow River,' said Leroy.

'It is, but Peg-leg calls it his private river,' said Kit.

Casey felt her thighs tremble as she struck out determinedly against the current. She had looked forward to a ride up the river by boat to the designated fishing spot, but now she took no pleasure in the high call of the great bald eagle and the emerald heads of the mallard ducks failed to attract her as they paddled away from the heavy splashing of the fishing party.

'Probably the same family as last year,' Kit said to Hank, eager to break the gloom which seemed to have settled over the group after the attack on their boat.

'Good eating?' queried Earl.

'Only for cats,' answered Kit. 'Their favourite food is the eyes of the salmon.'

'Yugh,' shuddered Casey. 'Why the eyes?'

'Well, unlike the merganser chicks who have a hooked lower beak to enable them to eat fish, it's easier for the mallards to prise out eyes with their stubby rounded beaks. That's why mallards taste the way the sockeye smell.'

Earl grimaced and glanced at Casey and Dursley. They were

plodding upstream together but apart. Neither had spoken to each other since Casey told her story of Inuit blood.

Hank, too, noticed the tension between them. 'Here, Dursley,' he said, pointing out a stretch of the river, 'start here at this riffle and work your way upstream. We'll meet where the river forks.'

Kit and Hank had long agreed to let Dursley fish on his own. He was a serious fisherman and the levity of the others annoyed him. He preferred to fish alone.

'You two come with me,' said Kit, striking out for the bank. 'We'll go up well ahead of Dursley and fish the opposite bank.'

'Bears?' queried Leroy, eyeing the dwarf scrub suspiciously.

'Hardly ever see them here,' said Hank.

'Richer salmon streams for them,' added Kit.

'Yeah. I seem to have heard that before.' Leroy stumbled, cursed and regained his balance.

'Watch it,' cautioned Kit, 'we're in an area of salmon redds and it's very easy to fall and slide into one.'

'How deep are they?' asked Leroy, peering myopically into the rippling water trying to find the round pits where the salmon spawned.

'Just under your chin and over Casey's head,' joked Earl as he strode easily upstream.

'Fish dig out these holes?' queried Leroy sceptically.

'The females use their tails plus the force of the current to wash away the gravel,' said Kit. 'Their tails are in tatters when the redd is finally ready.'

Leroy nodded but made no further comment. He peered down into the river as he walked, careful not to step into one of the redds, which sounded like a tank trap to him.

Hank glanced over his shoulder. He had decided to take Casey well away from Dursley, who seemed to have withdrawn totally from her after her story of her native blood. Hank hated to see the hurt and bewilderment in her usually sparkling eyes as she looked at Dursley, hoping for a sign of tenderness.

Dursley waded to where two streams met and twined before

joining the main river. He found the riffle tumbling over itself like fine lace which Hank had pointed out as a good fishing spot. Dursley selected two beads, one a bright peach the colour of fresh salmon eggs, and the other a dusty mauve to match the older eggs. He cast just below the petticoat of lace and quickly mended his line. It ensured that the current would not drag the line in a large lazy loop ahead of the eggs and hook, warning the trout that these were not normal eggs drifting away from a redd.

Kit watched him for a while before reluctantly moving away to teach Earl and Leroy not to throw themselves forward into the river when casting the heavier nymphs. She was still trying to explain to them that black leeches and nymphs bumping over the uneven river bottom would often tempt the trout to turn away from the current and follow them instead of waiting for eggs to pop into their mouths.

She turned round to watch Dursley for a few moments longer. It was a delight to watch an expert fisherman testing the river, tempting the trout. She studied the snap of his line as it flew back behind him. She nodded in appreciation at the fine tight coil at its tip as it sank to touch the water.

Heaving a sigh of resignation, Kit left Dursley to the solitude and beauty of the river. Dursley glanced up as Kit splashed her way through the shallows. She was as good a guide as any man he had met. He appreciated the way she steered the rest of the fishing party away from him, leaving him free to enjoy his fishing.

She trudged downstream to where Earl and Leroy were enthusiastically thrashing the water. The nymphs were dragged off the river bed and hung black and slimy on the hooks as the two men hauled them back over their heads and then beat them down on the water as if trying to knock the fish unconscious.

'Leroy,' called Kit, 'you will scare the trout to death if you do that.'

'Not a bad idea,' he answered.

'You could also try a stick of gelignite,' teased Earl, stripping in his line as if he had a great white shark on the hook, instead of a red sockeye which had darted at the nymph in anger to chase it and had managed to get the hook through its eye.

'You may have to just break it off,' said Kit as she reached Earl and studied the line where it sank into the water.

'What, a big one like this!' objected Earl.

'It's big, but it's an ugly old sockeye,' said Kit.

'Can't be,' objected Earl. 'Hank says once they enter the river to spawn they don't eat.'

'He's not eating. He went for your bait in anger. You've been hitting him on the head with it, now he's punch-drunk,' smiled Kit.

'I'm not losing another nymph,' said Earl. 'I'm down to my last two.' He reeled in the slack line and started slowly dragging the salmon to the shore.

Leroy gasped as the twelve-pound fish broke water. It bore no resemblance to the salmon he had seen lying red as strewn rubies on the river bed. The jaws had elongated and were lined with needle-sharp teeth. Its head was now a bilious green which clashed with the bright red of the body. The lower jaw was curved up into a vicious hook, giving the once beautiful silver fish a mean and vicious appearance.

'Looks like a killer,' said Leroy scathingly, relieved that Earl had not hooked into a huge trout.

Earl bit back the obvious retort and concentrated on dragging the sockeye up onto the mud.

'Belongs to the family Salmonoid,' said Kit. 'They evolved about sixty million years ago in the Arctic waters.'

'How do you know all this stuff?' asked Leroy.

'I'm an icythologist,' she said, enjoying his look of perplexity. She relented a little and explained. 'That means I make a study of fresh-water fish.'

Earl looked at her with admiration. He found 'book-learning' a mystical art. He had only gone to college because he played ball. He was big, strong and ruthless on a football field. His learning had been earned on his ability to block and tackle. At college he discovered another skill, his ability to coach. It was this skill which now earned him a very comfortable lifestyle; it also offered him the time to go fishing, a leisure sport which was very popular with the 'wealthy set' in the States.

'Watch its teeth,' Kit shouted as Earl bent down to remove the hook from the salmon's eye, where he had foulhooked it.

She put her foot on the fish to stop it thrashing and took out a pair of haemostats. Clamping the pliers onto the hook, she quickly whipped it out.

'Poor thing only has a few days to go,' she said. 'See, it's already losing pieces of flesh.' She pushed the dying fish back into the river.

'All right, guys.' She took Earl's rod from him and checked the length of the leader and the knot holding the black nymph and hook. 'What you need to fool these trout, and believe me they are no idiots, is a "dead drift".'

'Or a worm,' mumbled Leroy.

'You have to get the nymphs, or the mouse Leroy is using, to bounce along the surface as if it's in distress,' she cautioned, ignoring Leroy's interruption. 'If there is a slight drag on the line the trout will move away and not touch the line.'

'Yeah. Mend your line, mend, mend, mend,' mimicked Leroy, but cautiously. He was a little wary of Kit. She out-walked and out-fished all the guides, including Hank. She was a formidable force in an argument, especially if fishing was the subject. He had learned to watch her eyes. When the blue found deep in the heart of glaciers changed to the dead grey which heralded the approach of cold fog banks, he dropped out of the discussion and listened from the safety of the sidelines.

Kit's voice drifted over him as he watched her hook and land a fighting rainbow from the very pool he had been fishing from for the last twenty minutes.

'Knew he was there,' he said, as she held the rainbow into the current before releasing it.

So why didn't you catch him? thought Kit.

'You were right,' she said, remembering that the aggressive East Coaster was a client. 'You chose a good fishing spot, Leroy. If you get that dragging loop out of your line you'll be the terror of all the trout in the Katmai.'

Leroy smiled triumphantly at Earl. His lure hit the water, sank and immediately the current pulled his line ahead of the mouse on the bottom. Kit sighed and sat on one of the rocks, prepared for another long day.

'That's it, Casey,' said Hank excitedly. 'You've got it. A perfect mend.' They watched the luminous pink float warning her that her line was going to overrun the lure. Hank grinned as she automatically flicked the line upriver.

She dragged the weighted nymph from the river bed and cast again. Her eyes were dark and fathomless under the peak of her cap and she bit down on her bottom lip in concentration.

'You have the patience of your ancestors,' he said. 'You will make a good fisherman.'

Casey's face dropped. Hank could have kicked himself for reminding her of the conversation with Dursley about the Inuits.

'Come on,' he said, 'let's go further upstream. We'll give these fish a rest.'

Casey stepped back to join him. Her boot rested on the edge of a four-foot-deep redd and as the gravel of the funnel-shaped nest gave way she disappeared under the strong waters.

The cold took her breath away. She was gasping and struggling like a played-out trout when Hank reached her. He hauled her upright. She put her arms around his waist to steady herself and catch her breath. It was comforting to rest her head against his chest. She snuggled deeper into the safety of his arms.

The feeling of isolation and betrayal when Dursley ignored her after the disclosure of her ancestry, the fear of suddenly being underwater, anchored onto the gravel bed by the weight of her boots and waders as they filled with water, and the terror of drowning as the glacial waters rushed up her nose and down her throat had terrified and weakened her. She clung to Hank desperately.

'There, there,' he soothed. 'You've earned yourself a place in the Black Legs Lodge swimming team and you'll have a T-shirt to prove it.'

The lodge awarded T-shirts to those who 'swam' in the rivers. Casey smiled weakly, clamping her teeth together to stop them chattering.

Feeling the tremors run through her body as he held her close, Hank knew that he had to warm her before hypothermia set in. It didn't take long for the body temperature to drop dangerously low when the winds raced down from the tumbled mountains and added a wind-chill factor to a wet body.

Hank looked downstream to call Kit, but she was almost out of sight keeping Earl and Leroy away from Dursley, who had moved into a feeder stream and was fishing under a small lee on the opposite bank which seemed to have an inexhaustible supply of trout. He would remain there happily until someone found him and dragged him off to a shale spit for lunch.

Hank realized he would have no help with Casey. He half carried her to the shore, found a sheltered spot in a clump of stunted elders and left her. Soon he had a fire burning, fed with seemingly waterlogged driftwood. He threw as much wood on the fire as he could find, then hurried back. Unzipping the back pouch of his anorak as he ran across the pebbles, he pulled out a pair of blue thermal long johns and an expedition-weight vest. Years of guiding had taught him to carry extra underwear for his clients.

Casey sat on the wet turf. Her arms held her trembling knees to her chest but her fingers were blue and too numb to lace together. She had given up the attempt to stop her teeth chattering and her jaw ached. Tears streamed down her round face as she cried both for a love she thought she had lost and the misery of cold she had not known, even on Yorkshire shoots, with the wind knifing in from the North Sea defying all attempts to keep it out with Barbours, oilskins and fur-lined coats.

She knuckled away the tears as she heard Hank's return, but mascara ran telltale streaks down her cheeks. Hank took one look at Casey and knew that they had to move fast if she was not to be hospitalized.

'Strip,' he ordered.

Casey stared at him and remained huddled up, her body now jerking and shuddering as if in a seizure.

'We have to get you warm and dry, Casey,' he explained, pulling her up and tearing apart the Velcro straps of her waders. Casey stood still as a chastened child as he undressed her, bending her head dutifully as he pulled her sodden underwear over her head. Her breasts hung heavy and free, the creamy skin mottled blue with cold. He unzipped his anorak, took off his winter-weight shirt and dried her hair with it. Then he rubbed her back and buttocks until she winced with pain and the skin changed from the white-grey colour of dying salmon to a rich, deep pink. She held onto his shoulders as he scrubbed at her buttocks and pulled his long johns up high under her breasts. Eager as he was to have her dressed in dry clothes and sitting over the fire, he could not help noticing her nipples standing high in the cold, as if recently suckled.

He found a dry piece on his woollen shirt and rubbed at her breasts until they glowed, then he fitted the warm vest over her head. Quickly he put her into his lined windproof anorak and grunted in satisfaction as it hung well below her knees. Socks, he thought looking at her feet, blue with streaks of pink and white. Damn, I don't have a spare pair. He bent down and picked Casey up, slinging her over his shoulder as easily as he would a fishing creel. He carried her to the fire and sat her down with her toes close to the flames. He checked on the direction of the wind then seated himself close to her, acting as a wind-break.

'I'm sorry to have been so clumsy,' said Casey softly. Hank grinned as he noticed the colour coming back to her cheeks and the shudders lessening.

'I've slid down more redds than I care to remember,' he comforted her, as he unlaced his boots and peeled off a pair of thick marled fisherman's socks. The wind sliced through the thinner woollen pair he wore beneath them and he quickly replaced his boots.

'Put your feet in my lap,' he commanded. He rubbed her toes until they ached before he fitted his socks over her small feet. They came up to her knees. She leaned forward to warm her hands and face over the fire.

Hank took the opportunity to leave her and fetch her sodden clothes which he had thrown over an elder shrub. Digging holes between the pebbles he buried two upright pieces of driftwood and strung a length of nylon fishing line between them. Casey blushed as he wrung out her underwear and thick sweater and hung them over the line to dry. Hank turned her waders inside out until he reached the boots which he emptied of water. He laid them across the haversack, which he placed upright beside the fire.

He came back to her carrying a Thermos flask of coffee. As the metal cap burned her lips and the steam closed her eyes Casey realized how much she had enjoyed the touch of Hank's hands on her body.

She shivered as she once again felt his hands holding and rubbing her breasts with the coarse shirt.

'Still cold, Casey?' asked Hank, seeing her shudder.

Casey nodded guiltily and as he put his arms around her she snuggled up to him. He rubbed her back and arm, wondering why it felt so right to have another man's wife-to-be in his arms. The peace and silence of the wilderness seeped into him as he sat staring into the flames. He sensed that his destiny lay with this woman now nestling up to him. Overwhelmed with this feeling of tenderness he bent his head and kissed her hair lightly.

Though his touch had been light as the drift of a mayfly and quick as the beat of a gull's wing, Casey felt his lips. She lifted her face up to his. He looked deep into her dark eyes and saw his need echoed in the soft depths and tremble of her full bottom lip.

The wild call of the great bald eagle soaring high overhead seemed to seal and bless their tryst as their lips tasted each other.

They held time like eternity between their lips. As Hank tasted the sweetness of Casey's mouth, Trapper's words sang to the eagle's call.

Once you have found a woman who is rhythmed to you, hold her. Never let her go, for there is only one in the world who will beat to your rhythm.

Hank knew with certainty that this petite, dark woman was the one he had to hold. Her Inuit ancestors were part of this great wild land which had won his heart and like a jealous mistress refused to let him go.

'Whoa, bear.' Earl's hearty voice bounced over the river. It broke Hank and Casey apart. She opened her eyes. She was dazed and reached again for Hank. He held her hands in his for a moment and then moved towards the fire. 'The others are coming, Ticasuk,' he warned, using her ancestral name.

Casey smiled and Hank wanted to crush her to him, to feel again the softness of her lips and breasts pressing hard against him. Instead he stood up, walked to the makeshift washing line and turned her clothes around so that the heat could dry the other side. Casey threw the remainder of the pile of driftwood onto the fire and stood warming the back of her legs.

'What's going on?' queried Leroy, as he, Kit and Earl broke through the scrub willow and elder and out onto the open bank where Hank had built the fire.

'Looks like Delhi market on wash-day,' remarked Earl.

Kit quickly accessed the situation. She noted which of Casey's clothes were over the line drying and which of Hank's clothes Casey was wearing. Her eyes narrowed; perhaps her original assessment of the girl had been right. She was a threat.

Casey remained with her back to them pretending to rub the back of her hair to dry it. Hank was wringing water out of the toes of Casey's socks before returning them to the line.

'Bears?' he queried, his head still down over the clothes line.

'Aw, no,' replied Earl. 'Just singing the old fishing song, in case one of them was sleeping around someplace.'

'How did the fishing go?' Hank asked Kit, as he turned round to face them. He was certain that Kit would read his new love for Casey and guilt on his face.

'Not bad,' she answered, after scrutinizing his face and finding nothing to upset her. 'Earl hooked four good ones and Leroy three.'

'Five,' corrected Leroy.

'I said *good* ones,' answered Kit.

Hank was amused to see Leroy back down. Not many people stood up to Kit, he thought, well, not many sensible ones. He wondered what her reaction would be when he told her about Casey. It was not a pleasant subject to contemplate, so he regaled them with the story of Casey's mishaps.

'There must be an easier way to study a sockeye nest,' teased Earl.

'She is just after one of the lodge's T-shirts,' said Leroy, 'and she has the shape to fill it.' He winced in anticipation as Earl lumbered towards him. 'Come on, Earl,' he moaned, 'I only have two kneecaps and I'm not much good at walking on my hands.'

'Watch your mouth then,' warned Earl.

Casey laughed, a clear infectious sound. Hank was surprised to see no trace of guilt or anxiety as she finally turned round to greet the rest of the party. 'Thank you, Earl,' she said. 'It's good to have a gentleman looking after me.' Earl puffed out his chest and Leroy bristled. 'But in a way Leroy is right. Imagine me stumbling over the rocks with "Black Legs Lodge fishing team" wobbling all over my chest.'

Earl saw the joke and his deep roars of laughter complemented Casey's high clear notes. Even Kit joined in. Hank relaxed and grinned.

'Just as well fish only have good eyesight and not good hearing underwater,' said Dursley as he cut across the river to join them. Casey paled as she saw him.

It took Dursley a few minutes to comprehend the meaning of the washing line, fire and Casey enveloped in Hank's clothes.

'Are you all right, Casey?' he asked. She swallowed loudly, certain that he would read guilt in her eyes. She lowered her eyes, and crossed her arms over her chest as another spasm of cold shook her body. She did not answer.

'Casey fell into one of the redds,' explained Hank quickly, giving her time to recover. 'It is an unpleasant experience in these icy waters. But we seem to have warmed her up. Her clothes are almost dry.'

Suddenly Dursley was afraid. This woman standing silent and pale in front of the fire was not the sparkling, joyous woman he knew. 'Will she be all right?' he asked, picturing Casey in hospital with pneumonia.

'Perfectly,' comforted Kit, trying to ease Dursley's obvious distress.

Dursley realized with a sudden shock that if anything happened to Casey there would be an aching void in his life. To his surprise he found that he loved her enough to accept the native blood that a marriage with her would bring into his family. As he looked at the small shivering figure dwarfed in Hank's green anorak he was disgusted with himself for having ignored her and selfishly spent the morning fishing on his own, as far away from her as possible. He propped his rod between the branches of a willow. The yellow leaves fluttered softly onto the grey pebbles.

'Bubbles,' he said softly, as he reached her side, his voice now concerned and loving. 'I'm so sorry I wasn't with you.'

He put his arms around her and ran his fingers through her hair smoothing out the damp tangles. 'I love you so much,' he whispered as he kissed her neck below the ear. 'I need you so much.'

Casey let her head fall forward onto his shoulder. She felt so desperately tired and confused. She felt safe with Dursley, but knew that she had to be a part of Hank. Tears soon turned into racking sobs. Her body shuddered as violently as it had when the autumn wind iced her wet clothes.

'Hush, hush little one,' soothed Dursley, rocking her backwards and forwards. 'It's all right, everything is all right now.'

No, it's not, sobbed Casey silently. Nothing will ever be all right again. I can't marry you now. I have to tell you and I don't want to hurt you. I know that even though I still love you I must be with Hank.

Jumbled thoughts rushed through her mind. It's not possible to love two men, she argued as she rested in the familiarity of Dursley's arms, but I do. I could live contentedly with Dursley, but I know that I cannot live without Hank.

Hank watched Dursley hold and calm Casey and he wanted to shout: 'Leave her alone. She belongs in my arms. I should be comforting her, not you!' But the unwelcome and intrusive voice of reason persuaded him to keep quiet. Casey might have just turned to Dursley in shock.

As he saw her rest her head on Dursley's shoulder he had the sickening thought that perhaps their recent embraces and kisses meant more to him than they had to her. Casey was about to become the Countess of Edbury and enjoy all the privileges which went with the position. He could only offer her winters in Alaska, or ones spent in his flat. It was the top floor of a warehouse overlooking the Thames. An area habitable, but not yet glorified by property developers. Summers he could take her to Alaska where he collected material for the illustrations for a book he had been commissioned to write. The publishing house in London assured him it was to be the definitive book on Alaska. Judging by the handsome advance they had given him, he believed them.

Hank knew that these were but paltry temptations when compared with what Dursley Carrington, the sixth Earl of Edbury could offer.

He turned away, unable to watch Casey in Dursley's arms any longer. He busied himself checking and changing lures for Earl and Leroy. Kit took over the laundry and stood waving Casey's thick blue long johns over the fire.

'It's your client who did a sockeye swim,' she shouted across at Hank, 'so you buy dinner and drinks when we get to Anchorage.'

'Anchorage?' said Leroy. 'I thought we were here for another nine days.'

'We are, Leroy, but Stewart has to fly to Anchorage over the weekend to collect another cook to help Angela. Hank and I are going with him.'

Before Leroy could protest about losing Hank and Kit as guides, Kit continued, 'We have not had any time off for the last three months. We'll only be away for three days. By then you'll be teaching me how to fish. Bill and Len are fantastic guides.' She smiled at Leroy and his scowl vanished.

Earl looked up, leaving Hank to change the length of his leader. 'That means we have a chance at Heartbreak with Bill and Len,' he said, grinning at Kit.

'Heartbreak!' Dursley held Casey's hand in his, but looked up at the group with interest.

'A river you would love,' said Kit. 'It tumbles and turns over enormous rocks, then expands into deceptively wide, still stretches. One finds the fish lying behind the rocks or in the lee of the banks out of the current. Should you land one of those giants, trout fishing will never be the same for you again.'

The guides loved the testing river and guarded her jealously. They took few clients there, as the fish were prize fighters and had not grown to the scarcely believable size they were by being stupid. Heartbreak taxed both the mental and physical ability of everyone who dared fish her. A day spent fighting the river and being outwitted by the fish usually left clients disgruntled. Heartbreak was only an expert fisherman's dream. Kit loved the wild fish and the river with a deep passion.

'Bill and Len say it'll probably be the last time Heartbreak will be fished this season,' said Hank, hoping to excite the fishing team and lessen their resentment at losing Kit and himself as guides for a few days.

The thought of not fishing Heartbreak until the following year shocked Kit. She realized that she wanted more than anything else to spend the weekend on that wonderful river, not in Anchorage. Hank and I still have five weeks together until the lodge closes for winter, she reasoned to herself. It does look as if we'll have an early winter, which means that the weather will close down and Heartbreak will be inaccessible. I have to fish Heartbreak with

Bill and Len. Stewart can fetch the cook. She looked up as Casey coughed. A smile creased the corners of her eyes.

'Casey,' she said, 'why don't you go into Anchorage with Stewart to collect the new cook? A short break from fishing will be good for you. Spend a few hours in Nordstrom's. See if you can iron Dursley's Amex card flat.'

'I don't enjoy shopping,' said Casey. Everyone laughed.

'What!' exclaimed Kit, whose second passion was shopping. 'You have a Gold card and you don't enjoy using it? Casey, I don't believe it.'

'If anyone was crazy enough to give Kit a Gold card she would even give up fishing,' said Hank.

'You can try ironing my Mastercard as well, Bubbles,' said Dursley. 'I could do with a Patagonia neck warmer. This wind has found the secret of getting through zips and Velcro straps.'

Casey's first reaction was to reject the idea of being cossetted merely because she had fallen into the river. As Dursley held her away from him waiting for her answer, she remembered the force of the wind and iciness of the water. A few days away from the river did seem very inviting.

'Won't Stewart mind?' asked Casey, now eager to enjoy the luxury of a massage and sauna at the Captain Cook in Anchorage.

'Not at all,' answered Kit, 'and he'll probably fly through the Lake Clark Pass. Seeing mountains and glaciers at wing-tip level is an experience you will never forget.'

'Especially if he takes the wrong fork and you fly east side instead of west side – or is it the other way round?' said Leroy. He ignored Kit's frown. 'You end up flying vertically because the forks become too narrow to fly horizontally. The wrong fork finally peters out completely and only walls of rock and ice tower up the thousands of feet in front of you. The plane ends up frozen for all time,' he ended. He was repeating a story Bill had recited, about a cocksure young pilot flying the pass contrary to all advice and taking the fork which led only to death.

'Stewart has a few thousand hours of flying experience,' broke in Hank, seeing Casey pale and Dursley look anxious. 'He has also flown the Lake Clark dozens of times. He has passed the stage of having to prove himself.'

'You are perfectly safe with him as a pilot,' said Kit, moving purposefully towards Leroy. He found it necessary to visit the toilet and absent himself from her tongue. 'Flying the pass is an experience you should not miss, Casey. Stewart will enjoy your company,' she lied. 'He won't have Hank or me with him so he'll have no one to talk to.'

Hank listened to Kit, but instead of sharing the joke with her at Casey's expense, he was silent. The problem he had wrestled with since hearing that Heartbreak was to be fished over the weekend was resolved. 'I'll probably leave you, Bill and Len to take the guys to Heartbreak,' he said. Kit's eyebrows rose but before she could speak he continued: 'If you are not going to Anchorage, Kit, I'll take the opportunity to fly up to Barrow to spend a few days with Trapper Jack. I promised the old man that I would visit him before the season ended.'

Kit relaxed. Stewart could book Casey into the Captain Cook in downtown Anchorage. Hank would be miles away in the Inuit settlement on the edge of the pack ice, the northernmost human settlement in America.

It was a bleak, windswept place. She would never understand Hank's fascination for the region of permafrost, a desolate landscape where the ground remained frozen all year except for a few inches on top which thawed and became soggy during the short summer. He did not seem to see the sad collection of clapboard buildings. He ignored the rusty machinery, and junk lying around. She had once remarked to Hank that Barrow was Alaska's garbage dump. She had not repeated that mistake.

'I'll feel much better if Casey has you and Stewart to book her a suite at the hotel and arrange for a car and driver for her stay,' said Dursley.

Casey winced inwardly. She was always embarrassed when Dursley spoke of suites and chauffeur-driven cars, in the company of people who 'stayed over' with friends and took buses instead of taxis. She knew that it was merely his normal standard of living and he did it quite unconsciously.

Leroy and Earl were obviously wealthy, but Hank and Kit were not. Casey wanted to apologize. She looked across at Hank, but he was explaining to Leroy that pulling at a knotted line in frustration did not make it easier to untangle the knot. It usually meant cutting the line and joining on a new leader. Leroy seemed to be listening intently, but Hank knew that the next time he dropped his wrist on a back cast and dangled the line and hook in the tall grasses, he would again jerk at it furiously then curse the tight ball of nylon.

Casey looked away to find Kit studying her. 'Hank has only just managed to stop me dropping on my back cast,' she grinned, 'it's such a joy not to have to put down my rod after every cast and walk back into the grass to untangle my line from the seed heads.'

Kit smiled back. Hank would never be interested in anyone who floundered in the river and hooked up in the grass. Their ineptitude would drive him mad with frustration. He always found it inexplicable why clients could turn something as easy as fishing into such a difficult business. She decided she could relax and fish Heartbreak with an easy mind. Her mother, fully aware of the responsibility of protecting five attractive daughters, filled their days with admonishments and warnings about men.

'Remember, girls, that a gal who is liked by both men and women is never a threat. Your man is safe with her. Watch out for the ones who have no woman friends. They are the hungry ones.'

Casey listened to Kit and the men discuss the techniques employed to outwit the fish on Heartbreak. 'It's just as well that I won't be with you,' she said. 'Can you imagine me on that sort of river? I'd never stand against the wind.' The men laughed.

Kit smiled at Casey. 'Come, I'll show you a trout spa resort. It has fish which will make Leroy and Earl go as green as the backs of the sockeye with envy.' The girls giggled at the thought and linked arms. Two men watched Kit and Casey wade across the river arm in arm. One looked at the petite girl with love and possessiveness, the other with love and hope.

The night before flying to Anchorage with Casey had seemed never-ending to Hank. He had stayed out on the deck alone long after the generator plunged the lodge into darkness. He sat listening to the wild, forlorn cry of the loons on the lake. Only when the narrow ribbon of saffron which marked the line between land and sky was rolled away and water and earth became one in the darkness did he get up from his deck-chair and crunch along the gravel path to his cabin.

Kit lay on her side, her hands tucked between her knees like a child trying to keep warm. Hank slid into bed careful not to wake her and lay listening to her breathing as he wrestled with his conscience. Finally a knock on the door heralded a new day and released his brain from its twisted and tormented stirring. He had not found a solution to this new love which had come into his life at a time when he wanted no commitments.

He looked down at Kit lying beside him. He longed for hair which was dark, thick and glossy to cover the pillow, not fine and blonde. He wanted to caress breasts which lay soft and heavy in his hands, not ones which were small and hard. He wanted a woman who could curl up against his stomach and be enfolded in his arms, not one whose head and toes were level with him. His body ached for Casey.

'Going to miss me?' queried Kit, yawning and stretching.

Hank started. He had not realized that Kit was awake and studying him. 'Sure,' he answered automatically, lifting her leg which lay across his naked body.

'Then prove it,' she laughed and quicker than a bear pouncing on a salmon she straddled him.

'Kit, there's no time . . .' But his protests died away and were replaced by uneven breathing as she moved rhythmically on him. The feel of his coarse hair on the inside of her thighs excited her and Hank's fingers dug into the firm flesh of her buttocks as he responded.

'Better than fishing, isn't it?' said Kit as she rolled over onto her back, her lean muscular body veiled with perspiration.

Hank smiled at her, but was silent. He needed the hot stinging needles of the shower to wash away his guilt. He felt that he had betrayed Casey. The feeling sickened him. Even the knowledge that she was probably curled up beside Hank did nothing to dispel his miasma of gloom.

Kit smiled secretly as she watched him dress and pack a tote bag for his trip to Barrow. She knew that he was miserable. She was pleased that he would miss her. By the end of the season you won't be able to leave me, she gloated silently. If leaving me for a few days makes you so unhappy then you must love me. She sang as she pulled on layers of warm clothes to go under her waders. Heartbreak was a cold, unforgiving river and she was going well prepared.

Chapter Seven

IN AUTUMN, the fireweed bursts into white balls of wispy cotton. The ash berries lie red and rich as blood on the ground. The black and white spruce forests thunder with the roar of the rut of mating moose.

These huge creatures are the largest of the deer family. They stand higher at the shoulder than a man. Their racks spread the length of a man and they weigh as much as a large grizzly bear.

A male moose, his ridiculously large clown's nose belying his ferocity, stood at the edge of the light, white spruce forest. He had recently rubbed the velvet off his antlers; it lay in bloody clumps on the ground and pieces clung to the tree trunks. His rack was now sharp. He had stopped eating and was ready to battle for the right to mount a female. His roars had echoed across the hills and were answered by another dominant male who demanded the same female. The two bulls now faced each other.

'Look down!' Stewart gesticulated as he swung the plane into a tight turn. Casey had become accustomed to looking vertically down the wing of the plane and no longer clung to her seat certain that she was about to be catapulted out of the window.

'Moose!' shouted Hank in her ear. Casey felt his breath, warm and moist on her cheek. She sat still as silence, in case he moved away.

Hank prayed that the two moose would remain where they were and that Stewart would keep the plane circling clockwise. It gave him the opportunity to lean across Casey and look out of the window.

'They're huge,' she said, eyeing the two ungulates.

'Largest deer in the world,' announced Hank. 'You could probably fit under their bellies standing upright.'

The two males rushed at each other. Their racks smashed together. A clash Casey was sure she could hear above the roar of the plane.

Stewart circled lower and the larger moose tossed its head up at the plane angrily.

'Wouldn't like to meet up with him near a trout stream,' said Hank.

The smaller animal took the opportunity offered by the intrusion of the plane. It sneaked away into the forest to find a weaker adversary or look for another female.

'Wise boy,' grinned Hank, as Stewart straightened the plane, 'he'll live to fight another day.'

Casey kept her nose pressed to the glass as the angry animal pawed the moss and tossed its antlers, roaring defiance at the large noisy bird.

'Do they fight to the death?' she asked, turning to Hank suddenly. Her hair swung thick and dark as a black-out screen across her face and Hank longed to bury his face in it and hold her to him. But he knew from experience that Stewart had three-hundred-and-sixty-degree vision when he wanted it. He also held firm views on his staff having any relationships with clients.

Hank shuddered to think of Stewart's reaction if one of his staff fell in love, or had a relationship with a countess-to-be. He saw every lodge in Alaska closed to him as Stewart used his influence, and eased his wrath at losing a steady stream of British nobility as clients.

'Penny?' said Casey, trying to decide whether Hank's eyes were brown or green today.

Hank swallowed before answering, then decided that as the

noise of the engines muffled their voices it would be a good time to put his proposal to her.

'Ticasuk,' he said. Casey felt her throat and face grow hot. The name recalled the episode in front of the fire as her clothes were drying.

'Why don't you come up to Barrow with me? It's one of the largest permanent Inuit settlements in Alaska. Maybe you could learn something about your ancestors,' he added persuasively.

'I have a wonderful old Inuit friend there, Trapper Jack. He tells fascinating stories which have come down in his family over the years about the Inuits. He'll probably still be out at the hunting camp and will show you the eiders and animals he has hunted. It is his food supply for the long winter.

'Let him tell you about the other face of Alaska, the heavy, depressing face of winter, when the sun sets and does not rise for seventy days. Where temperatures can remain at minus forty-five degrees Fahrenheit for a week or longer.

'A time of darkness when people go mad and slash themselves with knives or tear out their hair, desperately needing light.' Hank saw her wavering and he continued talking. 'Let Trapper Jack tell you of the tundra. Seventy thousand square miles of flatness. A place where one can find beauty in summer but only a bleakness blasted by continuous gale-force winds in winter.'

Casey shivered involuntarily at the thought of living in complete darkness for months at sub-zero temperatures.

'He'll tell you about "perlerorneq".'

'What's that?' asked Casey, intrigued at the strange word.

'An Inuit word for the dreadful depression that a polar winter causes,' he explained.

'Oh, I'd love to go to Barrow with you, but I couldn't,' said Casey. 'It wouldn't be right.'

'How much do you know about your ancestors?' Hank insisted. 'When will you ever have another opportunity to see where you came from, to listen and explore? You are absolutely ignorant of your heritage. It's one you should be proud of,' he pleaded. He saw her hesitating. 'We can tell Dursley when we return that you wanted to explore your roots and it was a perfect opportunity to tag along with me. We need not tell Stewart anything yet,' he hastened to add, 'as my plane to Barrow only leaves later today.'

Hank grinned at her. Suddenly she broke into laughter, feeling free and happy.

'Why not indeed? You know I don't enjoy shopping, so let's play truant from the Captain Cook,' she said.

'We will book you into the hotel, say goodbye to Stewart and have lunch up in the Crow's Nest. I know the captain so we'll have a good window table. With luck we'll see a whale in the bay.'

Hank paused and combed his short beard with his fingers.

'I can never remember whether the restaurant overlooks Turnagain or Knick Arm,' he laughed. 'It's probably Cook Inlet,' he said lamely.

'James Cook certainly left his mark around the world,' grinned Casey. 'As Earl would say, not all limeys are useless.'

They laughed together. Now that the decision was made Casey looked forward to visiting Barrow. It gave her the perfect excuse to spend a few days alone with Hank. She wanted to be with him and learn to know him, away from rivers and fishing.

'After lunch, which hopefully will include giant king crab claws, we'll book you out of the Captain Cook and leave for the airport.'

Casey had been so engrossed listening to Hank plan their trip to Barrow that she had not noticed the plane climbing. She reached out and turned the small round vent in the window away from her. It had been blowing on her face and her eyes were starting to water in the cold air.

She now sat in silence, awed by the grandeur of the blue and white mountains reaching up to touch the sky. The sun polished the snow on the tips so that her eyes ached with their brightness and luminosity. In contrast, the crevasses and valleys folded into the sheer slopes were indigo blue, anthracite and forbidding.

Stewart flew into the break in the range and Casey gasped as the wing-tips seemed to brush the jagged black rock breaking out of the snow. She peered down from the window and drew back quickly. The mountains seemed to drop a million miles below the plane to the rocky valley. A place as fearful to look at as a fakir's bed of nails. Winds had curled the snow into towering waves and in places combed it flat as a freshly starched sheet pulled over the rocky mountain's flanks.

She smiled weakly at Hank as she caught his eye. Had she but known the terrifying might and beauty of the Lake Clark Pass she would have stayed at the Lodge. She was certain that in comparison to these mighty forces of nature, Heartbreak River must seem gentle as a country stream at home.

As the plane dipped and swayed, weaving its way through the upswept mountains in the eight-and-a-half-thousand-foot-high pass, Casey felt light-headed. The folding and unfolding of wind-swept ridges and ravines, the flashing of dazzling whites, pale blues and blacks made her as queasy as standing in a hall of crazy mirrors where images swirled and retreated with every move.

She closed her eyes for a moment, trying not to think about the incredible forces which had thrown up and cracked these towering peaks.

'Look right!' shouted Stewart, removing his headphones and turning round. 'We're now at the two forks. East side and West side. That fork leads nowhere,' he said, pointing at one of the forks. 'That's Dead Man's Bend.' He laughed as he glanced back at the instrument dial. 'No great visible difference between the two forks, is there? When you are here, you can see why the poor devils take the turn to hell.'

He settled his headphones back over his ears, signalling the end of any further conversation. He forestalled Casey's query as to how he knew he had turned in the correct direction.

She strained against the seat-belt to look back. The long broken walls of snow and ice seemed the same to her. She swallowed back her fear and sat pushing back the cuticles on her finger nails. She found comfort in the familiar activity, while the plane dipped and rose in the awe-inspiring chasm.

'The beginning of a new glacier,' said Hank, taking the opportunity to put his head close to hers and breathe in the warm perfume of her body.

Casey looked ahead to where he was pointing. For a few minutes her fear was forgotten as she marvelled at the enormous river of clear turquoise ice, shouldering its way imperiously through the mountains, gouging out rocks, covering crevasses, moving slowly, ever forward and downward, with eternity to time its progress.

'We have a few hundred thousand of those in Alaska.'

Mount Iliamna soared up, above the other peaks. It stopped at just over ten thousand feet. She wished that she could freeze time and imprint the grandeur of Lake Clark Pass on her memory for ever. Hank spoke, but she did not hear him. She stared entranced at this sample of nature's power and magnificence. She wanted to hug and keep the beauty to herself.

All too soon the mountains eased away from the plane and flattened out as the pass ended. Ahead lay the flat lands surrounding Anchorage bordered in the east by the Cughach Mountains, a dark smudge of gentian violet in the distance.

Casey fought back the feelings of guilt which once again surfaced, as Stewart circled Lake Hood waiting for permission to land.

She struggled to convince the small voice inside which kept reminding her that she had promised to marry Dursley and was therefore his woman, that as she was also part Inuit it was only natural to go to Barrow. But when she glanced at Hank who was studying the polychromatic float-planes, colourful as boxes of Christmas crackers lining the lakeside, she knew that he was the reason she was going to Barrow.

Her duplicity sickened her, but she was in the grip of an emotion too strong to be denied. She sensed that this land, twisted and tormented by the power and violence of nature, was to be her destiny.

'Seat-belts tight,' said Stewart as the plane circled lower. Casey could see wavelets ruffling the water. She automatically tightened the safety strap around herself.

'Yes,' she answered, but Stewart was already listening to his landing instructions. She could see a small frown of concentration between his eyebrows as he acknowledged them.

Casey did not realize that they had touched down until Stewart throttled back and the plane slowed to a gentle rocking on the water.

'He always does that here,' laughed Hank seeing her surprise. 'Likes to show the local aces how to really fly.'

Stewart turned round in his seat and his tiny grey pony-tail swung incongruously from the back of his baseball cap.

When Casey asked Kit why Stewart still wore a pony-tail, she replied that they believed it was to remind him of the horrors and atrocities of Vietnam. He had found peace and beauty in Alaska, but never wanted to forget just how disgusting man could be. 'It's probably part of what makes him such a good and fair boss,' she had added.

'Another lucky one,' Stewart said, smiling at Casey.

'Fantastic landing,' she said returning his smile. 'I still wait for the jolt as we hit water and it never comes. How do you do it?'

'Practice,' drawled Stewart. 'Practice and loving what you do lead to perfection.' He swung open his door, unclipped his belt and halfway down the steps he put his head back into the plane.

'Remember that,' he growled at Hank.

'Sure thing.'

Chapter Eight

HANK AND Casey flew towards the North Pole and Barrow happy and guilty as children playing truant. The possible consequences made the act exciting. The take-off from Anchorage had been bumpy. The plane swerved suddenly from one side of the runway to the other.

Eventually it lifted over the steel-grey sea and wove through a maze of cloud, dark as if sated with volcanic ash. As they approached Fairbanks the clouds changed to dazzling white and Casey put on her sunglasses.

It's beautiful, thought Casey, looking down at Fairbanks. The land was an artist's palette, swirled and daubed with indigo blues, grey-greens and the deep red and mustard yellow of lichens and autumn berries. Snaking across the palette was a large grey and milky-green river slashed with white shale spits.

The plane landed on a runway which ran parallel to the river, now a creamy coffee colour, its banks lined with float-planes.

They are as bright as the flowers in an English country garden, thought Casey. She felt a sudden prick of guilt at the thought of England and the two families preparing for her wedding to Dursley. What am I doing here? she chided herself silently. It's not too late for you to catch the next flight back to Anchorage and no one will know or be hurt. But when she looked at Hank she knew that this was where she had to be.

At Fairbanks, Casey left all her doubts behind her. She was

determined to enjoy the trip and discover as much as possible about the Inuit, her people.

Below them the dark green smudges of spruce and birch forests stopped abruptly as if the sharp crescent blade of a giant ulu wielded by an Inuit had rocked across the land and cut the forests sharply away from the Arctic tundra. The tundra reached away stained and waterlogged as an old sponge.

'It looks so bleak,' said Casey as the plane neared Barrow. She was stunned at the vast, desolate, flat wilderness.

The Arctic tundra defied the eye to mark either where it merged with the sky, now pallid and wan with sea fog, or vanished into the deep, dark waters of the Arctic Ocean.

'It's amazing what manages to cling to those thin, arid soils,' said Hank. 'Remember only the top few inches of ground thaws in summer. The rest is permafrost. It remains frozen ground all year round.'

'A freezing Arctic desert,' said Casey.

'That just about describes it,' smiled Hank, and he looked at his watch. 'We should be landing soon.'

The Comair vanished into thick coils of grey, as they flew into the ever-present fog which rolled in from the Arctic Ocean.

'Lucky it's still light enough for us to land,' said Hank, gesturing at the window. 'I was stuck here for four days on my last visit, waiting for the fog to lift.'

Casey suddenly doubted the wisdom of her decision. The thought of not meeting Stewart on time in Anchorage scared her. She had not yet decided what her new future would hold.

She had imagined the frozen North to be a romantic place. The drive through Barrow on the small tourist bus to the clapboard hotel soon dispelled her dreams.

The clapboard houses seemed to have been thrown together haphazardly. They teetered on the mushy ground with no foundations. It was difficult to tell where the grounds of one ended and the next began. Seemingly useless rusted junk covered most of the open ground. Snowmobiles, some new and some lying in pieces, added to the disorder. Beautiful, traditional hand-sewn kayaks made of sealskin were canted against battered aluminium boats. Hanging on sagging wooden washing lines or draped across the boats and hastily rigged wooden tables were strips of caribou, moose and seal meat, the red flesh turning black as it dried. Dogs were tied to poles on short leads. They yowled and whined as they smelled the putrefying meat. They were kept on leads to avoid any confrontation with rabid wolves outside the village. Pools of melt water, which could never seep away because of the frozen ground, added to the desolate scene. Overhead telephone and electricity wires wove intricate cobwebs almost blocking out the sky. The tangle of black wires seemed too heavy for the poles and they stood at acute angles to the ground. It looked like an abandoned film set.

The bus finally stopped outside a long clapboard building beside the sea. Casey gasped as she realized this was to be her place of romance for the next three days.

'Come, Casey,' said Hank, opening the bedroom door and throwing their bags down on the patched orange bedspreads. 'You must stand on the northernmost piece of land in the States.'

She was caught up in his excitement and ran with him down the hotel steps. The wind caught them as they rounded the corner of the hotel and faced the sea. The dark waves were held down by the weight of the ice-blocks. The water pushed up heavily against the shoreline which ran into the distance like a grease mark around a dirty bath.

I'll never complain about the wind again on one of Dad's shoots, she promised herself silently. Her eyes and nose watered and she doubted if she would ever be warm again.

Hank stood, legs astride on the grey beach, breathing in great lungfuls of the cold sea fog. The wind caught and curled his hair from under his woollen cap and it bristled up his deep red beard like the hair of an angry cat.

Studying Hank, Casey realized what attracted her so strongly to him. He was so obviously a part of nature, part of the elements. This was how man was meant to be, strong and free. She forgot the cold and the wind and ran to him. She wanted to share his love for the land and feel his excitement as he looked out to where the fog rolled in thick and cold from the Pole.

Hank tucked her head into the shelter of his armpit. Together they bowed their heads into the wind and walked to the edge of the sea for Casey to touch the icy water.

'How high does the tide come up?' she asked, eyeing the narrow stretch of beach.

'There is no tide. It's a tideless sea,' Hank answered. 'It's the east wind whipping up waves which gives the impression of a tidal ebb and flow.'

She dabbled her fingers in the dark sea.

'Imagine living in that!' she exclaimed. She drew back her hand from the water as if it had been placed on a hot stove.

'Makes swimming in the Katmai rivers a sauna bath, doesn't it?' laughed Hank as he rubbed her fingers between his palms until they were red and tingling.

Casey blushed as she relived their embraces in front of the fire. Almost as if he was reading her mind, Hank swung her around and bent his head to hers. She could smell the sea mist in his beard and the damp cowl of his polo-neck sweater. She lifted her face to his and tucked her hands under the elastic waist-band of his anorak.

The soft surging of the sea and their quickened breathing sang a song of love. Casey knew that once she had given herself to Hank there would be no other man. They remained together as the fog thickened and obliterated the hotel and the jumbled town of Barrow. It covered all the man-made ugliness and muted the howls of the dogs. Eventually they broke apart. Like sleep-walkers they found their way back to the hotel, guided by pin-pricks of light in the windows.

They giggled and laughed as they struggled up steps they couldn't see. The Eskimo lady at the desk looked at them in disapproval. Barrow was a 'dry town'. There was no liquor to be bought, though one could bring it in from another town.

The Inuit community had found that the natives, like most people who live close to the earth, could not tolerate liquor. To avoid fighting and all the troubles which trail along with alcohol, they had banned it completely.

Casey smiled at the woman as she asked for their key. The Inuit relaxed. The couple were not drunk, only in love. A smile lingered round her mouth as she watched them walk down the passage.

They reached the end of the corridor and fitted the key into the door of their room. Casey switched on the light beside the door, then quickly switched it off to avoid looking at the garish orange bedspread. Hank felt his way to the beds and clicked on the bedside lamp in its beige paper shade.

Their room immediately looked more inviting. The spreads turned to a deep peach and the walls were suddenly painted a soft cream. Hank sank into the bed which squeaked in noisy protest. He grimaced.

'Sorry, little Ticasuk, but this is the best in Barrow.'

'It's better than the barabaras my ancestors lived in, though not by much,' she laughed. She unzipped her padded anorak and hung it over the back of a chair.

'We don't have dried fish a few feet deep lining the walls and the floor,' Hank replied, throwing his cap onto the black television set standing on a poorly laminated chest of drawers.

'Neither did they,' retorted Casey, defending her Inuit family.

'Oh, yes they did. They lived off the layers of fish until the end of the winter. When they had eaten it all they could see the floor again,' Hank teased. 'Fortunately I love fish, so come here, my little Inuit,' he said.

Casey peeled off her clothes shyly and slowly. She walked across the room conscious, with every step she took, that she would never be a countess.

As she neared his bed her steps quickened. She had made her decision. Now she wanted only to feel Hank's arms around her and his warm mouth covering hers.

Hank leaned up on his elbow and studied Casey's naked body, glowing the peachy-pink of a Renoir nude, in the soft light of the cheap bedside lamp.

He forced himself not to kiss or touch her, but let his eyes caress her crevasses and depths.

'Do you wish to return your mail-order goods, sir?' she teased. She smiled up at him, her eyes dark and dreamy. Hank capitulated and let his hands and mouth follow where his eyes had explored.

'Oh, no,' he murmured, indistinctly, as his lips closed over her large rosy nipples. 'This is a catalogue order I'll keep.'

The bed squeaked and groaned as Hank dug his fingers into Casey's round buttocks, spreading them and bringing her up to meet him. He buried himself in her creamy body, delighting in her softness and voluptuousness.

Outside their window the pack ice growled and rumbled as the huge blocks ground and rode up against each other. The wind howled around the hotel, threatening to lift it up and to hurl it onto the black sea. Hank and Casey lay in each other's arms whispering dreams of the future, as the wetness of love dried on their bodies.

'Shower time, woman,' said Hank, finally rolling away from Casey and standing up. 'Or I'll never make the next two days.'

'You will,' said Casey throatily, 'believe me you'll have no trouble at all. See what I mean?'

Hank grabbed a dingy towel from the tiny shower room, which seemed to have been added as an afterthought to the bedroom. He quickly knotted it around his waist and turned on the shower taps, but he could hear Casey's laughter over the noise of the water.

He strode into the bedroom, picked her up in his arms and carried her kicking and protesting into the shower. He held her up with her legs spread around his hips and unknotted the towel.

'This is what happens to women who mock their men,' he said.

Casey's laughter changed to soft cries as the hot water flowed down their moving bodies.

The Inuit lady at the desk looked up as Hank and Casey dropped the room key on her desk.

'If you hurry you will still be in time for Pepe's,' she said looking up at the large brown wall clock.

'Pepe's?' queried Casey.

'North of the Border,' said Hank, completing the restaurant's name. 'They serve some great beans and red chili sauce.'

The Inuit woman smiled at the lovers.

She had not felt that way since her husband failed to return from a seal hunt with his friend Trapper Jack. They were returning to their boat which they had left in a flaw lead streaming with frost smoke. But the open water passageway had closed while they were hunting. They were stranded on the pack ice. Only one man returned to the village, Trapper Jack. He was the one who wore the traditional Inuit winter clothing made from caribou skin and wolverine fur.

She had pleaded with her husband to wear caribou and fox clothes, which she had stitched and looked after so carefully. But he had not listened. He discarded the delicate traditional winter clothing in favour of the modern European expeditionary winter wear and he had paid for his choice with his life.

After his death she had taken a job in the hotel. Seeing tourists dressed in expensive winter anoraks running inside to escape the cold strengthened her determination to join Trapper Jack's committee and make the Inuit children once again proud of their traditional clothing and culture.

'I suppose that a Mexican restaurant in an Inuit village is a reasonable thing to expect,' said Casey, as they ran to the boxlike building adjoining the hotel.

'It's not only reasonable, it's a sensible thing to expect,' she added a few moments later as they threw open the bright red double doors and were greated with a burst of jazz which sounded to her like Dave Brubeck.

The room was colourful, warm and loud with music. A passage lined with tables ran to the left of the doors and they slid into two vacant seats. Casey's eyes danced as she read the thank-you letters and posters from schools in the area.

'The proprietress is a great woman,' explained Hank, seeing

Casey reading the posters papering the walls. 'She does a tremendous amount for the Inuit community, especially the kids. They seem to look upon her as Mother Christmas.'

'Well, she's in the right place,' quipped Casey, then she was silent and her eyes widened as she stared in unwilling fascination at a young, husky man sitting at the table across the aisle. His breakfast had just been placed in front of him and he was methodically stirring the fried eggs, tortillas, sour cream and melted cheese into the fried beans and red chili sauce.

'He's eating enough for five men,' whispered Casey, 'and it now looks like something the dog threw up.' She looked away as glutinous streams of egg hung down from the youngster's mouth as he shovelled in the mixture.

'Table manners are not a requisite for a job up here,' said Hank. 'These guys work under dreadful conditions and need good filling food.'

'But why mix good food into such a mess?' protested Casey.

'Shh,' warned Hank. 'Here comes our breakfast.'

They looked up eagerly as their orders arrived.

'Eat up,' ordered Hank as Casey eyed with dismay her plate piled high with food. 'You'll need it. It's cold out in the Arctic desert.

'I have a thermometer which registers minus seventy,' he said, scooping the last smear of chili sauce from his plate, and wiping his mouth. 'They gave it to me the last time I was here as a prize for being the only tourist mad enough to visit Barrow twice,' he explained, forestalling the question in Casey's eyes. She laughed gaily.

'Do you think I'll be given one?' she asked.

'Don't tell me you want to come back here?' said Hank stunned.

'Oh, yes. We have to spend the anniversary of our love here every autumn,' Casey answered seriously. 'It'll be bad luck not to.'

Hank broke into deep laughter. The staff peered into the room perplexed at the hilarity. They were accustomed to the gripes, grouses and sour faces of tourists who came to Barrow expecting to see picture-book igloos, lovely fur-clad Eskimos, chewing sealskin, and carving beautiful copies of bears, seals and whales. The reality of the place left them feeling cheated and disgruntled.

Chapter Nine

TRANSPARENT SHEETS of ice Nilas seemed to have been lifted from the ocean and placed across the sky forming gigantic window-panes. The light shone through translucent, cold and grey.

'Wonderful day, isn't it, Ticasuk?' said Hank, squatting on the soggy tundra to examine a plant. Casey watched him as he dug into the tundra. He seemed indifferent to the wind, which stabbed cold and sharp as needle ice at her body.

'See, Casey – ' he held out a tiny leaf, its veins raised and unbroken – 'this has probably been here, preserved and perfect, for years.'

She forced her hand from the fur-lined pocket of her parka and instantly regretted it, as her fingers reddened in the cold. 'It's beautiful,' she said as she closed her hand over the leaf and thrust it back into her pocket.

'Do you realize that we are walking on top of a forest?' said Hank pulling the red woollen cap down over his forehead.

'We are?' replied Casey. Secretly she could not have cared what they were walking on. She only wanted to return to the relative warmth of the clapboard building which was their hotel.

'The last time I was up here with Trapper Jack, a British team was studying the Arctic eco-systems,' continued Hank. He was totally unaware of Casey's discomfort and increasing uninterest.

'It sounded a boring business,' he said, 'but within a few days I was completely fascinated.'

Casey nodded and stamped her feet, trying to warm her toes. Hank pulled at a tiny plant clinging to the ground.

'They sliced up one of these dwarf willows and counted over one hundred growth rings in a stem no thicker than your thumb.'

Casey looked down at the thickly matted carpet of plants beneath her feet. Hank had now quickened her interest in the tiny trees and shrubs lying like a coir doormat on the wet ground.

'According to the Brits doing the study,' continued Hank, his fingers still lifting and separating the plants, 'there is a difference of about fifteen degrees Fahrenheit in the first foot or two of air above the ground.'

'Why?' queried Casey, now totally absorbed in Hank's explanation.

'The dark earth attracts solar heat and the wind is less harsh,' he said.

'So the poor things have to keep down flat to survive,' she said, nudging at a matted clump of plants with her toe. 'It's tough to be a tree in the tundra,' she mused, 'the only water they have is when the top snow melts in summer and then they live in a soggy bog. Their roots get frostbite if they go down too low.'

'Low!' said Hank listening to her lament for the plants. 'In places the ground is frozen down to almost two thousand feet.'

'And the ice never melts?' she queried.

'Not ice, my little Ticasuk, it's the earth that is actually frozen.'

Casey shook her head. 'The Arctic must be one of the most difficult places on earth to survive,' she said.

'It is,' boomed a deep, ragged voice.

Casey spun round to face a short, squat man. His dark face was folded and seamed. His eyes seemed to look through her and on into the flat desolate distance. The hood of his parka was thrown back and his straight hair, thick and dark, flew wildly in the wind.

'Trapper!' exclaimed Hank with a broad grin.

Trapper Jack had told Casey and Hank to wait on the outskirts of the Inuits' traditional summer hunting camp until he came to fetch them. It was no longer safe, he explained, for tourists to wander into the camp. A group of Inuit hunters had finally decided to end what pleas and proclamations could not. They shot two tourists who entered their camp uninvited. When the uproar died down, their summer camp was once again inviolate. No tourists exclaimed over the cruelty of shooting 'darling bears' and eiders and seals. No groups came intent on persuading them not to hunt the whales which they were allotted each year to feed the villagers through the dreadful winter.

'It's so good to see you again,' said Hank.

He put his arm around Casey and pulled her forward. 'I want you to meet Casey Ticasuk Chargot.'

Trapper Jack's eyes widened a little at the name Ticasuk, but he merely smiled.

Casey was not hurt or surprised at the sparse greeting. Hank had explained that Trapper made no 'small talk'. He only spoke when out hunting or recounting Inuit folklore. She smiled at him as he handed her a brown skin garment which he was carrying.

'Put this on. It is caribou. You will be warm.'

Casey thanked him and gingerly eased the garment over her anorak. Trapper pulled up the hood and fastened it under her chin.

It was like stepping back into a dry sauna after a plunge in a cold pool. She snuggled into the animal skin and smiled happily. The wind had lost its bite and the day suddenly promised excitement.

Chapter Ten

DARK AND motionless as a submarine avoiding sonar pips, the giant rainbow lay under the overhang of the river-bank. The fish had chosen his spot well. His dark olive back merged into the darkness of the bank like a shadow at midnight. Years of being caught and released had made him cunning and wily. Water, crystal clear, raced past him. He lay finning with the minimum of effort, out of the thrust of the current. He could see fishermen or bears approaching; the spot was perfect. The fish left his refuge only to dart after floating salmon eggs, or to chase water voles and leeches.

Dursley, Earl and Leroy tiptoed through the grass behind Kit.

'Down,' she ordered and they immediately bent double. 'He is about twenty yards ahead of us, just where the yellow willow edges the water on the opposite bank.'

Leroy sat down and stretched out his legs. He was tired but relaxed. They had followed Kit like a group of boy scouts for the last hour, creeping up on the fish. There had been no bear scat on the path, trampled day-beds or deep claw marks in the mud to scare him. The sky was clear and the wind kept the worst of the bugs at bay.

This is the life, he thought as he broke off a grass stem and chewed it.

This was Dursley's fish. He and Earl had both had a turn

trying for a dark shadow which Kit insisted was a fish, but with no success. Leroy was still convinced that they had been casting to slime-covered rocks.

They had seen this dark outline from the opposite bank and crossed to a midstream island. Leroy was waiting for Kit to apologize to him when they discovered that he was right: the supposed rainbow was merely a submerged log. He knew that rainbow could not grow to the size of this shadow.

'You stay here with Leroy,' said Kit to Earl. 'This is a huge one. I don't want him alerted by four of us tramping through the shrubs.'

'Fine by me,' said Earl.

'That woman has steel-sprung legs,' moaned Leroy, massaging his calves, as Earl dropped down beside him.

'It's time Hank came back, at least he lets a guy have a breather every now and then.'

'It's because she's a woman,' said Earl, 'and has to prove that she is as good as any man. It's something about these outdoor girls.'

Leroy suddenly grinned. 'Imagine those legs around you,' he said, watching Kit and Dursley moving deeper into the shrub as they approached the fish.

'She'd snap you in half,' taunted Earl, annoyed that Leroy had been keeping up with him in Heartbreak, a river which was making his muscles ache and was yielding no fish.

He had been completely spoiled with the fishing in the other rivers in Alaska, where the trout seemed to fight with each other for the privilege of being hooked. The fish in Heartbreak were living up to the river's name.

'At least she'd get her legs round me,' retorted Leroy.

Earl ignored the gibe about his size.

'Just look at the two of them now,' he said, pointing to where Kit and Dursley were gingerly peering through a tangle of grass.

'That fish would have to have telescopic vision to see them,' muttered Leroy.

'Apparently the big ones do have, even your shadow alerts them,' said Earl, airing newly acquired knowledge from Kit.

'You'll have one chance with him,' said Kit to Dursley. 'Let's try a vole.'

Dursley grinned at her.

'Now hold rhapsody and let us look to the river! / Do you mark the regal presence in yonder glinting pool?'

'Orvis,' said Kit, recognizing the quotation. Dursley nodded in admiration.

Together they selected a hairy beige mouse lure and Dursley tied it on to the eight-pound tippet. He would have felt better using a ten weight with a fish of that size, but Kit insisted that these huge fish were too clever. He would see the thicker line in the water and they would lose him.

'Ready?' asked Kit, watching Dursley recheck his knots. 'I suggest you cast just above the spot where that willow is dipping its yellow leaves over the edge of the bank and wiggle it down to him.'

Dursley found that he was holding his breath. With all the care and precision of a golfer putting for a million dollars he studied the ripple of the water, the lie of the fish and the wind. Then he let out his breath and cast.

The line flew straight and high behind him, then whipped forward dropping the mouse into the water where it would seem to struggle downstream in distress over where the fish was lying.

'There!' shouted Kit, as the great black shadow moved away from the bank. 'Oh, no,' she said as it glided back to its former position. 'He was only window shopping. Try him again.'

'That's it,' she said to herself. 'He's lost it. The fish will never go for it now.'

'Again?' queried Dursley, surprised.

'Yes, he's not spooked,' she lied, knowing that the big fish would never rise a second time. 'It was a perfect cast. The mouse wobbled right over his nose. I have a feeling that if you can do it again, he'll take.'

Dursley found that his hands were wet and he wiped them on the sleeves of the thick shirt beneath his anorak. This time Kit held her breath as the line again whistled its cry of silence.

The mouse jerked and wobbled on top of the water as Dursley jiggled it exactly to where it would drift over to the rainbow. It was another perfect cast. It looked like a struggling vole to the fish and he could not resist it. There was a flash of movement too quick for the eye to follow as the giant rainbow twisted up from his hiding spot.

The water exploded and an arc of shimmering green streaked with pink rose up high. Its silver and white belly hung for a second over the water. As the rainbow felt the tension and pull of the mouse then the line, it jumped again. The water again exploded. In breathtaking colours the trout shook its head trying to dislodge the silver hook firmly lodged in its lower jaw. Kit clenched her fist and pumped her arm in excitement.

One part of her sympathized as always with the wild fish, urging it to lose the hook which was bending the trout to Dursley's will, but the other part exalted in the fact that they had lured him from his lair. Dursley now had the chance to feel the full fighting strength of the giants in Heartbreak.

Dursley's rod bent as if the tip would touch the spool, as the fish sank down heavy and unyielding as one of the green rocks lining the river bed.

'He's settling down to break your heart,' said Kit, straining her eyes to distinguish the trout from the rocks.

'Or my rod,' grinned Dursley, eyeing the bow bent into his rod with respect. 'I wish Casey was here to see this,' he said, hunching his shoulders to ease the tension and strain in his muscles.

And Hank, thought Kit. 'He will never believe that we raised "Tricky Dicky", a name the guides used for this particular fish since, just as the tabloid label give to a former United States president implied, he constantly outwitted the best of them.

'Just keep up the tension,' warned Kit, seeing Dursley stretch his fingers to uncramp them. 'We could be here for a long time.'

She stood legs astride, the wind flapping the collar of her jacket against her cheek. Her eyes never left Dursley's rod tip and the line. She polished her Polaroids and replaced them on her nose. The rainbow had vanished, merging perfectly into the colours of the river bed.

Earl and Leroy, who had jumped up yelling in excitement as the rainbow burst from the river, were now sitting down soberly watching the battle. They were chastened by Kit's wrath and smarting a little at being called idiots for rushing to the edge of the water.

'She's right,' admitted Earl grudgingly, watching Kit cross the river and speak quietly to Dursley, 'we could have frightened him into breaking the line.'

'Sweet Mary forbid,' answered Leroy. 'That woman would have killed us. I'd rather face a grizzly.' He paused. 'No, perhaps Kit would be better.'

'Hank will be as mad as a hornet when he finds that Kit put Dursley into a big one,' grinned Leroy. 'The guides are betting that we'd come back with the usual dry run.'

'Hope the fish moves before lunch,' said Earl looking at his watch. 'He's kept that rod down for almost half an hour.'

As he spoke, the tip of Dursley's rod whipped back and the rainbow once again teased them with his size and shimmering colours. For a moment he was held in a cone of cascading green water. Then he dived. Dursley's reel squealed in protest as the rainbow stripped off line in its frantic dash into the downstream current and freedom. He was left with only the backing on the spool. As he watched his line stream out he groaned, 'I had a hundred and fifty yards of backing on this reel.'

'Recover it fast!' Kit shouted. 'He's heading for the deep water at the fork in the river. If he reaches it we'll lose him.'

Dursley reeled in as fast as possible. His triceps throbbed with the unrelenting strain. 'This one's father was a giant salmon,' he puffed as he stumbled downstream after the fish.

Earl and Leroy could not resist the excitement and they scrambled up and pounded down the opposite bank, cheering and yelling encouragement, noisy as fans at the Yankee stadium. Their aching legs were forgotten in the excitement of the chase, as were Kit's warnings.

Kit kept pace with Dursley. She clenched her teeth to prevent herself yelling at him as he stumbled over the slippery rocks and the fish took the opportunity to strip more line from the reel. The rainbow found the current and seemed to fly.

Eventually the fish paused on its wild flight. Dursley took the opportunity to wipe the sweat off his forehead with the sleeve of his anorak and he breathed in deeply. He could feel his heart pounding in his ears. Chasing the fish over the rocks and in deep water had taken its toll. He still could not believe the strength and weight of this fish.

His nerves tingled. His whole being was focused on landing and holding this rainbow. At this moment it was the most important thing in his life. He had been pulling in twenty-four and twenty-six inch trout for days. But his arms ached with this one. He settled down for a long battle.

'Stay up on the bank, away from the fish,' Kit screamed, as she saw Leroy ready to jump into the river in his eagerness to see the fish which he thought had now given up the fight.

'Don't you dare come near. Don't even let it see you standing on the bank near it. It's only just settling down to fight.'

Earl nodded and dragged Leroy up to stand beside him.

Realizing that she had been harsh, Kit sought to make amends. 'If it scares, it will do another turn and reach deep water, then we'll lose it.'

'Not likely,' panted Dursley.

'We'll swim.'

Kit patted his shoulder. 'You'll get it. Just be patient, try to keep him pointing upstream and tire him.'

She felt a pang of pity for the magnificent fish deep in the water, trying to dislodge the hook and resist the persistent pressure of the rod. But her excitement at finally hooking the fish which

Hank and the guides had tempted fruitlessly for months overrode her compassion.

Puffballs of scrubbed white clouds now bloated into grey bellies pregnant with rain obliterated the sun. The wind strengthened. It funnelled down the river, giving Heartbreak its fearsome reputation.

'He's resting,' said Kit, 'you must keep pressure on him.'

Dursley knew that Kit was right, but he was standing deep in freezing water, bracing his legs against a current which threatened to lift his feet from the rocks. The wind which had cooled and dried his sweat now whipped into his collar, found and took away the warmth of his body.

'I know,' he snapped, 'I was fishing when you were still in nappies. Don't treat me like a child.'

Kit merely nodded. She knew too well the tension and fear of losing a 'big one'. She looked away from the line to check that Earl and Leroy were well back from the river on the opposite bank. As she did so the trout turned and headed upstream straight towards them. Dursley was taken by surprise. His line lay in a long lazy loop on the water.

'Strip in. Strip in,' screamed Kit.

Dursley pulled in the line by hand, desperate not to give the fish slack line and allow it to throw the hook.

They both turned and started the long struggle upstream against the current.

'I don't believe it,' panted Dursley as he battled back upstream. 'This fish is now dashing upstream, against this stinking current, as fast as he swam downstream when it was pushing him along.'

His heavy boots rolled on the smooth, water-washed rocks as he reeled in the line frantically. At times he had to stand still as the force of the current held him captive. He shook his head and was immediately blinded by rivulets of perspiration which stung his eyes. Kit pulled a bright green bandanna from her pocket, lifted his aviator style Polaroids and wiped his eyes.

'Thanks,' he said, as the river blurred then cleared.

'Comes with the service,' she grinned, 'now let's get him before he decides to run downstream again.'

'If he does that, I'll concede,' said Dursley.

Kit looked alarmed. They had to get this rainbow on film otherwise it merely became another fishing story.

'He has to be an IGFA record. A world-record rainbow,' she lied.

It worked. Suddenly Dursley was enthusiastic again. Bob, who had fished all of the 'hot spots' around the world, searching for that one great fish, would be furious if Dursley took a record rainbow on his first trip to Alaska. The record all fishermen hoped to land.

'I'd say he's a good eighteen-pounder,' continued Kit. She had been unable to judge the fish in its few breathtaking leaps for freedom, but her client was once again eager to overcome any ruses the fish devised.

She smiled as they stumbled up river shoulder to shoulder.

Earl eyed the new dark green haversack lying on the creamy spit of sand forking into the river. He looked upstream. Satisfied that Kit was totally engrossed with Dursley and the fish, he slid down the bank.

'Hey,' called Leroy. 'She'll skin you.'

'It's all right, the fish has taken them upstream. She's not watching,' reasoned Earl. He tore open the Velcro straps closing the haversack and pulled out blue plastic containers.

Leroy stood uncertainly on the bear path for a few moments, but, as Earl pulled out a Spam sandwich dripping with mayonnaise, his stomach grumbled. Forgetting about Kit's wrath, spooking fish or about grizzlies homing in on food, he joined Earl. Carefully they divided the lunch into four portions, taking only their share, as if to appease Kit. The coffee was black and hot. The large mug was lost in Earl's hands as he warmed his fingers around it.

The two men, now aglow with food and hot coffee, sat with their backs to the wind, content to let Dursley stagger up and down the river which had exhausted them.

The rainbow was now tiring of the persistent pressure. It was weary of its mouth being tugged and its body pulled. Abruptly it stopped. It felt the pressure ease. It immediately took the opportunity to jump, shaking its head vigorously. But the dark hook was firmly embedded in the skin of its lower jaw, even though the sharp barbs had been mashed flat.

Angry and tired of the battle it once again turned and tried to move into the main downstream current. The line remained tight and the trout no longer had the power to force its silver head into the deep, dark water, the refuge it now needed so desperately. It veered across the river to a place where it had so often found freedom. A gnarled root of the golden-leaved scrub willow, which was once embedded in the earth, now stood proud of the bank, its twisted tip dangling in the water.

'Don't let him cross the river,' said Kit, sensing where the trout was heading. 'He'll tie the line up in that root and break it.'

Dursley gritted his teeth and winced as his ankles twisted yet again on the rocks, but he held the rainbow away from the middle of the river. 'He's tiring,' he said as he recovered the line.

'Great. We'll bring him in to the shallows where we left the haversack. It's a good place to beach him, clear of rotting salmon and driftwood,' said Kit. Her voice was high with excitement at the thought of seeing and measuring the fish which had hurtled them up and down Heartbreak most of the morning.

She looked away from Dursley's rod and line to judge the distance to the sand spit and froze. It was much closer than she had supposed. Sitting right where they wanted to gentle the fish into the shallows were Earl and Leroy.

'Hey!' she yelled. The wind picked up her warning and whistled it upriver, away from the men. Realizing that they wouldn't hear her in the gale-force wind, she returned her concentration to Dursley, who was moving downstream more slowly now, reeling in steadily. She searched for an alternative place to land the fish. She found nothing but steep scrub-covered banks. Heartbreak foamed over exposed rocks or lay deceptively still and calm in wide stretches.

Please don't let those oafs move, she prayed silently as they approached the spit. Dursley had turned the rainbow's head and it was swimming towards the shallows like a well-trained gun dog.

'Don't relax,' warned Kit, feeling some of the tension drain from Dursley, 'these big ones have fight left in them even when you're holding a tape measure against them.'

As she spoke, Earl burped, stretched and stood up.

'That was good. Filled the cracks,' he said.

Leroy stood up with him and his boot rolled the silver top of the Thermos flask into the water. He waded in to catch it before it drifted into the current.

The rainbow was weary and ready to end the fight, but as the bright silver top flashed and sank in the water ahead of him followed by thrashing black boots, adrenalin raced through it. The fish twisted away from the shallows. The reel protested as line was stripped off once again by the powerful fish.

Dursley's shoulders slumped.

'Strip in and reel,' ordered Kit, sounding as fresh and eager as she had a few hours before. 'We've got him. He's really tired now. This is just an adrenalin run.'

Adrenalin run, like hell, thought Dursley as he watched the backing being taken off his reel. He tried to remember whether he had put on one hundred and fifty or two hundred yards of backing. Watching his line disappear down the river he hoped that it was two hundred. He had a feeling that he would need it.

Kit glared at Leroy. 'Where's your sense?' she hissed as she stumbled past the spit. 'Get up on the bank and out of sight. We're bringing him back here. If I see you anywhere near this place you're dead.'

Leroy did not even bluster as he joined Earl. They climbed up the bank and sat down on grass tussocks well screened from the sand spit. Neither spoke.

They had broken the unwritten fishing code of ethics and were chastened. They were sobered by the thought that they might have caused Dursley to lose his fish. Quietly they watched as Kit and Dursley disappeared downstream.

Dear Mary, mouthed Leroy silently, let them land the fish. Don't let him lose it.

As if in immediate answer the diminishing figures turned and started negotiating their way carefully upstream.

Leroy sank even deeper into the grass. A few no-see-ums braved the wind to settle on his neck. He did not even swat them, so determined was he that no movement of his would again spook the trout.

Earl sat cross-legged, burping and watching the bend of Dursley's rod as they approached.

'That's no fish. It's a supershark,' he said.

'Sshh,' cautioned Leroy.

'Fish can't hear.'

'No, but Kit can,' retorted Leroy. Earl was silenced.

'Well done,' congratulated Kit, as the powerful rainbow cruised slowly and wearily into the shallows.

She knelt in the river beside the shimmering fish holding the leader, fumbling in her vest pocket for the tape. Dursley had played the rainbow into the clear water lapping the edge of the sand spit four times. Every time Kit knelt to take the leader the fish spun around and sped downstream. They had followed it, terrified that the hook would eventually rip out of the white skin lining the trout's mouth and it would escape.

Now Dursley knelt beside her, ripping off his fingerless gloves. He wet his hands before attempting to hold the fish. He had no wish to damage the slimy protection which covered its scales and lay the fish open to infection. As his hand closed around its tail it struggled violently. Kit put her hand under its belly until Dursley managed to straighten the fish out and hold it securely below its gill rakers. The rakers beat like the wings of a scarlet butterfly, as the rainbow desperately sought for the oxygen it could find only in water.

'Thirty-six and a quarter inches,' breathed Kit as she held the tape in trembling fingers. She shook her head in disbelief. Once again she stretched the tape measure from the tail fin to the fish's mouth with the hook still dangling in the jaw.

'It is,' she shouted jubilantly. 'Just over thirty-six inches. Now let's get the girth.'

As her fingers, blue with cold, bound the tape around the fish's belly Dursley tightened his hold on it. It needed oxygen and writhed to find water.

'Just a moment,' Kit soothed, as if the rainbow was a fractious child. 'Just this one measurement and we will lay you in the water for a second or two then take some photographs.'

Earl and Leroy approached Dursley and Kit knees high and treading silently as if walking on rotting salmon.

'Cameras,' commanded Kit, not even looking up.

They spun round and returned each clutching a camera.

'Twenty-two inches!' yelled Kit. She punched Dursley on the shoulder almost knocking him over.

'You've done it, main man. You have a record river-run rainbow!'

Dursley, caught up in the excitement, forgot his English restraint and demeanour and punched Kit back.

'Superwoman,' he exulted. 'You are a fantastic guide. Without you I would have given up hours ago.'

Kit grinned at him, a boyish grin. She put her hand above Dursley's, round the fish's tail and below his, under the stomach, then twisted the line around her arm tightening the hook in its jaw before lowering the rainbow into the water.

Too often had she seen fish force their way out of a fisherman's hands when they felt the cold water close over them. Without the hook still embedded in the fish, the fisherman could only watch as his catch sped away before being captured on film. Earl and Leroy clicked as fast as their fingers could press the buttons on their cameras.

The rainbow's gills opened and closed rapidly as it absorbed oxygen. Happy that it was still healthy Kit and Dursley lifted it and held it with all the pride of parents at a christening, as Earl and Leroy photographed the magnificent trout.

'Whoever caught that fish is lying,' said Leroy.

The fishing party looked up at him in amazement and then broke into roars of laughter.

'Only an Irishman could say a dumb thing like that,' spluttered Earl. 'You really are something.'

He hit Leroy on the back. Leroy staggered and almost landed on top of Dursley and the fish.

'It's clever,' laughed Dursley. 'I must remember that one when Bob and I are fishing together.'

Leroy listened in dismay as his camera re-rolled the film.

'This idiot thing has finished,' he moaned.

'Not surprising,' said Earl, still clicking away with his camera. 'You must have taken at least forty-five shots of Dursley and the fish on a thirty-six-frame spool.'

Dursley closed his eyes for a brief moment and imagined Casey's joy had she been with him.

'I wish Casey could see this once in a life-time fish,' he said, as he unclipped a pair of silver haemostats from the pocket flap of his fishing jacket.

Casey's upturned mouth with its infectious smile and her dancing eyes flashed before him. He felt a deep pang of longing for the woman he was to marry.

And I wish Hank was here, to see me bring in a record, thought Kit silently.

Carefully Dursley clamped the needle-nose pliers over the hook and eased it from the rainbow's jaw.

'Hit it on the head,' commanded Leroy, his voice high with excitement. 'Take no prisoners!' he yelled.

Kit took her hands away from the fish letting Dursley have the joy of releasing his fish. She washed her fingers in the near freezing water, wiped them on her sleeves and stuck them quickly into the pockets of her anorak, gratefully finding the metal hand warmers which most guides used. 'We can't,' she said quietly, 'remember, this is a catch and release area.'

'Probably why they grow giants like this one,' said Earl, still taking shots of the fish as Dursley held it ready to let it go.

'Then it doesn't get into the IGFA record book,' said Leroy. He paled as the enormity of the thought struck him. 'So you spent all that time getting a record which isn't a record.'

'It doesn't seem fair,' said Earl, siding with Leroy. 'Record fish should be taken.'

Dursley smiled, but a little sadly Kit thought, as he knelt in the river and held the rainbow upstream where the current was gentle. It lay quietly in his hands and he felt a sudden pang of guilt. Perhaps he had overplayed and exhausted the fish. It would float away, its white belly up, showing that he had killed it.

The rainbow continued to lie motionless in the water, but as the current pushed into its gill rakers it drew in the oxygen and strength it needed. Spinning and jumping to shake the hook had made it dizzy. It rested as it re-orientated itself.

Dursley's thumbs pressed lightly into the bright pink streaks painted down its silver sides. It seemed as if nature, not satisfied with this fish's beauty, had sprinkled gold over the silver which lay above the pink stripes and dusted platinum where the silver merged with the pure white of its belly.

'It is so beautiful,' whispered Kit. Earl and Leroy standing on the edge of the sand looked at the rainbow with awe and not a little envy. The cold grey light found and struck the trout in the shallow water and it shimmered with all the glory of a rainbow painting a leaden sky.

Suddenly Dursley felt a ripple run up his fingers. The rainbow shuddered. As it strengthened and moved in his hands, Dursley felt a little of the wonder of a mother giving birth.

With a flick of its powerful tail it slid from his grasp and sped back to the world it knew. The fishermen watched soberly as the trout finned across the shallows and melted into the dark green depths of Heartbreak.

Chapter Eleven

CASEY LOOKED around curiously as they followed Trapper Jack to his shack on the summer hunting grounds. The hunting grounds were once a long way outside Barrow, but with the expansion of the town, the area now lay on its outskirts. The brightness of the sun belied the bite in the wind and Casey pulled at the drawstring of her hood. Hank looked down at her as she walked at his side and tucked her hair into the hood of her parka.

'My little Eskimo,' he murmured. As he said it he realized how much she looked like an Inuit in the traditional fur-rimmed parka. Her round face was correct, as were the colour of her eyes, but not the shape. They told of English blood, wide spaced and almond shaped, with no Mongolian tilt or slit. But her smile was that of the Inuit children, who danced sullen and expressionless for the tourists, but responded to a smile with an answering one which lit their faces and made them beautiful.

'You belong here by my side, Ticasuk,' he whispered. 'Together we can explore this magnificent land. An awesome land which defies anyone to disbelieve in the power of an Eternal Force.'

As he spoke Casey saw once again the climbing mountains of Lake Clark Pass and the grandeur of the enormous rivers of ice eating their way through the rocks. She squeezed his hand in response. 'When we flew through the pass I felt that God went there to rest, away from the mess we've made of his world,' she answered. They walked together quietly and in accord.

The Inuit men they passed seemed to ignore them. They were busy repairing the fat tyres on their snowmobiles, stretching walrus-skins over the thirty-foot-long umiak boats, repairing the one-man kayaks or fiddling with Japanese engines on the aluminium boats which were fast replacing the traditional light skin boats.

Casey paused to watch an Inuit carefully place pieces of an outboard he had dismantled between strips of drying caribou meat on an upturned boat.

'He'll have that engine fixed in no time,' said Hank. 'The Inuits have an uncanny knowledge of repairing machines which they have never seen before.'

'That's due to centuries of making boats and tools from bone, skin, driftwood or whatever was available,' explained Trapper, slowing his pace to stand with them.

'They have confused modern-day researchers with their innate knowledge of the working of modern machines,' whispered Hank, as Trapper Jack once again strode ahead.

'Well, that's one thing I've not inherited,' laughed Casey. 'I have difficulty threading a sewing machine.'

'That's why they accumulate all this junk,' said Hank throwing out his arm towards the tawdry collection of seemingly useless articles lying around. 'Over the years necessity put a price on everything they found. They still have the hoarding instinct, even though the North Slope oil find has made them wealthy and they can afford to buy what they need.

'I love you, Ticasuk,' he said. As he bent to kiss her, the wolverine fur lining her hood tickled his nose and he sneezed.

As they wound their way through the camp some of the Inuit men stared at Casey, their faces closed and their eyes expressionless. A shiver ran down her back.

Even though they were told at the hotel that they were very lucky to be in Barrow on a good day when the fog, which usually rolled twenty miles inland, had lifted and left the sun in its place,

Casey felt a dark, brooding menace lie thick as yesterday's fog over the prefabricated cabins which were replacing the driftwood and sealskin hunting tents.

Suddenly the Inuit carvings, showing figures with mouths stretched wide in hideous agony and shamans bound tightly to the backs of bears with walrus cords riding into the mystical and terrifying place of nightmares, seemed real.

Her subconscious spoke to her and reminded her of the times her ancestors had trembled to the dangers of the hunt. Yet she felt at ease and strangely excited in this makeshift camp set up on a bleak stretch of tundra edging the sea ice. It lay in the migratory paths of birds and near sea lanes used since time immemorial by the white Belukh whales with their grey calves, after their sojourn in the Beaufort Sea.

Now that Casey understood the reason for the junk which leaned against and surrounded the cabins, creating grotesque gardens of discarded implements, she concentrated on fascinating glimpses of the hunt as they wound their way through the cabins. She tried to imagine what it was like in winter. She could not imagine living in a place where the sun set for sixty-six consecutive days, a time of darkness when the dreaded Ivu, a gigantic piece of sea ice, broke from the pack and hurled itself inland like a demonic force, killing all where it landed.

The polar Inuit well knew the depression, the weight of life, 'perlerorneq', which drove many to the verge of madness. It happened when the only sounds in the unyielding blackness were the screeching of the north wind as it blew inland from the polar ice and the sickening crash of tons of ice twisting and climbing high over each other in the Stygian night of a winter which seemed to have no end.

'Look, Hank,' called Casey. She tore her thoughts away from the depressing Arctic winters as she ducked beneath a line hung with creamy white eider ducks. The wind fluffed up their feathers exposing the soft down. The birds seemed alive as they hung by their necks, twisting and dancing in the wind.

Hank was in close conversation with Trapper Jack. Casey had

to call a second time before he heard her and stopped. She was now running her fingers through the yellow-tipped fur of a polar-bear skin which was clamped over the line alongside the geese. Trapper Jack quickly called out to a man who was approaching Casey from behind. An old tyre lever hung from the man's hand. Trapper then shouted across to her.

'Do not touch anything from the hunt. Walk with us. It is better so.'

Sensing someone behind her, she turned to the Inuit hunter.

'I'm so sorry,' she apologized. His only reply was to tighten his hold on the lever.

Casey felt her arm immobilized in a grip which made her wince with pain. Trapper Jack stood beside her, talking persuasively to the hunter. His argument seemed to placate the man, though his eyes when he looked at her were still hard and cold as black frost.

'I was only admiring the skin,' explained Casey as Trapper Jack and Hank hurried her away from the hunter's shack. 'I have never touched the fur of a bear before, I always thought they were white, but that one was peachy yellow in places.' Her voice was trembling. She fought to control it.

Trapper realized how shaken she was and kept his lecture for later. He had quickly warmed towards Casey and her obvious interest in everything around her. Now was the time to calm her. He spoke of the bear.

'The hair of a polar bear has no colour at all. It seems white only because of the refraction of light from the sun. You felt the thick wool under the stiff outer guard hairs. The guard hairs are hollow and don't let its hair mat when it's wet.'

Casey listened to Trapper Jack, wide-eyed. Her encounter with the hunter had upset her, but she wanted to know everything about this immense, wild land where beauty and cruelty were lovers. It had captivated her instantly and completely. She realized that Trapper Jack was a telescope through which she could see and understand the people and the country. Her people, her country. After the initial shock at the barren landscape around

Barrow, Casey had seen only the inventiveness of the Inuits. They fascinated her.

'Remember that you are now in the Inuit summer hunting camp.' He paused as he sought words to explain the sacred nature of the hunt.

'Even though the young men now hunt with automatic rifles instead of our beautiful carved spears, they still respect the inner spirit of the prey. This "Inva" is very important to us. The animal must die knowing of the hunter's great respect and appreciation.

'You, as a non-Inuit, are destroying this inner spirit of esteem by touching the prey. There must be respect, even in this time of change.'

'I'm sorry,' said Casey abashed.

'When do you return to Anchorage?' asked Trapper Jack, suddenly changing the subject. He pretended that he did not notice the quick look of desolation cross Casey's face, or her hand seek Hank's and clasp it tight.

'Tomorrow,' answered Hank, hating the thought of returning to Kit and Dursley and all the recriminations which must follow.

Trapper Jack stared out to sea, across the strip of dark grey water to the ice moving in huge blocks like an armour-plated animal. He breathed in the cold sea air as deeply as a bear scenting prey.

'I smell sea fog,' he said, staring out towards the polar ice-cap. 'Mark Air will not fly for a few days.'

Casey bounced from euphoria to dismay within a few seconds and it left her feeling nauseous. It meant that she had Hank to herself for a little longer, but it also meant that Stewart Saunders would find out that she had flown up to Barrow with Hank. She had hoped to be back in the hotel when he arrived to collect her, then no one would have known. The few precious days in Barrow would have been their secret. She would have found an excuse to break off the engagement to Dursley. Once the family anger and Dursley's hurt had been assuaged, she would return to Alaska, Hank and a life she now knew was hers.

Hank put his arm around her shoulders and squeezed her to

him. She drank in his strength, thankful for the momentary refuge in his arms.

'All things are planned, Ticasuk,' he murmured comfortingly. 'Nothing happens by chance in this cosmic universe of ours. It may not be what we want, but it is meant to be. We'll face it together.'

Trapper Jack pretended not to hear them. His face, seamed as patched pants, was inscrutable.

'We leave to hunt polar bear tomorrow. Why don't you join us?'

Hank immediately looked at Casey and was hesitant.

Trapper paused in front of the entrance to his skin and whalebone tent and studied this English girl with an Inuit name. He narrowed his eyes and saw his daughter when she was about the same age, young and enthusiastic. He shook his head. He had not seen her since she was lured to Prudhoe Bay by a burly youngster working on the North Alaskan pipeline. He had heard that she had renounced her Inuit breeding and had become an 'American babe'.

Here he had a British girl who was obviously captivated by her thin trace of Inuit blood. As he turned from her, he smiled. Fate had given him another daughter. He would teach her the love and the loveliness which lurked beneath the ugliness of all she saw.

'Ticasuk,' he called, and Casey hurried to his side. 'Remember that our people are trying to mould an old culture with new. It causes problems. Come and witness the courage of the Inuit hunter, Ticasuk.' He pulled aside the walrus-skin flap to his tent and motioned them inside. 'We will hunt with the guns, not the traditional twenty-foot spear we used in my youth,' he reassured them. 'It will be much safer.'

'Hunting polar bears is always dangerous, Trapper,' disagreed Hank, again looking at Casey.

'Oh, I would love to go, but how on earth did you hunt bears with only a spear?' said Casey, hoping to distract Hank from his obvious fears about taking her on the hunt.

Trapper Jack smiled as he thought of the days when he was young, out on the ice floes, tracking an animal he could barely distinguish from the ice. Throwing sticks at it, to enrage it and entice it to rush down on his spear. Then the dreadful noise, as he felt the full power and rage of the animal impaled on the shaft, held away from him only by the crossbar. The fear as he twisted the spear within the writhing bear, slicing and tearing its insides, hoping to cut through vital organs quickly, before the bear pulled free and maddened by pain shredded his body.

'It was one of the marks of a man,' said Trapper, wisely not explaining the hunt to her. Women never seemed to grasp the heady excitement of the kill. They saw only the blood and felt the pain.

'Perhaps you had better stay in the hotel,' he said to Casey, suddenly doubting the wisdom of including a woman, an English girl, on a hunt for one of the most dangerous and cunning of all animals.

'I think Trapper is right, Ticasuk,' agreed Hank, remembering all the horror stories of hunters being stalked and killed by the bear they were hunting, or the ice floe breaking away from the main ice-pack and bears and hunter floating away, never to be seen again.

'Oh, no, please no,' pleaded Casey looking at the two men. 'I couldn't bear to be alone whilst we wait for the plane to leave,' she said, turning to Hank.

Hank knew exactly what she feared on their return to Katmai. The hunt will make time pass quickly and she won't have time to worry about Dursley, he thought. 'Let's take her, Trapper,' he said, and Casey exhaled a breath of relief. 'She is a tough girl and I'll look after her. She'll be my responsibility.'

Trapper remained silent for a while. His gnarled fingers stroked a fish lure, beautifully crafted in bone, which he had picked up from a table nailed together from driftwood. He nodded and handed Casey the bone lure.

'One day, when you return to our land of ice. I'll teach you how to fish in winter and teach you of Arktos, the Great Bear from the land beyond the north wind.'

Casey smiled her thanks. Deep down her heart sang in silence.

Trapper Jack knew that she would return to Alaska to live with Hank. He saw her cheeks flush and her eyes dance with love as she looked up at Hank. 'You have found the one whose heart beats to yours,' he said quietly. 'Let her go, Hank, and your future will be a long cry of silence.'

Casey looked from one man to the other, perplexed by the words barely heard.

'Everything in this universe of ours beats to a pre-ordained rhythm. Spring pulses into summer, which in turn daydreams into autumn then sleeps as if dead in the grip of winter.

'Animals understand and live with the rhythm of life. We are the only species who fight against it. That is why we will be destroyed. The Great Life Force will not tolerate aberrant species,' Trapper said. He smiled a little sadly at Casey as he seated her on a rough wooden stool, hastily swept clean of knives and bone shavings.

'Listen, little English Inuit, and remember these words. I feel that you will need them in the near future. I know that you will.

My fears,
These small ones that seemed so big,
For all the vital things
I had to get and to reach.

And yet
there is only one great thing
To live to see the great day that dawns
And the light that fills the world.'

Trapper's voice was deep and rang out loudly in the small tent. Casey felt her skin prickle. She repeated the last verse to herself silently, hugging it close, as a talisman. She was amazed. She had accepted Trapper as a Mission-educated Eskimo who hunted, trapped and fished for a living. She had not expected philosophy and poetry, from him.

Hank laughed. 'Trapper is a poet. He has had two books published on poetry and one on Inuit legends.'

Trapper acknowledged the compliment with a small nod as he lit a gas stove and prepared three mugs of coffee.

'Would you tell me one of the Inuit legends?' asked Casey as she wound her fingers around the cup of coffee, enjoying its warmth.

Trapper sipped noisily. His eyes ranged the tundra constantly from the small window in the tent. 'I will tell you one of the most famous of our legends. It concerns bears in general, not polar bears, but it shows the respect due to all bears.' He closed his eyes as he visualized the story he was about to tell.

'One day a beautiful young woman went out from her village to look for berries. She met a young man who was both good looking and kind. She immediately liked this young man, so when he asked her to go with him she did. They made love on the tundra and the summer sun warmed them.

'When winter came the man dug a den on the hillside for them. She went to the den with him, but she was now beginning to suspect that he was not a man. He grew very hairy and when she watched him hunt animals he looked like a bear, yet when he was with her he looked like a man.'

Hank moved across the room quietly and sat at Casey's feet with his arm over her legs.

'That winter the woman gave birth to two children in the den. She forgot her family and other life in the village.' Trapper paused, and took another noisy mouthful of coffee. He held out the pot to Casey, who shook her head, wanting him to continue with the story.

'They were happy, the woman and the bear,' said Trapper. 'Then came spring. The woman's brothers set out from her village to hunt bears, as they did every spring. They came to the woman's den. The bear man heard them and before he went outside he sang a song to his wife, a song of respect for bears, and he told her how to boil a dead bear's head and sing the song of praise.

'The woman's brothers shot the bear as he left the den. She

returned to her village with her two children. There she taught the people how to love and respect bears. She taught them to boil a hunted bear's head and sing the words of praise.

'As the years passed the woman's body grew hairy. One day her brothers teased her. She immediately turned into a bear and killed her whole family.'

Casey drained her coffee, her eyes still fixed on Trapper's face as if willing him to continue.

'People who live near bears have always held them in high esteem and often address them as members of the family,' broke in Hank. 'Some ethnic groups believe that they are descendants of bears.' Hank looked to Trapper for confirmation.

Trapper nodded. 'We believe that bears possess great powers. There has always been a relationship between bears and ourselves. For centuries humans and bears shared the berry fields and salmon rivers. Bears never looked upon humans as prey.' He sighed and picked up a knife he was carving. The handle depicted a bear flying high over the tundra.

'That time is over,' he said quietly. 'Now there are too many humans. They do not respect the bears. They are no longer content to share the rivers. They want it all and chase away the bears. The bears will soon begin to hate and hunt humans. Instead of being our revered ancestors the bears will become our feared and hated enemies.'

'Why do you hunt bears, then?' queried Casey. She wondered for a moment why she did not find it at all strange to be sitting in a sealskin tent talking to an educated man about ancestors who were bears. Trapper bent over his carving. The silence grew long and painful.

'Because bear, like walrus, seal and whale meat, is necessary for the survival of the Inuits through the months of winter. They are not hunted to lie in front of some fireplace, Ticasuk,' explained Hank, realizing that Casey had broken the rules of hospitality and Trapper was not going to answer.

'This is a brutal, harsh land. Even though royalties from the North Alaskan oil pipeline have enabled them to have supermarkets and fly in fresh flowers for their homes, they still rely on their quota of whales and bears for meat to stock their underground ice larders. They need walrus and sealskins for their kayaks and winter clothes.'

Trapper listened silently, nodding occasionally.

'They are grateful to the animals they kill. They look upon the death of the animal as a gift and don't dwell on the kill.'

Trapper Jack looked across the tent at Hank. In the dim light Hank's face was intent and earnest as he tried to explain the ceremony of the kill to Casey. He bent over his carving once more, streamlining the bear's torso so that it resembled that of a man. He was content. Hank understood their way of life. He had learned well. It would be fitting for him to marry Ticasuk. Even though the girl had only a trickle of Inuit blood, it was enough. They would both be children of a country that the Universal Spirit had kept beautiful by ensuring that only a handful of people who had great strength and love for the land could survive the winters.

Yet when he looked at Casey, Trapper felt uneasy. Their way would be hard.

'We must leave Trapper to rest for tomorrow's hunt, Ticasuk,' said Hank. Casey stood up obediently, but Trapper stayed her by holding up his hand, not much larger than hers.

'First we must find you clothes,' he said, pointing at her fur-lined down anorak disparagingly.

'That will get wet. Then you freeze to death quickly.'

'But . . .' said Casey, ready to explain that her anorak was top-quality winter gear.

'My nephew died last year,' said Trapper softly. 'Like so many of our youngsters he discarded our traditional skin and fur clothing in favour of the new American polar polypropylene expedition-weight wear. Their snowmobile, another dangerous invention, broke down and they tried to walk back to camp.'

Trapper broke off and shook his head at the thought of another grave in the white-fenced area for his family, far out on the tundra, beyond the now disused DEW aircraft and radar station. The Inuit had ignored the neat camp. The Inuit interests were survival on the ice and tundra, not politics.

Casey immediately swallowed her protests about wearing skins for the hunt, and turned the subject away from what obviously still hurt Trapper.

'Why don't you like snowmobiles?' she asked. 'I thought they were a wonderful invention for snow and ice conditions.'

'Trapper has spent all his life with his dogs,' explained Hank. 'It's difficult to change to machines . . .'

'And dangerous,' added Trapper. 'If you're caught out in a snowstorm or whiteout you can curl under the dogs and sleep it out. They make a great blanket. If the storm lasts too long you have food.' He sniffed. 'Try eating a snowmobile!'

'Oh, no, Trapper,' said Casey with a grimace. 'You would not eat one of your dogs?'

'Always take along one or two mean critters that I hate,' he said, rummaging in a box at the back of the tent.

Casey opened her mouth, but Hank silenced her with a warning look.

'Here,' said Trapper, triumphantly holding a pile of clothng over his arm.

Casey quailed inwardly. They looked like goods picked over by a thousand hands in Petticoat Lane street market.

Hank winked at Casey as Trapper thrust another parka made of caribou skins and wolverine fur into her arms.

'Almost all Inuit winter clothing is made of caribou killed in autumn before the deep fur matting makes it too heavy and uncomfortable to wear,' said Hank, saving her the necessity of replying.

Casey winced as Trapper gave her boot liners made of bird skins turned inside out and boots soled with polar-bear fur for silence when walking on snow.

'Most of your British expeditions now use Inuit clothing,' said Trapper, seeming to sense her discomfort. 'It is better to live than to be fashion conscious, Ticasuk.'

'Thank you, thank you so much,' said Casey, suddenly contrite at having hurt his feelings and seemingly rejected his offer of warm clothing. 'I really am very grateful.'

Tomorrow you will be, he thought as he watched Hank open the flap of the tent. He hurried to join them, unwilling to let them walk unguided through the hunting camp.

Trapper watched the couple walk hand in hand down the grey road. Casey stopped to pick an Arctic poppy from the tundra. She stood on tiptoe to tuck the delicate yellow flower into the band of Hank's baseball cap and the wind threw back the hood of her parka.

He watched as Hank held Casey's hair away from her face and bent to kiss her.

He glanced at the sky as he turned to thread his way back through the summer shacks and tents. The first wisps of fog streamed in on the wind, grey and thick as an unkempt moustache.

Chapter Twelve

STEWART SAUNDERS paced past the picturesque ACVB Log cabin with its sod roof and garden overflowing with late autumn flowers. He scowled at the visitors as they hurried into the cabin to obtain maps and information. This was the fifth time he had walked past the cabin. He studied the five-thousand-pound jade boulder outside the door and walked round and round the abstract sculpture dedicated to William Seward. The sculpture confused him as much as the purchase of Alaska, a seemingly barren and useless piece of land, had confused the Americans at the time.

He walked back to the mile post in front of the cabin, proclaiming Anchorage to be the Air Crossroads of the World. His grey pony-tail blew like a windsock in the wind, which whined across downtown Anchorage.

Angrily he kicked at one of the ornamental cabbages lining the walkway to the cabin. He glanced up at the cabin guiltily as the burgundy-tipped leaves canted over into the earth. Hastily he bent down and straightened the plant, stamping the ground well down on either side of it.

Surely that idiot woman can find the corner of 4th Avenue and F Street, he growled silently. The town was laid out by army engineers. Even the most stupid cannot get lost.

He pushed back his cap and squinted into the distance where the white peaks of the Chugach Mountains flashed bright as neon lights as they rose up to embrace the sky. Their beauty only made him more irritable. That was where he wanted to be, back in the wilderness, away from this city whose municipal boundaries enclosed an area the size of the state of Delaware.

'Damn women,' he muttered, 'undependable lot.'

'Morning there,' chirped a young voice directly behind him.

Stewart swung round ready to deliver a lecture on tardiness.

'Right on time,'she smiled as she pulled up the sleeve of her Day-Glo orange anorak. 'Well, almost. It's only two minutes past ten.'

'And you were to be here at nine,' said Stewart curtly.

'No, siree,' she replied. 'The arrangement was ten and I apologize for being two minutes late.'

Stewart decided to keep the lecture for later. It had been difficult to find a cook this late into the season. He could not afford to fight with this one in Anchorage, where she could just walk away and leave him stranded. Once they were at the lodge she could not turn on her heel and tell him to keep his job, not unless she wanted to hike out.

'Come on, then,' he growled gruffly, 'we have to collect some people at the Captain Cook, plus one of my guides. Probably won't be able to leave before lunch now.'

Ginger smiled secretly and congratulated herself, as she fell into step beside him. Angela had warned her that Stewart was mostly bark with not much bite, but advised her to stand up to him right from the beginning, or he would make her the whipping boy of the lodge.

Well, Mr Stewart Saunders, she thought as they waited to cross the road to the mustard-brown high-rise hotel which overlooked the Cook Inlet, I think you and I understand each other.

Stewart looked at his watch as they pulled open the heavy glass doors to the hotel. He hoped that Dursley was not annoyed by the delay. He had come up with Stewart to meet Casey. Well, he will have Casey, thought Stewart with a concealed grin, they haven't seen each other for three days. He probably won't even notice the time.

He strode past the shops lining the long walk to the reservation and bell captain's desks. The windows were crammed with paintings, Inuit sculptures and clothes to tempt the tourists. He shook his head when he thought of the fall in the number of tourists a few years ago, when the news media told the world of the Katmai coastline painted with the black oil of death, as almost three thousand square miles, encompassing the most important commercial fishing areas and the incomparable beauty of Prince William Sound, were drowned under a flood of Alaska crude oil from the damaged tanker *Exxon Valdez*.

He and many lodge owners were convinced that the damage done by the oil spill would affect tourism to Alaska for years to come. It was difficult to persuade the public to spend their precious lesiure time and money in a place they were convinced was a graveyard of smothered birds, fish and wildlife. Television had convinced them that the beauty and wildlife were damaged for ever.

He grunted as he walked past the Pantry. The open-air café was usually buzzing with hungry tour groups. Now only a few couples were scattered in the non-smoking area. He searched for Dursley and Casey but the English pair were not in the café.

'Then, my good man, I suggest you contact your air terminal in Barrow and find out when my fiancée will be back in Anchorage.'

The bell captain looked up in relief as Stewart hurried across to where Dursley was demanding the impossible.

'Dursley,' he said, concerned at the barely concealed anger on the earl's face.

'Casey is not here,' clipped Dursley, his voice sharp, 'and neither is your guide Hank Butler.'

'No, Hank went up to Barrow to visit his old mentor Trapper Jack,' said Stewart.

'So did Casey,' snapped Dursley.

Stewart was silent. There had to be an explanation for this.

Listening to Dursley drum his fingers on the desk, Stewart realized that he had to find an acceptable explanation and quickly.

Ticasuk. This time his memory fed him exactly what he needed. He remembered the guides gathering in his cabin to report on the day's activities. Kit and Hank had told him of Casey's claim to Inuit blood. Laughingly they had spoken of the future Earls of Carrington being addicted to dried fish and Inuit ice-cream, a nauseating blend of cloudberries, ice and blubber.

'Barrow is the northernmost human settlement on the continent,' said Stewart. 'It is an Eskimo settlement. I'm sure we'll find that Casey persuaded Hank to let her join him. She seems very interested in Eskimos and their culture.'

Stewart wisely decided not to remind Dursley of the native blood in his fiancée's veins.

'It's most unlike Casey,' said Dursley, only slightly mollified.

'She'll be safe with Hank. He and Kit have been together for years. I'm expecting a wedding invitation, probably before the end of the year,' lied Stewart.

It worked. Dursley relaxed. He turned to Ginger and smiled. 'Dursley Carrington,' he said, holding out his hand. 'Please forgive my rudeness in not greeting you earlier, but . . .'

'Howdy,' answered Ginger, plugging the chewing gum into her other cheek. 'Don't worry, I understand. The last guy I was with met a babe on one of the glacier tour boats. He worked on the boat. We too had an understanding, but he preferred the new understanding with her.' She chewed her gum happily, unaware that Stewart's hands were itching to throttle her. 'Life can be a crock of – garbage.' She quickly amended the last word and lapsed into silence, as she caught Stewart's eye.

'You must forgive these kids,' said Stewart, deliberately placing himself in front of Ginger and waving her away with his hands behind his back. 'They don't realize when they are being rude. They think it's friendly and helpful.'

'The malaise seems to be general,' answered Dursley, looking around for the bell captain, who had wisely found pressing business in another part of the hotel.

'What were you trying to find out when I arrived? Can I help?' asked Stewart, silently cursing Hank.

He listened to Dursley's explanation about the fog blanketing Barrow, and the ineptitude of the airways personnel in not being able to predict when their aircraft would be airborne again.

'When touring up in the Arctic you are totally dependent on the weather,' explained Stewart calmly. 'That fog is a real pain in the arse. It can ground planes for two to three days before it lifts. But don't worry, let me make a few phone calls and we'll find out what the forecast is for that area.'

Dursley slumped down in one of the leather armchairs and watched a baggage trolley which seemed like an enormous brass bird cage trundle past. He felt drained.

When he heard that Casey had booked out of the hotel with Hank almost immediately after Stewart left for the airport, he felt as if a heavyweight had landed a full punch in his stomach. He buckled as disbelief stunned him. Till now, he had accepted Casey as belonging solely to him. Not many girls throw away the opportunity of becoming a countess. It was generally considered in London society that Casey Chargot had made an excellent catch.

This was the first time in his privileged life that he faced the thought of another man taking what he considered to be his. He did not enjoy the feeling. It left him stunned and nauseous.

He needed to see Casey, to hear her laugh, to feel her as she stood on tiptoe to put her arms around his neck. He needed to smell her breath as warm and musky as the highbush cranberry in the birch forests. He ached to see her and tell her that he loved her. He wanted to hold her and explain that ancestry and blood lines were not important. He flogged himself mentally for his coldness towards her when she told of her Inuit blood. He loved her so much . . .

Casey, he cried silently. *Please still be here for me!*

He felt his eyes burn. Quickly he pinched the skin over his nose. He looked up as the chair beside him belched air under the weight of a body.

'Got it,' said Stewart as the leather seat relaxed beneath him. 'It's a two-day fog. They should be here the day after tomorrow at lunch-time, which means we'll be back at the lodge in time for a whisky before dinner.'

Dursley pulled his lips into a smile and heard himself thank Stewart for the information. But he died a little inside. It meant another two nights without Casey. He wanted to explain so many things to her.

'Tonight dinner is on me,' said Stewart. 'There is a little place down the road which serves the best king crab in Anchorage.'

Ginger edged across the reception area, watching Stewart's hands, ready to return to window shopping if they flicked her away.

'You may as well come with us,' he said ungraciously. 'It seems as if Angela will have to manage for another two days on her own. You can take over the early morning shifts when we arrive. It will give her a break.'

That will take some of the cheek out of her, he thought with satisfaction.

Ginger nodded. Tumbling out of bed at four-thirty in the morning did not bother her at all. 'Suits me fine,' she replied, winding an elastic band around her frizzy ginger hair, now tamed into a bushy plait. 'I'm used to getting up early and working hard. My family are Sourdoughs not Cheechakos.'

Stewart grimaced. The old-timers never missed an opportunity to let newcomers know that they were superior.

'What's that mean?' asked Dursley, happy to have something to take his mind off Casey and Hank in Barrow together.

'Cheechakos are newcomers like Stewart,' said Ginger. 'My family were promysheleniks, Russian trappers, who came over from Siberia in the mid-seventeen-hundreds in search of furs.'

'And hunted the sea otter to near extinction,' added Stewart, stung at being called a Cheechako. 'The mother often floated on their backs holding their babies on their bellies,' he explained to Dursley. 'A good whack from a paddle was enough to kill them.

They lost more pelts than they took, as the mother and baby normally sank to the bottom of the sea before they could haul them out and skin them.'

Ginger ignored the remarks. She preferred not to think of the bloody period in Alaskan history when the fur traders forced the Aleuts, who were skilled at hunting from boats, to hunt the sea otter for them. They found that holding women and children hostage usually persuaded the Aleuts to take to their boats. Those who didn't were shot.

'And Sourdoughs obviously trace their history back to the original settlers,' said Dursley. 'But why call them Sourdoughs? What is sourdough?'

'It's simple. It's a "starter" for bread. All the old-timers used to have a jar of sourdough with them when they travelled. It's a mixture of yeast, sugar and flour which is added to mashed potatoes. Store it in a closed jar for three days and it's ready.'

Ginger grinned at Dursley. 'They'll probably have sourdough rolls at dinner tonight.'

Dursley's eyes followed another baggage trolley as it rolled down to the front doors. He wished that it was collecting Casey's luggage. He could see her trotting alongside the huge trolley smiling as she walked towards him. Lost in thought, he missed what Stewart was saying.

'Is that all right?' asked Stewart.

'Sorry, yes. What did you say? Forgive me, my thoughts were elsewhere,' said Dursley, sitting up straight in the chair.

It's not over yet, thought Stewart, as he studied Dursley. The man is hurting. If that fool Hank has done anything stupid, I'll have every fishing lodge in the Katmai closed to him.

'When a man loves a woman,' Dursley sang happily off key, as the hot water stung his back. He held his face up to the shower head, washing the soapsuds away from his eyes and choking on the words of the old Percy Sledge song.

'He sounds happy,' said Ginger in a loud voice as she and Stewart walked past the door to Dursley's suite. 'Happier than you are.'

'Shhh!'

'It's OK, the guy's awake.'

That's the trouble, thought Stewart as he hurried Ginger down the corridor. He quailed at the thought of Dursley opening the door at six o'clock in the morning to see him whisking Ginger out of the hotel.

'Must have been the wine,' he said. 'I should stick to beer.'

'You did fine,' smiled Ginger, 'especially for a guy your age.'

'I'm not talking about how but why I did it at all,' grunted Stewart, smarting at the back-handed compliment she had given him.

'The same reason every guy does,' she answered, braiding her hair back into a plait. Stewart had not even allowed her time to shower. 'You wanted to.'

Stewart was quiet as they waited for the lift, but as the doors slid closed and it began the long descent to the ground floor he knew that he had to broach a subject which had kept him awake most of the night. 'Have you? Do you?'

Ginger laughed unselfconsciously. 'Don't worry, I've been on the pill for years.'

Stewart still looked worried and tugged at the zip of his windbreaker.

'Ah,' said Ginger. 'The Big A. That's what's worrying you.'

Stewart nodded and coughed. 'These days one has to be careful,' he said.

Had his fun, now he's scared, she thought as the lights on the panel flicked to show which floor they were passing.

'Well . . .' She paused and pretended to think. 'I may have had a test before Bud, he's the guy working up on the pipeline, or was it after Stephen on the oil tanker in Valdez. Anyways, it's no damn good. They give you an "all clear" and five years later the bug wakes up. Whapoo, you're a goner.'

Stewart blanched and felt ill. He could not believe that he had gone to bed with Ginger. He didn't even remember much about it. Now he was one of the thousands waiting in the queue to see who had been chosen as victims. It wasn't even any use blaming her. Kids nowadays felt they were immune to the disease. They were bored with it. They needed something new to talk about. It did not attack the young and if it did, it certainly would not choose them.

'Don't worry,' said Ginger as she swung out of the lift on the ground floor. 'Live for today. There may not be a tomorrow.'

He wondered what the chances were of finding another cook. He realized that he had to have breakfast with Dursley and then take him to the airport to meet Casey. He conceded defeat. 'Never again,' he swore. 'Never again.'

Ginger grinned at him impishly over her shoulder. 'See you at the airport, sir!'

Two days later, the clock on the air terminal showed that the Mark Air flight from Barrow was now an hour late. Stewart watched Dursley pace up and down the room.

'Go and ask when the damn plane will be here,' he whispered to Ginger. She had asked four times in the last hour, but seeing Stewart's thin lips compress as his eyes followed Dursley, she stood up. As she kicked her tote bag under Stewart's chair, a voice, thin and metallic through the loudspeakers, announced the arrival of the aircraft from Barrow, Prudhoe Bay and Fairbanks.

Stewart breathed a sigh of relief, smoothed down his moustache, pulled his cap deeper over his ears and went to join Dursley. Hank had better come up with a damn good story, he thought, as he watched the passengers slosh through the mud and ash.

The line trickled away to the last few passengers but there was no sign of Hank or Casey. Stewart spun on his heel and strode to the desk before Dursley could react.

'Why, yes, sir,' answered the young girl. 'We have another

flight due in at two o'clock. Your friends will be on that one. We've had a backlog because of the Barrow fog, but everyone will be here today.'

Relieved, Stewart thanked her and went to find Dursley and Ginger.

Chapter Thirteen

CASEY AWOKE to find Hank leaning up on his elbow. He was studying her face with the intensity of a man about to go blind. She smiled at him sleepily, but his face remained grave.

'What's wrong?' she asked, now worried that something dreadful had happened. 'Have they phoned from Anchorage? Is Dursley sending a plane to fetch us? Can't we go on our bear hunt?'

Hank smiled and put his finger lightly over her lips

'Hush, little Ticasuk. Everything is fine. I was just wondering how it is possible to love someone so completely in such a short time.'

When you find the one who moves to your rhythm you will know it. The words, like an old melody, returned to haunt him. I do know it, Trapper, he thought. I have found her and I will do everything in my power to keep her. He smiled and bent down to kiss her. Casey giggled.

'My beard tickles your face,' he teased, moving down her body. 'Let's see how your tummy feels. We can also test . . .'

The small black pocket calculator/clock chirped on the bedside table. Hank switched on the light and checked the time.

'Saved by the squeaks,' he said as he patted Casey's warm round buttocks. 'Out of bed now, like a good little Eskimo wife. Out and find a polar bear for your man.'

Casey's desire to take part in the mystery and danger of a

white bear hunt overrode her need to be with Hank. She dutifully padded into the shower cubicle, squealing and hopping from foot to foot, as if walking on ice-cubes.

'You would make a wonderful go-go dancer in one of the strip bars down Vegas way,' Hank said, leaning against the door to the bathroom.

Casey tried in vain to cover her breasts. Hank strode into the cubicle and held her hands behind her back. Her breasts were thrust forward, the nipples puckered and hard in the cold morning air.

'Don't cover yourself,' he said softly. 'They are beautiful.' He let her hands drop and Casey stood quietly as he scrutinized her.

Hank's obvious pleasure in her body and his lack of inhibition had stunned Casey at first. She found herself studying the veneer on the wooden furniture or picking at threads on the orange bed covers when he walked around the room tumescent and eager to take her. Now she was learning the joy of nakedness and finding pride in her body.

'If you don't get back under that shower, the hunting party will have left the summer camp,' he said, settling back against the door frame.

Casey had never bathed in front of anyone in her life. It had always been a private time. Now she had no option. Hank was not going to leave the room and they had to meet Trapper.

As she ran the tablet of soap over her body and the hot water streamed down on her, Casey found that she enjoyed Hank watching her ablutions. I probably would make a good stripper, she thought, as she soaped her breasts and dotted foam on the nipples. The size of her breasts had been an embarrassment to her when she realized that men spoke to her but focused their eyes on her breasts. She had learned to ignore the lascivious stares. She ran the soap down the cleft of her buttocks then bent over to retrieve it as it slid from her grasp and skidded around the floor of the tiny shower.

'Hank,' she said, her voice high with mock surprise as she looked at him. 'I thought we were going hunting.'

'We are,' he answered huskily. 'This will keep till later.'

For a fleeting instant a picture of Dursley with a towel tied around his waist flitted across her vision. He always waited outside the bathroom door of their cabin at the lodge until she had showered. Dursley would never intrude on her privacy. It was not the thing a gentleman would do.

As she luxuriated in the last few seconds of hot water streaming over her, she compared Hank and Dursley. In bed, Dursley was like a lovable puppy, warm, wriggly and cuddly. They always made love under sheets or blankets. All actions were gentle and hidden from view. Hank stripped back the bed-coverings and made her observe and enjoy the act of making love. He was powerful and demanding. He played her to the point of exhaustion. He then watched her pleasure with a smile before taking his own.

Casey shivered beneath the steaming jets of water. She felt that by comparing the two men she was betraying Dursley. She admired and was very fond of Dursley and had no wish to hurt him. Guiltily she stepped from the cubicle into the tiny towel Hank was holding up for her. She rubbed at her body ineffectively and goose bumps rose on her arms.

'Let me dry you,' said Hank. She spread her legs to keep her balance as he rubbed her body to a rosy red.

'Now into the clothes Trapper gave you,' he commanded, and went to take his shower.

Casey looked towards the bathroom as she sneaked a set of white thermal underwear from her bag. She had no doubt that sealskin underclothes were the warmest for this hunt. But it was not yet winter, she reassured herself. Hank and Trapper would not know that she was wearing good British expedition-weight underwear. She heard the shower taps being turned off. Quickly she dragged on the clothes made of caribou skin, careful not to tear them in her haste. The bird's feathers felt strange as she slipped her small feet into them before pulling on the boots. She ran her hand over the polar-bear fur. It felt soft to her touch, not like hollow guard hair needles at all. She carried the konagen, which the Russians had named a parka, over her arm.

'You'll need to put that on,' warned Hank as they stepped into the small lounge-cum-reception area of the hotel. 'We have enjoyed summer in Barrow. It was yesterday.'

Casey struggled into the parka and walked across to the stuffed polar bear in the glass case. In the sharp grey light which crept in from under the sea fog the bear seemed alive and menacing. The long canine teeth and the shining molars gleamed bright as porcelain. Its brown glass eyes glittered and Casey felt that it was looking at her. Not in anger but in sorrow. It had the face of a gentle dog with small ears set far back on its head, she thought.

Grandfather bear, she said silently. I greet you and it's with great respect that I join the hunting party today. Forgive me.

She shook herself mentally, not believing that she was actually talking to a stuffed bear. 'Must be the clothes I'm wearing,' she muttered. She stood in front of the case for a while longer studying the animal, which itself hunted as skilfully as the hunter and often ended having the hunter as its prey.

The polar bear's face was more elegant than the concave one of the grizzly, she decided. It had a high protruding nose ending in a deep black button. Its neck seemed long and sinuous. Its shoulders were narrow and its hips wide. It's what fashion magazines would call 'pear shaped,' she thought.

'It doesn't look nearly as strong or large as the Katmai grizzly bears,' she said, turning to Hank who was handing in their room key.

'Did you send the message I gave you to the Captain Cook Hotel in Anchorage?' he whispered to the receptionist.

'Here it is,' the Inuit lady said proudly, pulling a piece of paper from under the reservation book.

'Oh, no,' groaned Hank. 'It is very, very important that message. Why did you not send it?'

'We tried, but this is Barrow, not Olitok Point with a DEW

station. Sometimes things work, sometimes not.' She smiled at him sweetly.

Hank sighed. 'Please see if you can find something that works today and send the message.'

He decided not to tell Casey that their message had not been relayed to Stewart and Dursley. He wanted nothing to upset the precious days they had together. They could face all the unpleasantness on their return.

'Are they more dangerous, Hank?' Casey asked again.

'A brave man dies but once. A coward dies a thousand deaths,' quoted Hank in answer to her question. 'They say that in hunting a polar bear on ice, it is the brave man who dies a thousand deaths.'

He walked across the room and stood in front of the case with his arm around Casey's shoulders.

'It looks so streamlined in front.'

'Those streamlined legs and shoulders can stun a Belukh whale with one blow. They can also flip up a four-hundred-pound bearded seal.'

Casey's eyes widened. 'I suppose you are going to tell me that it moves fast as well.'

'It climbs over ice rubble forty foot high as if stepping onto a sidewalk. It's as agile and supple as a cat. It can streak at twenty-five miles an hour when necessary,' answered Hank, laughing. 'A little faster than you can, Ticasuk,' he teased.

'Agreed, but only because of these clothes,' she retorted.

As they walked to the door the Inuit receptionist looked up at them. 'I hear that today you will hunt for polar bear with Trapper Jack.'

Casey was stunned. How could this woman possibly know what was only decided yesterday afternoon? She merely nodded.

'Remember, we believe that when we die our spirits enter animals. So all animals must be treated with great respect, especially the bear.'

Again Casey nodded but her fingers tightened around Hank's

and she was thankful to leave the small room dominated by the polar bear, glowing a ghostly white in the pearly-grey light of dawn.

Trapper Jack was waiting for them. 'I ordered food for you,' he said, as Casey looked in horror at the plate piled high with eggs and hash. 'Eat it, today you will need warmth in your stomach.'

Hank nudged Casey's leg as they slid onto the seat opposite Trapper.

'Thank you, Trapper,' she said weakly and picked up her knife and fork.

'I have a snowmobile outside. The only thing they are useful for is to move around Barrow quickly. We will meet the others at the landfast ice. The bear they have found looks as if it may move out onto the ice.' Casey frowned and Trapper hastened to explain. 'Along the shoreline a run of stable ice forms. A flaw lead usually separates this landfast ice from the moving ice-pack. This open water is a highway for sea animals. Bears know this and go there to hunt. We follow the bears. It is safer to hunt on the landfast ice.'

'Then the bears should keep away from the polar ice-cap,' said Casey. 'Why don't they?'

Hank grinned and squeezed Casey's hand. 'You are like a child, Ticasuk. Always questioning,' he teased.

'It is good to ask, there is no better way to learn,' said Trapper.

'Let's hope that this bear stays away from the pack ice,' said Hank soberly.

'The caribou herds have not been as plentiful this year. Many bears seem to be moving out early,'said Trapper, continuing his conversation with Casey. He drained his mug of black coffee.

'I feel it will be an easy hunt. The bear is hungry, he is checking aglus, sniffing to smell if a seal has used them recently. When we arrive, he will hopefully have settled down to wait at one.' Trapper wedged a fork piled high with hash into his mouth before continuing. 'In this fog we should be able to creep up close enough for a shot before he senses us.'

'Senses us?' queried Casey, trying to hide some of the egg beneath the brown hash. Hank and Trapper smiled at each other as her questions continued.

'Oh, yes. Ticasuk, the polar bear is the most formidable of all animals. Our people learned how to hunt by watching the bears hunt seals and walrus on ice.'

'Oh,' said Casey, eating a little to please Trapper. 'So your people are like the little Bushmen in the desert in southern Africa. You too live happily and in harmony with nature and the animals.'

Hank looked at Casey quizzically as he dribbled syrup over his waffles and it oozed into the hot hash and browns.

'Dursley told me about them,' she explained. 'He and his father hunted there.'

Hank's smile faded. She was immediately contrite for mentioning Dursley. She felt for his leg under the table and squeezed it.

Trapper shook his head and his straight black hair seemed to stick out like porcupine quills.

'No, we find great joy in life and in living. But we do not live happily with nature. Here nature is too cruel and fierce. We live in terror of her might. We are filled with "kappia" and "ilira". The animals we hunt are dangerous and the ice and sea they live in raise terror in our hearts. It excites us to hunt, but there is always a dark dread in our souls.'

'Apprehension and trepidation,' Hank interpreted the Inuit words, 'and it's easily understandable when you realize that a rock is a feature in this flat Arctic tundra, constantly whipped by gale-force winds and storms.'

Trapper called for the bill and Casey stopped chasing the egg yolk around her plate, relieved that she could leave it.

'Eat up,' commanded Trapper. 'There are no Wimpy Bars out there.'

She breathed in deeply and shovelled as much as she could into her mouth. She washed it down with the dregs of her now lukewarm coffee, wiped her mouth and smiled across at Trapper. He nodded and they left the room.

'You sit behind me. Hank will be behind you, to stop you falling off,' said Trapper as the snowmobile roared into action. Casey fought back the urge to cry out as the road fell away beneath them and they seemed to be moving in space. She breathed in the fresh air, trying to quell her panic, but the wind set fire to her nostrils. She bent her head and buried it in Trapper's back. Hank put his arms around her and hugged her tightly.

What am I doing here? she thought. *Finding your Inuit blood*, her small inner voice answered.

But I didn't realize that my ancestors lived this sort of life, she protested.

The bike bucketed into a melt pool in the road. Her teeth jarred and she concentrated only on holding on. Eventually the seemingly interminable bike ride ended. Hank lifted her off. She now bitterly regretted wearing her own underwear, instead of the soft sealskins Trapper had given her.

'Always listen to people who live in the area,' Hank had warned her, when they were in the plane on the way to Barrow. 'Don't look for English or even American traits in the North Slope Inuit. I find them extraordinary people. The words "courage" and "tenacious" must have been coined here.'

Casey pulled her parka hood tight around her face and the wolverine-fur lining stood out thick and straight in the cold air.

Figures came and dissolved in the polar fog. She could hear dogs barking but could not see them. She felt for and found Hank's hand. The swirling grey light disorientated her and she felt as if she was moving though she knew she was standing still.

'Stand astride and press down hard into the tundra,' said Hank, immediately understanding her plight. 'It's like a "white-out" when skiing. You'll soon get used to it.'

Casey nodded, not trusting herself to speak. She kept tasting the hash and eggs. She forced herself to think of clear apple cider and lemon barley water and it seemed to cleanse her mouth.

'The sled is ready,' called Trapper as he emerged from the

grey curtain which cut off sight and masked all sound. His figure was squat and dumpy in the traditional skin clothing. Over his outer clothes he wore a white oversized shirt.

'Camouflage for the ice,' he explained before Casey could question him.

Casey turned her eyes to the old but obviously well cared for .338 Remington magnum which he carried.

'Is that enough gun for a polar bear?' she asked Trapper. He looked at her in surprise. He had not expected the English girl to know anything about rifles. Hank had told him that her family had a rough shoot in Scotland. He could expect her to know a little of shotguns but was surprised that she had recognized his rifle.

'This is a spare rifle. We always take one on a hunt,' answered Trapper, tapping his 30-06. 'Most of our hunters use this model. I am one of the few hunters who does not use it.'

'I always thought that the perfect gun for most large animals was a Holland and Holland .375,' she said, echoing Dursley's choice of gun for hunting in Africa.

'A fine English gun' – Hank broke into the conversation – 'but here, hunters tend to use American guns.'

'Of course,' said Casey. 'I didn't think. May I see it, please?' she asked Trapper. He smiled as he handed her the rifle.

Trapper felt that Casey's interest in rifles showed her ancestral love of the hunt. Inuit women traditionally took part in the hunts. They usually rowed the large umiak boat leaving the small versatile kayaks for the men to chase the prey at sea. They were also skilled at dismembering the animals into small manageable pieces.

Casey held the rifle and wrinkled her nose at the lingering smell of benzine, then sneezed.

'Oil and grease freeze in this cold,' explained Trapper, 'so we clean the guns with benzine, then use powdered graphite to lubricate them.'

Casey nodded as she stroked the wooden stock. I must tell Dursley of the graphite, she thought. It will interest him.

Immediately the nauseous feeling returned. Dursley. She had to face him in a day or so and she was dreading it.

A voice called harshly and urgently through the mist.

'The sled is ready,' said Trapper, 'at last they have untangled those fool dogs. Let's go. You can ride in the sled,' he offered Casey, as they almost fell over it in the gloom.

She looked at the dogs. They were much smaller than she had expected and were still snapping at each other and tugging in opposite directions. They seemed deaf to the commands. 'No, thank you, I'll walk,' she answered, tucking her hands deep into her pockets.

'Once the lead dog takes over and starts pulling they all settle down,' Trapper reassured her.

'Until the first snow drift,' laughed Hank. 'Or "grey ice", when they decide to stop in the middle instead of moving over the buckling new ice.'

Trapper joined Hank in reminiscing about past hunts and Casey listened to them fascinated.

Suddenly the dogs stopped. All sound ceased. Casey was conscious of the ice beneath her boots and the wind ripping unhindered across the vast desolation behind her. She felt very vulnerable. The words *kappia* and *ilira* beat with a monotonous strike in her eardrums.

Somewhere ahead of them, invisible in the fog, was Nanuq, the polar bear, a skilled and savage hunter.

Casey resisted the urge to glance behind her. She fought to keep her imagination from creating an image of the bear, huge and hungry, swinging his powerful legs like a pendulum as he ran, holding them wide apart to cool down his body heat, the paws flapping loosely inwards as he moved.

She held her breath. There was a soft flapping somewhere ahead of them. She strained her eyes until they stung but could not penetrate the swirling grey ice fog. Her breath puffed out in little vapours of mist as she released it.

*

The great male bear, *Ursus maritimus*, was hungry and irritable. He needed to eat every five to six days. His last meal had been on the beach when he had gnawed at the half-frozen hide and blubber of a seal which had washed up on the stones, round, and cold as ice-cubes.

The seal had allayed but not appeased his hunger. He swung over the ice in his splayed loose-limbed gait to where he saw a cloud of vapour steaming in the cold air. Vapour always meant open water and open water meant easier hunting. Testing the wind, he moved slightly until eventually he was downwind from the seals' breathing hole.

Cautiously he slid towards the aglu flat on his belly. He stretched his forelegs out in front then slid his hindquarters up to meet them.

His huge frame was not silhouetted against the skyline, but merged with the tumbled ice. His camouflage was perfect. The bear chose a place well away from the aglu and dug a hole through the foot and a half of ice cover. The bear then lay down over the hole. His white fur lulled any seals swimming under him into believing that the ice was still solid overhead and they were safe.

The hours passed. Time was meaningless in this terryifying landscape. The silence was so thick and intense that it strangled all sound except the sharp crack and groan of ice.

Suddenly the bear's small brown eyes moved fractionally. The surface of the dark grey pond stirred. The ripples buckled the young ice circling it.

A sleek black head broke the surface of the water. The seal looked around quickly, well aware of the danger of being out of the water. He saw a rounded yellowish white hump to the right of his hole, but it looked like all the other lumps of ice and he ignored it. His eyes probed the icy moonscape ceaselessly as he breathed in the air he needed.

Imperceptibly the bear edged itself backwards. It slid stealthily and silent as a thief into the hole it had gouged in the ice. The dark water closed over its head and all was still. It swam easily as an otter towards the seal. As the seal breathed in its last lungful of icy air and again submerged, the bear struck. Its canines sank deep into the seal's neck and crunched the vertebrae. Blood flecked the grey ice and instantly froze into maroon rosettes.

Only the churning and frothing of the water and globs of crimson blood rising to stain the surface told of the death struggle deep below the ice. Soon all was silent. The polar bear broke the mirrored surface of the pool as he clambered out of the open water and struggled up onto thick ice. It carried the heavy seal high and easily. It dropped the seal as it shook its coat. Droplets rained down, soft as tears, on the dead body of the seal.

The bear moaned softly as it rolled into the snow blotting the water from its fur.

It raked the seal towards itself leaving a snail's trail of dark blood on the ice. Within minutes its powerful, sharp teeth ripped off and chewed the thick black hide and blubber. The bear then eagerly swallowed the exposed warm red meat. It scattered the intestines and other viscera across the ice. They lay like streaks and lumps of red, purple and brown oil paint on a pure white canvas.

The bear ambled away moaning contentedly to itself. As it walked its tongue cleaned its fur and mouth of all traces of blood and blubber. The polar bear is a lonely creature who wanders the white wastes, always moving, always hunting, always solitary. The great bear approaches only three things with trepidation, man, the killer whale and the walrus.

It was the first of these creatures, who, using powerful binoculars, watched and admired the skilful seal kill. It was man who was now going to hunt the mightiest of hunters on this creaking, shifting ice.

'There he goes,' said Trapper Jack's brother. His hands were blue with cold and his fingers cramped. He had not replaced the caribou-skin gloves which he had tucked into his pocket as he fiddled with the setting on his binoculars. He had no need for the binoculars as, like most Inuit, his vision extended three to four miles. But, like snowmobiles, binoculars were new and coveted.

Quickly he tugged on his gloves and beat his hands together. He winced as warmth gradually returned to his fingers.

There were smiles of anticipation and a palpable air of excitement between Trapper Jack and his two brothers as they broke open their rifles and chambered rounds of Nosler partition bullets into the 30-06.

'Into the sled,' said Trapper, almost carrying Casey across the snow. The stocky Siberian huskies were barking and biting each other in excitement. They pulled at the traces, almost over-turning the sled as they tried to sniff at a new trail of black blood leading from the ice towards the hunting camp.

Someone had earlier dragged a bleeding seal carcass across the ice, hoping that the smell would attract one of the 'early' bears on the ice, to follow it.

The lead dog turned round to join in the mayhem, pulling the sled sideways. Within seconds the sled, packed with food, extra clothing and ulus, their crescent-shaped knives, toppled over, scattering carefully wrapped goods across the ice.

Casey waited for the men to curse and yell as they tried to untangle the dogs and right the sled. To her amazement they merely laughed as they hurriedly restored order.

'But the bear is moving away,' she said to Hank. 'What is the joke? They could lose it.'

'Inuits do not lose their tempers when things go wrong. They laugh instead,' explained Hank. He then moved away from her to hold two of the dogs which had been entangled, before they could rejoin the fray.

'Stupid fool,' grinned Trapper as he retied one of the huskies into its traces. 'You will be the next one to go into the pot.'

Casey shuddered. The thought of eating dogs revolted her. At home their dogs were treated well and loved as much as the children.

That's England, she thought, trying to peer through the fog, which had now lifted a little. It was drifting in veils of light and dark grey across the ice. She felt dizzy and still a little nauseous as she squinted at the swirling landscape. There was no horizon, no shadows and no depth. It was a whiteout. She knew that it was caused by light travelling at a particular angle in one direction, which had the same strength as all other light travelling at any angle and in any other direction. In the exceptionally clear atmosphere of the Arctic it is difficult to determine distance.

Don't try to compare your gentle and civilized life in England with this unforgiving land. Remember, your Inuit ancestors learned to live and survive here. Be proud of it.

Casey was still chiding herself silently when Trapper grasped her by the arm and led her to the sled. She held back a little, unwilling to trust herself to the team of dogs snarling at each other, but now standing still. Trapper tucked a caribou blanket around her and called to the lead dog. Her head snapped back as the dogs took up the slack and pulled forward. She clutched at the skin blanket as the bottom fell out of her world. She wanted to scream and ask Trapper to stop the sled; instead she buried her face in the skins. Once her eyes were closed and she was warm, her panic subsided and she found to her surprise that the ride was more comfortable than she had expected.

Not as bad as Dursley's old Range Rover on the moors, she thought. She put her hand behind her neck to support it from the sharp halts every time Trapper's brother stopped to use binoculars to locate the bear.

At one stage they waited for half an hour as he patiently moved the glasses across the ice, carefully inspecting every lump and rounded mound.

'Looks as if we've lost it,' whispered Hank, bending down over the sled.

'How do they know where they are and how to get home?' asked Casey peering at the whiteness, cut only by the grey of the fog. 'Where is east and west?'

'Up here there is no east or west to use for direction,' said Hank. 'The sun is not reliable. It does not always rise in the east and set in the west. There are also fewer stars. The Inuit are guided by the winds and currents, the flow of a river or a flaw lead in the ice.'

Casey rubbed her hands together and hoped that they would be able to find the hunting camp again. The thought of being lost out on the ice and hemmed in by swirling fog horrified her.

'Don't worry, Ticasuk,' said Hank as if sensing her distress. 'These men are old and wise hunters. We are safe.'

Casey now hoped that they would not find the bear even though she knew that the fur, blubber and meat were precious to the Inuit. At home she could pick up pricked grouse and break their necks with a quick flick of the wrist, but somehow a polar bear was different. She felt it was the very spirit of loneliness and it should be left to its solitary wanderings in this wasteland of ice.

Trapper's brother smiled suddenly. 'Kiviakatitaktok, it appears and vanishes,' he said as he lowered the glasses. He handed the binoculars to Hank. Hank stared into the shimmering whiteness and shook his head. 'I see nothing. Certainly no bears.'

'Ticasuk,' said Trapper, handing her his Zeiss, 'see if you can see him.'

Casey held the glasses to her eyes and adjusted them slightly. She moved them fractionally from left to right.

She remembered Dursley saying that when looking for game, look for movement, not colour or size. The flick of a tail, the twitch of an ear is what betrays them. But Dursley was talking about Africa, not the monotonous spaces of the Arctic on a day swirling with grey fog. Here there was no perception of size or depth. A ptarmigan could vanish when it crouched only a few feet away. A bear could be a large animal far away or a small animal up close. Animals could rise in the air and fly away as you approached, or they could appear to be rocks and glaciers, large and menacing.

Casey was about to hand the binoculars back to Trapper when she thought the end of an ice ridge moved. She stared at it until her eyes watered. She was rewarded. It did move.

'There,' she said triumphantly. 'It's sitting on the far ice ridge at about two o'clock.'

Trapper and his brother nodded approvingly.

'Good spotting,' congratulated Hank.

'Won't the bear see us?' asked Casey as the sled lurched forward.

'Nanuq does not have excellent eyesight,' said Trapper. 'We can move much closer before releasing the dogs. Perhaps you should walk with us now, Ticasuk.'

She swallowed back her protest. Hank had warned her that the bear would be held at bay with dogs. While the huskies ringed the bear, taking turns to dart in and nip his legs keeping it occupied, the men would come up and shoot it.

'It's no worse than riding to hounds,' Hank had reasoned.

'But that's traditional and it's only a fox,' she had protested. 'They are considered vermin and are shot on most estates.'

'So is hunting bears and whales traditional here,' countered Hank.

Sitting huddled in skins and furs with the wind howling across the ice, Casey could understand the need to trap and hunt. It had been so easy to sit at home in warmth and safety and condemn these people for killing whales and taking pelts.

The paid trouble makers and placard shakers should be forced to spend a winter here, she thought as she put her head on her knees to break the force of the wind frosting her face. They would then sing another song about the so called senseless killing of animals for profit.

Fixing her gaze on the ridge where she had seen the bear, she nevertheless willed it to sense danger and leave. But its belly was full and warm. The polar bear was content. He would now move deeper and deeper onto the polar pack ice. Occasionally he would cross the path of a sow in oestrus. Then the deep silence would shatter to the roars of converging bears as they fought to mount her. Bloodied but triumphant the dominant male would continue on his lonely way. Grunting and moaning, only to keep other bears away, not to be sociable.

The dogs inhaled the scent of the bear deeply at the aglu and were now racing towards the ridge. Casey was thankful that she was not in the sled as it bounced and jerked across the ice. She plodded beside Hank, using his large frame as a wind-break.

'All right?' he asked tenderly, putting his arm around her shoulders and squeezing her to him. Casey merely nodded; her lips were so cold that she was afraid to speak. Her teeth would chatter, giving away the fact that her face was bitterly cold. She wanted to do nothing which would spoil the enjoyment and excitement of the hunt for Hank.

They're like little boys playing cops and robbers, she thought, watching the stealth with which the men approached the ridge. Even the dogs had been quietened, a feat she would have considered impossible a few hours ago.

'Do you still have your old Contender?' asked Trapper quietly.

'Yes.' Hank patted the pocket which ran from shoulder to waist inside his jacket.

'Contender?' queried Casey. Silently she thanked Trapper for making her wear the caribou clothing and boots soled with polar-bear fur.

'It's a real cannon, a Thompson Contender,' answered Hank, pleased with Casey's apparent interest in guns. 'The round is a necked-down .444 Marlin Case to .375.'

Casey's eyes crossed, but she kept her expression bright and enquiring, fixed on his face. She had been about to query the term 'necked down', but years of living with a family who loved guns, dogs and children, in that order, had taught her that explanations of guns and ammunition were interminable and usual incomprehensible. She let Hank's explanation rush past her like the Arctic wind. Suddenly she realized he had stopped speaking and was obviously waiting for her to say something.

'It's more powerful than a .44 magnum,' he explained, naming a gun she would probably have heard of. 'With a muzzle brake it makes a hell of a noise, but doesn't have that much recoil.'

'Can you shoot bears with it?' she asked, hoping that he would say yes. It would be comforting to have a man with a gun at her side.

'It'll take out any of the big five. If the animal is shot in the right place,' Hank corrected himself.

'When we let the dogs go, stay with Casey,' Trapper warned Hank. 'Have your handgun ready in case.'

Hank nodded and Casey shivered. Now that the time had arrived to confront the bear she wished she was back in the hotel room. Even the cigarette burns on the veneered furniture and bath-tub were more acceptable than being out in this swirling white desert. They were about to confront the sea bear, a creature which hunted as silently and successfully in the black waters beneath the ice as it did on the ice or on land.

Casey jumped as the dogs were released from their traces. They rushed past her turning on each other snarling, biting and screaming before following the lead dog across the ice. She dug her hands deep into her jacket. The dogs streamed away in single file, ominous as a brown lead suddenly opening in the ice.

The bear heard the dogs. They were strong and savage, bred for these conditions and hunts. The bear's long neck snaked from side to side as it peered at them. Then it stood up on its hind legs, towering ten feet into the air. The wind brought with it the scent of an animal it instinctively knew and feared. It was man, a predator more powerful and deadly than itself. It moaned again, a sad cry in the silence.

Casey held Trapper's binoculars to her eyes and she gasped as the bear rose up. 'It's magnificent,' she breathed. She was afraid.

'Yes. Nanuq is our grandfather,' answered Trapper.

The bear turned to run. It instinctively headed for a lead of open water where it could dive and find safety. But in its contentment after its meal it had hemmed itself in comfortably against the wall of ice rubble. The rubble hung suspended in huge blocks over its head and sheared up high on both sides. It was a perfect place to shelter from the wind, but now it formed an ideal trap.

Though the bear could bound over a thirty-foot ridge as effortlessly as a cat, it started to scramble around the rubble. But too late. The lead dog reached it and circled the bear barking hysterically. Within moments the rest of the pack surrounded the bear. The noise was deafening as they darted in to nip at its feet.

They kept the bear spinning allowing it no rest, no chance to escape. The bear made small groans. Its canines were white and pointed in the dark purple of its mouth. Foam flew out, spattering the dogs, as the bear swung from one dog to the other trying to kill its tormentors. Its hindquarters were well protected by the three-inch-thick layer of blubber beneath its black skin. But the dogs tore its legs and sides.

'Chase will live to hunt more bears,' nodded Trapper approvingly, as the lead dog kept to the right side of the bear.

'Inuit believe that polar bears are left handed,' whispered Hank.

Casey closed her eyes. One of the dogs had misjudged the bear's reaction. Five recurved claws swung out and ripped open the dog's belly. It howled and crept towards them, dragging its entrails behind it. They made an obscene stain on the purity of the ice.

Casey gagged and prayed for someone to shoot the dog, to put an end to its pathetic howls. But the men never took their eyes from the massive bear. They knew how swift and dangerous it was. Until Nanuq was dead their attention would be riveted only on him.

The bear caught a second dog and spun it thirty foot into the air before it smashed into the rubble wall, staining the translucent blue ice a dirty red. Trapper Jack and his brother hurried forward. If the bear killed and maimed too many of the dogs the rest would slink away. They were brave only in a pack.

As they circled to the right of the bear the hunters were eager and alert. Their blood raced to the ancestral thrill and danger of the hunt. They did not see an angry animal bayed at and tormented by dogs. They were hunters and responded to the hunt with the non-rational mind we have when we dream. Their senses became one with the land, the ice, the wind and the animal. The shots which would end its life were only the end of a primeval experience. Being part of the land and the raging elements was important, not the dead bear.

They sighted their rifles on the whirling bear, waiting for a good shot, just behind the shoulder, which would rip through the pumping lungs and explode the heart.

All the men were skilled at skinning and dismembering animals. They clearly saw the powerful ligaments and the strong ribcage protecting vital organs. They mentally traced the path their bullets would take as they bored into the animal, if not bursting its lungs and heart then smashing its vertebrae, paralysing and finally killing Nanuq, the sea bear they loved and honoured.

Trapper's brother fired just as the polar bear turned and scooped up another dog. Its claws sank effortlessly into the dog's neck cutting off the animal's terrified scream. The bear's heavy foreleg was stained bright red as blood pumped up from the carotid artery. The bear swung the dog around. Drops of scarlet encircled them both, bright as sparks of a Catherine wheel, as it whirled the dog around its head. With a howl of pain and bewilderment the bear shook the dog free from its claws. It spun round biting at the burning pain in its back leg.

It tried to stand, but the leg was shattered and hung useless. It tried to balance on three legs, but on the ice it could only teeter like a cripple.

Casey closed her eyes and bit her lip to stop from screaming. Tears froze on her cheeks burning her skin.

'Let Nanuq escape,' she breathed, knowing that the bear was doomed. If it did get away it could never hunt and would starve to death. She changed her prayer to: 'Let it die quickly. Don't let it suffer.'

As if in answer, another shot cracked out. It echoed against the ice ridge. Casey listened to it sickened and sad, until it faded away soft as a whisper. All was silent.

The bear, turning to tear at its hind leg, had presented Trapper with the shot he needed. Nanuq lay huddled on the ice. A pool of red darkened quickly as it froze on the silky white surface.

Casey opened her eyes slowly. She hated men and hunters. She looked up at the tumbled ice ridge fully prepared to face Trapper and his brother with her bitterness, but to her amazement they had tied the remaining dogs together, wedged the harnesses beneath an ice rock and were now solemnly revolving around the bear in a stately stilted dance. With their white camouflage shirts and brown skins they looked like ptarmigans, half of their bodies winter white and the rest still the speckled brown of summer.

Casey shivered as the words they were chanting struck an ancestral chord deep within her. Her anger and bitterness slowly gave way to understanding and a deep love for the bear.

Instinctively she understood that Life went into Darkness and back into Life. Life merely handed on the torch to another. There was no death. Life itself never died. Nanuq was being honoured and his spirit would live on in others for ever.

Casey Ticasuk Chargot removed her gloved hands from her pockets and clapped slowly in time to the chant. Standing in the fog, Ticasuk, the white girl from England, joined in the song of praise to Nanuq, and the icy wilderness which was his home.

Hank took his gaze away from Trapper and his brother. He had seen Inuit honour the kill many times before and it was always moving. He looked down at Casey but did not touch or speak to her. She seemed to clap the strange, slow rhythm as if in a trance. My little Eskimo, he thought, how I love you. Life without you would be like this place, cold and dreadful. Hank shook himself, he was becoming maudlin.

It must be the bear hunt, he reasoned silently. But he knew that he was now committed to Ticasuk. She had in a very short time become his life.

Trapper lifted his leg high to stamp it down and then paused. The slow sound of clapping drifted into his song. He looked down to where Hank and Casey were standing side by side. He and his brother smiled and gestured for them to come up to where they were honouring Nanuq.

'Come,' said Hank, touching Casey gently on the arm. She shook her head as if awakening from a deep sleep and held back.

'No, Hank. I don't want to see the bear butchered,' she said.

'Skinned,' he corrected. 'Come and let Trapper show you the

massive muscles. Come and see what an incredible creature the polar bear is beneath that pelt. It's fascinating. Please. Honour the bear.'

Casey, unable to resist his plea or his smile, reluctantly followed him.

Trapper and his brothers were now deftly slicing the skin on the inside of the legs and opening it up from the belly to the chin. Quickly two of them peeled back the heavy pelt and it steamed in the cold air. Working swiftly with the sharp, crescent-shaped ulus, they scraped the hot red meat and blubber away from the pelt.

Casey tried not to breathe as the hot stomach gases escaped. She pretended to wipe her nose with her glove but left the glove covering her nose and mouth. The men dismembered the joints and cut the bear into large portions. The women in camp would skilfully cut it up into small pieces.

Trapper never stopped talking. He pointed out the passage of the bullets to Casey, pretending not to notice her blanch as he held up the jellied heart and lungs.

He explained how the ligaments worked. Trapper captured Casey's interest. She found that she could touch the dead animal. Something had changed. It was now an object to be examined and wondered over. It was no longer a terrifying and mysterious creature. She ran her hand down the long doglike nose and stroked the hair inside its tiny ears. She tried to close the lids over its soft brown eyes while Trapper washed the blood from the pelt with blocks of ice, but the eyes were frozen open.

'Live happily in your new body,' she muttered quietly.

Trapper smiled. He had watched as Casey moved from repugnance to fascination. There is still much of our blood in you, he thought with satisfaction. He passed his small strong hands across the bulging shoulder and foreleg muscles. He sliced out the liver which was so high in vitamin A that it was never eaten for fear of illness and death.

'The flesh of a bear must never be eaten raw,' he warned Casey. 'Warm caribou flesh is good after a hunt, but the uncooked flesh of a bear makes you ill and your hair falls out.'

'*Trichinella sprilis*,' whispered Hank. 'A parasite found in most polar bears. The liver is worse. It has toxic levels of Vitamin A. Eat that and you think you're going to die.'

Casey shivered, not at the thought of dying, but of eating raw liver. 'Dursley says one of the joys of hunting in Africa is cooking the liver of buck over an open fire and eating it, immediately. . .' She paused, seeing Hank's smile fade.

'Go on,' he said, controlling his dislike of hearing Dursley's name. This was their precious time together and he did not want the English earl intruding, even in thought.

'After they have shot it,' she finished lamely.

Hank reached out and held Casey's face, tiny behind the fur lined hood in his hands. 'I love you,' he mouthed, and she smiled.

The bear's pelt was carefully wrapped and placed on the front of the sled. The huskies were kicked and beaten away as the men worked quickly to stash the meat onto it. They covered it with sealskin and bound it down tightly.

'Tonight we will eat well and all our friends will join us. The women will cook and we will sing and dance the "dances of the hunt". Bear stew is always good,' said Trapper. 'Will you join us?'

Trapper's brother looked surprised. They knew that Trapper considered Hank to be the son he never sired, but Hank and Casey were still 'tanitz', outsiders. They and their friends disliked the ever increasing groups of tourists who trooped through the small burgundy and grey Mark Air Terminal and sniffed with disdain at their Inuit way of life.

They had seen and understood the sniggers as the bus drove the tourists around Barrow. These people understood nothing of the Inuit love for this inhospitable and most violent of lands. They did not even listen when the guide stood them out on the tundra and showed them the beauty of the Arctic poppy, its translucent lemon petals glowing and opening, in defiance of the howling winds. They merely glanced at the great white snowy owls perched on hummocks, the only mounds of raised earth in the flatness. The ptarmigan, Alaska's national bird, was ignored as the tourists fought to clamber up the steps of the bus and escape the icy gale which sliced through their borrowed jackets with the ease of an ulu through soft blubber.

Casey looked up at Hank and squeezed his hand hard, willing him to refuse Trapper's invitation.

'Thank you,' she heard him say and she blanched. She knew she would throw up if offered any of the bear meat. 'But it is our last night here. They say the fog will have lifted by morning.'

'We understand,' smiled Trapper, smoothing the sparse, wispy hairs on his chin. 'It is necessary to be together when one is young.'

Casey smiled in relief and instantly put her arms around Trapper and hugged him.

'Thank you, Trapper Jack,' she said. 'Thank you for everything.'

The old man's expression did not change but Hank thought he saw a twinkle in his dark eyes.

Trudging back to Trapper's tent in the hunting grounds Casey found that she was hungry and wished that she had eaten all of her breakfast. Her mind swirled with images of the hunt. The bear, the blood, the sharp rifle cracks and cries in the silence. The soft moans of the bear. It now seemed part of a dream, a strange, disorientated, swirling mixture of beauty and cruelty.

'If we cannot offer you bear stew, then you will eat "tailpipe ptarmigan",' decided Trapper.

He spoke to his brother who drew up the dogs and unwrapped a shotgun from one of the parcels on the sled. They were now on landfast ice, within sight of the tundra plain. Trapper's brother walked away from them.

Casey watched him idly as he walked away. They had ptarmigan in Scotland but she had never heard of a tailpipe species.

'Trapper,' she said, 'what is. . .' Her words were lost. A group of ptarmigan which had been huddling behind a small mound of ice exploded into the air, their cries raspy and harsh. Two shots rang out in quick succession and Casey jumped. She looked up into an open patch of dove-grey sky and watched as two speckled birds tumbled down, feathers falling like snowflakes around them.

'He would do well at an English shoot,' she said, as Trapper ran to kick the dogs into silence.

The birds were skinned and the breasts split out. Trapper pulled a beige skin thin as paper from the sled. He wrapped up the breasts and handed them to his brother, who quickly walked ahead to where they had left the snowmobile. Lifting the cowling, he wrapped the breasts securely to the tailpipe. The snowmobile roared into life and bumped away over the tundra.

Trapper watched the machine veering round hummocks and roaring over the matting of plants which clung onto the thin, acid soil. The thick tyre treads crisscrossed a web of old tracks spun into the vegetation. Casey wondered if the marks would vanish or remain for ever, turning into shallow melt pools in the tundra.

'Soon you will taste tailpipe ptarmigan,' said Trapper happily. 'Grouse are also good cooked this way, but rabbits are the very best.'

Casey realized it was an honour to have been included in the hunt and she was determined to eat the ptarmigan no matter what it tasted like.

Trapper's brother returned about twenty minutes later and halted in a cloud of black fumes which tested her determination to eat the game bird.

Trapper handed her a piece of pink meat. It smelt slightly fishy but she stripped out a piece from the centre, trying to avoid the meat which had rested against the sealskin.

She bit into it and found that it was surprisingly good.

'It tastes a little like chicken,' she said, smiling up at Trapper and his brothers.

'Only better,' answered Trapper, licking his fingers.

Casey dug into the pocket of her parka and found a handful

of tissues. Carefully she wadded the outside pieces of the ptarmigan into the tissue, pretended to wipe her nose and then stuffed the ball back into her pocket.

She looked back over her shoulder as she and Hank left Trapper's tent and trudged along the coastal road to where they had left the car. The fog had lifted and a watery light washed the hunting grounds with silver.

The huskies lay in a huddle, their backs to the biting wind. They tucked their noses deep into their bellies for warmth. As an eddy wafted the scent of meat drying on racks across to them they lifted their heads and howled. In the distance a wolf answered. His high, lonesome song lay on the wind.

Casey reached up and tucked her hand into the pocket of Hank's jacket. 'The fog has lifted,' she said softly. He nodded and his fingers curled around hers. They were silent. There was nothing to say.

Chapter Fourteen

THE WIND flung open Casey's anorak as she walked carefully down the steps from the aircraft. A light drizzle made the treads slippery and she held onto the handrail. Hank walked behind her carrying her bag over his shoulder. She longed to turn around and look at him for comfort. They had decided that nothing would be said to Kit or Dursley until they were both in the privacy of their cabins at the lodge.

Hank was certain that Kit would be reasonable. After all they both knew that theirs was only a passing affair. As he consoled himself with this thought he remembered his last night with her. She had spoken of a 'Hank junior' someday. He had mumbled, 'Fine,' and turned over to sleep. That was only pillow talk, he assured himself. He watched Casey's dark hair spread out black and full as a storm cloud above her collar. He longed to put his arms around her and feel her softness up against him. To see her lips curve up in a smile. He wanted to the world to know that Ticasuk was his.

Dursley watched Casey walk into the terminal. He wanted to vault over the bags, cases and cardboard boxes littering the floor. He wanted to swing her up into his arms and never stop kissing her.

The few days without her had seemed a lifetime. He now knew without a doubt that his future lay with Casey Chargot. He wanted everyone to know, but his breeding stopped him from displaying emotions in public. He did however allow himself to hug her and whisper in her ear. 'I've missed you so much, Bubbles.'

No problems there, thank goodness, thought Stewart as he watched Dursley put his arms around Casey and hold her to him, for once disregarding the public.

'Dursley,' Hank said, holding out his hand. 'It's good to see you again.'

Dursley seemed relaxed. Hank mentally thanked Stewart for whatever he had done to keep Dursley happy. But when he met Stewart's eyes he realized that there was a price to pay. He did not look forward to their arrival at the lodge. He greeted Ginger perfunctorily and turned away to take the bags out to the van. He did not want to see Dursley greet Casey.

Casey felt Dursley's lips on hers and they were the lips of a stranger. She forced herself to respond. Later she would be able to talk to him. Not now.

'Bubbles, it's so good to have you back,' said Dursley linking his fingers behind her waist and holding her to him. 'Let me look at you.'

Casey struggled not to cry as he studied her face. She felt so guilty. He was such a gentleman. In a strange way she still loved him.

How can I possibly love two men? she thought as he smoothed her hair away from her face and tucked it behind her ears. Perhaps in different ways, as they are different men, she reasoned. But I belong to Hank. I belong to this land and this life. She glanced up as Hank walked past, with the heavy bags bumping against his legs. Quickly she lowered her eyes in case they told tales of her love for him.

Hank waited for the party at the truck. He pulled up the collar of his jacket and stamped his feet, splashing the hub caps with chocolate mud. 'Fascinating,' he heard Casey say as she came out of the terminal arm in arm with Dursley. He felt all the fires of rage and jealousy burn in his belly, but he merely smiled over their heads, avoiding their eyes.

'Did you know that when we landed at Deadhorse Airport in Prudhoe Bay we caught a glimpse of that eight-hundred-mile pipeline which carried the crude oil down to Valdez?' babbled Casey. She was talking about anything and everything, desperate not to be questioned in front of Stewart and the new cook about their stay in Barrow. 'The Eskimos of the North Slope are paid by the oil company. They apparently get royalties on all the oil piped out. They have to be the only community who don't pay taxes but actually have money paid to them at the end of each year.'

Dursley opened the door of the van for Casey to climb in. His hand rested on her rounded buttocks for a moment. Hank saw Dursley's fingers caress them. He hurled Dursley's leather bag onto the oilcans they were taking back to the lodge to lubricate the generator.

'Hope your bag looks like the aftermath of Valdez,' he muttered softly.

'All loaded?' asked Stewart.

'Done.'

Stewart grimaced and swore silently as he listened to control. 'Mist is down on the pass. We'll have to sneak around the mountains then fly home the long way round.'

He clamped the headphones back over his ears and his grey pony-tail shook as the black cap slipped sideways.

'Not in a very good mood, is he?' queried Ginger, sitting hunched up beside Hank on the narrow middle seats.

'Stewart doesn't like talking unless there is a good reason,' answered Hank, trying not to glance over his shoulder at Dursley and Casey sitting in the sling seats behind him.

Ginger moved the wad of gum from one cheek to the other. 'Really!' she said, weaving a world of meaning into the one word. 'That must depend on where he is and who he's with.'

'Yeah?' answered Hank, studying Ginger for the first time.

So much for Stewart's supposed dislike of the casual relationships between the staff at the lodge, he thought. Given the chance he does exactly the same. Hank looked at her and then at Stewart. A faint smile twitched his lips. This information could be useful if

Stewart started berating him about Casey and being back at work late.

'Dirty old man,' he muttered.

Ginger giggled.

Casey looked across at her. She hated the way her ginger plait brushed Hank's shoulder as she laughed. That's where I should be sitting, she thought. That is my man. You've no right to be flirting with him.

Dursley felt her stiffen. 'Don't worry,' he comforted her. 'The mist cannot be very thick. Stewart would never fly in dangerous conditions. He is good and has nothing to prove. It's those who keep trying to impress everyone who end up in crashed planes.' He stroked her fingers. He seemed not to notice when she pulled her hand away pretending to look for a tissue in her pocket.

Casey smiled at him weakly. 'I'm fine, just a little tired,' she reassured him.

'I'll treat you to the famous Earl of Carrington massage this evening,' he said gently.

Casey shivered inwardly. She still had to face Dursley when they were alone in the cabin. Suddenly she wanted the flight to last for ever.

Kit stamped her legs and the gravel scattered around her feet.

'Stewart will have you on your knees smoothing out his pathway again,' warned Angela. Kit grinned at the beige gravel and kicked out a divot with great satisfaction.

Each pebble was precious to Stewart, as it had all been ferried to the camp. It made the slippery paths easier to walk on. It also kept the ever-present mud from clogging into sticky patches on the boots and dropping off in the cabins.

Kit looked up into the sky, once again willing the float-plane to appear. The clouds were heavy and dark but no plane was hiding in them. She now regretted the impulse which made her join Angela at the jetty to welcome the passengers with a tot of brandy.

'Peg-leg Pete says that it'll snow before morning,'said Angela, balancing the tray of brandy glasses carefully as the wind threatened to topple them into the lake. She did not seem to notice the cold or the gusting wind. 'And he was sober,' she added.

'Then it will snow. Peg-leg is never wrong about the weather,' said Kit.

'Stewart will be stunned to see our new boat. He swore that fish would turn into bald eagles before Peg-leg replaced the one he hacked up.'

A low drone halted the conversation. Both girls looked up at the dark speck wavering in the immense grey vault over them.

'They'll need the brandy,' predicted Kit as they watched the plane flop gracelessly as a wet butterfly onto the choppy water.

Kit waited for the door to open before she strode out onto the jetty. She gave Stewart the thumbs-up in salute to a good landing in bad conditions. She felt a prick of excitement as she grabbed the rope and waited for Hank to jump down and help dock the plane. She had worked out a plan to persuade him that marriage was now both necessary and desirable. It meant falling pregnant and being unable to terminate the pregnancy because of religious scruples. The last bit would be difficult. But she was sure that it would work. She would have to pretend that she was a closet Christian.

The few days he had been away had persuaded her to hang up her fishing rod and settle down to raise his children.

She had proved herself in the world of men and was tiring of being one of the boys. Now she was ready to try motherhood.

'Hi there,' said Hank, avoiding her eyes.

'Hi, yourself,' answered Kit. He must be feeling queasy, she decided.

'I propose a toast,' said Kit, holding up a glass of brandy, as they stood shivering in a small group on the jetty. 'To Dursley and his world-record rainbow.'

Hank, Stewart, Ginger and Casey stared at Kit in amazement.

Then a babble of voices broke out, drowning the cry of the loons tracing the lake edge.

'Marvellous,' said Hank, pumping Kit and Dursley's hands.

'Magnificent,' added Stewart, still a little stunned at the news. 'Had I but known, Dursley, I would have taken Anchorage TV time and let every fisherman in Katmai turn bright green and break their rods with envy.'

Dursley had waited, thus allowing Kit the honour of breaking the news to Stewart. Kit could hardly contain her pride as Stewart punched her on the shoulder and Hank questioned her closely on the catch. He wanted to know every detail. She had to describe every rock they stumbled over and every move the fish made.

He groaned when she described Leroy and Earl's part in the day. He picked up a second glass of brandy, not realizing that he had already downed one.

Kit said nothing. She knew that Hank never drank spirits, but it suited her plans to have him a little drunk this evening.

Casey congratulated Dursley, breaking away from his embrace as soon as she decently could. She was delighted that he had his record. 'You do realize that Bob will hate you for ever?' she said.

'I will send him a fax from the hotel when we are in Anchorage,' he said. 'It will go out to his club.'

'His club,' echoed Casey. 'Oh, Dursley, that's both mean and brilliant. All his friends wil be there to enjoy his chagrin.'

The party now glowed with brandy which lay warm and deep in their stomachs. They walked up the manicured path to their cabins to unpack their bags, tensions and problems forgotten for the time.

'Whew,' said Hank as he stumbled up the wooden steps to the staff quarters. 'Angela must have poured a heavy tot.'

The little room was warm and inviting. He collapsed onto the bed, holding the side to keep the room from spinning and the bed from falling. Kit looked at him and smiled. This was perfect.

'Let me take off your boots,' she said. 'Close your eyes. It's still an hour to dinner. Stewart will not have his meeting until afterwards. Just relax, big boy.'

Hank heard her soothing voice and closed his eyes. Kit sat on the edge of the bed. She unlaced his boots, pulled off his socks and drew the blanket up over his feet. Carefully she tucked her strong fingers behind his belt buckle. She paused as he mumbled and kicked out at the blanket. She undid the brass buckle and slid the belt out of the trouser loops. The zip opened easily; she held her breath as she eased the heavy green corduroy material down his long muscular legs.

She breathed easily again when she saw that he was wearing his elastic boxer shorts and not his tight bikini underwear. She tugged at the waistband gently and pulled them down to lie with his trousers on the wooden floor.

Quickly she added her thick denim slacks and thermal long johns to the pile of clothing.

She tiptoed into the bathroom and walked out a few minutes later shaking a thermometer. There was a wide, contented smile on her face as she crept into bed beside Hank. She ran her experienced fingers lightly up the inside of this thighs, then straddled him, and as she started moving, he groaned. He dug his fingers into her buttocks, holding her down onto him.

'This must be quick,' muttered Kit as she ground her pelvis in a hard circle over Hank, 'if he wakes up properly, he'll go for the packet of contraceptives beside the bed.' Suddenly Hank arched.

'Ah, Ticasuk,' he whispered, 'my lovely little Eskimo.'

Kit bent low over him not believing what she had heard.

Ticasuk. That was Casey's Chargot's second name. The discussion on blood lines came back to tease her. She felt an overwhelming anger for Hank, now lying flaccid beneath her.

How dare you fall for that helpless little-girl act! she fumed silently. Wait until Dursley and Stewart hear about this. You won't even find a job on one of the commercial fishing boats in Prince William Sound. You'll be finished and you deserve it.

She wanted to pummel Hank's chest, shave his red beard with a fish knife, burn the thick hair on his chest and pull out his curling pubic hairs one by one.

'Oh, I hate you, Hank Butler,' she whispered, 'we were going to have such a wonderful life and family.'

At the thought of a family she calmed down a little. I knew I couldn't trust her. Small broads with wide smiles are always dangerous. Men, the idiots, feel they must protect them. It's the men who need protecting. Well, Miss Casey Ticasuk Chargot, this man is mine. You may have conned him into your bed, but he's now back in mine and that is where he will stay.

Carefully Kit eased herself away from Hank. She raised her legs and doubled a pillow beneath her buttocks. Everything is perfect for conception. I'll order a home pregnancy testing kit and it'll be here in a few weeks. Then let's see you squirm and Casey try to take you when you know that you are to be a father.

The room was dim and warm. The stove's black chimney vent rattled in the wind. In the distance the wild, free cry of a loon nesting on one of the small lakes bounced across the opalescent waters of Nonvianuk. The wind carried snatches of the song into the room and lulled Kit to sleep.

The loon, her emerald and anthracite feathers burnished by the evening sun, sailed across the darkening waters to join her mate. They called again and yet again. The calls, eerie and chilling, cried in the silence which hung heavy and suffocating between Casey and Dursley.

Dursley sat on the edge of the bed. His head was bowed in his hands and his fingers pulled at his dishevelled hair. 'No,' he said in a small bemused voice, 'no. You don't, you can't mean this.'

Casey's heart ached as she looked at the man she had been about to marry.

'I'm so very sorry, Dursley,' she said as his shoulders started to shake, 'I'm just not good enough for you. You'll find a perfect wife in London. In a few years you won't even remember my name.'

At the mention of London, Dursley looked up at her. Even in

the dim light she could see the tear stains on his cheeks. She put out her arms and then let them drop.

'Bubbles, everything is arranged. Our families, our friends, they all expect our wedding!' He stood up and walked towards her. Instinctively, she backed away and he stopped.

'Come home with me,' he pleaded. 'Things will seem normal there. You are entranced with this place, the beauty, the untamed wilderness. I do understand, Bubbles. Believe me, I do.' He slumped down on a hard wooden chair set before a small screened window overlooking the snow-capped peaks of the mountains which both topped and tailed the lake. 'You feel you have found your roots and that you must now live in Alaska.'

'That's only part of it,' said Casey in a small voice, her eyes swimming with tears for the pain she was causing a man who certainly did not deserve to be hurt. 'There's Hank.'

Dursley winced at the name, but kept his voice low and calm. 'Don't you understand, Bubbles, my love? Young Butler is part of this wild country which attracts you. You would not have the same feelings for him in London.'

Casey thought of the rusted tangle of debris and leaning poles which was Barrow, the harsh and inexplicable attraction of the tundra, the silence and beauty of the huge snowy owl sitting hunched on a hummock in the wind-rippled landscape, the might of the polar bear at bay, Trapper Jack offering her a slice of 'muktuk', assuring her that blubber was as good as gum.

She felt Hank's body up against hers as they stood on the beach with its iced pebbles looking out at the terrifying expanse of polar pack ice.

'No, Dursley. It's much more than that. I would never have made a good countess. I would have embarrassed you and your family.' She combed her heavy fringe away from her eyes and Dursley cried silently at the familiar and loved gesture.

'To hell with all of that,' he said. 'I love you and want you to be the mother of my children. I don't want someone looking for a title. One of the many reasons I love you, Bubbles, is because you are unimpressed with titles. You just wanted me.'

'I still do,' Casey blurted out and then cursed herself when she saw the glow of renewed hope on Dursley's face. 'I mean as a friend,' she said quickly. 'I want to love you as my friend.'

'And I want to love and have you as a woman,' he answered heavily.

A sudden pounding on the door startled them.

'Who's there?' called Casey, relieved at the intrusion.

'Me,' said Leroy and Earl in unison.

'The Laurel and Hardy team,' sighed Dursley.

'Peg-leg Pete is here to hand over the new boat,' called Leroy.

'And to apologize,' added Earl.

'Never! He said Stewart could have the boat but he could—' Leroy's voice faded as a hand muffled his mouth.

'Come on, we're waiting for you. The new cook is great. We've got popcorn and chipolatas with drinks tonight.'

'Coming,' said Dursley, standing up like a boxer making it to his feet after taking six counts.

'Dursley?' said Casey hesitantly as he held open the door letting the wind chase out the warmth.

'Don't worry, Bubbles. I will not tell the lodge of your new love.' He straightened his shoulders and smoothed down his hair, which the wind immediately tangled as he stood on the top step waiting for her.

Casey's heart clenched, as if squeezed in a giant fist. She had never loved Dursley as much as she did now, watching him prepare to be jovial and face the others in the lodge. She sought his hand. They always walked hand in hand to the lodge.

'No, Casey,' he said, as he tucked his hand into his pocket.

'Don't make it worse than it is. We'll pretend in front of the others, but not when we are alone!' He forced his mouth to open in a smile as they passed Earl and Leroy pounding on the door of Hank's room.

Casey froze and her stomach churned as Kit's voice rang out clear and hard.

'Belt up, guys. We're coming.'

Dursley glanced down at Casey quickly, but her face betrayed no emotion.

It's not Hank, she thought wildly. She is in the room with someone else. Hank would never . . . Casey clenched her teeth to stop from shouting his name. She knew he was not in the room. He could not be there. The colour in her face had drained and her lower lip trembled slightly.

'Casey!' shouted Earl. 'It's good to see you again. Seems as if you were away for a year.'

'He pined for you,' said Leroy, making sure he was well out of reach of Earl's boot. 'But it's given my kneecaps a rest.' He grinned and dodged as Earl lunged for him.

'Come on!' yelled Earl, giving the door a final resounding thump.

Hank opened his eyes slowly. The room had stopped spinning but he had a sick feeling deep in his stomach and it was not due to the brandy. He let his eyes roam around the room before turning his head to the person he sensed lying beside him.

Oh no! he groaned silently as he saw his boxer shorts tangled with Kit's cotton panties on the floor.

As the realization of what had happened sank into his fuddled brain he lurched off the bed and staggered to the bathroom. The wooden walls shook as he slammed the door behind him and hung over the toilet.

'Brandy,' said Kit, smiling sweetly as he emerged wiping his mouth. 'It's no good for your head and stomach,' she paused, 'but fortunately it doesn't affect the important parts.'

Hank collapsed onto the side of the bed and held his head in his hands. 'How could I? How could this have happened?' he agonized.

'Oh, it was quite easy,' said Kit. 'You wanted me and you took me.'

Hank shook his head in mute denial. Then he remembered his

dream of Ticasuk. She had been with him. He remembered feeling her warmth and softness over him. Ticasuk! No, it had been Kit.

'What am I going to do?' he said softly.

'Well, we could do it again,' laughed Kit, 'but the comedy act is outside demanding our presence in the dining-room. Peg-leg is about to apologize publicly.'

She swung her legs off the bed and walked slowly and carefully to the bathroom. Hank heard her voice muffled by the sound of water running into the basin.

'I cannot believe that he is going to apologize. It must be senility. Hacking boats, destroying ancient barabaras and claiming the river as his private domain is more in keeping with the old guy,' shouted Kit from behind the closed door.

She came back into the room, her face scrubbed and shining and her damp hair slicked back into a tight pony-tail.

'Kit,' said Hank tentatively, 'there's something I must tell you.'

'Not now. We're late. Earl will knock the door down if we don't leave.' She stepped into her panties and pulled them up high over her flat, taut stomach.

'Here,' she threw his trousers across the bed, 'tuck away your tackle.'

Hank ignored the corduroy trousers. He knew that he had to tell her about her his love for Casey. The longer he waited the more difficult it would be. He took a deep breath and rubbed at the scar beneath his eye.

'Kit,' he said loudly. His voice sounded as harsh as the cry of the bald eagle. 'I love Casey Chargot and intend marrying her as soon as possible.' He gabbled the words, spitting them out as if they were putrid pieces of fish, and his voice broke in embarrassment. 'I am sorry,' he ended lamely.

'That's all right, Hank. I understand. She's small and cute and curvy. What else is there to do up in Barrow?'

Hank sighed. His guilt changed quickly to anger at Kit's refusal to register what he was saying. 'Marriage, Kit, marriage. I want to spend the rest of my life with her.'

Kit turned round to face him, resting her back up against the closed door. 'We so seldom get what we want in life, Hank. I think you've put your mail order in a little late.' She ran her hands over her belly. 'You have already started your life commitment and it's not to Casey Chargot.'

Hank looked at her aghast as the import of her words hit him. 'We've always agreed that our relationship was casual, Kit. We've always taken precautions.'

'Always?' queried Kit, looking at the closed drawer beside his bed.

Hank wrenched open the cupboard. Lying in the middle of the drawer surrounded with old fishing lures and bead patterns was his new packet of contraceptives. It lay untouched, pristine in its cellophane wrapping. He sat staring at it in silence, long after the door closed softly behind Kit.

Casey looked up as Kit flew into the lounge of the lodge. The wind smashed the door closed behind her and the pictures of loons and wolves which cluttered the walls swung drunkenly on the hooks. Stewart stopped pouring bourbon for the men and frowned at her.

'Sorry,' she called, 'it's this damn snow wind. Should be fun for those fishing the Henley tomorrow.'

Casey's heart sang. Kit was alone. Hank had not been in the room with her. Everything was all right.

Kit smiled at Casey. She felt trimphant. Poor little thing, she thought, Alaska is not for you. Go back to your own social circle. Enjoy your theatres, regattas, polo and Wimbledon. This frontier is for people like Hank and myself, not you, little Casey Chargot.

'That's us,' said Dursley, studying the list pinned to the log wall which notified the clients of where they would be fishing the next day. 'What's different about the Henley?' he asked, turning to face Kit.

'Wonderful river,' she said. 'It was gouged out by the retreating glaciers, apparently radio-carbon measurements show that the moraine is about nine thousand years old.'

'Moraine,' said Dursley, 'so it's bleak and windswept?'

Earl edged up to listen to Kit's explanation. He was still amazed that a girl should have such a wide knowledge. He was compiling a list of facts with which to stun his friends when he returned to the locker rooms of his world.

Dursley met Kit's eyes and smiled. 'They gazed and gazed and still the wonder grew. How one small head could carry all it knew,' he quoted softly.

'What's that?' queried Earl.

'A few lines from a poem. They pertain to a village schoolmaster and the villagers' amazement at his knowledge,' answered Dursley, looking round for a place to put his empty glass.

Kit took it from him. 'Refill?' she asked.

'No, thanks. Only one when I'm fishing. I need all my wits for these trout. I don't need to see two trout and double nymphs every time I cast.'

Kit laughed. She became involved in a discussion about the Pacific plate and the North American plate, two tectonic slabs of the Earth's crust, which slide over its surface. Earl helped himself to another plate of popcorn and chewed furiously as he tried to understand how new crust is produced at centres on the bed of the ocean and circulated up into the Earth's interior at subduction zones.

'A subduction zone lies right beneath Katmai,' Kit said wickedly, grinning at Earl.

He choked on a handful of white popcorn. It all sounded horribly dangerous to him. 'You see, the Pacific plate is not as dense as the North American plate so it dives under it and goes down to the Earth's interior.'

'I know what goes on down there,' said Earl, wetting his finger and cleaning the scraps of popcorn from his paper plate. 'It's so damn hot that everything melts, then, whammo, it all bursts out on top and we have more volcanoes.'

'That's a pretty good description,' laughed Dursley. 'Not scientific, but descriptive.'

He enjoyed the opportunity of talking to Kit. The girl was knowledgeable and spoke well. It helped to stop his mind spinning and swirling like a springhatching of insects. Every time he looked at Casey he wanted to scream, pick her up and take her back to London.

'We have tons of volcanoes in Alaska,' said Kit, looking at Earl. 'At least eighty, many are still active.'

'Any around here?' said Leroy, coming to join the group.

'Oh, yeah. Trident erupted in 1933.'

'About sixty years ago,' said Leroy, relief flooding his voice.

'Just about time for another bang,' said Earl, enjoying the look of dismay on the little Irishman's face.

Leroy turned away and filled a plate with popcorn, popping two chipolatas on top.

'Come and listen, Casey,' Earl called across the room to where Casey sat on the edge of the stone fireplace. She was quiet and unsmiling. She shook her head, but Earl was not content to leave her alone. He lumbered across the room, hoisted her to her feet and propelled her back to join the group around Kit.

'We were talking about volcanoes,' Kit said. 'The day before you and Dursley arrived we were fishing in an area which in places is still covered in white volcanic ash from the eruption of Nova Erupta.'

'Ah,' broke in Dursley, 'of course, wasn't that the largest explosion the world has seen for almost two thousand years?'

'It was certainly the biggest in the twentieth century,' answered Kit.

'Then what are we doing here?' squeaked Leroy, looking at Earl accusingly. 'There must be safer places to fish.'

'Safer perhaps, but certainly not better,' said Dursley, remembering his battle with the record trout.

A deep voice broke into the conversation. Casey swung round. It was Hank. He had come into the lounge and joined the circle silently.

His hair, damp from his shower, was combed flat and he had trimmed his beard. Casey dropped her eyes, she could not look at him with Dursley watching her. She stretched out her hand for some of Earl's popcorn.

'But you don't eat it,' Earl protested.

'I know.' Chewing popcorn allowed Casey time to still the thumping of her heart.

Hank deliberately looked over Casey's head at Earl. He did not want to meet Dursley's eyes. He burned with shame and anger when he thought of how he had kept his part of the bargain he had made with Casey to tell Dursley and Kit the truth as soon as they arrived back at the lodge. But he could not decide whether Casey had told Dursley. They both looked calm and interested in Kit's discussion about volcanoes. Let's join in, he thought. At least it'll pass the time until Angela and Ginger call us to dinner.

Dursley, determined not to accept Casey's new decision without a fight, turned to Hank. He would not allow the new man in her life to see that he was hurting.

'That was your President Woodrow Wilson, was it not, who declared Katmai a reserve, but it was only to preserve the Valley of Ten Thousand Smokes?'

'Yeah,' agreed Hank, 'but remember that it was not a reserve, only a monument. In '42 Roosevelt added all the islands within five miles of the coast.'

'These must have been the ones messed up with oil from the *Exxon Valdez*,' broke in Leroy, eager to air his knowledge as well. 'I remember my booking agent telling me to forget fishing in Katmai. It would take decades to clean up eleven million gallons of oil drifting in from the Sound.'

'You can tell your agent he's crazy,' said Kit, winking at Dursley. 'Show him a photograph of Dursley's fish. That will convince him that the salmon are still coming up the feeder streams to spawn and the trout are still getting bigger and fatter on the eggs.'

'What is the valley of Ten Thousand Smokes?' asked Casey.

She felt that she ought to join in the conversation, even though she had no interest in anything whatsoever, except the outcome of her and Hank's stay in Barrow. She needed to talk to Hank, but knew it would be impossible until they were fishing the Henley River together the next day.

'According to old Bob, it's the most devastated yet eerily beautiful place he has ever seen,' answered Dursley, smiling at her. Hank grimaced. Casey could not yet have told Dursley of their love for each other. He obviously still considered Casey to be his fiancée.

'The smokes or fumaroles have almost all died out now,' he continued, 'as the ash has cooled and no longer vaporizes the surface and underground water.

'When Bob saw it, fountains of smoke still played across the whole burnt-out valley. Apparently he sat for hours looking down at the place where the forces of nature swallowed a mountain seven and a half thousand foot high. Then it turned the desolation into a modern work of art by painting circles of brilliant red, gold, black, orange and blue around the fumaroles.'

Kit saw Earl frown, but decided not to interrupt Dursley's story by explaining that hot steam dissolved minerals from the ash. When they touched the cool surface of the rocks, the minerals became brilliant encrustations. Earl, she knew, was finding it difficult enough to understand Dursley's English accent. She would not add to his discomfort. She turned her attention back to Dursley.

'Bob says that even today when he closes his eyes he can still clearly see the black River Lethe raging in its chasm and the enormous columns of pure white smoke which rose endlessly to meet the sky. There he believed for the first time that there is a Universal Force which created this cosmos.'

'He meant God,' said Casey softly.

'God, Universal Force, Divine Spirit, whatever one wishes to call it,' said Dursley. 'The valley certainly changed Bob.'

'Awesome,' said Earl.

'No one can live in this untamed country, close to the beauty and terror of nature, without believing,' said Hank.

Casey looked up at him and smiled. She knew that one day she would see the valley with Hank.

Dursley felt ill. He had lost her. That smile confirmed her words. Suddenly he recalled a magazine cutting which his mother had pasted to the door of the library. It showed an enormous heron holding a kicking frog in its beak. The frog had stretched out an arm and had the heron's neck in its tiny grip. The caption read: *Never give up. There is always a chance.*

Dursley smiled bleakly. Yes, Mother dear, he thought, I've as much chance of marrying Casey as your frog had of strangling the heron.

'So . . .' said Earl, licking the grease from his fingers. The conversation had confused him. 'This Katmai was made a reserve, to protect a dead valley which still smoked after a volcano erupted?'

'No. You dummy,' said Leroy, eager to air the little knowledge he had gleaned from the pamphlet in their cabin. 'It was your friend Jimmy Carter who made this place so huge. He added another million acres to it. Almost three and a half million were declared a wilderness and Katmai became a national park, not just a monument.'

'Yeah,' drawled Earl, disbelieving Leroy's sudden knowledge of Katmai. He looked at Kit and Hank for confirmation. Kit nodded. Stung, he turned on Leroy.

'Now give me one other good thing Carter did. You voted for him, not me.'

'Never,' lied Leroy, 'I wasn't crazy.'

A sharp thumping on the counter with a metal soup ladle heralded dinner. Earl broke away from the group first and headed for the large dining-room. The saffron light of evening stained the large glass windows and the room seemed to float on the opalescent waters of Lake Nonvianuk.

Dursley took Casey's arm.

'Come, Bubbles,' he said. Casey obediently walked with him to their table.

*

The guides spread out to sit at tables with the clients. Kit and Hank chose separate tables. They were not paid to enjoy their meals. Bored by the same endless questions, some guides resorted to mumbling into their beards, others to sneaking an extra glass of wine to sweeten the ordeal.

Dursley found that one of the fishermen at their table had fished the Henley the year before.

'Not only is the river great, but rafting surely beats walking over tundra. Remember to wear belts over your waders and tighten them,' he cautioned. Casey was about to question this advice when he continued: 'That river runs real deep and wide and the current is a mean b—pardon me, ma'am,' he said, looking across the table at Casey.

'Please go on,' she grinned, eager to know more about the river they were to raft down the following day.

'If the guide loses it, the raft will hit one of the banks and it'll be a long, cold dive.'

Casey shivered as she thought of it.

'You don't want your boots filling with water or you'll have a Mafia funeral. The good old "lead shoes" one.' He guffawed as Casey paled.

'Last time we were on the Henley a grizzly nearly gave us all a Mafia funeral. Our raft scared it. Only when it had scrambled out of the river and up the bank did it recognize us as humans. It turned round to dive back in on top of us. Bill put a cracker shot under its tail. I think it's still running.' They all laughed.

'Thanks for the advice,' said Dursley, trying to tuck his thick peanut sauce out of sight under a piece of bread.

'The fish are swell on the Henley. If you can find them,' interjected another diner.

'That's why we fish at this lodge. I swear these guides think like fish. They find them were no one else does.'

Dursley was satisfied. It was always exciting to fish a new river. He smiled at Casey. 'It'll be a fun day tomorrow,' he said, 'You'll enjoy rafting down the river instead of walking.'

'Stumbling, you mean,' said Casey, admiring Dursley's determination to carry on as if nothing had changed between them. You are strong, she thought with admiration as she watched him grimace as he cut into a slice of fresh salmon masked in peanut sauce. It's one of the things I love about you.

'Have some of mine,' she teased. Her spirits suddenly lifted. Dursley was going to make it easy. It would be her and Hank's secret until they left the lodge.

Dursley gagged slightly. She knew that he loved his fish with no sauces, especially salmon. He felt that sauces merely demonstrated the chef's talent to the detriment of the delicate flavour of the fish.

Dursley glanced across the row of tables to where Hank was seated. Silently he laid down the battle lines. He was certain that if he could get Casey back to England, then Hank and Alaska would become only wild and lovely memories.

Chapter Fifteen

THE WIND moaned and whined like a sick child as it swept across the flat land bordering the Henley River. The rolling landscape with shallow ponds sparkling between the rocks, silt, clay and rubble, told of the great glacier which had retreated twelve thousand years ago. An age when almost the whole of Katmai was dead and buried under ice. But peat moss and scrub willow quickly grew on the wetlands and the new moraine soils left behind, as the ice gave way to the warming earth.

Casey watched Hank swing the huge blue canvas sausage containing the rubber raft onto his shoulder. He grunted as his body accepted the weight. He set off at a shambling, lurching trot up the slope. He knew that once he started he had to use that momentum to reach the top of the hill or the weight of the raft would slide him back down the muddy path.

'Whew,' panted Earl as he held onto a scrub willow root to haul himself up the path. 'Hank should enter the triathlon. He'd break all the records.'

'Yeah,' agreed Leroy, wheezing behind him, 'the guy's awesome.'

Dursley was silent, also determined to make it to the top of the ridge without stopping.

Kit was helping Casey. 'Climb with your head forward,' she said. 'It's the heaviest part of your body.'

Casey merely nodded her thanks. The beauty of the autumn tundra stunned her. She had only been away for a few days and in that time the hills had exploded into deep golds and crimson. White lichens gleamed like broken porcelain in the glory of autumn. She wanted to stoop down and pick the berries which hung black and red close to the ground. She remembered that fishing was the priority, so she contented herself with sideways glimpses as she plodded up the path, but she was unable to resist a bright red plant growing in the path. It looked like a strawberry bush. She bent down and picked a leaf.

She jumped guiltily as she heard Dursley say, 'Come on, Bubbles. Give me your hand and I'll help you up here. Last night's snow has melted and turned the mud into a skating-rink.'

She uncurled her fingers as she stood beside him and studied the leaf. 'Look, it's a sockeye plant.'

'I haven't heard of that one before,' said Kit as she stopped beside them.

'See, it has dark green edges and the centre is deep red. The same colours as the sockeye when it has spawned,' explained Casey.

Dursley put a finger gently under her chin and lifted her face. The hood of her anorak blew off and her hair blinded her to the look of anguish in his eyes, but not to the tenderness in his voice.

'Bubbles,' he said softly, 'you are so lovely.' He dropped his hand and turned away to continue up the path.

'You're a lucky woman to have found Dursley,' said Kit, 'I'd marry him fast. He's too good to lose.' She watched Casey's reaction closely. She was determined to see her leave with Dursley at the end of the week.

Tears stung Casey's eyes and she swallowed hard. She would not cry.

*

As they reached the crest of the hill Casey gasped. Standing on the desolate plateau, ugly as a modern sculpture, were the crumpled remains of a Piper Cub. Only the twisted framework and rusted engine remained.

'Not a lucky one, this,' said Earl.

Kit laughed. Dursley walked over and inspected the remains of the aircraft.

'It was a perfect landing. But the guy had caught salmon in the Naknek and stashed them behind the seats. He went down to the Henley for a few large trout to add to his catch, and the smell of fish attracted two sows. I guess they finished the salmon, then found that the acetone-based dope painted on the canvas of the light aircraft was delicious, so they ate the aircraft.'

Dursley clambered from the wreckage, shaking his head.

'Ate and enjoyed it,' said Kit. 'Now let's move on or Hank will yell.' She led them to the cliff edge.

The sun had not risen high enough to melt the snow on the side of the hill lying in shadow. Snow nestled thick and white as rabbits' tails in the pockets and hollows of the scrub and tundra. It was a winter landscape and beautiful.

Far below them the Henley River spread and circled through the grey flat lands. It seemed deceptively shallow and placid. At the foot of the hill the spawning sockeye glowed like spilled red wine in the crystal water.

Casey blanched as she looked down at the precipitous path plunging to the river bed. 'It looks as if a giant has bitten a huge piece out of the hill,' she said.

'A giant did. A glacier,' said Kit.

'We have good and bad news about this place,' said Earl, standing close to Casey.

Casey looked up at him enquiringly.

'The bad news is that we have to get down this track and the wind is not going to be any better once we're on the river. The good news is that once down we don't have to climb back up. Hank says that Stewart is collecting us downriver.'

Casey laughed. Dursley looked round. He had been peering over the edge watching Hank's progress. It was the first natural, unforced laugh he had heard from Casey since their return to the lodge.

It'll work, he thought. Casey will realize that Hank was just a respite. She will, in time, understand that she was merely afraid of all the implications of marrying into my family. She subconsciously found what she thought was an easier and less complicated love. I'll be able to show her that their relationship could never have succeeded. The incredible emptiness and silence of this place has affected her. Give my girl a taste of Sloane Street shopping, the roar of traffic in Knightsbridge, London buses and black taxis, and she will forget all of this. Casey Chargot will still be the Countess of Carrington.

'Come on down! Dursley first.' Hank's voice rose up faintly on the wind to where they stod huddled and a little apprehensive on the skyline.

'When it gets steep, sit on your fanny and slide,' said Kit.

Casey burst out laughing at the affronted look on Dursley's face.

'You mean bottom,' she said to Kit, choking with mirth. 'In England a "fanny" is something men don't have and it is certainly nothing to slide on.'

Earl and Leroy stared at Casey for a moment and then hit each other on the back and raised and smacked palms in 'high fives'.

Hank had no idea as to what had caused the mirth, but he saw his fishing party reeling around helpless as gulls in a gale. He looked upriver. There was a party ahead of them. Five men from a nearby lodge. 'Come on!' he bellowed, cupping his hands to his mouth.

He hated anyone else on the Henley. He considered it to be his river and in the lodge he was certainly the acknowledged expert on its moods and vagaries. Not only had he named all the best fishing spots, but the staff teased him that he had also named the fish. They insisted that the fish now knew him so well that when they were hooked they swam to him with their mouths open to have the hooks removed. Hank enjoyed the reputation he had gained on the Henley and was eager to show off his skills to Casey and also to Dursley. He felt that Kit's record trout catch with Dursley had undermined his authority and skill. Today he was going to regain both.

Holding his rod high in his left hand Dursley sat down at the top of the path. He eased himself forward by walking his heels in the mud.

'Watch your fanny!' yelled Leroy.

'Butt,' corrected Earl and the two collapsed into hysterical laughter once again.

'Bottom!' shouted Casey. 'Don't tear your waders!'

Kit nodded approvingly as she watched Dursley slide down. His knees were drawn up high. He used his right hand to clutch at shrubs and roots to break the speed of the slide.

'Neat,' said Hank as Dursley stood up at the bottom of the path and twisted round, trying to check the seat of his waders. 'Here, take over the foot pump and I'll see if you've done any damage.'

Dursley started pumping up the rubber raft and soon realized that his thigh muscles were not as strong as he liked to think they were. By the time Hank pronounced himself satisfied that Dursley's waders were still watertight, his legs were screaming in protest.

'Thanks,' said Hank. 'Let me have it.'

Dursley pretended to busy himself with his rod and line, but he watched the ease with which Hank pumped up the boat. The thought of those powerful legs entwined with Casey's sickened him. He moved away to sit on a rock, first wiping off the cloth of snow. He looked up at the skyline, where a puppet show was being executed.

'It really doesn't matter who goes first,' reasoned Kit, as Earl and Leroy jockeyed for position at the top of the precipitous path which was now a mud slide.

'If Earl goes first, he'll groove out the Grand Canyon,' groused Leroy, 'and I'll be buried in it.'

'Leroy's so scared that by the time he gets down the salmon will have spawned and died and the trout all left for richer grounds,' retorted Earl, elbowing him in the ribs.

Kit raised her eyebrows at Casey. This was worse than a school picnic.

'I'll go,' said Casey, smiling at the two men sweetly. 'After all, it is usually ladies first.'

'But . . .' said Leroy. A brown wading boot thumped into the back of his ankle, cutting short his protest.

'Yeah sure,' said Earl. When he returned to the Lower Forty-Eight, he was going to find a girl like Casey for himself.

'Give me your rod,' said Kit. Casey thankfully handed over her Hardy, six weight. Kit inspected the graphite rod, made a few test casts and decided that she preferred her Sage nine weight. Six is a bit light for the Henley, she thought, especially in this wind. But Hank obviously feels that is all she's capable of handling.

She turned her attention back to Casey, but she had gone and Earl and Leroy were peering over the edge shouting encouragement as she careered down the hill. Dursley and Hank had both walked across the snow-flecked pebbles and were waiting for her at the foot of the path.

'She certainly pulls in the guys,' muttered Kit. 'With a bit of luck she'll break her neck.'

Casey was enjoying the slide. It was like skiing, only on her bottom. The shrubs flashed past. The wind watered her eyes and reddened her cheeks. Her cap flew off.

She looks like a raven flying down the hill, thought Hank fancifully. He wished Dursley had remained seated on the rock fiddling with his fishing gear so that he could catch Casey up into his arms to break her headlong slide.

Should have stayed and pumped the raft, thought Dursley, glancing sideways at Hank, whose eyes were fixed on Casey.

'No,' roared Hank suddenly, causing Dursley to jump. 'Leave the branches! You're going too fast to brake now.'

His voice cut through the wind which was numbing her ears.

Casey pulled back her hands, which she had stretched out to grasp at a willow to break her speed. She closed her eyes. The slide was no longer fun, it was scaring her.

'Watch out!' yelled Hank.

'Be careful!' shouted Dursley, but with closed eyes Casey did not notice that she was veering from the path.

'Oh no,' said Earl as he watched Casey hurtling into the dense scrub willow, peat moss and snow. A mound of snow exploded as a group of winter white ptarmigan flew up into the wind, squalling their indignation.

Carefully Casey opened her eyes. She was alive. Sore but alive. The slide had ended.

Hank and Dursley were at her side within moments, helping her to her feet and leading her down the last short stretch.

Hank hung back as Dursley put his arm around Casey and tenderly brushed the mud from her face and twigs from her hair. Hank felt as nauseous as if he had a belly full of flat beer. Casey had obviously not told him. He dragged his attention away and studied the river. The wind had changed from the whine of a child to the bluster of a bully. Hank narrowed his eyes.

The surface of the grey river now seemed to be covered with thousands of tiny white gulls, their tapered wings cresting the waves. Wind changed the Henley from a fisherman's dream to a nightmare.

They had to launch the rubber raft now, or they would spend the day on the bank. If the wind did not drop Stewart would be unable to land on the river. They would then have a fourteen-hour hike over the moraine to the shores of Nonvianuk, where a boat from the lodge would eventually find them. Hank disliked long hikes. They increased the chances of a grizzly contesting their presence in his territory.

Hank thought of the Contender tucked into his haversack and he was content. He appreciated all the rules of the reserve, but on this occasion it was a good feeling to know that he had his hand cannon. Instinctively he patted the pockets of his shirt inside his waders. Yes. The cracker shots to scare off the bears were tucked into the left pocket and the soft-nose ammunition was in the right.

Hank was about to turn round and shout up at Kit when something smashed into him, hitting him behind the legs with all the force of a swipe from a grizzly's paw. It knocked him off his feet and as he fell forward onto his knees, the frozen pebbles seemed to bore through the rubber knee padding on his waders. He was certain that he felt a bone crack.

Carefully he pulled his hands from the snow drift that bordered the river. He twisted his head over his shoulder to see Earl and Leroy in a tangled lovers' heap on the ground. Hank stood up, smearing his wet hands on the back of his waders. Pain seared his knee. He swallowed down all the things he wanted to say to the two men on the ground.

'Hank. Are you all right?' called Casey as she extricated herself from Dursley's solicitous cleaning-up operation. She slithered across the stones to where he stood rubbing his knee.

'Fine,' he answered, testing his weight on his knee. It was probably fractured, he decided.

He gave a mirthless grin as he thought of Stewart's reaction when he heard that his guide would have to go back to Anchorage for an X-ray and treatment. He decided to see the group safely to the beach at Rainbow Run before taking out the first-aid box and binding his knee in a crêpe bandage.

Kit hurtled down the slope like a heli-skier, gathered herself neatly at the bottom and strod towards Earl and Leroy.

'I told you two to cool it,' she said. 'If Hank's knee is damaged, you will row the Galley Stretch. Believe me, you'll both wish you'd listened by the time you've rowed a laden raft down that heavy stretch of water.'

'It's OK, I'm fine,' said Hank, wincing as he bent down to lift the raft.

Kit watched with narrowed eyes as Hank hobbled to the edge of the river dragging the raft behind him. You won't be after a few hours in this wind and freezing water, she thought. And I can't manage the raft on my own. She fumed inwardly at Earl and Leroy.

Leroy had launched himself onto the path ahead of Earl. With a roar of outrage at being tricked, Earl had followed immediately. Kit was left holding his cap, the only thing she had managed to grasp in an effort to stop him. Earl's weight had driven him onto Leroy and they rode down twined together tightly as a wind knot.

In spite of her anger Kit smiled as she studied the group lined up at the water's edge. The brown mud stretched across the seat of their waders gave them the appearance of a group of nursery school children who had soiled their pants.

Casey climbed onto the fat rubber front of the raft and hung her boots in the water. Surreptitiously, to give herself something to cling to, she twined a piece of the wet tow rope around her hand as she watched Earl and Leroy prepare to climb into the boat.

The raft scraped over the river bottom and milling salmon, then swung into the current. Casey winced, waiting for the rubber to tear. She soon forgot her trepidation and leaned forward watching with fascination the ever-changing pattern of fish as they darted away from the dark shape overhead.

Hank bent into the oars and forced the raft to the middle of the river, away from the men already fishing on the bank. Dursley was studying their casting techniques, which were certainly different to the two-handed version he used at home. The men were fishing in Eye Opener, the least likely, yet one of Hank's most favoured spots on the river. Hank was delighted to see, from their disgruntled looks, that they were not taking any trout from this spot.

Casey stared up at the towering brown cliffs as the raft floated past. Guano dripped down the rocks and soil like white icing, and the gulls rode the wind. Their swept-back wings powered them into the gusts. They swirled, soared and tumbled as if part of a wild mating dance. The birds circled the waterworn pebbles endlessly searching for decayed and bloated salmon. Their raucous cires and screeches suited the harsh landscape.

Earl and Leroy, chastened and quiet, sat on the wooden plank behind Hank, keeping well out of the swing of the oars. Leroy held tightly onto the side of the raft. He shuddered every time a rock rasped along the rubber bottom of the dinghy or a gust of wind rocked it over to one side. He breathed a sigh of relief when Hank eventually shipped the oars and let the raft drift towards a narrow spit of land jutting into the river.

'We'll fish here,' said Hank. He nodded at Kit, who stepped out of the dingy onto the shallow wash and held the tow rope.

'Earl, you out first,' ordered Hank, 'and slowly.'

He waited until Earl had waded to the beach before allowing Leroy to climb out. Dursley made a point of holding Casey as she slid off the front of the dinghy. Hank and Kit then dragged the boat over the smooth pebbles and onto the bank.

'Rainbow Run,' said Hank proudly. 'We'll fish here until lunch. I wanted you to spread out so that we cover the whole run. This is a "take no prisoners" run,' he explained to Casey and Dursley, whilst smiling at Casey. 'We don't want that other gang butting in on our fishing spot.'

'We'll beat them off with our rods,' laughed Leroy, relieved that they would be out of the rocking raft until lunch.

'You won't have to beat them off,' said Kit, 'but don't dangle your egg pattern in front of them as they pass.'

'It's a tough, mean river,' explained Hank. 'We play hard here. We keep our lures a secret.'

Yeah,' agreed Earl, 'let them find their own egg colour to fish.'

Earl and Leroy had learned that their guides were dedicated to the art and skill of hooking and landing the really large rainbows. They spent months working on lures to tempt and trick the massive fish. Over the years, the trout had everything short of gelignite thrown at them. The Black Legs guides were convinced that the large 'Granddad' trout gave them marks for ingenuity as they tried out their new lures each year. This river had one or two of these old 'flashers' who kept the guide's excitement at fever pitch. On their days off, they headed for the river hoping to hook 'the one really great fish'. Their fear was that one of the casual fishermen would 'luck into' a flasher, lose it and no one would ever know how big it had been. These 'flashers' seemed to have computerlike memories with a list of the guides and lures used over the years punched into them.

Hank sent Dursley up to the top of the run almost out of sight of the boat. 'Work the run slowly,' he said, 'there are some great fish along the far bank. It needs a good long cast. You are the man to do it.'

Dursley nodded. 'Look after Casey,' he shouted over his shoulder. Good move, he thought as he ploughed his way back upstream. The wind and current brought him to a standstill every few minutes. Hank thinks he is clever in getting rid of me. That should deflate him and show him that I don't consider him a threat at all. She can fish with you today, but at the end of the week she'll be with me on the plane home. Dursley plodded on painfully. The waves slapped against his thighs and splashed his face.

He was surprised at the strength of the wind as it gathered its forces from the river-banks and raced over the open water. For a moment he wondered whether it was wise to let Casey fish the river in these conditions.

But soon he was totally absorbed in casting low over the water to outwit the wind. He was fishing 'blind' today as the chopped surface effectively masked the fish beneath.

'You take Earl and Leroy to the middle stretch and watch out for the "gusher",' Hank commanded Kit. 'I'll fish on the bend with Casey. The wind should not be as bad for her there.'

And you'll be hidden from the rest of us, thought Kit. Well done, big guy, but remember, you are now mine. Mine and little Hank's.

Kit was certain that she had conceived. The timing could not have been more perfect. Like many women who confound medical science by intuitively knowing what their bodies need to heal, she knew that her pregnancy and Hanks lifelong commitment had started.

'Hook on,' said Hank to Casey as he picked up two rods from the dinghy and made his way into the river. Casey felt strangely embarrassed to walk arm-in-arm with him downriver; though she had done it since the first day they went fishing, things had now changed. Suddenly it seemed intimate. She was certain that everyone could see the difference.

She glanced back over her shoulder. Dursley was a speck in the distance and Kit and Earl were helping Leroy to his feet. He was sitting in a few inches of water, looking forlorn and miserable.

Casey stumbled as the wind hit them. Hank put his arm around her waist to steady her. She longed to lay her head on his chest and close her eyes.

'Oh, Hank,' she said, and in the wind her words were but a whisper. 'It's all so awful. I had no idea that it would be like this. It seemed so simple and beautiful in Barrow.'

'It is. It is,' consoled Hank, tightening his grip. 'We love each other and will be together. Just remember that. Never forget it, Ticasuk, no matter what happens.'

Casey looked up at him. She had a green ski cap pulled down low over her forehead and the hood of her fishing jacket zipped up to her chin. He could not see her eyes behind her polaroid glasses, but her full bottom lip trembled.

'Come,' he joked, 'is this the girl whose ancestors hunted Nanuq on the polar ice pack with only a spear? You have courage, my Ticasuk. Now you must use it.'

Casey stumbled again and, with little regard for the pain in his knee, he half-carried her across the river. 'It's Dursley,' she said, as he put her down on the beach. He felt a weight, heavy as a lead sinker, hit and settle in his stomach. Casey was going to stay with Dursley. 'He is being such a gentleman and I know that he is hurt. I feel so bad and selfish.'

Hank rejoiced in silence, keeping his face grave and his voice concerned. Casey had told Dursley. There would be no going back. She was his.

He led Casey to a patch of elders and scrub willow which shielded them from the rest of the party and from the wind.

'Ticasuk,' he murmured as he enfolded her in his arms and tasted her lips.

Casey smelt the clean perfume of soap in his beard. Lingering traces of Deet, sprayed onto his cap, tickled her nostrils. Then she inhaled his breath, warm with the musk of his desire and she opened her mouth to him.

She heard a rough rasp as he tore open the broad velcro straps of her waders.

No! she wanted to protest. No, not here! Dursley! Earl! Leroy! Kit! But she found her fingers suddenly warm and agile, unbuckling her belt and rolling the deep blue thermals down to her ankles.

She did not feel the wet spargum moss squelch beneath her buttocks or even the bite of the odd insect hidden away from the wind in the scrub. All that mattered was Hank, his weight pressing her down and her shudders as her body trembled and delighted to his touch.

I will never forget this. It is perfect, thought Casey, lying quietly as a child as Hank dressed her.

The wind bent the elders over and they formed a tent for the lovers. Through the branches she could see the glaucous-winged gulls streaming before the wind, their strong yellow beaks open as they screamed and called to each other.

'This is how one should make love,' whispered Hank as he helped her to sit up. 'This is how it was meant to be.'

'The earth as a bed and the sky as a canopy,' said Casey lazily.

Hank kissed her softly on her mouth.

'Don't let it go.' Leroy's voice, sharp as a fish hook, struck and dragged them apart.

Hank peered around the bushes. He grasped Casey's fishing-rod, whipped his plastic container of lures from his fishing-vest lying on the pebbles and bent over the line busily mending the leader and retying the lure.

Casey quickly pulled her tackle boxes from the pockets of her vest and started sorting out the already perfectly neat hooks and lures.

She looked up innocently as Earl and Leroy floundered past. The wind and current propelled them faster then they could walk.

'A good one?' called Hank.

'A monster!'

Kit shook her head in mute denial as she followed the men. They swayed down the river as if it was a pinball alley and she waited for them to topple.

Neat, mused Kit, as she glanced at Hank and Casey, both busy readying their rods to fish. I thought Hank would have her on her fanny in the bushes. He's slowing down.

She gave a smug smile of satisfaction as she hurried to catch up with Earl and Leroy who were now waist deep in water and holding onto each other nervously, the fish forgotten in the fear of being sucked under and washed downriver.

'Does Kit know about us?' asked Casey as she watched her walk confidently after Earl and Leroy.

Hank kept his head low over the line, pretending to struggle with the knots. He was afraid that Casey would read the guilt in his eyes if he looked at her.

'Yes. I've told her.'

Casey waited for him to continue but he was silent. She was about to press him for details when she remembered a remark made by one of the lodge girls when she first arrived. 'Kit's one of those who always warms the bed of the best-looking guy. Hank will need all the rubbers he can find.'

The laughter and the girl's voice came back clearly. It had been Angela, though at the time the men and girls were still only a mishmash of names and faces to her. Her fingers trembled as she re-sorted the hooks. A large, firm hand closed over hers and the hooks dropped back into the yellow box.

'It's you I love, Ticasuk,' said Hank. 'Kit and Dursley are from our past. The present and the future belong to us.'

A bank of cloud pushed along by the wind covered the sun. The river lost its silver glitter and tarnished to a sombre grey. The gull's bodies, usually white and crisp as Irish linen, looked stained and grubby as they rode its crests and troughs.

Casey shivered. Instead of Hank's words comforting her they seemed to tempt fate and be a bad omen. She smiled up at him.

'I know, Hank. We have found each other and that is the most important thing in the world.'

Hank limped back to where he had put her rod. He had taken the opportunity to bandage his knee before he replaced his waders, but his knees had taken the brunt of his weight as he knelt over Casey. Pain now screamed at him with every footstep.

Casey noticed how he tried to mask his limp. She insisted on going into the river alone.

'I want to show you how my casting has improved,' she lied. 'You must stay on the bank and watch.' She did not want him standing in that freezing water, supporting her and being buffeted by the wind. 'I won't wade in too far,' she said.

Her words were prophetic. The wind caught her and toppled her onto her knees almost immediately. Quickly she struggled up, before Hank came to help her. 'It's perfectly all right,' she called as the wind upended her a second time. She reamined seated in the four inches of water and laughed over her shoulder at Hank. 'This is the Chargot way of fishing in a gale. This way it can't blow me over.'

'And neither can you cast,' reasoned Hank. 'Can you reach that rock?' He pointed to a waterwashed rock standing proud of the waves a few yards off shore.

'Sure.'

Casey clenched her teeth. She swore as the wind dragged her glasses to the end of her nose. She walked over the rocks as if treading on crystal balls. She reached the rock. The water was now above her knees. She could feel it pulling her boots, trying to slide the felt soles off the polished bottom.

Determined to show Hank that she was as independent and confident in the river as Kit, she launched herself at the rock only to slide down the greasy green side.

Hank roared with laughter and waded over to help her. 'Into my arms, Ticasuk,' he said. Happily she twined her arms around his neck and he lifted her up high and sat her on the rock.

'I feel like a weather-vane,' she said as the wind buffeted her.

'You don't look like one. You're wearing enough clothes to last a month on the ice-pack.' He grinned lewdly. 'And I should know.'

As her cheeks flushed he felt a tenderness he had seldom known. He bent over and kissed her cheeks, then her nose and finally her lips.

A long low whistle separated them instantly.

'Do all your clients get that sort of encouragement?' Kit's voice rang loud and clear as it bounced across the water.

'No. Only pretty ones,' retorted Hank, turning around.

'That cuts you out, Leroy,' guffawed Earl.

'But you qualify, Earl,' said Casey, relieved that the incident was going to become merely something to joke about.

'No, thanks. I like my men to shave,' he answered.

'Where's the monster?' asked Hank, eager to change the subject.

The following twenty minutes was a litany of woe as they all relived the loss of Leroy's trout.

Suddenly Casey jerked her rod up fiercely. The tip bent almost double. Her delighted shrieks drove the gulls from the water. They spun high and light as scraps of paper in the gale.

Hank caught her by the back straps of her waders, slid her from the rock and propelled her downsteam after the fish.

'I can't walk on water, Hank! Put me down.'

'He has you stripped to the backing,' said Hank holding her even higher. 'If you don't retrieve line he'll break off.' The group listened to Casey's protests until they died in the distance.

'Hank will burn the burgers if he messed with Dursley's

woman,' said Leroy righteously. Earl nodded in silent agreement. He secretly wished that he was in Hank's position.

'That's nothing,' said Kit airily. 'On these lousy days when the Willawaws gust up to fifty miles an hour Hank often does a bit of flirting. It keeps the women from bitching and leaves the men to fish in peace.'

Satisfied with the explanation, Leroy and Earl went back to cursing the wind, the waves and the fish in that order.

Hank's call for a lunch break was welcomed with cheers.

'I'll fetch Dursley,' offered Kit quickly. She needed some time alone. The morning had been a nightmare. She had unravelled wind knots and retied leaders until her numb fingers ached. Seeing Hank standing guard over Casey in the river had not lightened her mood. Neither had the patches of moss squashed high into the back of Casey's anorak.

Dursley needed little persuasion to reel in and take a lunch break. Kit questioned him closely about the wedding plans as they struggled downsteam, fighting the wind which threatened to pitch them into the water. By the time they reached the designated lunch spot, she was satisfied that she had nothing to fear. Casey was definitely set to become the new Countess of Carrington.

The sun appeared as they sat on the hard, wet pebbles sipping mugs of rich bean soup. They were sheltered by the high riverine bush from all but the strongest gusts of wind.

As the food warmed their bellies and the sun falsely promised to warm their faces their spirits rose. 'Oh, look,' said Casey pointing to a break in the thick foliage. It framed a hill, soft and glowing with the crimson and golds of autumn lichens and bushes heavy with berries. Tumbling over each other were two bear cubs, gold as the leaves they tore from the soggy ground in their play.

'Cute,' said Earl.

'Yeah, real neat. When they're small,' qualified Leroy.

'The smallest is a yearling, probably born this summer,' said Hank. 'The other one looks about three. Wonder where the mother is?'

Leroy looked around nervously.

'With one that young, she'll be close,' said Kit.

He relaxed. That meant she would be on the other side of the river. He prised a packet of chocolate mint cookies away from Earl and leaned back against the bank munching contentedly.

'They look so beautiful and harmless,' said Casey, shaking her head to refuse a third slice of walnut bread.

'About as harmless as a hand grenade with the pin pulled out,' mumbled Hank, trying to swallow a wedge of bread with his soup. 'Keep well clear of cubs. There's always a four-footed Sherman tank near by.'

Everyone laughed. Dursley leaned over to Casey. She looked so beautiful and contented sitting crosslegged on the cold stones. 'A little different from Henley-on-Thames, isn't it?' Dursley said, wiping a dribble of soup from Casey's chin with the tip of his finger. He watched Hank's expression as he licked his fingers.

I like you as a man, he thought, as Hank looked away. But you want Casey, try and take her.

'It certainly is,' said Casey, holding out her mug to be refilled. She vividly recalled the beautiful stretch of river running past the town of Henley-on-Thames. She and Dursley had met there when Sir Bob Franshaw, holding a bottle of Dom Perigon in one hand and two crystal champagne flutes in the other, tried to weave his way unsteadily to where Dursley was sitting on the grass with a group of friends. His feet behaved magnificently until he saw Casey. He stumbled and the champagne poured down the front of the antique lace dress Casey was wearing.

'It's all their fault,' Sir Bob had said as Dursley came across to see what his friend had done. He pointed at Casey's breasts swelling up cream and smooth from the low lace bodice. Casey had laughed and accepted both Sir Bob's apologies and Dursley's invitation to dinner.

'Do you remember?' they said in unison and burst out laughing, enclosed for a minute in a world the others could neither join in nor understand.

That's it, exulted Dursley. Keep reminding her of the good times we've spent together. Bind her to you with memories. You have more of those than Hank. The poor blighter has only one weekend to build on.

At the thought of the weekend in Barrow, Dursley felt the familiar pain flooding through him, quick and unpleasant as fish poisoning.

'What's the fishing like here?' he asked Hank, determined to concentrate on rainbows and not images of Casey in Hank's arms.

'We don't usually fish this stretch, but only because there are so many other excellent spots,' said Hank, eyeing the deep stretch of water at the foot of the opposite bank speculatively. 'Have a few casts while we clean up here,' he suggested.

Hank swept all the cardboard plates greasy with leftover salad into a black bag while Kit carefully wrapped up the uneaten cake and cookies.

'Come and join me,' Dursley called to Casey. She hung back, embarrassed to have to cast with the party watching her.

'Go on,' urged Hank. 'Show them how good you are.' Casey looked at him appealingly. 'You really do throw a mean line now,' he said. 'Go and show Dursley how we fish.'

Touché, thought Dursley. Casey picked up her rod, stripped out line and remembered Hank's instructions. She kept her elbow in at her side and using it as a fulcrum swung the rod back.

'Short back. Pause for the line to straighten. Short forward. Tip high,' she muttered to herself. She was delighted to hear the line sing its song of silence as it whipped forward.

'Atta girl.' Leroy and Earl whistled and applauded. When they saw the tip of her rod bend and the reel race, they jumped up and extracted their rods from the elder bushes they had used as rod racks.

'Stay on the shore. Play him from here,' shouted Hank, judging the size of the trout by the movement in the rod.

Casey nodded and walked slowly down the beach away from the party. She was going to land this fish without any help.

'There's a feeder stream at the end of the beach,' shouted Hank as Casey grew smaller in the distance. 'Don't try to cross it, and check that it's clear.'

Casey nodded.

'Clear of what?' asked Leroy. Hank looked at Kit and quickly she answered.

'Bears, Leroy. Sows often fish the feeders with their cubs. The water is shallow and it's easy to scoop out the dying salmon. They are also unlikely to come across dominant bears who guard the good fishing spots.'

'Only females, that's neat,' said Earl with relief. 'It's those big, mean males who give me goose bumps.'

'A sow with cubs ranks next in line to a dominant male,' said Kit. 'And she is more likely to charge, to protect her cubs.'

'See a sow with young cubs and you'd better have your skywalking boots on,' added Hank, stuffing the rubbish bag in the bottom of the boat, to be taken out on the float-plane once they returned to the lodge.

'Put it in the haversack,' said Kit.

'I don't like having the haversack too full.'

Kit was silent. She knew that Hank carried a Contender and liked to be able to get at it quickly. It was illegal to carry guns in the reserve but Hank felt that a dead bear was preferable to dead or mauled clients.

The blonde sow shouldered her way through the willow and elders lining the river. They stood higher than a man. She grunted softly to the two young cubs who ambled behind her. The one cuddly as a soft teddy had been born that summer and the sow was still very protective of him. The other was about two and a half years old. He would soon lose her protection and learn to fish for himself and avoid confrontations with the other two thousand bears which lived in the Katmai.

The smallest cub bumped into her and grunted. It had been

looking over its shoulder as it ran from the nipping teeth of its brother. She lectured them both in soft moans and grunts and cautioned them to remain silent. She stood up on her hind legs to look over the shrubs lining the feeder stream before taking them into the open.

She stared across the water myopically. Her nose seemed to stretch like elastic as she quested the wind. Suddenly her flared nostrils, keen enough to track an animal by the scent of its footprints, were filled with the sour stench of humans. Standing at the mouth of the feeder stream was one of the two-legged creatures.

Casey heard a *whoof*, low and threatening as a guard dog. Strange, she thought. I wonder how dogs survive here? *Dogs!* her subconscious cautioned. *There are no dogs here. In the Katmai it's bears who whoof. They warn you, then they charge.*

She looked up. For a moment she saw only the shrubs bowing to the wind. Then, highlighted and pointed out by the sun, she saw two gold fluffy ears.

Part of the autumn colours, she thought desperately. But she knew that those round ears, downy and soft, belonged to a bear large enough to peer over the high shrubs.

'Stick it, break it off.' She heard Hank's words from long ago. She had never asked him how to break off a trout which was determined to take off downstream. Her fingers tightened on her rod; she was too terrified to release it and let it float away. She reeled in but regained little line. The rainbow was putting on a fine fighting display. She resorted to stripping in the line by hand and within seconds she had loops of pale nylon lying across her boots. 'Please break off,' she begged the fish, 'please, fish.'

Whoof.

Casey heard the sound clearly but the bear had disappeared. She had been afraid when she could see part of the grizzly, but now that it had vanished she was terrified. She felt very small and vulnerable facing a bear on its terrain.

'Bear!' she shouted, warning the fishing party. She tried to walk to where Dursley and Kit were now discussing lures on the bank near the picnic spot, but the nylon line twined around her boots, making her movements clumsy and ungainly.

'Break off and walk slowly towards us,' shouted Hank as he tore open the haversack and scrabbled for his Contender. He pulled it free of the spare underwear and boxes of tackle. His fingers trembled as he patted his pockets looking for a cracker shot to scare off the bear.

The more adventurous of the two cubs sensed his mother's anger and distress. He pushed around her, risking a slap with her paw, but she was totally absorbed with the danger that a human presented to her cubs. The human had not immediately left the vicinity. Therefore it was challenging her.

The stronger cub pushed through the tangled branches and tall grasses. His brother sat behind the sow mewing indecisively. Suddenly he decided against the boredom of waiting for his mother to move. He crept up on his brother jut as the older cub broke through the scrub onto the river. He pounced, delighted with the success of his stalk.

Both cubs rolled over snarling in mock battle. The bank gave way. They tumbled into the river in a spray of stones and mud. The youngest screamed for his mother as it tried to find a footing on the slimy rocks. The older shook the water from its coat and stood, miserable and dejected as a wet cat, looking over his shoulder at the bank. He waited apprehensively for the nip and slap he would receive from his mother.

'Cubs!' shouted Hank. The scar became a white gash on his cheek, but his attention was focused on Casey, stumbling towards them trying to pull free from the line now tangled tighlty as wind knots around her boots.

With a roar the sow exploded from the shrubs. She launched herself far out into the river, soaring over her cubs, intent on killing the human who blocked her stream and now also threatened her young.

Casey stared at the golden bear flying towards her. In a split second the sow became one of the Inuit flying bear carvings. She almost expected to see the shaman, the wise man, bound to its back.

'Curl into a ball. Protect your head.' Hank's voice drove her to action. As the sow landed in the river, water, like a tidal wave, swamped her. She dropped her rod, covered her head with her arms and screamed in silence as she waited for the agony she knew must come.

'Dursley!' she heard Kit and Hank bellow. 'Don't run. Stand still!' But Dursley, mad as a dervish, set off down the beach, his arms windmilling and his voice cracking as he screamed: 'Whoa, bear! Bear, whoa. Bear! Bear!'

'Damn fool,' cursed Hank as he stumbled after Dursley. He dragged his right foot forcing it to bear his weight. Pain pulled his face into the lines of an old man. 'Now I can't get a clear shot.'

The bear did not even pause to shake the water from her coat. She could see Casey clearly. She was determined to take the danger away from her cubs. They were now both sitting in the river, scared and bemused by her anger and actions.

A shot rang out. The sow jumped as the cracker shot exploded under her hindquarters. Usually the violent explosion was sufficient to turn a grizzly. But this sow was enraged and intent on Casey.

'Shoot the damn thing. Don't play with it,' screamed Dursley as he ran on towards Casey.

Hank had already chambered a soft-nose bullet into his handgun but Dursley's stumbling figure made a safe shot impossible.

'Stay with Earl and Leroy,' he shouted over his shoulder at Kit. He felt pain cutting like a bandsaw across his leg. Something ground in his knee, assuring him of painful operations and a permanent limp. He ignored the frantic messages his body was sending. He had to reach Dursley and take him out of the way.

His order to Kit had been unnecessary. Leroy and Earl were already hidden deep in the scrub. Only Earl's rounded butt was visible.

Kit watched in sick fascination as the sow reached Casey's

rolled-up figure. 'One has to give her guts,' she whispered. She was not certain that she could remain still in the same circumstances. She closed her eyes, not wanting to see the sow tear Casey apart.

Casey gagged as water washed over her face, but she kept her arms locked tightly behind her neck and over her head. Her shoulder muscles corded and screamed in protest as she forced her chin down onto her chest.

'Nanuq,' she mouthed, then changed her pleas to suit this grizzly. 'Grandmother bear, I honour and love you. I mean you no harm.'

The words surprised her; they seemed to come from someone else, but they comforted her. It stopped her seeing those great recurved claws and long canines behind her closed eyelids.

'This is what it must feel like to be mad,' she said.

The sound of her voice helped her to remain curled up tightly.

'Screams, voices. Things you can't see but only hear. Darkness and dread that only you can feel.'

Suddenly she sensed a huge presence over her. It became dark as a polar winter. She smelt the stale stench of rotting fish. She was on the ice and Trapper was slitting open the big white bear. It was the sickening stench of belly gases that she smelt. No, this was the breath of the blonde grizzly. It was the hot slime trickling down her neck.

She finally capitulated. Her screams rose as high and shrill as the calls of the gulls, now mere specks in the sky as they wheeled waiting to return to the feeder stream.

Hank stood in an agony of indecision. His love urged him to run to protect Casey, but his knowledge of bears told him to shoot this one or it would maul and probably kill them all.

Dursley's ruse worked. The sow caught sight of his figure running towards her as she stood over Casey. Immediately she left Casey to chase him. Her hind legs seemed to reach forward over her ears as she ran. Casey's body tumbled then lay on the grey pebbles like a played-out fish as the grizzly hit her before turning to chase Dursley.

He pounded on, drawing the bear away from Casey, praying that Hank would manage to shoot it before it was too late. He was fully aware of the danger. He had acted as instinctively as had the sow. He to protect his wife-to-be and the sow her cubs.

'Curl up!' shouted Hank, needing a clear shot at the bear which had almost reached Dursley. He also wanted Dursley to protect himself as much as possible.

Dursley obeyed immediately. Pain shot up his thighs as his knees hit the stones.

A shot rang out. The grizzly roared and spun round. She clawed frantically at her shoulder, trying to kill the pain which burnt inside her. The bullet had ripped through the muscles of her shoulder shattering the bone. It made a black jelly of her lungs before by-passing her fast-beating heart. The bullet mushroomed perfectly and lodged deep in her.

Hank wheezed his breath in relief. He knew it was a good shot. Now he could turn his attention to Casey. She had climbed stiffly to her feet and was staggering towards Dursley and the bear, like a child learning to walk.

Kit's scream drew Hank's attention back to the bear.

He stared at the grizzly in disbelief. The shot had stopped but not killed her. Maddened by pain and rage, the sow turned back to Dursley. He looked deep into the dark red of her mouth.

The sow's teeth were stained by the juices of roots and berries. Scraps of rotten fish were wedged deeply into the gaps between them. He remembered no more. His brain closed down its complicated circuitry.

The leathery scalp covering his skull moved and slid like the scruff of a puppy's neck beneath the grizzly's teeth, but it protected him for only a few moments.

The bear's jaws tightened, putting tension on the skin. The skin tore and the sliding movement of teeth on scalp stopped. She now had purchase on the skull. Like a dog with a chicken bone her teeth cracked the scalp driving fragments of bone through the dura mater, tearing the final material protecting the brain.

Sharp as steel nails, driven deep by a giant's hammer, the teeth sank into the grey junket-like substance. They tore the blood vessels feeding the brain, with no respect for the extraordinary anatomy, beauty and fine circuitry of the human brain.

The torn network of blood vessels now seeped blood into the creamy grey convolutions of Dursley's brain. The build-up of pressure due to this haemorrhage oozed creamy curds of bruised brain out of the skull and they hung there, obscene, like globs of mucus clotting a child's nose.

Hank was so close to the sow and Dursley that aiming was not necessary. He lifted the handgun and pumped a shot into one of her downy ears. She roared and sank down on Dursley wearily, like a tired old lady.

'Help!' screamed Hank as he struggled to roll the bear away. The horror of the attack pumped adrenalin through his body. It kept him moving, dragging his leg behind him. Kit's boot flew through the air and landed firmly on Earl's bottom. 'Come,' she commanded, as Earl and Leroy sheepishly crawled out of the undergrowth. 'Help Hank.' She could hear Leroy praying as they ran down the stony spit of land.

Earl locked his arms around the sow's head. His muscles bunched and strained as he and Hank heaved it off Dursley.

Leroy gagged and barely reached the edge of the river before he threw up. He remained kneeling on the shoreline with his back to the party grouped around Dursley.

Casey, white faced and numb with horror, sank onto the stones. The grey pebbles quickly stained red with congealing blood. She stroked Dursley's face, mumbling incomprehensibly, begging him to open his eyes. Blood stained her fingers and soaked into the cuffs of her anorak. She was unaware of anything except the man she had hurt and wronged, lying at her feet.

Kit ripped open the first-aid kit. She and Hank tried ineffectually to staunch the blood which ran down and round Dursley's neck like a red muffler. It cobwebbed the stones, making a lace pillow for his head.

'Get the rest of the coffee in the Thermos into Casey and put my jacket around her,' Hank ordered Kit, watching as spasm after spasm shook Casey.

'Dursley?' questioned Kit.

'Do as I say!' roared Hank, holding a pad of gauze tightly against the holes in Dursley's skull. 'We don't need two casualties here. She'll have to help us lift him and move him to the boat. We need all the help possible.'

Kit ran to obey, jerking Leroy to his feet and taking him with her.

'Is he . . .?' asked Earl soberly, trying not to look at Dursley's head.

'Yes. He's alive,' answered Hank, 'but we must get him to a hospital, and fast.'

The two cubs, terrified by the shots and roars of agony from their mother, slithered back across the rocks, scrambled up the bank and hid in the thick brush. The younger sniffed at his mother's footprints and mewed for her softly. When she did not come to comfort him, he nestled close to his brother and shut his eyes.

'Hi, guys.' A man's voice rang out across the water. Hank and Earl spun round. Casey kept stroking Dursley's face, her eyes like a madwoman's, glazed and unfocused.

The five fishermen who had been fishing together up the river at Eye Opener came drifting round the bend in their dinghy.

'Jumping cows!' exclaimed their guide, interpreting the scene quickly. He rowed to the pebbled shore and beached the raft. 'A goner?'

'No, but we need him out of here.'

'No problem.'

Hank and Kit stared at the guide.

'I'm from Peg-leg's place. His two guides have headed for King Salmon and sanity. Peg-leg set off after them this morning, hoping to persuade them to finish the season, so I volunteered to take these guys out fishing.'

Kit still looked confused. 'So?' she said.

'So, I'm Peg-leg's pilot, my float is quite close. I'll go fetch it.' He studied the stretch of water and frowned. 'Usually wouldn't try a landing here. But what the hell. The mood Peg-leg is in, the loss of one plane can't make him any worse.'

Kit and Hank stared at each other in silence as the dinghy vanished around the bend in the river. A small, uncertain voice broke into their relieved silence.

'Is he all right? He will be all right, won't he, won't he, Hank?'

'With Peg-leg's plane to fly him out, he has every chance of fishing here next year,' answered Hank, as he tried to stand up. He rested his weight on his left leg and held onto Kit's shoulder. His right leg hung useless as torn waders.

'Well, you certainly won't be fishing here next year if you don't have that knee fixed,' said Kit.

'The two most important ones are Dursley and Casey,' answered Hank, his voice hoarse with pain. 'She must have cracked or broken ribs and hopefully has no internal injuries. The swipe that sow gave her could take a man's head off.'

'Luckily she's well padded today,' answered Kit.

Hank looked at her quickly but she returned his stare, guileless as a child.

'Her anorak and sweaters may have helped and . . .'

Her voice was drowned by the roar of a float-plane. Kit found herself biting down on her lip as she watched the pilot circle then prepare to land on the short stretch of water. The acid taste of blood in her mouth made her unclench her teeth.

She closed her eyes as the roar of engines rose in a deafening crescendo and then whimpered into silence.

'He did it,' she breathed. 'He made it.'

'Casey, come and help Hank,' called Kit, using the only ruse she could think of to draw Casey away from Dursley's side.

Casey heard. Concentrating on each footstep, her breathing shallow and fast, she walked to where Hank was seated on the side of the dinghy. Earl and Kit were immobilizing his leg in splints fashioned from aluminium wading sticks borrowed from the new fishing party.

The pilot and men had removed the wooden seats from the dinghy and were lashing Dursley to them as quickly as possible.

They bound his neck onto the plank trying to immobilize his head. His face was now a grotesque crimson mask. The wadded cloths seemed unable to stem the red tide. He lay with the chilling stillness of the dead.

'I'll call your lodge as soon as I've the altitude to pick them up,' said the pilot, climbing up the steel steps to the cockpit. 'Do you know which hospital they should call?'

'Humana, I guess,' said Kit. 'Though Providence is also good. The guy is an English earl so let's go for the best in these circumstances.'

'You've got it,' he answered, smiling at her as she held the rope and steadied the plane.

He would have felt more comfortable if Kit was in the plane with him, but they could not leave Leroy, Earl and his four clients to find their way down the river alone.

Leroy had refused to continue downriver without Hank until Kit showed him that she had the handgun. She proved that she could use it by putting a shot through his fishing cap, which hung on an elder branch fifty yards down on the beach.

The seats had been removed from the float-plane and stowed in the hold to make room for Dursley and Casey's makeshift stretchers and Hank with his immobilized leg.

The pilot sighed as he eased the plane around and warmed up the engines. It would be a long flight before he could hand his passengers over to a medical team.

'It'll be a long flight, girl,' he said, talking to his plane. 'Wind is gusting at thirty knots. But wind is workable. You and I know that.'

'What's that?' asked Hank, hearing the pilot mumbling to himself.

'We'll be flying into turbulence with this south-wester and probably fog. I'll try to get up to over two thousand feet. That should be high enough to call your lodge.'

Hank nodded. Stewart would then call for the emergency mobile truck to meet them on the landing strip beside the river at King Salmon. There a physician assistant would take over and rush the three of them to the airport. Knowing Stewart's efficiency, the medevac plane from Anchorage would be ready for take off as soon as they arrived. The pilot's duty would then be over and he could return to Peg-leg's place.

Hank grimaced mirthlessly. He could imagine Peg-leg's reaction to the news that his pilot had taken Stewart's clients to King Salmon. He would be over at the lodge demanding a replacement for his Avgas immediately. 'You can buy clients cheaper than you can buy an aeroplane' was one of his favourite sayings.

'How long?' whispered Casey, looking up at Hank. She too had been strapped to a plank and wedged firmly into the Beaver.

'In this weather it will take about forty-five minutes to Naknek River,' said Hank, looking at the pilot for confirmation. 'Then Dursley will be in a medivac plane, which is as good as an emergency ward,' he comforted. 'Dursley will be all right,' he added with a conviction he did not feel. He took Casey's hand away from Dursley's masklike face. Her hand lay cold and lifeless in his. He started to rub her fingers but she withdrew her hand and tucked it into the pocket of her jacket.

It seemed obscene to her to be holding hands with her lover while Dursley fought for his life beside them.

'It's all my fault,' she said. Hank had to bend forward to hear her. His knee screamed at the slightest movement. He gritted his teeth as pain dripped beads of sweat on his forehead. 'He's here like this only because he loves me.'

Hank was silent. It was true. There was nothing he could say to comfort her.

'And I no longer love him.' As she voiced the denial of her love, her shoulders started shaking. The pent-up reaction to the horror set in.

Hank bent over her stretcher and held her to him as she screamed out her anguish and pain.

The pilot glanced around and quickly turned back to his instrument panel. Now he understood why bush pilots were never told about the case they were to collect. There had been too many accidents when a pilot, realizing how serious the case was, 'stretched the envelope'. They 'pushed too heavy' and crashed. They flew these rescue missions in conditions they knew were treacherous.

Alaskan bush pilots are an extraordinary breed of men, thought Hank as the plane dipped and swayed. They fly to some of the most inaccessible places and in the most treacherous weather conditions in the world. It had stunned him when he first arrived in Alaska to learn that a pilot with three to four thousand hours of flying time was considered merely a novice. He was only accepted as a good pilot if he had fifteen thousand hours of flying to his credit.

The experienced pilots knew that flying and surviving in appalling conditions was an accumulation of years of mistakes which they learned to eliminate. A pilot who made the same mistake twice ended up as a statistic.

Hank shuddered. He was happy to wade the rivers. He had no desire to be part of a job like bush flying which could not be taught, only learned.

Peg-leg's pilot listened to Casey for a few moments then he clamped his headphones over his ears and settled them down. His reputation as an excellent and hard bush pilot was well deserved, but he could not listen to a woman crying. The headphones gave him the silence he needed to concentrate on outwitting the fog now wiping the tundra.

The only thing the man flying the Cessna Conquest to Anchorage would be concerned with today would be the weather conditions during the two-hour flight from King Salmon to Merrill Field, a private airfield where the plane could taxi to the back entrance of the Humana Hospital.

He would not be told of the bear attack or the conditions of the patients. Peg-leg's pilot envied him. He would not have to fly with the mental picture of a man with a crushed skull.

*

Suddenly the plane dropped.

'We're here,' said Hank.

The Beaver dipped and rocked as it rode the river to the jetty. A van waited to transport the patients to the Cessna.

Peg-leg's pilot greeted the nurse and paramedic who were waiting beside the Cessna with unfeigned relief. He felt twenty years younger once the transfer was made and Dursley and Casey were strapped into proper stretchers. In the plane the oxygen tanks, defibrillation machine and packs marked *sterile* frightened Casey. She was in a world where death seemed very close. The ventilator and intubation equipment seemed inadequate to hold it at bay. The gleaming metal, coiled tubes, dials and knobs were not part of her world and therefore alarming.

She watched the paradmedic bend low over Dursley. Guilt flooded her and she fought not to vomit. She refused to allow her thoughts to test the future. She still had to learn to live with the complications of the new present.

The paramedic and nurse unwound the stained bandage from Dursley's head. Hank watched as the paramedic's lips compressed when he saw the fragments of grey matter in the now congealing blood. No, the paramedic thought silently. Brain matter oozing out with blood. I'll have to alert Humana.

He knuckled his fingers and pressed down hard and sharp onto Dursley's sternum giving the patient a painful stimulus to test the depth of his subconscious reactions which would fight their way from the depth of his coma. Dursley lifted his arm and pushed at the paramedic.

'Bloody swine!' he swore. His eyes opened for the first time since the attack. They were hurt and angry.

'Leave him!' shouted Casey. 'Hasn't he suffered enough?'

Hank held her close. 'Shh,' he said. 'He has to do tests. He won't hurt Dursley unnecessarily.'

'Will Dursley live?' Casey asked the medic.

The paramedic ignored both Casey's outburst and her question. He had no answer for her. He merely studied Dursley and pulled out his Glascow Coma Scale, ticking off the various responses to pain, to shouted commands and to eye reactions.

'He will, Ticasuk. He will. Soon this will all be only a nightmare,' comforted Hank. He smoothed her hair, glued to her forehead with a fine sheen of sweat. Then he turned his attention back to the paramedic.

Dursley's verbal, motor and eye response to the painful stimulus gave him a ten out of fifteen on the scale. 'Not too bad,' said the medic as he eased a needle into Dursley's cubital vein and quickly set up a drip.

'What's that?' asked Casey softly.

'It's haemacale, blood volume expander, to replace the fluid he has lost,' explained the paramedic. He turned to Hank and Casey.

'Now let's see what we can do for the two of you.'

He noted where Casey winced when he ran his fingers over her ribs. Probably one or two cracked ones, he thought. 'They'll X-ray you at Humana.'

He resplinted Hank's knee and felt the strong leg muscles. 'You'll probably get away with a padded brace. Most of you guides have legs like steel. A brace should hold this.'

'Break or fracture?' queried Hank.

'It will have to be X-rayed but I'd bet on a fracture.'

Peg-leg's pilot watched the Cessna roar into life and head for Anchorage before he walked back slowly to his Beaver. 'Runways are so boring,' he said, kicking the wet Tarmac. As he climbed into his float he realized that if his group had not spent so much time at Eye Opener, they too could have been attacked by the sow. He raised his eyes to the grey vault overhead which seemed to stretch to eternity. 'Thank you,' he mouthed as he prepared his aircraft for take off.

As the Cessna sped on its way to Anchorage sobs started shuddering through Casey's body again but she pushed Hank away weakly as he tried to hold her. Any movement jarred her. She gasped for breath as her lungs seemed to be held in an ever-tightening vice.

Not wanting the medivac nurse who was seated in the back with them to hear her, Casey gestured for Hank to bend close to her. 'We are paying for our love,' she whispered. The colour had drained from her face leaving her as pallid as Dursley.

'No, Ticasuk,' said Hank fiercely. 'Never even think that. It's not true.' He put his hand over hers and this time she twined her fingers into his. Pain was now gnawing at her, hungry as a bear. She needed the strength and comfort Hank could give her.

'I love you so much,' she said, looking up into his eyes which were only inches above hers as he leaned over the stretcher, 'but I can't leave Dursley like this. I owe him my life.' She felt Hank's beard, thick and soft, as he rested his head on the edge of the stretcher.

'No, no, Ticasuk,' he murmured shakily. 'He saved your life, but you don't have to sacrifice our future. Getting through this will be tough. But not tough enough to break us. You must believe me.'

She lifted her arm weakly and her fingers stroked his beard.

The nurse seated on one of the jump seats was about to order Hank back to his seat, but she looked away as their wet cheeks met and Hank's mouth covered Casey's.

Chapter Sixteen

A LITTLE under two hours later the Cessna circled the square hospital building. The emergency team were standing just inside the silver-wire gate waiting for the plane to taxi to the helipad. The paramedic had already contacted them by radio and relayed the severity of the injuries that he had been able to ascertain.

Casey's side still hurt, but only when she twisted or bent suddenly. Hank was relieved to see how much more easily she moved as she was helped from the plane.

'I can walk,' he heard her protest to the emergency team. But she was placed on a stretcher. Hank started to hobble stiffly across the Tarmac, as the team raced with Dursley's stretcher through the high-rise car park for hospital staff and into the trauma room. The Humana team knew that they were bringing in a man with a compound depressed skull fracture. They moved quickly.

The neurosurgeon, a man labelled a 'top-shelf' doctor by all who knew him, had been alerted, as had the anaesthetist who had been stopped in his plane which was lined up on the runway at Merrill Field. He wistfully gave up his fishing trip and returned to Humana.

All the preferred theatre team who worked with the neurosurgeon had been rounded up and were waiting by the time the gurney carrying Dursley was wheeled into the trauma room.

'You're a lucky lady,' said one of the team to Casey. 'We have

Professor Matt Siebens here with us. A great guy. Just back from a lecture trip to Seattle. He's the best in the States, a trauma expert and a world authority on bear attacks.'

'Is he a neurosurgeon?' asked Casey.

'Neurosurgeon? The word was invented for him.'

'He's a miracle maker,' added one of the women.

'Well, he sure gets enough practice,' laughed one of the men, who looked as if he still played on a football team and could lift all three gurneys single-handed. 'The "Forty-ninth" is a great state. If guys aren't beaten up by bears or moose they are flying into mountains or falling down glaciers. Prof. Matt has to be the most experienced guy in broken skulls in the world.'

Thank you, whispered Casey silently to her God, whom she knew without doubt was the Divine Life Force. Thank you for having Prof. Siebens back in Anchorage in time to treat Dursley.

'Dursley's family?' she asked Hank.

'Don't worry, Ticasuk. Stewart will have contacted them already. He is highly efficient.'

Casey gulped. The thought of Lady Edbury in Anchorage was almost as unpleasant as the bear attack.

She felt a desolation, harsh and cruel as the polar winter, press down on her at the thought of having to return to England with Dursley and his family.

The gurneys were pushed through the bright orange swing doors.

'Where is Dursley?' she asked, searching round the small trauma room, her voice thin with apprehension.

'Don't worry,' said one of the OR nurses, walking into the room and patting her arm. 'He is in the very best care.'

'Let's look at you, young lady,' said a doctor not much older than Casey. She was about to ask if he was qualified or a student, but suddenly it didn't matter. Her body relaxed as he ran his fingers along her ribs and her eyes closed, she was so tired.

'Nothing seems to be broken,' he said to the trauma room sister. 'Possibly one or two ribs are cracked, but I'd like her X-rayed.'

Casey only opened her eyes a fraction later when she heard strange voices talking over her. The room was dark and cold.

'She's certainly a lucky one,' said a nurse. 'The radiologist says there are only two cracked ribs, lungs are fine. She'll ache until those ribs have mended, but that is all.'

'Not many have only sore ribs after a grizzly has swatted them,' answered a disembodied voice. 'But she was well padded. I thought we'd be here till dinner taking off all her thermals.'

Casey closed her eyes quickly and pretended to be sleeping.

'Wheel her back to the trauma room. They'll strap her up and dress her.'

Casey opened her eyes in the bright lights of the trauma room to see Hank anxiously waiting for her. He spoke to the nurse in low tones and hobbled across. His crutches squeaked on the polished floor.

'Hank,' she said, 'what has happened to you?'

'Nothing, Ticasuk,' he reassured her, kissing her lightly on the cheek. 'Just a chip off my knee-cap. It may twinge a bit in winter. It'll remind me of Earl and Leroy,' he joked, wanting to see her smile. 'It's not even in plaster, only this damn awkward steel brace – sorry, sister,' he said with mock humility.

'Much more of that, young man, and we'll have you in plaster up to your waist,' she warned.

Casey smiled at the banter and Hank breathed in deeply with relief.

The air of urgency in the trauma room was controlled. It seemed as if there was no dire necessity to move fast.

Casey stood up from the hard chair, which had been pushed into a corner out of the staff's way. Hank held out his hand to her and then dropped it. She carefully walked across to the gurney. One of the nurses held out her arm to bar the way. The casualty officer shook his head. May be the last time she sees him alive, he thought to himself.

Casey bent over Dursley and gently stroked his cheek. She felt so helpless. Where was the neurosurgeon? Why were they not more concerned with Dursley? Everyone seemed to be moving so slowly and casually. Did no one care about him?

The casualty officer knuckled down hard on Dursley's sternum. Dursley opened his eyes, but his gaze was disorientated. He lifted his arm slowly. It dropped to his side; he was unable to push the man's hand away. There was no longer any purposeful response. He grunted softly, unable to talk or swear at the pain.

'Where is the surgeon? Why isn't he here?' cried Casey.

'He is on his way,' lied the sister reassuringly, patting Casey on the arm. She well understood the fear and uncertainty experienced by families in the trauma room.

The casualty officer turned his attention back to Dursley. He noted his eye and motor responses and checked them against the Glascow Coma Scale. Matt Siebens would want them straight away. His staff revered Matt Siebens as a doctor, loved him as a man, but were wary of his temper if they were slow or derelict in their duties.

The casualty officer frowned and motioned to the sister to take a blood-pressure reading. The paramedic in the Cessna had radioed them a GCS reading of ten. It had dropped to eight during the two-hour flight from King Salmon to Anchorage. He moved quicly to the telephone. There was no doubt about the patient's worsening condition.

Hank's eyes followed the casualty officer to the telephone then he looked back at Casey. She seemed so small and forlorn standing beside Dursley's gurney. He had to force himself not to hobble across the scrubbed tile floor and join her.

She needs this time with Dursley, he thought. When his family arrives from England she will have to make a decision.

The thought of her deciding to stay with Dursley out of a sense of duty and sympathy appalled him. He dropped his head into his hands. Surely she wouldn't deny their love?

'All right?' queried a soft voice.

Hank looked up to see one of the nurses bending over him solicitously.

'Fine,' he stretched his mouth into a grin. 'Just wondering how I'd do as a male nurse. I'll probably be looking for a new job after this.'

The nurse looked at him appreciatively. 'Don't take it too hard. If they fired a guide for every bear scare or attack, you guys would be an extinct breed.'

Hank smiled. He knew and usually enjoyed the effect he had on women. But his world had changed since meeting Casey. He now wanted to share his dreams and life with only one woman. Thoughts of their future together tumbled through his mind like water-washed pebbles. For a short while these thoughts blocked out the smell of antiseptics and the austerity of the trauma room.

Professor Matt Siebens listened carefully, the phone pressed tightly to his ear. His Siberian husky laid its head on his legs and looked up at him appealingly, hoping to be invited to jump up onto the couch beside him. But he merely fondled its pointed ears absentmindedly.

His long delicate fingers belied their strength, built up by climbing mountains in summer and glaciers in winter. These dangerous sports both relaxed him and fed him the adrenalin high he needed as a release from the trauma of the delicate operations he performed.

As the head of the trauma room spoke to him, he built up a mental picture of Dursley's brain. He well knew the damage which could be caused by the pointed canines of an eight-hundred-pound bear. A human skull would crack as easily as breaking an egg shell with the sharp tap of a ballpoint pen.

Matt pushed the dog's head from his lap as the casualty officer described the two-millimetre grey pieces which were embedded in the dark blood clotted on the bandage.

'Good news is that it sounds like a posterior parietal compound depressed fracture,' he said. 'Let's hope the eloquent areas are not affected.' His husky whimpered and scratched at his leg for attention. But Matt was already repairing what to him was the most superb and mystic organ in the human anatomy. 'Bad news is that the haemorrhage may not have stopped the brain tissue coming through the wound. Are the . . .?

'The theatre and team are ready and waiting, Matt.'

'Good. I want a skull X-ray, a cervical spine X-ray and a CT scan of the brain,' he said briskly. 'Have them ready for me when I arrive. Give me fifteen, no, make it ten minutes.'

'Fly carefully. Try to keep four wheels on the road,' the officer answered. 'We need neurosurgeons here in Anchorage.'

Hank broke out of his reverie to hear Casey shout.

'No! Let me go with him!'

The nurse locked her arms around Casey's shoulders and forcibly dragged her away from the gurney.

Hank stood up gingerly. His new crutches squeaked as he swung them across the floor to the nurse.

'The Earl of Edbury has to be taken for scans before the surgeon arrives. It will be easier and quicker to have the scans and X-rays done if she stays with you.'

'Come, Ticasuk,' soothed Hank. 'We both want what's best for Dursley. We aren't any help here.'

Casey buried her face in Hank's anorak and her shoulders shook.

'Here, take this.' The nurse held up a cup and white tablet.

'I don't want any drugs.'

'These are so harmless that we use them for babies and children,' the nurse reassured her, but Casey only tightened her lips.

Hank gestured to the nurse over Casey's head and she handed him the mug and tablet. She watched as he gently led Casey out of the trauma room. They turned right into the small reception-cum-waiting-room. Casey sat in one of the square light-wood chairs and stared sightlessly at the framed pictures of bald eagles and wildlife on the slate-blue walls.

She opened her mouth obediently as Hank popped in the pill and she drained the plastic mug of water quickly. Hank put his arm around her shoulders and she rested the back of her head on his arm. She hooked her fingers into his, finding comfort in the strength and warmth of his hand. The nurse frowned as she turned back into the trauma room.

Strange, she thought. The girl seemed crazy about the earl, but she obviously has something going with the guide as well.

'Ticasuk,' Hank whispered, 'when things are bad, think of all the good times you have enjoyed. Make your mind concentrate on happiness.'

'Happiness?'

'Yes.' He started telling her old fishing stories and Inuit fables. Her mind followed his voice and soon she was back on the ice with Nanuq and Trapper Jack.

They both started as they heard their names called. The nurse walked into the small room accompanied by a man who looked as if he had just left a basketball game.

Matt Siebens ducked his head slightly as he walked through the doorway. He had played basketball at school and a great future was prophesied for him. A few pre-med courses changed his future from the glamour and wealth of a basketball player to the testing skill of handling the most mysterious of all human organs, the brain.

'Miss Chargot.' His voice was surprisingly soft. Casey had expected to hear a deep, loud bellow to match his physique.

She prepared to stand up, but he placed a large hand on her shoulder and held her firmly in her seat. He sank into the chair beside her and stretched his long legs out in front of him. He seemed completely unconcerned and relaxed.

Casey felt the tension which had squeezed her throat at his entrance drain away.

Matt studied her carefully whilst appearing to scan the paper in his hand. Every nerve in his body urged him to hurry into the theatre. His fingers itched to start repairing the damage done to one of his beautiful brains – he considered all brains to be his and remembered the intricacies of each years after he had performed the delicate operations – but first he had to alert the family of the possible consequences of operating on the brain.

Unlike some of his colleagues, who preferred to hit both family members and patients in the solar plexus, winding and sickening them with the worst possible scenario, arguing that any later complications would then seem mild in comparison, Matt preferred to hold out a life-belt of hope for them to cling to. Compassion and sympathy were the tools of his trade, not cold, hard facts, easy to assimilate by the medical men but callous and terrifying to the layman.

As he waited for the signal from his sister telling him that the scans were all done and waiting for his appraisal, he turned over the paper from the casualty officer noting the drop in Dursley's responses. He was now seriously worried about that blood clot forming deep in the brain.

Quickly and reassuringly he drew the outline of a skull on paper. Casey watched him in fascination. As his quiet voice explained the intricacies of a skull repair, she exhaled and relaxed. She now knew that Dursley was safe. Matt Siebens would save him. This was not the sort of man who would let Dursley die. She smiled as she watched him hurry from the waiting-room in response to a signal from the sister.

'Great guy,' said Hank. 'Dursley will probably be back on the river to finish this trip.'

Casey gripped his hand. 'Not this trip, but he may return in a few years to fight the rainbows.'

'We'll be here to meet him,' said Hank.

Casey opened her mouth and then closed it again. She would have to talk to Hank about their future, but not in this austere waiting-room.

*

Matt strode into the darkened room with its TV screen. It took a few seconds for his eyes to adjust to the gloom. He peered through the glass panel which allowed him to view his patient.

Dursley's thick waders had been cut off his body. He was in a thin cotton hospital gown. The casualty officer, worried about the time it could take to do all the X-rays and scans, had inserted an endotrachial tube into the unconscious man to keep his airway open and protect it in case of vomit.

Matt Siebens nodded to himself. The man seemed robust and healthy. It was easier to work on a body which was not abused. Smoking, drinking and eating to excess produced bodies unable to withstand the rigours of brain surgery.

He turned his attention to the TV screen. His expression was inscrutable. The machine projected layer after layer of the brain onto the screen, quickly and neatly as peeling an onion. He breathed an audible sigh of relief as the images showed no compression of the brain stem. Working in that area was like crossing one-inch-thick ice alone. He had been worried that the tremendous force of the bear's jaws closing on the head could have caused secondary damage high in the neck.

The screen now moved to sections from the site of the injury. He could clearly see the fragments of bone driven into the brain by the canines.

'Parietal compound depressed skull fracture with a cerebral laceration,' he murmured.

Suddenly he bent over the screen as if standing closer would give him a clearer image and enable him to see even deeper into the brain. His eyes were the pale, translucent blue found in glaciers which had recently calved into the sea. His theatre staff insisted that the lack of colour in his eyes enabled him to see through the brain and that accounted for his extraordinary success as a neurosurgeon.

He held up his hand for the radiologist to freeze the frame. Yes, the white smudge he had noticed a few slices earlier was now clear. The blood vessels feeding the brain were torn and a clot had formed beneath the bone fragments. He could see how the blood clot was compressing the yet undamaged brain beside the injury, displacing it and so threatening further loss of brain function. The process would continue the total destruction of the brain if left unchecked.

Matt felt the familiar rush of adrenalin bristle the hair on his forearms and tingle his fingers. Dursley Carrington, Earl of Edbury, would die if the clot was not removed.

His sense of urgency and excitement vibrated through the room. Hospital staff moved swiftly to their practised positions for the familiar battle with death.

They ran another GCS as the gurney rolled smoothly towards the operating room. His position had not deteriorated. It still held steady at eight.

The theatre staff had trays of gleaming instruments ready to place on the sterile blue sheets high above the patient once he was on the table. They whispered together quietly, adjusting their burgundy theatre caps while Matt carefully shaved Dursley's head. They watched him run his fingers over the skull, pausing every now and then to probe a bump.

His theatre sister grinned at Matt's registrar. Her dark eyes twinkled impishly. 'Our Matt rides again. His six shooters are blazing. A grizzly has taken a scalp.'

The registrar frowned at her. He disapproved of levity in the theatre. The sister was well known for her total disregard for authority and her somewhat bizarre sense of humour.

'The Forty-ninth is worse than the Wild West,' grumbled the anaesthetist half-heartedly. He had been up most of the night, whilst surgeons tried to save a pilot. Young and too eager to please clients booked on a bear and moose hunt, the pilot had 'stretched the envelope', flown into fog, tried to turn back and found a mountain in the way. The clients were killed instantly and the young man would never fly again.

Matt listened to the theatre-room banter as he completed shaving the skull. There was a time when he had considered marriage and his theatre sister ranked high on his list. She was erased from the list of hopefuls when he realized that she did not enjoy hanging from rocks by her fingernails, or testing her endurance to the limit by crossing glaciers and slithering on ice-covered mountain slopes.

The talking and laughter faded as he studied the unconscious Dursley. His skull was now white and naked and looked defenceless in the bright lights. The deep red holes made by the incisors and the jagged gashes gnawed into the skull by the bear's lower jaw seemed as obscene to Matt as graffiti splashed across the walls of the White House.

He forced himself to walk and not run to the basins to scrub up after shaving Dursley's head. This was always the worst time. He had seen and felt the head, planned the outlines he would follow to make the incisions. He knew instinctively where the brain was damaged and was eager to open up the skull to reveal its secrets.

The anaesthetist had assisted Matt with many a case. He held the neurosurgeon in high esteem, but not even the famous Matt Siebens pacing the OR like a caged bear was going to make him hurry. Coldly and precisely he set up his drips and checked his instruments. He ran his hand over Dursley's head and allowed himself a small smile. Whatever Matt did, he did well. The head was close shaven. There was no need for him to make any final touches.

Matt was not a fanciful man but every time he stood in the operating theatre waiting impatiently to take his place at the head of the operating table, listening to the soft strains of Mozart trickling into the cold room, it seemed that the OR staff performed a stately minuet as they moved forward and then retreated from the unconscious body on the narrow table.

Their movements were smooth and silent. Each had a part to play in this macabre dance with death. They flowed towards the body and inserted a catheter. They hung bags to hold the yellow fluids from the bladder. Then they retreated and collected eye pads to protect the eyes during the long hours it would take to complete the delicate operation.

An arterial line was set up instead of a blood-pressure cuff.

Wires were untangled and knobs were turned, tuning in the ECG. The metallic sonar-like pings would reassure the staff that Dursley's heart was accepting the strain of the drugs and the steel instrument probing his brain.

Finally the staff formed a circle around the operating table. A pause had come in the dance and Matt was now invited to join. He stepped onto the centre stage and took up his position in front of the Mayfield clamp at the top of the table. The device held Dursley's head in a vice-like grip, preventing all movement during the delicate stages of the operation.

Fresh latex gloves were rolled over his fingers. He clasped his hands together lacing his fingers, forcing the creamy rubber gloves into a close fit. Dursley was on his back, but a heavy bolster wedged firmly under his shoulder kept his head and neck in the position Matt had chosen. He was tense with eagerness. Nervous energy formed an almost palpable aura around him. He looked around the room checking that everyone was in place and everything in order. His staff had learned not to change anything from Matt's chosen position.

He personally cleaned Dursley's bald head with disinfectant. The head was now his. He grasped every opportunity to handle it before cutting it open. With a sure hand he drew dark blue lines across the back of the skull. Without these lines the shaven skull would be like an egg, featureless, once it was draped in sterile sheets. It would be impossible to know where to make the important incisions. He would be totally disorientated.

At a nod of his head slender needles were slid into the demarcated area, infiltrating the scalp with a solution to stop excessive bleeding once Matt opened the skin. They well knew the flood of blood which would be released from the rich network of vessels feeding the scalp. Matt waited, trying to control his impatience and excitement as they stitched blue drapes onto the scalp to help absorb the red tide. He lifted his hand and gestured for them to shift the overhead lights. Satisfied with the lighting he closed his eyes.

'Grant my hands the skill I need for this operation,' he prayed. 'Be with me and guide me.'

Most surgeons prayed before operating on the human body. Every neurosurgeon known to Matt certainly did, though many denied it, feeling that it might be construed as a sign of weakness. Matt had no such inhibitions. Every time he felt the brain pulse beneath his fingers he knew he was feeling the soul, the part of God he knew was in every human body. It never failed to humble him and fill him with awe.

He found the other organs in the body fascinating, but had no desire to operate on them. To him, the brain was holy. It was the very essence of the person. Every operation he performed on this intricately beautiful organ was an act of worship.

The staff waited until Matt opened his eyes then draped Dursley's head in sterile pale blue sheets leaving only the demarcated area open.

'Pit-bull fighting,' said Holly. The anaesthetist laughed. The operating area did look a little like a bull pit. Dursley lay at the bottom of the table. The round overhead lights beamed down bright as a tropical sun. The trays of instruments placed high up on the draped sheets could, with a large stretch of the imagination, be trays filled with cash for betting on the outcome.

'Dr Siebens is one pit-bull terrier and . . .' Her voice and the laughter trailed away as Matt returned to the table freshly scrubbed and gowned.

'And death is the other sister,' he said, 'now let's work, and take this one for ourselves.'

'Kick death in the backside,' agreed Holly.

Matt laughed. He had a deep, rich laugh, unlike his gentle voice. Catching his eye above his mask Holly felt a twinge of regret at what might have been.

What the hell, she thought. We would have only met for coffee in the canteen. I would probably see more of him in the theatre than I would have in bed. No thanks.

She turned her attention to the operating table. 'Only the

"crown of thorns" today,' she quipped, knowing that they would all work in virtual silence once the operation started.

'The "iron mask" and the "rack" were not available, sorry, Doc. I did try for them.'

Matt shook his head but his eyes smiled. He had once called the Mayfield clamp a crown of thorns. The name had stuck as the clamps fixed with sharp pins to grind into the skull did look like an instrument of torture.

He carefully sited the clamp over Dursley's head, placing the two steel pins on the one side which, with its opposite number, would sink deep into the skull holding it immobile. He tightened the clamp and the ratchet groaned as it forced the spring-loaded pins deep into the bone. Holly groaned with it.

'Are we crazy or something? The poor guy already has holes in his head and now we are giving him more.'

'Scalpel, sister,' Matt demanded, ending the levity.

Instantly Holly became a serious dedicated theatre sister. She slapped the sharp cutting instruments firmly into his hand. As the razor-sharp blade traced the blue outlines, blood, like molten lava, welled up and flowed over the scalp. Soon the sheets were stained dark red.

Retractors were quickly inserted. The tonglike instruments held the bleeding cut wide open whilst deft hands worked swiftly to clamp Dandys forceps on the seeping galea. If these blood vessels were not sealed quickly Matt's fingers would be paddling blindly in a pool of blood.

Soon the almond-shaped opening was bristling like an angry porcupine with the forceps. The scissor tops jostled together like lucky charms on a bracelet. Holly stretched rubber bands over her hands and neatly gathered the jangling heads of the forceps into tidy steel pigtails.

The scalp on which small beads of blood hung now lay open. Peering at the wound through his glasses Matt went cold with anger. Fragments of Dursley's hair and threads from his green fishing cap were trapped amongst the bone fragments, some of which tilted inwards. Others cut the dura with their sharp edges.

Silently he cursed the bear. Every thread and strand of hair would have to be extracted.

Matt held out his hand for the air-driven drill. He was now ready to drill the burr hole through the pink skull. Holly swallowed hard. This was the one part of the operation which still made her queasy with the high-pitched whine of the drill as it bored into the skull and the stench of charred bone.

She breathed in deeply, grateful for the cold air in the austere room.

The whine stopped abruptly as the drill broke through the bone and automatically switched off.

Holly breathed a sigh of relief. She had a profound mistrust of computers and computerized machinery. She was certain that one day the drill would not automatically switch off. It would continue to drill, plunging into the brain as if beating egg-whites.

A groove was now nibbled from each side of the burr hole around the depressed fracture. About as easy as clipping an elephant's toenails, thought the anaesthetist glancing up from his monitors for a moment. He watched the muscles in Matt's arms thicken and relax and his knuckles whiten with each two-handed snip.

As if reading his thoughts, Matt said, 'It's not strength that does it. One just has to have the knack, then it's fairly simple.'

'The knack, plus hands hardened to steel from clinging to rock ledges that not even a bald eagle would feel safe on, or be crazy enough to try landing on.' The anaesthetist shook his head. 'You're awesome, Matt. You fix broken skulls every day, yet for relaxation you do the one crazy sport that's almost certain to end in a bust head.'

'Or leg or neck,' added Holly.

Matt grinned. He knew they were right. Rock climbing was dangerous, but it commanded all of his concentration. In a strange way it was like climbing in and over one of the brains he loved.

'There,' he said, as he flicked up his wrist and broke off the last piece of bone. The fractured area was now freed from the skull. The 'nibbling' was always time consuming and delicate, yet hard physical work. It took years to perfect the technique he exhibited.

The light ting of Dursley's measured heartbeat was loud in the silence as Matt carefully lifted the bone fragments from the white dura, the outermost and thickest of the three membranes covering the brain. The theatre staff held their breath as Matt folded it back reverently.

He adjusted his glasses and glared at the damage caused by the grizzly's teeth. The dura was stained and torn where the canines had penetrated the protective layers. Matt seemed to hold time in his hand as he skilfully extracted the fragments of bone driven through it and into the brain substance. Carefully he moved the fine top of a suction device and bipolar forceps into the depth of the torn brain, removing clotted blood and damaged tissue. He could not afford to hurry. Every fragment and piece of foreign matter had to be removed.

He waved his forceps in the air and Holly placed a tray beneath them. He dropped what looked like a small clot of blood onto the tray.

'Grizzly hair and material. Probably threads from his fishing cap,' he explained.

Holly put the tray to one side. Patients often wanted the stuff fished out of their brains. She would not want to be reminded of the attack, but many enjoyed having the weird mementoes with them.

Matt, hunched over Dursley, did not notice the muscles in his shoulders spasming in protest or the ache in his cramped fingers. He was totally absorbed in cleaning out his beautiful brain. At last, satisfied that no fragments of foreign material remained in the ripped, creamy convolutions, he straightened up. He ignored the immediate tremors of pain from his relaxed muscles and tendons. His eyes were still fixed to the damaged brain.

'There!' he exulted. A blood clot, thick and slimy as a slug, oozed from deep in the laceration he had just cleared.

The theatre staff stood quietly awaiting the urgent action which would follow its appearance.

'Time for enemas,' joked his assistant as she held up an

instrument which looked like the bulb of a Victorian enema apparatus.

Immediately gloved hands, busy as ants, surrounded the depression. They had to clean and close the wound without causing another blood clot, damaging vital blood vessels or causing another haemorrhage. It was an unvoiced nightmare that they might stitch up over an unnoticed slow blood seep.

Soon the theatre was filled with the slobbering sounds of a sucker removing blood and the soft squeak of rubber as the assistant pumped saline solution from the enema bulb to gently irrigate the brain, washing out the last of the blood clot.

Holly wrinked her nose as the bipolar diathermy needle singed closed the seeping blood vessels. It smelt to her like a Sunday roast burning. Patties guided the accurate needle. As the thin sterile squares were laid gently on the brain they stained at the actual spot of bleeding. The buzz of the diathermy needle immediately sealed off the potential trouble maker.

The anaesthetist glanced up at the round clock on the wall. Three hours. This one had taken longer than predicted. Probably because Matt found material fibres deep in the brain, and spent longer than usual probing the area, he thought.

Eventually, satisfied that nothing was still bleeding and all foreign matter had been removed, Matt bent low over the brain. He watched the creamy convolutions rise and fall to the pulse of Dursley's heartbeat. Softly as a sigh he placed a fingertip on the exposed brain as if in benediction. Thank you, he whispered silently.

He unfolded the white dura mata and stitched it closed with self-absorbent material. The brain, once again, had some protection.

The anaesthetist checked all his readings and yawned. If the weather held, he could probably persuade his pals to forgo watching the Dallas Cowboys play ball on television, and join him for a day's fishing down at Katmai. He glanced at Dursley having a plate inserted at the back of his head. No, probably not Katmai. They might try Kenai River for rainbows before the season closed. It would probably be his last fishing trip for the year. The trips before winter set in were always a very special. The trout were big and hungry and the air rolled with the thunder of a million wings, as birds migrated from the dark and the freeze they knew must come. 'Blest with a magic power is he, drinks deep where others sipped, and wild things write their lives for him in endless manuscript,' he quoted, unaware that Matt had paused and was looking at him.

'Dreaming of steelheads?'

The anaesthetist jerked himself back to the bleak operating theatre. 'No,' he lied. 'I was quoting Seaton and wondering when Katmai will be closed to tourists, hunters and fishermen and left to the bears.'

'Not as long as sporting licences are paid and there is money to be made,' predicted Matt. 'Bears will have to share the land and rivers with us. Occasionally the odd bear will object and we'll be here at Humana to clean up the mess.'

Matt eventually stretched and cracked his knuckles. His assistant would supervise Dursley's move to the Intensive Care Unit.

'Now for the hard part. Care to join me while I visit the relatives?' he asked the anaesthetist.

'No thanks,' his colleague demurred. 'I signed on to be tough when I took this job, but not that tough! I need to settle him in ICU.' He thought quickly. 'Take Holly. She's good at this sort of thing. That babe makes a craniectomy seem as serious as a grazed knee.'

Chapter Seventeen

CASEY LOOKED up at the clock in the small reception room off the operating complex. 'Almost four hours,' she said.

Hank kneaded her fingers gently. 'Brain operations take for ever, Ticasuk,' he soothed. 'Four hours is nothing.'

'Have the Carringtons contacted the hospital yet?' she asked, suddenly changing the subject.

Hank slowly unwrapped a stick of chewing gum from his pocket and offered one to Casey before answering. 'Lady Edbury is happy that Dursley is in such excellent care.'

He had accepted the call from Lady Edbury as Casey was having her ribs X-rayed. After twenty minutes of listening to her comments on inefficiently run fishing lodges, incompetent guides and doctors who operated in Alaska only because they were not acceptable in large cities at well-known hospitals, Hank's patience and good manners ended abruptly. He affected a laconic American drawl. 'Ma'am, this call is being terminated. We have a great input on these hospital lines. All calls over ten minutes are cut.' He put down the phone to expletives that no lady should know, let alone use.

'Yes, Ticasuk,' he said, answering Casey's question. 'Everything is fine. The family will be here tomorrow.'

The painkillers they had given him when they set his knee into the brace were wearing off. Pain gnawed its way from his knee up to his head. It felt as if Peg-leg was attacking his forehead with an axe. He had refrained from asking a passing nurse for pills as he wanted to be strong for Casey.

The casualty officer who admitted Dursley, Hank and Casey joined Matt and Holly on the walk to the reception room where crumpled Styrofoam mugs testified to the long wait.

'The knee and ribs should spend the night here,' he said referring to Hank and Casey. 'We'll pop a pill down their throats and they'll have a good night's sleep.'

'Probably need it, after this brush with the bear,' agreed Matt.

'They'll be popping pills for weeks to kill the nightmares,' prophesied Holly. 'Perhaps pills won't be necessary,' she amended as they walked through the half-open door, the carpet muffling their footsteps.

Hank and Casey broke apart. Casey flushed guiltily, but Hank unselfconsciously brushed the tears from her cheeks with his thumb before turning to greet the doctors.

'How is he?'

'How is Dursley?'

'The operation was a success,' said Matt, using the five magical words the family needed to hear. 'The patient is well but still unconscious. He is now in Intensive Care.'

'You may be able to see him tonight,' whispered Holly, reading the appeal in Casey's eyes. 'If Professor Siebens agrees,' she added hastily, noticing ice freeze the warmth from Matt's eyes.

'We need the ribs and the knee to overnight at Humana,' broke in the casualty officer, mindful that he might be needed in the emergency centre.

Hank and Casey looked at him, slightly puzzled.

'He always uses the injuries instead of names when referring to emergency cases,' explained Holly.

'But . . .'

'We already have accommodation downtown,' explained Hank.

'That was an order, not an invitation,' said Matt. 'You were admitted by the casualty officer and you will be discharged when he is satisfied with your condition.'

Hank and Casey had tasted the edge of Matt Siebens's legendary cold displeasure. The blood drained from Casey's face and her lip trembled, much as she tried to hold it steady. Like shadows at midday Matt's bad mood vanished.

'I know it's been hard,' he said, resting his hand on her shoulder. 'It's not often one is used as the ball in a bear bowling alley. We want to be certain that we have missed no hidden injuries. So stay with us tonight. Tomorrow you can talk to your friend.'

'Talk?' said Casey.

'Yes. He should be up in two to three days.'

Casey smiled.

'But no fishing for a while,' he teased as he turned to leave the room, 'and certainly no more playing with grizzlies. They are too tough.'

'We have a two-bed ward free for tonight,' said the casualty officer, studying a list clipped to his board.

Hank nodded.

'My mother-in-law will throw a floppy,' said Casey.

'Mother-in-law? I have you down as Miss Casey Chargot.'

'I should have said future,' amended Casey.

Hank placed his hand over hers and Matt noticed how her fingers instinctively curled into his.

Matt glanced at Holly and regret hung for a moment in the air, warm as steam over a seal's breathing hole. It vanished as quickly as the steaming air once the seal dived back into the black icy waters. Matt's life was the exploration of the human brain. It was a vast and wonderful subject. One which left no room for all the joys and problems of living with a woman.

As they strode down the passage his mind was checking the operations scheduled for the week ahead. His schedule was full and that meant a week of happiness.

*

The Countess of Edbury flicked open a delicate lace handkerchief, dusted the seat of the cab and studied the white lawn cloth for any signs of dirt. 'Dirty, grimy place this Anchorage,' she pronounced. She ignored the driver's explanation that it was the remaining volcanic ash from the explosion of Mt Sitka. Most had been removed, but some clung stubbornly to window-ledges and hid in the drainage system of the city.

'Should have been cleared away immediately,' she declared. 'Just like that oil spill. No one moved until everything was covered with black muck. It broke our hearts to see all those poor birds on television. Gross inefficiency, that's what's wrong with this place.'

The cabby tried to defend his city, but once in full cry the countess was difficult to stop or to stem. Her brother and other family members whom she considered important enough to make the trip were squeezing into the cab behind hers. They had borne the brunt of her ill-humour on the tiring flight from London to Seattle and then on to Anchorage. Her brother hoped that the long flight would have exhausted her. But she continued to find fault with everything and everyone. Her dislike and distrust of anything foreign seemed more acceptable in England than it did in the States, where they were the foreigners.

'Humana Hospital,' he said to the driver and promptly closed his eyes.

I hope Casey has alerted the staff to Agnes, her mother-in-law, he thought.

A few moments later the cab rolled towards Humana to the accompaniment of loud irregular snores.

Chapter Eighteen

CASEY STUDIED the two narrow beds in the ward. The sheets were drawn across them tight as a drawing board. They looked cold and uninviting. She barely glanced at the gleaming apparatus fixed to the wall at the head of the beds. She reacted to the heavy antiseptic smell which permeates hospitals with all the fear of a pheasant to the odour of a fox. She hugged herself and shivered as she walked over to the square window.

The sky was a clear, cold grey, sullied with clouds tattered as beggar's trousers. Light aircraft still buzzed between the clouds like flies. She stared sightlessly. She realized that she would have to talk to Hank. The Carringtons would arrive the following day and she would have no time alone with the love she must now abandon.

'Hank. I have to talk . . .'

The door to the ward flew open and a nurse bustled in. Efficiency hung like a neon sign over her head.

'Twenty-four-hour bed rest has been prescribed for the two of you plus these pills.'

'What are they?' queried Casey, looking at the plastic container suspiciously.

'Painkillers and something to give you a good night's rest. With no nightmares,' she added. 'Here are your gowns. Towels are in the bathroom. Toothbrushes and paste will be provided and added to your bill.'

There was a gentle knock on the door and a waiter appeared holding a pad and a menu.

'Your order for dinner, please,' he said.

Hank grinned at Casey as they placed their orders. 'I could get to like this treatment.'

'The catering is done by an outside firm. We pride ourselves on the standard of patient care here at Humana,' the ward sister said shortly.

'Of course, Sister,' smiled Casey.

'I'll be back after dinner to tuck you in and see that you both take your pills.' Her voice softened a little. By all accounts they had endured a tough day.

'Whew!' Hank breathed out as the door closed behind the crisp rustling skirts. 'I wouldn't like to be caught pinching her popcorn.'

'She would make you replace double the amount you took and still hit you with the empty box,' said Casey.

Like winter travellers crossing thin ice, knowing that once they stopped their static weight would break through the crust and they would not survive long in the sub-zero temperatures, Hank and Casey approached the subject of Dursley with extreme caution.

Once words were spoken, they would be irrevocable. Secretly Hank felt that the bear attack had given Dursley an unfair advantage in the unspoken 'battle' for Casey. He pitied anyone who had the misfortune to be near an *Ursus arctos horribilis*. They were terrifying creatures when angry. The mental scars inflicted by a bear attack remained with one long after the physical ones had faded.

A wounded man evoked sympathy. Hank was afraid that blood would bind Casey to Dursley tighter than love would tie her to him. He knew that he had to let her talk. She needed to gather her feelings and come to a decision.

Gently he lifted her up and sat her on the high narrow bed. She winced, but was silent. He placed white pillows behind her, attempting to make her comfortable. She reached out a hand and ran her fingers through the silkiness of his beard.

'Oh, Hank.' Her voice broke and tears swam in her dark eyes. 'How am I going to live without you?'

The dreadful chill of an Alaskan winter froze Hank. She had decided. She was going to marry Dursley.

Instinctively he did not protest or beg her to change her mind. Instead he turned away and fiddled with the knobs of the radio. Within minutes country and western music jigged happily around the room, dispelling the clinical coldness.

Keep the conversation light, his intuition cautioned him. She is still in shock and depressed. Make her laugh. Make her understand that she does not have to sacrifice her life because of an accident.

'Ticasuk. Do you realize what my future will be without you? You leave me with only two choices. One is to send my photograph and statistics to *Alaska Men* magazine. If I include a good-looking dog, I can expect at least three hundred letters from unhappy women. Up here men outnumber women eight to one.' He saw a spark of interest light Casey's face. 'In some places further north it goes up to thirty-five to one.'

He pulled as doleful a face as possible. 'Not many women come up to hunt moose or shoot bear. None of them will be my Ticasuk, so all the letters will remain unanswered. The second choice is to join the Eveny in the Soviet Arctic and herd reindeer.'

'Like Father Christmas, but you'll have to bleach your beard,' said Casey with a shadow of a smile.

Hank gave himself a silent 'high five' salute. He was succeeding. She was responding and smiling.

'The only clothing to keep one warm is reindeer fur. So not only will I look like a two-legged reindeer, I'll smell like one!'

'That should attract the Eveny ladies,' retorted Casey.

'I understand that most of the ladies remain in camp.'

'Wise decision,' interjected Casey. 'At seventy below zero who wants to be out looking after reindeer?'

'They only see their men once a year. Occasionally more often,' he amended.

'If that was practised in all Third World countries, their population explosion would be solved.'

'Ticasuk, you are wicked.'

Hank was delighted that she was showing an interest in the nonsense he was talking. He called up old, almost forgotten information about the Eveny reindeer herders. He wanted to keep Casey amused and keep her mind off Dursley and the Carringtons.

'At seventy degrees below zero your breath freezes instantly and is called a "star whisper" as it tinkles to the ground.'

'Oh, that's beautiful.'

'This is a beautiful land, Ticasuk,' he said softly. 'It is your land. Don't turn your back on it. Stay here where you belong.'

Casey dropped her head into her hands. Hank mentally kicked his fractured knee. How could he have been so stupid. For a few minutes he had her to himself. Then he threw it away. Fool, you deserve to be in *Alaska Men* with all the hopefuls, he chided himself.

There was a deferential knock on the door of the ward. It opened to the squeak of a wheeled trolley.

'Dinner is served.'

Casey brushed at her eyes and ran her fingers through her hair. To her surprise she found that she was hungry. She broke off a piece of sourdough and ran it round her plate mopping up the lemon sauce which masked the salmon. 'Better than that peanut sauce,' she commented.

Hank grinned. 'No one likes it, but in a lodge the most important person is the cook. She has to be kept happy, so everyone eats it, gags and says it's wonderful.'

Casey laughed. She found it difficult to be miserable in Hank's company. 'If Angela heard you, your diet would be dog biscuits, unflavoured ones.'

The dinner trays were no sooner cleared away when the sister bustled into the ward. She made Hank feel like a schoolboy thankful to be sitting quietly at his desk and not throwing spit balls when the teacher walked into the room.

'You first,' she said, helping Casey down from the bed. She scooped up the hospital gown from the end of the bed as she swept her into the bathroom.

Sensing what was about to happen to him, Hank grabbed his cotton gown, struggled out of his shirt and stuck his arms into the gown's sleeves. It felt cold and uncomfortable as it flapped around his legs. The casualty officer had pulled a large pair of drawstring pants over his brace. He kept them on, tightening the drawstring.

The sister plumped up Casey's pillows and watched her swallow the painkillers.

'Please may I leave the sleeping pill till later, Sister?' she pleaded. 'I promise that I will take it if I can't sleep.'

The sister nodded. She glanced across at Hank who was now lying flat and immobile beneath the tightly stretched hospital blankets.

'You need some help in the bathroom,' she teased, keeping her face expressionless.

'I'm fine, Sister. Goodnight, Sister. I won't need sleeping pills, not after today,' he said, pulling the sheets up under his chin.

The sister grinned at Casey with the special look women have between themselves when men think they have outwitted them. She closed the door quietly behind her.

'Remember those pink pills will chase away any nightmares,' she said.

Hank breathed a sigh of relief and opened his mouth to talk to Casey. She had her eyes closed and seemed to be drifting off to sleep. He turned his head so that he could look at her, but the events of the day soon closed his eyelids and he slept.

Casey opened her eyes as she heard the first gentle rumbles which he insisted were definitely not snores. Her ruse had worked.

She lay in the twilight which seemed to stretch to daybreak and she longed for the dark. Her mind, active as a salmon guarding its redd, darted from one subject to the other but they all ended up with the same major problem, her love and desire for Hank and her promise to marry Dursley.

She lay listening to the soft voices of the night staff at the nurses' station. Occasionally the wheels of a trolley squealed as it was hurried down the corridor. A door banging and a telephone ringing were all that broke the quiet of the night. At last darkness managed to oust the lingering light and Casey's brain gained the deep sleep it needed.

Casey awakened suddenly as if shaken. She lay rigid, straining her eyes to see if there was anyone in the room. As the queasiness abated, she eased herself out of the bed, wincing as her ribs protested at the movement. Suddenly the clinical ward seemed claustrophobic. She needed to breathe in the crisp night air or at least look outside through the sealed windows at a place which was not enclosed by walls and fear. She drew back the blinds and stood frozen. The heavens were alive. Greens and pinks drifted across the sky soft and delicate as the opening strains of a symphony then furled into deep S-bends and folded back on themselves in the crescendo, only to once again float and spin, playing on the wind as the symphony throbbed into silence.

Casey felt a sense of awe and deep serenity as she watched the heavens dance.

You have to believe in God if you live in this grandeur and beauty. She heard once again Hank's half-forgotten words. Now she realized what he meant. She felt the peace and stillness of spirit which pervaded her when she was in some great and ancient cathedral. Tears fanned her cheeks but they were tears of cleansing and she did not wipe them away.

'The aurora borealis,' whispered Hank, as he came up and put his arms around her. Casey leaned her head back against his chest and was silent. For the first time since their trip to Barrow she felt at peace. It was almost as if the magnificence and tenderness of the auroral display had spiritually strengthened her.

'The Inuit say it's the spirits of the dead holding torches so that they can hunt in the black of winter. Some believe it is the play of unborn babies.' Hank's voice was soft and gentle, as were his hands as they caressed her. 'Trapper Jack believes that if you whistle softly the curtains of light will approach you.'

Casey smiled. She was content and happy for the few hours they had before dawn awakened the hospital and brought the Carringtons.

'It seems to fill the sky,' she whispered, covering Hank's hands with hers. 'What do you believe it is?' she asked.

'I know what it is. It's energy released as visible light, due to an electric discharge in the ionosphere,' he answered. Then, sensing her incomprehension, he tried to simplify his explanation.

'Jetting towards us from the Sun is a gas of ionized particles called the solar wind. As the solar wind swings around the Earth it generates an electric current. The easiest way for the current to reach the Earth's surface is along force lines in our magnetic field which curve down in the polar regions.'

'Ahh,' said Casey.

'It's particles from the left flowing into the polar regions which cause the colours we see. But I like to think that it is the Eternal Power who created this Universe, showing us the magnitude of beauty he is capable of creating.'

'I like that,' said Casey. 'I also like the Inuit explanations. I prefer them to the scientific one.'

'So do I,' agreed Hank, and he kissed her gently behind her ear.

'It's so large,' said Casey, watching the delicate curtains of bleached pink and green unfurling across the sky. 'It touches the ground. Or is it like a rainbow, you never find where it touches?'

Hank kept his lips to her skin and murmured: 'It's hundreds of miles long and almost two hundred foot high. It never comes lower than about one hundred foot above the Earth.'

Casey shivered as Hank's tongue traced the outline of her ear.

'It appears to touch the Earth because we are not able to accurately judge the depth in space of objects of an unknown size, especially when they are moving, like the aurora.'

Hank's knee screamed in pain as he stood behind Casey. But the time they shared watching the aurora borealis was too precious to break. They stood joined together, bound in love as if in front of an altar, until the banners of light separated into patches, pale as new clouds, with the advent of dawn.

'Hank,' whispered Casey as she turned to face him. Her expression was calm and peaceful. He knew that she had reached a decision whilst watching the heavens dance. 'If you wait for me I swear that I will come back to Alaska and marry you.'

'But . . .'

Casey put her finger over his lips to quieten him. 'I must return to England with Dursley. As soon as he is well, I will break off our engagement and come to you.'

'Oh, Ticasuk, Ticasuk,' said Hank, and his voice broke. 'I am so afraid that once away from me they will change your mind.'

'I promise you that you will be the only person to change my mind. If you decide you no longer want to be married, or you find someone else, I will understand. But as long as you still want me I will come back to marry you.'

As the lovers impressed on their memories the feel, taste and smell of each other the sky lightened behind them heralding the end of their privacy.

A diffident knock on the door announced the arrival of breakfast and broke them apart.

Chapter Nineteen

PEG-LEG PETE stood on the pebbled beach hemming the front of his lodge. He dug his stick deep into the wet earth between the grey stones to steady himself from the gusting wind as it lifted his carefully plastered hair and exposed his pink scalp, swinging the wispy strands around his head like a tattered flag. He raised his hand, shading his eyes from the shimmering grey sky, as he tried to identify the float-plane sinking down to land on the choppy water.

'Idiot,' he muttered as he recognized the primrose-yellow plane with the enormous mosquito painted black and stark on its side. 'Only Saunders would be fool enough to land in these conditions.'

He was irritable. His plane and fishing party had not yet returned. He knew that his pilot would 'sit out' the weather if it turned misty or too windy to fly, and that would mean a group of cold and disgruntled clients and no repeat bookings for the following year.

The wind caught the yellow plane just as it was about to settle on the white caps. One wing dipped into the lake and Peg-leg smiled. Saunders was about to burn the gravy. His smile vanished as he watched the wing lift from the water and the plane steady itself. It rocked slowly towards the shore.

'Another lucky one,' he said grudgingly.

Peg-Leg scowled as he watched Kit swing down the steps, grasp the tail rope and wade towards him.

Not only had Saunders managed to save his 'float', he had

also brought his girl fishing guide along. Peg-Leg believed that fishing was a sport for men only. It infuriated him to see a woman guiding. When reports of the record trout she had put Dursley into reached him he went on a two-day drinking spree and destroyed a barabara. He was now awaiting a visit from the Katmai National Park and Reserve Officers, with some trepidation. He glared at Kit as she dragged the plane to the shore.

Sensing trouble, Stewart closed down the motors and left the plane ahead of the fishing party. Kit thankfully waded back to the plane to help the clients into the water and onto land. They were unwieldy in their thermal waders and boots.

'Off my water!' shouted Peg-leg, waving his stick at Stewart and almost overbalancing as a gust of wind hit him in the ribs. 'Get back to your tart Lodge where you belong. Out of—' He broke off in confusion as he recognized his own clients wading towards him.

'Sure,' said Stewart. 'OK, Kit, load the gear and guys back into the float. They can spend the night with us.'

Leroy huddled into his seat in the plane listening to the argument. He was not going to face that madman again.

'Come on,' urged Earl. 'Let's help Kit. She can't hoist that canvas bag ashore on her own.'

Leroy shook his head emphatically. He was not going to be anywhere near Peg-leg when he learned that Leroy had accidentally stuck his fishing knife into Peg-leg's rubber dinghy.

Leroy had been trying to help Kit deflate the dinghy and stuff it into its canvas bag. A rope had snaffled the top of the bag. Leroy slashed at the rope which gave way easily. The knife continued its downward path and sliced into the dinghy, easily removing the air valve.

'You're going to let a woman carry the can?' said Earl, trying to shame Leroy into helping him.

'She's bigger than me and probably stronger,' answered Leroy, tightening his seat-belt.

Peg-leg calmed down the moment he saw his clients obediently turn and follow Stewart back into the water.

'I didn't mean you guys,' he quickly amended. 'Come on. There is whisky and a fire waiting. We'll warm you inside and outside.' He laughed self-consciously, but no one joined in.

'OK,' said Stewart, 'that's probably as good an offer as you'll get today. We'll unpack your gear.'

'Enjoy the whisky,' called Kit as the party trudged to the lodge.

Peg-leg was so relieved that he offered to hold the rope and steady the plane while Kit unpacked the fishing-rods. Taking advantage of the situation, Earl strode up to him and dumped the canvas sack at his feet. 'Your dinghy. It got in the way of a knife. Needs some repairs.'

Peg-leg looked up at the man towering over him and merely nodded. He needed to speak to Stewart to find out where his plane and pilot were.

'Ornery son of a b—' he muttered as he hobbled to where Stewart was talking to Kit. He knew that he would have to apologize to Stewart before he could speak to him, but he was damned if he would do so with that woman listening.

Kit nodded in response to something Stewart said. She turned and plodded back to the plane, smiling her thanks to one of the fishermen who was now holding the rope restraining the plane.

Leroy watched as the waves chopped around her legs and splashed up to her waist. She had lost the rubber band around her pony-tail and her hair was as matted as a crow's nest. She was tired and cold. Shock was setting in and she wanted to be back in her cabin.

The thought of Hank in Anchorage worried her. What would happen to them if he was unable to complete the season? She needed to have him with her until the home testing pregnancy kit she had ordered arrived. She needed him to sleep beside her every night for the next few weeks.

She needed to assure him that the egg, which she was certain was already adhering to her endometrium and dividing into the thousands of complex cells it would need to become a baby, was fertilized by him. Fancifully she believed that she could feel it. She wondered whether she could persuade Stewart to let Hank do administrative work at the lodge for the remainder of the season; that way he could not deny paternity. She smiled, a weak smile.

The bear attack had softened Stewart. He was worried and distracted. She would probably never have a better opportunity. She made her decision as she was about to climb into the plane. Leroy shivered and pulled his cap lower over his eyes as the wind threatened to drag him from his seat.

'Is the heat out there too much for you?' asked Leroy, just as Kit was about to close the door and return to shore to confront Stewart about Hank's future at the lodge.

'Leroy, you are gross and a slug,' she said and slammed the door.

'Women!' muttered Leroy. 'My mother was right, bless her heart. "Never marry, my boy, for the only woman you can ever trust is your mother."'

He had meant his remark to Kit to be sympathetic. Now he watched as Stewart threw his hands in the air and shook his head. To his surprise, a few minutes later Stewart stuck his hands up high in the pockets of his wind-breaker and nodded. Kit had regained her usual jaunty stride as she waded back to the plane. She waited for Earl to settle into his seat then stuck her head in the doorway.

'But a nice slug,' she said.

'What was that all about?' asked Earl, easing the seat-belt to fit across his stomach.

'Just something between Kit and me,' leered Leroy.

'Dream on, 'cause that's all you'll ever do,' retorted Earl.

The waves clung to the floats like lovers about to be separated as the plane dipped and rose in the water. Lake Nonvianuk was showing her temperamental side. Stewart swore silently as he fought to lift the plane from the water.

Leroy clung to his seat as the wind sided with the water and tried to tip the floats under the waves. The plane creaked and groaned as it accepted the punches and blows of the wind. He eased his fishing cap from his head and placed it on his lap. He needed a receptacle in case he was unable to control his queasiness.

He closed his eyes and silently said his 'Hail Mary' as the plane seemed to bounce between the translucent grey of the sky and the deep leaden grey of the lake.

Stewart held the plane. He alternately cursed the weather and his bad luck that the bear had chosen to maul Dursley. Not only was he a good guy, but the attack would almost certainly mean a drop in what was becoming a lucrative and steady stream of fishermen from England. They would remain fishing with two-handed rods on their safe English rivers where grizzlies, moose and wolves were unknown.

The light, cold and grey as steel, made the loons look like rubber decoys as they quickly paddled to the safety of the bank. The float-plane circled overhead. They looked up at the huge yellow bird and the female screamed her chilling yet beautiful call. It echoed eerily across the water and was then lost in the thin spruce forests running down the lake.

Chapter Twenty

HOLLY FROWNED as she studied the operating slate for the day. She bit her lip as she ran her finger down the list, trying to find a break when she could leave the theatre for half an hour. She dearly wanted to see the Countess of Edbury. Matt Siebens had been adamant in his refusal to allow her to join him and the senior ward sister when he did his ward rounds and checked up on Dursley, and she knew that it was hopeless to argue with him. He may have held her in his arms and whispered words of love into her hair, but he had made it clear that she was not to presume on an old love affair.

'I've never seen a real live countess and I'm going to see this one,' she muttered quietly. 'All I need is an early break which will give me time to slip into the ward and see her son. It has to be after Matt has left or I'll be looking for a job as a nurse aide.'

The strident call of the telephone demanded her attention. She answered the phone and suddenly she smiled. If she left the theatre now, it would work.

The first operation of the day had been delayed due to the patient's adverse reaction to the pre-medication. She glanced at the watch pinned to the breast of her uniform. Matt should be finishing his rounds, she would be safe. Quickly she smoothed down her hair and straightened her uniform.

She left the theatre walking briskly and purposefully down the corridor. She wished to present a picture of a dedicated concern to the countess. Holly hurried past the Intensive Care Unit. Dursley had spent only one day under constant surveillance and was now in a private ward.

She paused as she heard raised voices from the small anteroom near the private wards. She grinned as she heard Matt's voice. It was cold and hard. He was obviously angry.

'Madam, your son has and will receive the same treatment as every other patient in our hospital and that is excellent, spelt in capital letters.'

'Our family dates back to—'

'I understand, madam. Please rest assured that because he is an earl he will not be penalized and given inferior treatment. The War of Independence ended animosity between England and the States a long time ago.'

'I am not accustomed to being spoken to in this manner. I will . . .'

'Your main concern should be your son's condition, not the tone of my voice nor the phrasing of my sentiments.'

Matt watched as the countess's shoulders slumped and her face crumpled. He relented only a little.

'Your son was brought in with a posterior parietal fracture. A compound depressed skull fracture,' he explained.

The countess paled and scrabbled in her handbag for a handkerchief.

'We performed a craniectomy—'

'Craniotomy,' corrected Dursley's uncle.

Matt scarcely paused in his explanation. 'Slivers of splinted bone were removed from the brain releasing the blood clot which had formed at the base of the injury.' He paused and looked at Dursley's uncle. 'The craniectomy was successful.'

'Will he be normal?' asked the countess.

'We can expect some spatial disorientation. It could last for a week or a month.'

Matt forestalled her next question. 'At the moment there is a lion under his bed.'

They all looked at him in total disbelief.

'When you go in to visit look under the bed. Assure him that the lion is still fast asleep. Only then sit down and talk. He will want you to do the same when you leave. Humour him. It will pass.'

Matt glanced at his watch, picked up his clipboard and turned to the door. 'He will probably walk with a slight limp at first. We will have him mobilized tomorrow.'

'But my son is seriously ill. How can he possibly be expected to walk so soon?' The countess twisted her handkerchief into a tight knot, wishing it was the callous American's neck between her hands. 'If it's a matter of money to keep the ward for him . . .'

Matt tensed and like an angry grizzly seemed to rear up over them. 'Money?' he snapped. 'No, madam. It's a matter of your son's health! Good day to you.' He resisted the urge to slam the door behind him.

So much for the politeness of the upper class, he thought. Not even a thank-you. He strode down the corridor with his head bowed, reliving the unpleasant interview with Dursley's mother and relatives. He did not notice Holly slip into one of the wards.

She smiled brightly at the nurse doing her morning rounds. 'Sorry, wrong ward,' she said. She could not leave the ward until she had given Matt sufficient time to leave the area. She strolled around admiring the flowers and greeting the patients.

The nurse stared at her for a moment, then returned to her duties. She was not going to be late and endure matron's wrath just because the theatre sister was acting strangely.

Holly peeped into the corridor. It was empty. Raised voices attracted her to the anteroom.

'Odious man.' The countess's voice carried clearly through the closed door. 'Imagine my poor boy living with a plate in his skull. Incompetence, that's what it is. Had the operation been done at home by a decent neurosurgeon from Queen's Square, instead of this overgrown, unpleasant, incompetent man . . .'

The door burst open and Holly walked in. The countess looked up in surprise.

'Hi,' said Holly, knowing that the familiar greeting usually annoyed the English. They disliked the American's casual use of their language. Her anger at hearing Matt termed incompetent burst through her restraint.

'Any of you guys seen Dr Siebens?' she asked. Before any of them could answer she continued speaking. All the devils of anger chased out caution and coloured her words.

'He digs into brains.' The countess gulped. 'He is a great guy. But when he's angry, strong men piddle and weak ones crawl into rabbit holes.' Holly gave no one a chance to answer.

'Tell the hunk that his theatre sister is looking for him. We have some more pulped brains to sort out today.'

She swung out of the room and paused outside the door.

'We must remove Dursley from this dreadful place and these dreadful people immediately,' she heard the countess say. 'I do wish he had listened to me. I've begged him for years not to go to these barbaric countries. But he will insist on hunting in that Third World Africa and now Alaska.'

'The States are hardly Third World,' interjected her brother unwisely.

'You call that man and that awful woman decent?' Her voice rose and Dursley's uncle set about calming her before they went in to see Dursley.

Holly smiled. The countess might have the most beautiful, unblemished skin, hair coiffured into an elegant French roll and the most stunning pearls Holly had never seen, but she was not going to denigrate Matt or the Humana Hospital.

She walked past the door to Dursley's room then turned back. She had better see the patient, it would give her an excuse for being away from the operating theatre. She knew that if Matt suspected she had been anywhere else he would check up on her movements. She certainly did not want him to know of her visit to the countess.

She opened the door gently. There was a soft murmur of voices from the ward. A petite woman with hair that Holly longed for, thick, straight and glossy, sat beside the bed holding Dursley's hand. Flanking her was a tall craggy-faced man who seemed to be thoroughly uncomfortable in the clinical ward.

Both men were tall and good looking, thought Holly, and her mind assessed their bodies. The patient with his little-boy looks aroused the maternal instinct, she decided, whilst the one with a beard and a scar under his eye recalled Mother's advice to keep your legs crossed.

Holly bent down and peered under the bed. 'The lion is fast asleep, sir. Looks as if he'll be like that all day.'

Dursley smiled his thanks while Casey and Hank looked at her in amazement.

'I'm Holly,' she said to Dursley. 'Your theatre sister. Dr Siebens did a magnificent job on your brain. He definitely saved your life. The man works miracles.'

'I met him this morning,' answered Dursley weakly. 'He's most impressive.'

'Right on. He's awesome.'

Holly eased the pillows beneath Dursley's head. Covered in bandages, it lay like a rounded field mushroom on the crisp cotton pillowslip.

'And you have an awesome brain, according to Dr Siebens,' she added as he winced. 'Dr Siebens says he can always tell when the brain he's operating on is well used and intelligent. Dummies have scrawny little convolutions in the brain. Yours are plump and great.'

'There has to be an easier way to find out if one has a good brain,' said Dursley.

Holly studied his face. 'You'll do,' she said, pleased that he was able to joke about the operation. 'I'm due in the theatre in ten minutes,' she added, seeing the time on his bedside clock. 'Just wanted to say hi and tell you that you're going to be fine.'

Dursley smiled his thanks and closed his eyes. He was still drowsy from the medication.

'Lions?' whispered Casey as she followed Holly to the door. 'Is he touched?' Holly frowned. 'I mean is he mad?'

'No, merely a little spatial disorientation,' replied Holly, repeating Matt's description to the countess. 'Pretend to see what he sees. It'll pass in a few weeks.'

'Thanks,' said Casey, relived to hear that Dursley's brain had not suffered any lasting damage. He had been asleep when she and Hank tiptoed into the ward, so they had not had to lock up the lion. Holly noticed her stiffen as the strident, demanding voice of Dursley's mother rang down the corridor.

'Good luck,' she said conspiratorially and squeezed Casey's arm.

Holly sighed as the theatre doors closed behind her. The Countess of Edbury had been disappointing. She had expected someone regal and elegant.

Like most Americans bereft of their own royal family, she followed the television coverage of the British royal family assiduously.

'Sister . . .' Matt's voice stopped her dreaming and she prepared herself for another long day in the theatre.

Chapter Twenty-one

CASEY BREATHED a sigh of relief as the British Airways Boeing gathered speed and lifted off the runway. Her breath misted an irregular circle on the plate-glass window of the Anchorage International Airport. Hank leaned forward and wrote *H. loves C.* across the patch.

Casey flushed and scrubbed at the patch with the sleeve of her anorak before a group of young backpackers sprawled on the carpet near them could comment.

'Casey.' She spun round, recognizing Earl's voice. Her neck and cheeks were still pink. She moved away from Hank's side, relieved that the tell-tale patch was no longer visible on the window.

'Where is Dursley?' asked Leroy, coming up behind Earl. He ducked as Earl lashed out at him for being tactless.

'We hoped to see him and say goodbye before our plane leaves.'

'He is still in Humana. You have missed his family by a few minutes,' answered Casey. 'They have returned to London. I will be going back with Dursley, plus a doctor to care for him on the flight. We hope to leave soon.'

Before Leroy could ask any embarrassing questions Hank intervened. 'Casey couldn't go back with the family now as the plane is fully booked. The doctor attending Casey will not allow her to travel in Economy. He insisted that she has a reclining seat for the journey.'

Earl nodded soberly. Stewart had kept them informed of the threesome's progress. 'We missed you,' he said.

'It gave me a rest. The bruises on my knees are now yellow,' said Leroy, keeping a watchout for Earl's foot.

'Yeah,' mocked Earl, 'dummy here can't upset Kit, so my foot hasn't had much exercise.'

Casey laughed. 'How is Kit?'

'She hasn't been the same since Stewart brought back a parcel for her the last time he was in King Salmon,' answered Earl.

'She's like a cat with cream on her whiskers,' added Leroy. 'Must have been some parcel. The girl is all smiles. Even kissed Earl goodbye.'

'Shut it,' growled Earl, but Leroy was ready. He slipped behind Casey and put his hands on her shoulders.

'You can't hit a lady, especially one with cracked ribs,' he said.

'How's the leg?' asked Earl, turning to Hank and changing the subject.

'Should be fine for next season. I'll be at the lodge as a desk jockey for the rest of this one.'

A metallic female voice, common to all airports, rang across the room calling passengers for the flight to Seattle to collect their boarding cards. Earl and Leroy hoisted their tote bags and shook hands with Casey and Hank. On his way to the check-in desk Earl suddenly turned around, strode back, bent down and kissed Casey. She stood on the tips of her toes and hugged him.

Hank and Casey watched as he joined Leroy. Leroy said something and grinned. Hank and Casey burst out laughing as Earl's sneaker caught Leroy on his knee.

'That yellow bruise will be purple again,' said Casey. She waved as the two men joined the queue and filed from the room.

As the door swung closed behind them she realized how fond she had become of the two men in the few days they had fished together.

'I'll miss them,' she said, 'both of them.'

'They made a great Tom and Jerry team, but they are good

guys,' Hank answered. He put his arm around her shoulders and guided her carefully to the front entrance of the building. 'Stewart tells me that they'll be back next year.'

The fresh wind caught them as they left the building and Casey staggered into Hank. Her bag caught his braced leg and he almost groaned out loud. Biting down on his lip he hailed a cab. He eased Casey into the back seat and gingerly climbed in beside her.

'What's wrong with the pair of you?' queried the driver. 'Been playing with bears?'

'Something like that,' answered Hank curtly, cutting off the conversation. The driver shook his head, peeled a stick of gum out of the wrapper, turned up both the heater and the radio. They jolted back to Anchorage at the prescribed fifty-five miles an hour.

Hank had arranged with Stewart to take the responsibility of putting Casey and Dursley on the flight to London once Matt Siebens decided Dursley could travel.

Stewart had thankfully headed back to the Lodge. He had joined the countess and her family for dinner. To Hank and Casey's amazement, he was silent throughout the meal. Occasionally he nodded, smiled or shook his head.

'Couldn't understand a damn word they were saying,' he later confided to Hank. 'Why don't they just talk English?'

Hank had grinned in sympathy. The first few years when he spent the Alaskan winters in England he had often wondered whether the English were talking English or some strange dialect. Without the time he had spent in London he doubted whether he could have understood the countess either.

Chapter Twenty-two

HANK CHECKED Casey's luggage as the bell-boy off-loaded it from the gilded baggage trolley. The boy's hand closed quickly around the tip and he left the corner suite with a knowing look at Hank. Hank pretended not to see or understand the look and closed the door quickly behind the bellboy.

He flung his cap onto the settee and ran his fingers through his cropped hair. It stood up spiky as a hedgehog.

'You look like a loo brush,' laughed Casey. 'But a nice one,' she added as he feigned shock. She turned back to face the expanse of glass which overlooked part of Cook Inlet and Knik Arm.

'Look!' she said excitedly as a funnel of water rose high in the air, and cascaded back into the sea in a shower of fine mist. 'Whales, Hank. Oh, how magnificent.'

'It's very lucky to see whales,' said Hank.

'Now you are beginning to sound like Trapper Jack.' Casey studied his face, but it was serious.

'Every good Inuit knows that,' he teased, then he was quiet. 'Up in Barrow in the old days they used a circle of stretched sealskin like a trampoline to toss a young girl up as high as possible to sight the whales.'

'I've heard of the blanket toss but I thought it was a routine used for tourists.'

'No,' said Hank. 'They have no hills or trees or multi-storeyed Captain Cook Hotels. In the old days they needed height to spot the belukhs or bowheads as they passed from the Bering Sea region and rounded Point Barrow.'

'To kill them,' said Casey, winding open the bottom of the window, hoping to have a clearer view of the whales blowing.

'But not for profit, Ticasuk. Chasing whales in open sealskin boats is not a sport. Inuits need and use every part of the whale. It is part of their very existence.'

'They were about to harvest these poor whales trapped in the sea ice a few years ago. Do you remember a Russian ice-breaker came in to smash a way through the ice for them?' said Casey.

'Documenting the plight of a small group of people or animals awakens the conscience of the world. They go crazy, spend millions and end up only putting a plaster on leprosy,' disagreed Hank softly.

'But those whales—' interjected Casey.

'They spend their lives cruising in these polar seas. Hundreds probably leave their migration too late, thick ice covers the sea so they're unable to break through and breathe and they die. The news media kicked the world into awareness, but it was the skill of the Inuit, not great ice-breakers which saved those whales. Remember that, my love.'

'Oh, yes,' said Casey. 'They cut breath holes in the ice and led them to open water, didn't they?'

Hank nuzzled into her neck, breathing in her perfume, wanting to smell and remember her for ever. 'They did, my little Ticasuk.' His grip tightened around her. 'What am I going to do without you?'

Casey put her arms around him, ignoring the pain spreading across her chest. 'Patience, Hank, that's what we'll both need.'

'*Quinuitug*,' he answered softly, lifting her hair from the nape of her neck and letting it fall back in a heavy swirl of ebony. 'The Inuit word for the deep patience practised in the Arctic,' he explained. 'Without that seemingly never-ending ability to sit motionless and wait, few would survive.'

'But we will,' answered Casey. 'Patience will be easy because we have our love.'

Hank rested his chin on her head. His eyes were troubled. Having met the Countess of Carrington he understood some of the pressures that Casey would have to face. He was afraid for her. Afraid that without him beside her, she would capitulate and accept marriage to Dursley.

As if reading his thoughts, Casey raised her hand and stroked his cheek.

'I'll never stop loving you. No matter how long it takes for Dursley to recover. I will come back and marry you, Hank Butler. That I swear.' Her eyes were warm and wet with tears as she turned to him.

'And I swear that I will wait for you, Ticasuk. The whales out there are our lucky omen.' Their lips met and for a short while happiness was theirs.

Neither heard the doorbell ring.

'Sorry, sir. I rang three times and then used the pass key,' said the young man, balancing a tray with an ice bucket on his shoulder.

The gold foil top of a bottle standing deep in the ice caught Hank's attention. He had forgotten that he had ordered king crab and champagne to be sent up to the suite. The expense would cut deep into his share of the tips left for the staff by the fishing clients.

Seeing Casey flush as she turned away from the waiter to stare out to sea, he knew that he would give everything he possessed if it could keep her with him.

Casey squealed as Hank cracked the crab's giant claws. She ducked as the juice sprayed across the table. The flesh was white and succulent.

Their mood lightened as they sipped the champagne. They watched the sea imitate the ever changing and subtle shades of the sky as the sun streaked and washed it in peach, gold and silver.

'We are so lucky,' said Casey, licking her fingers and pushing away her plate stacked high with cracked and empty red claws. 'We have found each other. Think of the millions of unhappy people searching for a love and always finding the wrong one.'

'Lucky we are,' grinned Hank. 'Do you realize that I have a battered knee? You have battered ribs, but between us we still have some parts in good working order!'

Casey looked at him in amazement, then burst into giggles. She had not felt this free and happy for days. The dreaded countess had left Anchorage. She had arranged for a doctor to accompany Dursley and Casey to London. Dursley was going to be fine.

Casey had committed herself to Hank and was determined to return as soon as possible. Any doubts or indecision had vanished along with the vapour trail of the Boeing.

'Let's try out the working parts,' she laughed and led the way into the bedroom.

A few hours later the waiter arrived to clear away the plates. He rang the bell again. There was no answer. He opened the door.

The soft cries of a woman singing her song of love greeted him. He felt his breathing quicken. He kicked himself mentally for accepting and offering to deliver the message slip from the bellboy whom he met in the lift.

Keeping his eyes averted from the open-plan bedroom which led from the sitting-room, he collected the empty glasses and plates as silently as he could. He was terrified that they would see him and believe he was a voyeur. He would drop the slip in the doorway as if it had been pushed under the door.

The hair prickled on his forearms as Casey's voice rose and hung trembling in the air. Sensing that with the climax he was about to be detected, he hurried from the suite not forgetting to put the slip of paper on the carpet. He closed the door with a soft click.

'Let's stay here for ever,' murmured Casey, nestling in the crook of Hank's arm.

'We could try. At least until tomorrow when we have to be at the hospital to have your ribs re-strapped and . . .' He stopped.

He did not want to think of her leaving the hospital and Anchorage with Dursley.

'Ribs?' said Casey, sensing why he had cut his sentence short. 'They have just been cured. I'm going to tell that young doctor that I've found a marvellous cure for cracked ribs.'

'You are perfect,' he said as he kissed the nape of her neck. Her skin was soft and damp and tasted slightly salty.

The lovers awakened to a room washed in apricot and ochre. Cook Inlet, like a mirror, reflected the beauty of the setting sun. Hank hated the soft rays which streamed into the room. They heralded the beginning of the short night. Darkenss would last but a few hours and a new day would dawn. A day when Casey returned to England.

He would no longer be able to touch her. His mind raced ahead and scanned the long months he would be without her. Despair, deep, dark and oppressive, tortured him. He tightened his arms around Casey. He laid his cheek on her full breasts, finding comfort in the rhythmic beat of her heart.

Casey, sensing his distress, pressed his ear deeper into her breasts and ran her hand gently over his hair, trying to comfort him.

She longed to hold this moment and use it when she was alone in England. But she knew that like a sepia photograph it would blur with time.

The dying sun caught the fountains of water spouted by the whales and changed them into glittering cascades of gold and silver. The water shot up high from the breath holes on the mammals' heads, burst into a million droplets and fell, short lived and breathtaking as fireworks.

It was a glorious display but one unseen by Hank and Casey. They lay entwined, murmuring endearments and planning for a future they still believed would be theirs.

The room was still dark when Hank heard the door creak as it was inched open. He kept his eyes closed. If he saw Casey, he knew that he would not let her leave. He had to love her enough to let her go.

As the door closed he pulled her pillow over his face and screamed his anguish into the soft down.

Casey paused in the corridor. She almost turned back to their room, thinking that Hank had called out to her. Casey held the slip of paper tightly in her hand. She would read it in the good light in the lift. They must have put it under the door when we were asleep, she thought. When all remained silent she pressed the square button for the elevator and slipped quickly into its brightly lit interior. The lift was crammed with a sleepy tour group and Casey stuffed the message slip into her pocket. She would read it later.

Hank held the pillow tightly to his face as if clinging to Casey. Her perfume clung with all the promise of a lover's kiss to the white cotton pillowslip. He sobbed his fear and longing for her into the pillow. When he became aware of the sodden cloth covering his eyes, he threw the pillow from him and it hit the wall with a dull thud. With the act came a voice from the past.

You have the power within you to gain what you want. You are the power. Believe in yourself. See what you want. Use your power and you will have your desire.

'Trapper Jack,' whispered Hank. He picked up the pillow again, inhaling the whisper of the elegant perfume Casey used. He placed the pillow neatly at the head of the bed. He swung his legs over the edge of the bed and groaned as the leg in the brace protested.

'I must contact Trapper Jack and confirm that I will be in Barrow this winter,' he muttered as he hobbled to the bathroom. He felt drained of emotion but calm, almost detached. He would visualize a future with Casey. It would happen.

The lift shuddered to a halt and Casey waited for the tour group to shuffle out. It was still far too early to leave for the airport. She had to settle all hospital and incidental expenses before leaving for London with Dursley.

The countess had lined up some of the city's most eminent specialists to check on the operation performed by Matt Siebens. The old lady had been a little stunned when her doctor in London not only knew of Dr Matt Siebens but spoke of him with great respect. Nevertheless she would not be happy until the further examinations and scans had been performed.

Casey quickly found her Gold Amex card and settled the hotel bill. She decided to dawdle over breakfast in the Pantry, the open restaurant downstairs, until it was time to drive out to Humana. She would settle the hospital account then leave for the airport.

As she pushed her waffles and maple syrup around in the yellow yolk which spilled from the fried eggs she imagined Hank upstairs. He was so close. All she had to do was go to him.

Suddenly she remembered the message slip in her pocket. As she read the words the room swam. She pushed her chair back, knocking it over, and ran down the stairs and out of the hotel. The waitress looked at the toppled chair. In her hand she held the bill. 'Take it to the desk,' said the girl at the till wearily. The waitress shook her head. The young lady did not seem the sort to have a free breakfast and run before paying the bill.

Casey did not allow herself to look back at the massive building as the taxi bumped its way out to the hospital. She murmured a silent farewell to Hank and a promise to return as soon as possible.

The words on the white slip burned into her. *Urgent. Please come to the Earl of Edbury's room as soon as possible. We need your help.*

Chapter Twenty-three

KIT SWEPT her freshly washed hair up into a top-knot on the crown of her head. She fastened it with a blue ribbon.

'For luck,' she whispered. 'It's going to be a boy.'

Hank was expected back at the lodge with the new party of clients that Stewart's pilot was collecting at King Salmon.

Kit fiddled with the bow. She licked her forefinger and dabbed her dark eyebrows into straight lines. She stared at herself in the small mirror on the door of the wall cabinet. 'Not bad,' she said and dabbed a little gloss on her well-shaped lips. She looked at the toilet. The plastic seat looked cold and uninviting. 'Still fifteen minutes before they are due to arrive . . .'

Quickly she slid the small window closed. Immediately the sharp wind was shut out. She scrabbled in her toilet bag and placed a small plastic disc beside the basin. She picked up a Styrofoam cup and gingerly sat on the seat. She shivered as her warm flesh retracted from the icy plastic.

'Come on. Only five drops,' she urged, pushing back the cuff of her thick plaid jacket to check the time. She knew how particular Stewart was about his staff waiting in the main lodge to greet all new arrivals.

She was very much in favour at the moment and was given his most important clients to guide. She wanted her status to remain unchanged, but she had been unable to resist doing one last pregnancy test before Hank arrived.

She grinned as the cup grew heavy. Her blonde hair swirled around the bow as she bent over the plastic disc.

'Five,' she said, as the last drop of urine dripped into the small indentation in the disc, which would confirm her pregnancy.

Her eyes narrowed, she drummed her fingertips on the plastic basin as both the result and control panels above the indentation remained clear.

Slowly a blue line appeared across the result panel and edged into the control section as well.

'There!' she said exultingly. 'A little Hank.' She took a final look at herself in the mirror and hurried from the room.

Now to tell Angela, she thought. By breakfast, everyone, plus Peg-leg across the lake, will know that I'm pregnant with Hank's child.

As she jogged up to the lodge she worked out the more serious implications of having a baby. Now that she was guiding, the idea of staying at home and changing nappies no longer pleased her. She totted up the months quickly on her fingers. 'Damn,' she swore. 'I won't be ready by May, when the lodge opens. If I'm not here Stewart will hire a guy to guide and I'll never get back in.

'June. I could just make it by June if Aunt Lily will look after the kid.'

Kit had a spinster aunt who was convinced that men were inferior creatures who had crept into creation by mistake. She adored children and had adopted one Chinese and two Thai babies.

'She'll love mine,' said Kit. 'It'll be the closest thing to a baby of her own that she'll ever have. I'll point out to the old bird that her genes are in its blood.'

'Talking to yourself, Kit? It often happens at the end of the season. That's when the strain tells.'

Kit looked up to find Stewart standing on the wooden deck outside the lodge. He leaned against the flagpole with his hands dug deep into his windbreaker. The handsome dark blue Alaskan flag, with its eight gold stars depicting the heavenly positions of the Great Bear and the North Star, lay straight on the wind, as did his pony-tail.

There will never be a better time, thought Kit. Tell him, and secure your job for next year.

She swallowed hard before talking. She feared Stewart's probable reaction. One has to play hardball for what one wants, she thought. She brushed away Hank's certain anger and embarrassment when she had to tell him that Stewart knew he was the unborn child's father.

'Stewart,' she said, 'I need to talk to you. It's great to find you alone.'

He gestured to one of the deck-chairs in silence. Experience had taught him that when his staff needed to have a personal talk, they usually wanted something. He sat in silence staring out across Lake Nonvianuk, waiting for Kit to begin. He found the silent wait usually unnerved his staff and halved their requests.

Stewart showed no reaction to Kit's story about her and Hank's deep love for each other and their plans to marry at the end of the season, but he allowed himself to raise an eyebrow at the news of the pregnancy. 'Does Hank know?'

'No. I've only found out myself, but he'll be thrilled. It's what we've always wanted.'

Stewart's other eyebrow joined the first. Hank had said nothing about marriage when he had recently offered him a guiding contract for the next two years. He shrugged silently and continued to watch the sun, which seemed to form sheets of Nilas on the shimmering waters of the lake. The surging waters seemed to ride these imaginary sheets of transparent thin ice, high up on each other, until they shattered into crystal shards and fell back onto the wavelets.

Stewart screwed up his eyes against the dance of light. Kit watched him anxiously, unaware of, and uninterested in, the beauty which captivated him. 'I'll be able to guide by June,' she said.

Stewart turned his back to the beauty of Nonvianuk and stared at her.

'This lodge has no place for babies,' he snapped. 'If you want to be a mother then your place is at home with your child.'

Kit thought quickly. It was no use appealing to him. His staff knew that he was unmoved by pleas.

She stood up and thrust her hands into the back of her jeans. She was taller than Stewart and now had the advantage of looking down on him. 'I want to be a guide,' she said, 'and a guide here at your lodge. I am good and the men accept me.'

Stewart could not fault her argument. He turned his attention back to the lake, while he sorted out this latest hitch to his fishing arrangements for the coming year.

'I have arranged for my aunt, down in Florida, to look after the kid while I'm guiding. I'll be able to be with it for the rest of the year,' lied Kit unashamedly.

She stared at Stewart, willing him to look at her. She had long discovered that most men are inherent cowards. They find it easy to be angry and say what they truly mean in letters or over telephones, preferably phones with answering machines attached, but face to face they need to be 'good guys', liked and admired.

Stewart looked at her and her dark brown eyes stared right through him. Damn kids and their hopping hormones. But she is right, he thought. The girl's a damn good guide and there's no harm in having a good looker to take the men out on the rivers.

'We'll try it for one season,' he capitulated. 'But you'll sign a contract forfeiting pay each time you fly off to Florida. You have to decide what you want to be, a guide or a mother. You can't be both.'

Can't I, hell! thought Kit happily. She had won the first round.

At the drone of the float-plane they both looked up. The pilot was circling the lodge, allowing the clients their first glimpse of the magnificent setting, exciting them for the week ahead. The staff trickled out, prepared to show enthusiasm and joy at the arrival of the newcomers.

'Second last lot,' said Bill as he strode out onto the deck, 'only one to go and the season is over.' He grinned at Stewart and to his surprise had the grin returned.

Watching someone else fly his plane made Stewart feel as helpless as a bald eagle with clipped wings. He longed for the freedom to roam the skies, but was bound to the lodge. He had taken Hank's place and was guiding, a job which he found arduous and tiring at his age. For once, he too, would welcome the end of the season. He was pleased that he had decided to close the season early. The fish had thinned out and the guides were having to work harder to find good trout.

He did not want his lodge to lose its reputation for showing the best trout, both in quantity and quality, so the buildings would be boarded up against prowling bears and moose during the winter months. He and most of the staff would move down south to the States.

Ginger, Angela's assistant in the kitchen, was to remain in Anchorage. Her idea of heaven, she confessed to Angela, was a State where men outnumbered women seven to one. Stewart had not renewed her contract for the following year and it did not surprise her. She was a good cook and enjoyed sharing the guides' beds. But she knew that she was a constant reminder to Stewart of his infidelity. Why he worried about the one night they spent together she could not understand: men were fun, they were there to be played with. He was the only one married one she had been with who showed any remorse and Ginger found it all very boring.

Just like a man, she thought. He does something that he is ashamed of and I'm the one to suffer. I don't get my contract renewed. She had not told anyone at the lodge about the night she had spent with him in Anchorage as she needed the job. But when she left at the end of the season, Angela would be the first to know. She was determined that not only would the staff know of his infidelity but also his grunts and groans during their love-making session. That'll take the mustard off his hot dog, she thought happily.

The staff studied the group as they walked along the gravel path. Kit immediately looked for Hank. He seemed to be putting a little weight on his leg, but the brace gave him a pronounced limp.

The clients were made welcome and taken to their cabins. The guides gathered around Hank eager for news of Dursley and Casey.

'Congratulations,' said Stewart, joining the group.

'Yeah, it's great being able to hobble,' smiled Hank, a little uncertainly.

Kit looked at Stewart appealingly. She put her hand on his arm. He relented.

'I mean for the success of Dursley's operation,' he said lamely.

'Yeah,' answered Hank looking from Kit's pale face to Stewart, as if seeking an explanation for the strange congratulatory welcome. 'I reckon the congratulations should go to Doc Siebens. He did a marvellous job on Dursley.'

At the mention of Matt Siebens, Hank was immediately inundated with questions from the guides about his own condition and Dursley's operation. Kit took the opportunity to slip into the kitchen with Angela, leaving Hank seated on a deck-chair with his leg resting on a bench.

The noise and confusion which always heralded new arrivals had died down and the lodge once again nestled into the deep stillness of Katmai. Hank hobbled to the office beside the lounge. It would now be his job to issue fishing licences and fill in dozens of forms.

He ached for Casey. He could smell the soft flowery Chanel perfume she used. He could still taste her breath. Her smile was deeply etched into his memory. The silk of her hair slid through his fingers.

He sighed as he sat down and drew a pile of papers towards himself. The door opened and he started as a soft voice said, 'Hank.'

For one glorious moment he thought it was Casey. He looked around to see Ginger leaning against a filing cabinet smiling at him. Ginger made him uncomfortable. He believed that in the mating game men should play the dominant role. He was unaccustomed to woman who made their desires clear and invited men into their beds.

'Congratulations,' she said, then added: 'Daddy.'

The words lanced Hank sharp as the barbs of a fish hook. He sat upright and banged his brace on the side of the desk. The pain flashing through his knee, plus his dislike of Ginger, hardened his words. Suddenly the memory of Kit straddling him was a cold douche to his anger. He realized that Kit must have told the girls that she was pregnant. 'Daddy!' he sneered. 'The first or the fourth?'

'Men!' exploded Ginger, thwarted in her desire to see Hank break down at the news. He had been the only guide not to share her bed and she had not forgiven the slight. 'It's all great fun until the game gets serious, then you want to sit on the sidelines.'

Hank deliberately turned his back on her and pretended to shuffle through the papers on the desk.

'This is what you'll be doing in future,' she taunted. 'A nice nine-to-five job in an office, then back home to wife and baby.'

Hank ignored her, though her words bit and smarted like a cloud of white-leg bugs. Ginger turned to leave the office, happy that she had been the one to break the news. She collided with Kit, whose thin lips and set face warned her to leave the room as soon as possible.

'Bitch,' hissed Kit. 'You knew I wanted to tell him.'

'It's OK,' laughed Ginger. 'New daddy is delighted with the news.'

'He is?' Kit's face softened and she squeezed Ginger's arm. 'Thanks. You're a pal.'

Kit stepped into the room, patting the blue bow on her top-knot. 'Hank,' she said softly. When he didn't answer she tiptoed up to the chair and kissed him gently on the nape of his bent head.

He swung around, lashing out at her. His arm caught the side of her neck. She reeled back staring at him in horror.

'I want no part of you or your lies,' he said. His words, soft and controlled, frightened her more than the smack had.

'But it's ours, Hank. We are going to have a baby.'

'You are.' He stared at her. She read only hatred and dislike in his eyes. 'You are despicable. I am going to marry Casey. To hell with you and your schemes. You knew there was nothing serious in our relationship. I will not be coerced into marriage. Go and find the kid's real father. I'm not the only one you've had.'

He spun his chair round to the desk, then suddenly swung back to her.

'Get your gear out of my room. I want nothing to do with you. I don't even want to hear your name!'

'But Hank!' Tears welled up in Kit's brown eyes. She scrubbed at them, angrily. Tears were a sign of weakness. Hank was the father and she would see that he accepted the responsibility.

'Crying may work with your other lovers, but not with me.'

'Crying may not, but a paternity test certainly will. You will accept this child, Hank Butler, even if I have to go to court.'

Her words chilled Hank. Fighting Kit was not going to work. How could he explain Kit's child to Casey? He wanted to scream at this woman who was threatening to ruin his life.

Hank knew Kit well enough to know that she would not bow to threats. She would fight back. He knew that she would not hesitate to involve Casey if her plans were thwarted.

Kit watched his fingers move away from the scar on his cheek. As he ran his fingers through his beard she knew that she had won.

Let her think that she has won this argument, thought Hank. Given time I can probably persuade her to have an abortion. She does not really want to settle down to family life. The girl is a born fisherman and an excellent guide. She has a great future in that field.

'Kit. I'm sorry,' he said, holding out his hand to her. 'It's just that Ginger shocked me with the news. Come and sit down. Let's discuss this.' Seeing her hesitate to touch the olive branch, he said, 'You know that I'll stand by you. I wouldn't leave you alone.'

Kit relaxed and sat in the wooden arm chair opposite him. It was going to work. She almost smiled.

'Our lives will of course change,' he continued. 'There will be no more of this nonsense of flying up to Alaska and round the world to guide and fish in exotic fishing spots. Home will be the four-letter-word from now on.'

He grinned inwardly as he saw her face fall and her fingers pluck at the fleece of her Patagonia jacket.

'A mother's place is at home with her child. I know you feel the same,' he added. 'I will try and find an office job, so that I can be home at six to play with baby and have supper.'

Kit started to look unhappy. This was not what she had envisaged at all.

'If I don't make enough money, I may have to fit in some guiding, probably up here. The pay and tips are good. You, fortunately, are a very capable woman and will manage fine without me for a few months.'

Kit coughed, but Hank continued talking, not allowing her to have a say.

'We will of course have another baby almost immediately. I believe in large families and all born close together. That way they make great playmates. Who knows, we may even have a baseball team of our own. The Butler Busters. Doesn't that sound great?'

Hank infused as much enthusiam into his voice as possible. The more enthusiastic he became about their future, the more nervous and unhappy Kit seemed. This was not turning out as she had envisaged at all. Suddenly she remembered the contract she had just wrested from Stewart.

She looked out of the small window framing the spruce trees running down to the lake. She would have to give up all of this beauty and freedom if she married Hank and gave her child Butler as a surname. She had not realized what strong opinions Hank held on families and children. She was certainly not a brood-mare and the thought of a large family nauseated her.

It was only since meeting Hank that a child had played any part in her future. One child was her ideal, preferably a boy whom she could take fishing.

Hank was still talking, painting fiendish pictures of a future full of dirty nappies, whining babies, night feeds, doctor's bills, school clothes and fees, perhaps a secondhand car and a bank loan for a downtown apartment.

'You do understand, Kit, that we'll have to tighten our belts. Any royalties from my book on Alaska will only come in once the book is in print. I still have at least a year's work to do on it. With babies . . . well.' He opened his hands and shrugged his shoulders. 'But we'll manage. Don't worry. Life will be fine, just different.' He coughed and fingered his scar. What he said now would either condemn him to a loveless marriage or set him free.

'I'm sorry that I was hard when I heard of your pregnancy, Kit. It was like being swiped by a grizzly.' He paused as he saw once again the blonde sow poised over Casey. He had to convince Kit that marriage to him was not at all desirable. Casey had both his word and his heart.

'I had no idea that you wanted to give up fishing and settle down to being a housewife with babies.'

'I don't . . .' Kit bit her lip. The words had escaped her control.

Hank was silent. He unclipped a card of trout flies from the shelf. Lovingly he stroked and examined the flies, all painstakingly tied to resemble the insects and gnats which hung over the rivers in summer. He flicked the black, brown, red and white feathers of the black gnat, Coho fly and polar shrimp, making the lures come alive.

He knew that each one would remind Kit of a particular river or a special fish. In her imagination she would see the trout twist into the air, water washing its spotted body. It would hang suspended in space for a few seconds, beautiful in silver and pink with its mouth wide open. She would watch, see it gulp the fly and spiral down into the river depths. She would feel its weight and strength as she struck and the hook lodged deep in its mouth.

Hank hoped that reliving the excitement would make her realize that her future lay in guiding, in striding down the virgin streams trying to outguess an old and wily rainbow, not in becoming a mother.

'Eighteen years,' he murmured, flipping at the tail feathers of a gnat. 'That's what we'll devote to each of our children. Eighteen years of our undivided attention.'

Kit gasped. She was horrified. Hank was becoming more and more excited at the prospect of devoting the rest of their lives to raising a horde of children.

Idiot, she chided herself. Why didn't you find out his views on children before you used him to be inseminated?

'It was a mistake,' she whispered. Hank did not even look up. He seemed to be totally engrossed in the card of flies. The silence suffocated her. She stood up and paced the small room.

'Hank. It was all a dreadful mistake,' she said loudly.

'Kit!' said Hank covering the fishing licences with the card. 'Do you mean to tell me that you don't want the baby? Because if you are saying that it was a mistake and you want an abortion, you must realize that I can't marry you.'

Kit nodded dumbly.

'You know how I feel about children. My wife must be prepared to be a proper mother and give herself totally to the care and upbringing of my children.'

'Hank, this is not a living baby. If it was born now the cells would just collapse. It can't breathe on its own, so it's not alive,' explained Kit.

Hank shook his head sorrowfully.

'Don't you see, Hank?' Kit continued, desperate to make him understand and help her. 'I believe that it is cruel and evil to bring a child which is unwanted into the world. We have thousands of abandoned babies waiting for adoption or being patched up in hospitals because they were abused.'

Her blue bow loosened as she shook her head in agitation. The long streamers hung down over her eyes. Angrily she jerked the ribbon from her hair. She stuffed it into her pocket and bent over Hank.

'You're right. One has to devote almost two decades to a child. We have no home, no capital and only temporary jobs. It would be cruel to allow these cells to split, re-form and grow into a baby.'

Hank pretended to consider her argument. 'Babies are wonderful little things and I could not be part of allowing an unwanted baby to be born.' He ran his fingers over his scar. 'As you say. It would be cruel, Kit.'

Nearly there, thought Hank with relief.

He's going to agree, thought Kit. 'The lodge is closing early. We could fly to Florida where they have a clinic. The procedure only takes a day.' Kit breathed in deeply. 'Would you come with me, please, Hank?'

Every fibre in his body screamed *no*. He wished to have nothing to do with Kit. Her duplicity appalled him. Yet common sense told him that if he wanted Casey, he must see the pregnancy ended so that she could not blackmail him in the future. He nodded without speaking.

'Thank you. Thanks so much. You're an awesome guy.'

'Fishing licences ready yet?'

The door opened and Stewart stood in the opening, scowling. 'OK, break it up, Mum and Dad. Hank, I need those papers. Now.'

'Two minutes. They are almost ready.' The door slammed.

'Please don't tell the others that I'm going to a clinic, Hank. I'll just say that I had a miscarriage. Please.'

Hank was scrawling across the necessary licences and nodded.

Kit watched him for a minute, then left the office, closing the door quietly behind her, almost afraid that the click would disturb him and make him regret his decision to accompany her to the clinic.

She felt like dancing along the pathway to the main lodge, where the clients were gathered waiting for their licences. Their disgruntled faces soon lightened as she told them a spurious story about monster rainbows which had stripped two fishermen down to the backing on their reels that morning.

'Had they been with our lodge, the fish would have been in long before the backing even showed!' she boasted. The men loved the banter and soon the room was once again noisy with deep voices and laughter.

'Pity she's decided to have babies,' said Stewart as Hank handed him the wad of licences.

'I've a feeling she'll be back fishing as usual,' answered Hank.

Stewart's bushy eyebrows rose and met over his nose.

'These home-testing kits are a pain, more mistakes made by them than by a first-time fisherman.'

Stewart smiled in relief as he looked around the full room. Kit was certainly an asset to his lodge and he would be happy to have her on his team in the new summer.

Chapter Twenty-four

THE ENGLISH night nurse looked at her watch. She had been hired from a private agency by the countess, who distrusted the hospital and staff. She was certain that only an English nurse could give her son the twenty-four-hour care she felt he needed. The agency omitted to inform the countess that the English nurse on their books was now more Alaskan than the Sourdoughs: she had been born within the sound of the Bow Bells but had nursed in Alaska for thirty years.

The nurse shook her head. She had sent the message to Miss Chargot at least two hours ago. Her training told her to contact the ward sister and tell her of Dursley's ravings, but the dollars pressed into her hand and the instructions from the overpowering countess had made her contact the woman she had promised to call if she was at all worried about her charge.

A soft but insistent knocking on the door of the ward took her from the side of her patient and into the corridor.

'Bears? Death? Brain haemorrhage? Marriage now?' Casey was stunned.

According to this night sister Dursley had started ranting and raving about three hours ago, pleading with the bear to kill him, calling for Casey, crying out to marry the woman he loved.

Casey felt a flush of guilt warm her face and neck. She and Hank had been making love three hours ago and promising to remain true to each other for all of eternity. She had not once thought of the man lying alone in the cold, dark ward.

'I must see him,' she said, pushing past the nurse and tiptoeing into the ward. She stopped short of Dursley's bed. The pale man covered in sweat, mumbling and throwing his arms around, was hardly recognizable.

'Bubbles, Casey,' he called as his arm hit and knocked over a glass of water on the table beside his bed.

Casey left the nurse and ran to Dursley. She put her arms around him and rested her cheek on his. He was hot and wet. A sour smell hung around him.

'It's all right, I'm here now,' she crooned. 'I'm with you, everything is going to be all right.'

'Love me, Bubbles,' he mumbled.

'I do, Dursley. I do.'

Fear trembled her voice as she held him close. The nurse had said that if her presence did not calm him then she would have to call the ward sister and alert Dr Siebens as his obvious distress could cause a haemorrhage in the brain. That would mean another operation or death.

'And they go quickly once the brain bleeds. I've seen them,' said the nurse, airing knowledge she did not possess.

Casey's voice seemed to calm Dursley and he opened his eyes. They were dull with pain and drugs but fixed on Casey. 'Marry me, Bubbles,' he whispered.

'But . . .' Casey began and Dursley immediately thrashed around twisting the bed sheet into a soggy rope.

'Now, Bubbles, now,' he pleaded.

Casey looked up at the nurse. She was terrified. She did not want Dursley to die.

'You have to calm him down,' said the nurse, her short, firm fingers on Dursley's wrist, feeling his pulse flutter and race like the heartbeat of a trapped bird.

'Marry. Marry,' cried Dursley.

'It's not possible. We are in a hospital,' answered Casey. Her tears of fear, and of compassion, joined the film of sweat gleaming on Dursley's face.

'It is,' said the nurse. 'There is a religious minister on this floor. He was called in to see a dying patient earlier this evening and he is still with the man. He could marry you here now,' urged the nurse. 'Then if that young man dies at least you will have given him his last wish. He loves you.'

Casey looked up at the nurse; and as instinctively as Dursley had acted when he rushed down the beach to draw the bear away from her, so Casey now acted to help the man to whom she owed her life.

'Call him,' she said, and listened to the high squeak of heels as the nurse hurried down the corridor.

'Dursley,' she whispered, putting her head beside his on the pillow. 'I will marry you now. A priest is coming.'

There was no reaction. She felt ill. She should have agreed immediately. Now it was too late. The wound had opened deep in his brain and blood was seeping out. Dursley would die. She squeezed her eyes closed.

'Please don't let him die,' she prayed. 'Please keep the blood away from his brain.' She eased herself carefully up on the bed beside Dursley and cuddled close to him, holding him to her, trying to give him strength from her body.

The trauma of parting from Hank and the shock of seeing the deterioration in Dursley had exhausted her. Her eyes closed and she slept with him in her arms.

It took some time for the nurse to convince the preacher that her patient could be dying and his only wish was to marry his fiancée who was now in the ward with him. The nurse was a spinster who read too many romantic novels. She saw herself as an angel of mercy, bringing joy to two people, one of whom was an earl. This was better than any of the stories she devoured so eagerly. His mother, the countess, would probably send her a handsome gift, preferably dollars, to mark her appreciation when she heard of the part she had played in arranging the marriage, thus saving her son. The nurse's eyes were bright with dreams as she pleaded with the minister.

Casey opened her eyes as she heard heavy and light foot steps together beating a tattoo on the tiled floor of the corridor leading to Dursley's ward.

Dursley moaned and groped for her hand. 'Marry?' he whispered.

The nurse felt Dursley's pulse and nodded. 'Wonderful. It's beating normally.'

Casey smiled at her, then turned to the preacher, a man from a religious sect unknown to her.

'Does he understand what is happening?' the preacher asked, looking at Dursley dubiously.

'Yes,' said Dursley opening his eyes.

Tears of relief washed Casey's face. Dursley would be all right. She would save him.

'Ring?' asked the preacher, looking at Casey.

'Ring?' echoed Casey, looking around the ward vaguely.

'Here. Take this.' The night nurse eased a cheap silver band from her finger and handed it to Casey. The new crisp dollars in her bag would doubtless buy her a better ring, perhaps even a gold-plated one.

'Do you take this man . . .' For a frightening moment Casey saw Hank standing beside her, proudly claiming her as his wife. She pushed the image away and concentrated on the preacher. She heard herself say, 'I do.'

With the two words the significance of the commitment she had made suddenly terrified her. Hank. Her family. Dursley's family. What had she done?

Saved the life of the man who saved yours. A little voice spoke to her. She listened and grew calm. It was done.

The preacher shook hands with Casey, blessed Dursley and hurried back to his friend, a member of his flock, lying in a ward at the far end of the corridor.

Casey sat beside Dursley until he fell into a calm, peaceful sleep. Both she and the night nurse breathed sighs of relief. Casey because Dursley was saved and was not going to die, his brain would not tear apart, and the night nurse because she would not have to explain to the sister-in-charge why she had not reported the deterioration in Dursley's condition immediately.

'Nurse,' said Casey, standing at the window with her back to the room, 'would you call in at the Captain Cook Hotel and drop off a note for a friend of mine? I want him to be first to know the good news,' she added, sensing the nurse's hesitation to agree. 'I know that you have had a long and tiring night but I'll pay for a cab to take you to the hotel and then to your home.'

She turned to face the nurse. 'Please. He is a very close friend of ours.'

The nurse nodded and hurried across to the nurses' station to find a pen and paper.

Casey watched as satin ribbons of cerise and pale lemon broke and lifted up the darkness. What could she say to Hank? How could she ever explain to him why she had left his bed and come to the hospital to marry Dursley?

> My darling – the promises I made to you will never change, no matter what happens to me in the time we are apart. You have my heart and my love for all time.

The paper became soggy as it soaked up her tears. The pen tore through it, leaving jagged holes.

Casey filled the page, trying to explain that she knew Dursley would release her from her vow once he was home and completely healed. Her heart fluttered and she felt queasy. Dursley might, but she had taken a solemn vow. Would her God forgive her and understand? Doggedly she wrote on. She poured out her love and fear of the predicament she was in to the one man she believed could understand her actions.

The nurse coughed. It was now light in the ward. She had enjoyed a tiring but exciting night. She wanted to go home to relive in the privacy of her small room the only adventure she would probably ever have in her lonely life.

Casey sighed and folded the paper. She scrawled *Mr Hank Butler* in large letters on the outside and handed it to the nurse. She crossed the room and took her place on the hard chair beside Dursley's bed to wait for the doctor to examine him and release him as fit to fly home. She felt empty. As drained of emotion as the vast Alaskan sky, now pale and colourless beyond the windows of the hospital. The new Countess of Edbury dropped her head on the edge of Dursley's bed. Her hair swung over her face and she slept beneath a shroud of black silk.

The nurse grandly called for a taxi. She bored the once garrulous driver with her endless and aimless chatter. He sighed with relief as he dropped her at the Captain Cook. He waited until the high doors swung closed behind her, then executed a tight circle and with tyres squealing he left both the hotel and his fare behind. Someone else could suffer her on the last leg of her journey, he decided. He was paid to be patient, but not that patient.

The nurse stared around her, trying to remember every small detail of the decor to impress her friends. She found her way to the desk and asked for Hank.

'Mr Butler checked out half an hour ago, miss. Is it important?' asked the girl behind the desk.

'No not, at all. Just a message to say friends of his are married.'

The girls eyes flicked back to her computer. 'I see. Well, if that is all ma'am.'

The nurse was a little cowed by both the woman and the soaring hotel bustling with tour groups. She hurried towards the glass doors with their ornately carved heavy wooden edges. As she passed the Pantry she crumpled up the note and dropped it into a bin at the foot of the steps.

A man waiting in the queue to be seated at a breakfast table flicked the long grey worm of ash from his cigar into the bin and the ashes fell like tears on Casey's letter.

Chapter Twenty-five

EDBURY HALL seemed to doze, contentedly as a cat, in the early winter sunshine. The woods glowed as the sunlight fingered the ochre, gold and russet leaves. Stray beams highlighted the thick carpet of fallen leaves. They rustled to the scratch and scurry of golden brown pheasants and grey rabbits. The estate lay dreaming and was beautiful. Casey pressed her hot cheeks to the panes of glass in the high drawing-room windows. Tears trickled slowly as snails' tracks down the glass.

'Casey, Casey, please don't do this.'

Dursley eased himself from the leather chair in front of the fireplace and limped across to her. He placed his hands on her shoulders. His fingers sank into the soft cashmere of her sweater. Casey turned away from the window, framing the gentle beauty of the English countryside, and buried her face in his chest.

'Dursley, I do love you, but . . .' She choked and he waited until she regained her breath. 'If I stay with you, a part of me would always long for Hank. Eventually I would make both of us unhappy.' She looked up at him. Her tear-streaked face and racking sobs tore at his heart. He kissed her lightly on her pink-tipped nose.

'You know that I would take you on any terms I could get you, Casey. I also know why you went through the marriage ceremony in the hospital. I appreciate the love and concern for me which made you do it. But after our visit to Alaska I know that keeping you to your vows and remarrying in a large London ceremony would be caging an eagle.' He paused and stroked her hair, burnished to a high gloss by the sun pushing through the paned window.

Casey tightened her arms around his neck. She knew that life on this peaceful estate would be wonderful. But she now had the wild beauty of Alaska injected into her veins. Like the silver salmon battling to return to the spot where it had been spawned she had to return to the land which had been home to her ancestors. She had to see again Nanuq, on the terrifying splendour of the Arctic ice-pack. She needed to hear a deep, authoritative voice call her Ticasuk.

Her sense of duty told her that she was behaving badly and was breaking a solemn vow and promise. She was hurting a man who did not deserve such callous treatment. He would probably live on drugs for the rest of his life to calm a brain irritated by scar tissue. She should stay at Edbury Hall and marry Dursley in public as planned. It was her duty to repay the man who had saved her life and would now suffer for his actions.

But her love for Hank and need for the great silent spaces of Alsaka pulled her inexorably away from the security and love of her family and friends.

'Why don't you use the phone in the library?' asked Dursley rocking her gently in his arms. 'It's private. I'll wait here for you.'

'Oh, Dursley.' Casey now sobbed out loud. 'I don't deserve you.'

'I know, as the Yanks say, I'm one awesome guy,' he answered with a laugh. He was relieved to see a watery smile break through her tears.

'Awesome you are,' she agreed. 'Also kinda neat.'

Dursley smiled until she left the room. A large part of his life would end when Casey went to Alaska.

'Damn you, Bob Franshaw,' he muttered as the huge double doors closed behind Casey. 'Why didn't you suggest fishing in Tasmania or New Zealand? She could find no Eskimo roots there.'

He stood looking out at the well-clipped lawns leading down to the golden woods. Suddenly harsh honking attracted his attention. The sky was laced by flighting ducks. They flew with their long necks outstretched, each seemingly intent on overtaking the other and leading the formation. Dursley watched them until they disappeared over the copse in the valley. He turned from the high windows and limped slowly back to the button-back chair in front of the fire. He lifted his leg onto the petitpoint footstool and closed his eyes. As his eyes closed so the grizzly reappeared and he relived once again the day of his attack. He whimpered softly and twisted in his chair.

The leather chair standing tall and proud behind the great oak desk creaked as Casey sat down. She allowed herself a few minutes to savour the magnificence of the library.

Dursley's great-grandfather believed that books were as necessary to life as breathing. Both were needed to exist. He had spent his life time collecting and reading the great philosophers, travellers and biographers. Their works now rested on waxed oak shelves which ran from floor to ceiling around the three walls of the room. The fourth wall was broken by two enormous windows through which one could step out into a walled garden.

Between the windows were paintings of Africa, meticulous in detail, by Thomas Baines. But the one which always attracted Casey was of great turquoise cliffs seemingly suspended in space, where glaciers had calved into the sea. Whaling ships sailed across the canvas awash in the wake of enormous whales and sled teams dragged pelts and raw meat across the ice.

The search for the North-West Passage attracted not only men like Captain Cook, but also Dursley's great-grandfather. He had confined his romanticism to books and paintings on the unknown Arctic wastelands.

As Casey stared at the painting of the Arctic, she remembered something written by Edmund Carpenter. Dursley had quoted it to her when he first proposed a fishing trip to Alaska. The words had made an impression and now she recalled them clearly. *It is simply there – untouched, silent and complete. It is very lonely, yet the absence of all human traces gives you the feeling you understand this land and can take your place in it.*

She felt comforted by the words and repeated them softly as she paged through her diary, looking for the number at King Salmon which could be used to radio through to Black Legs Lodge on Lake Nonvianuk.

She dialled the number. Nervously she drummed her fingers on the desk as she waited, praying that they had the radio switched on at the Lodge.

Casey kept her eyes fixed on the Arctic painting as if it would bring her luck as the phone continued to ring unanswered. She scrabbled through her diary to check the date on which the lodge was due to close. The air waves crackled with noise but no voice broke into the squawks and screeches.

'Hank,' she whispered. 'Hear me. I know that you are on office duty.' She gulped, and looked out of the window at the gardeners pruning and preparing the plants in the walled garden for winter. The colourful annuals had been dug up. The tumbling yellow and white butterflies had gone. The garden was plain and grey, waiting for spring.

'Please, Hank, please.'

Casey was about to replace the receiver and try to contact someone at Peg-leg's Place when a female voice, indistinct and broken, came across the line. It was Ginger. Casey was almost in tears of relief. She had managed to raise the lodge and would soon be able to speak to Hank.

'Hank?' came back to her metallic and distorted.

'I leave here tomorrow. I stayed because I'm not going to the Lower Forty-Eight, I'm spending the winter up here.'

Casey kicked at the desk in frustration. She didn't care what Ginger was doing. The line was breaking up. Ginger's voice was becoming more indistinct. She had to speak to Hank.

'Hank!' she shouted. 'It's urgent. Get Hank.'

'Can't. The lodge closed early. Everyone has left.'

'Number or his address?' screamed Casey.

The gardeners looked up at the library windows and then returned to their work. What went on in the big house was no business of theirs.

The line crackled and suddenly cleared.

'Hank has left with Kit,' Ginger said. 'Their baby is due quite soon,' she lied. 'I think they've gone to her family, but I have no address.'

Silence deep and pregnant hung suspended on the air waves.

'Casey? Can you hear me, Casey?' Ginger continued trying to get a reply for a few minutes then she shrugged and switched off the radio receiver. She had plans for the afternoon, with the handyman Stewart had left to finish closing up the lodge. Those plans certainly did not include looking up telephone numbers and addresses for some hysterical client in England.

Casey's fingers ached before she dropped the phone. She sat cold and unfeeling as the great glacier in the painting. She concentrated on massaging her fingers, not allowing herself to think.

The squealing of wheelbarrows beneath the library windows brought Casey out of her trance of disbelief and pain. The gardeners were packing up their equipment and going home. She would have to face Dursley. She knew that once she told him the news, he would renew the pressure for their society wedding to go ahead as planned.

Hank, her heart screamed. Did you not understand my message? Why did you not trust me? I swore I'd return. You know the marriage was only to save Dursley.

She walked across to the large painting and ran her fingers lightly over the sled dogs and the snow. The feel of the oil paint seemed to soothe her. She started as the door opened and Dursley entered the library.

'Successful?' he asked as he came towards her.

Casey nodded. Suddenly she knew what to do. She hated lying to Dursley but if he knew that Hank had fathered a child he would not let her leave his side.

'I'm leaving for Anchorage on the next flight.'

Dursley paled. He had hoped that the inevitable could be delayed. He slumped down into the chair she had just vacated.

'Bubbles?' Casey turned at the gentleness in his voice. 'I will always be here for you. If things don't work out.' He held up his hand to stop her protestations. 'Everyone needs a friend. Let me be yours. If after a year or two you find that Alaska has been a mistake, Edbury Hall is here for you.'

Casey put her arms around him. 'I wish that I could marry you,' she whispered.

Their lips met in a long, tender kiss which sealed his love and her friendship. They did not hear the library doors open.

'Now, now. Dursley, you know I dislike these public displays of affection. In my day . . .'

Dursley closed his ears to his mother's monologue on modern-day manners.

'Isn't it time for tea?' he asked. The question successfully diverted her attention to the maid, who was late with the tea tray, and the footman, who had not stoked up the fire.

'Since I have been occupied with your wedding plans, the staff have become quite lax in their duties,' his mother complained. The impatient ringing of a bell brought the tea and the fire was stoked up and crackling in the great brass grate.

Dursley heaped a spoonful of clotted cream onto his scone and bit into it with relish. A white crescent was left pasted to his upper lip.

'You will have time to tighten up the discipline again,' he said. 'I am not going to marry Casey.'

The delicate Limoges cup and saucer trembled in his mother's hand. She placed it carefully on the polished mahogany tea table before replying.

'Would you repeat that, Dursley?' she ordered, her words grating and cold.

'Casey Chargot has released me from my offer to marry her.' Casey merely nodded, deeming it wise to remain silent. 'She will be leaving London on an extended visit to Alaska. I will of course, meet all costs.'

'You will?' hissed the countess. 'You cad. I am thankful that dear pater is not here to hear this. How can you bring such shame to your family? No one in our family has ever reneged on a contract.'

Dursley was relieved that he had acceded to Casey's wish to keep the hospital marriage a secret from the family. His mother would never have forgiven them.

Then, to Dursley's surprise and Casey's dismay, the countess burst into tears. Dursley had never seen his mother cry. Not even at his father's funeral. She had always been the strong one in the family.

He was immediately contrite. He could stand up to his mother when she was strong and arrogant, but he could not see her weep.

'Mother, dear. It is better this way. A lot has changed since the bear attack. I find that I'm not ready to accept the responsibilities of marriage. I need time to heal mentally.'

She dabbed at her eyes with a lace-trimmed handkerchief. She had grown quite fond of Casey. Her mind immediately tested the future. This would mean that she could line up some girls from good 'old' familes for her son. She was certain that he would soon be ready for marriage.

Casey looked at Dursley with love and admiration. He had accepted the blame and given her the perfect excuse to return to Alaska. He glanced at Casey, gave her a quick wink and continued talking to his mother.

'Casey,' said the countess, suddenly finding a deep affection for the girl, now that she was leaving. 'You will always be welcome in my home. If you should ever need anything . . .' Her voice tailed off as Casey smiled at her.

'Thank you, Lady Edbury. I accept that. You have a very special son. The girl who marries him will be fortunate. I'm really sorry that it will not be me.'

The countess nodded, took a sip of her now lukewarm tea

and excused herself, allowing Casey the honour of a kiss on the cheek. She had phone calls to make. It would take days to alert all her friends and cancel the wedding plans.

'You *are* a very special man, Dursley. Thank you for doing that,' said Casey, as the heavy library doors closed behind the countess.

'I love you, Bubbles,' he said. 'That love will always be there for you.'

Casey tried to smile at him but her lips quivered.

'Now don't you cry on me as well,' he teased. 'One crying woman is enough to cope with for the day.'

She picked up a piece of shortbread and pretended to nibble at it to compose herself. Why can't I stay here and marry you, Dursley? she thought, as she flicked the sugar from the plaid skirt. Without Hank there is nothing left in Alaska, and I have lost him.

She rejected the thought as it crept into her mind. She knew that she had no good reason to return to Alaska. In her despair she was running to where she had once found love. She knew too that only if she saw Hank and Kit together, or Hank told her that Kit was having his baby, would she finally believe that she had lost him.

Like everything in life which is too terrible to contemplate, she pushed away the image of Hank as a father. She tucked the thought deep into recesses seldom used in her mind. It was the only way she knew of clinging to sanity.

Dursley and Casey sat quietly in front of the fire listening to the crack and hiss as flames ate into the walnut logs from trees on the estate which had crumbled with age.

They faced each other silent and as emotionally drained as a couple in the aftermath of a bitter argument. The maid entered and drew the curtains closing out the damp English twilight.

'Sir, madam wishes me to tell you that the car is at the front to take Miss Chargot back to London.' Dursley merely nodded his dismissal.

Now that the time had arrived to leave, Casey found that she wanted to cling to Dursley, to stay with what was familiar.

Suddenly she was afraid of what she would find in Alaska. Her decision to rush off and find Hank seemed madness.

Dursley ran his fingers through his tousled hair and struggled to his feet. He held out his arms and Casey went to him. For a moment she clung to him, burying her face in the rough wool of his sweater.

She pulled away and fixed a bright smile onto her lips.

'I will never forget you, Dursley. You will always be one of the happiest memories of my life.' She fought to control her tears. She would not add weeping to their parting.

'You will always be a part of me, Bubbles.'

The footman appeared as if on cue and held open the library door. Dursley kissed Casey tenderly. She turned and walked quickly from the room without looking back. The worst part of her decision was over. The parting with Dursley. Now she was alone and faced the formidable task of finding Hank somewhere in the States.

Dursley's cry was one of silence as he heard the heavy brass door handle click into place as the doors closed. In a way he understood Casey's need to return to Hank and the silence which is part of the wild beauty of Alaska.

Chapter Twenty-six

CASEY SAT at the small round breakfast table in her room at the Captain Cook Hotel.

The pencil in her mouth was gnawed down to the lead and it tasted strangely metallic as she rolled it around with her tongue. The table was strewn with timetables and scraps of paper black with telephone numbers. She stared out at the panoramic view of Cook Inlet, but for once it gave her no pleasure. She had been in Anchorage for two weeks and was no closer to tracing Hank than when she arrived.

He seemed to have left only three contact addresses at the hotel and airlines. One was the fishing lodge, one a postal address in King Salmon and the other was the flat he used in London. She had even contacted the ski resorts where he mentioned he occasionally instructed in winter. They had no new address for him.

'These guys move around. They fish up North summer, then fish down South or ski winter. Not even their families seem to know where to contact them.'

In desperation she had then decided to contact Stewart Saunders at his home in Idaho, but the only address he had for Hank was the one he used when he stayed in London, doing research in the British Library on the early fur trade in Alaska.

Stewart had confirmed that Kit was pregnant and had left with Hank for Florida but he did not have an address. He had seemed surprised at Casey's lame explanation for trying to trace the couple. 'You want to give them a christening present? But you have no address to which to send the gift!' He had not noticed any particular friendship between Kit and Casey.

Suddenly he remembered a letter lying at the bottom of the sack of post which his pilot had taken to King Salmon. It had been addressed to Casey Chargot and was in Hank's handwriting. The pilot had returned to the lodge with the unposted letter and Stewart had put it on his desk intending to post it when the lodge closed. It was still there. He made a quick decision. It would be wise to forget about the letter. Casey was engaged to Dursley and he wanted no scandal with his staff.

Casey received the impression that Stewart did not seem to know or care when the baby was due to be born. 'One can never tell with these tall, slim kids. She could be one, or seven months pregnant. But she has a contract to guide at the lodge again this summer.'

Casey had replaced the receiver. The news was true. Hank and Kit were together. Hank must have misunderstood the message she left with the night sister, or was so hurt and angry that he went to Kit.

No. I will not believe that. Not Hank, she shook her head violently and tears flew with her hair. She called the Airways to book a seat back to London but as a voice answered she replaced the phone. She chewed at the pencil in her mouth, flaking pieces of cream and brown paint on her lips.

She toyed with the idea of flying to Florida, but good sense prevailed. She recognized the futility of wandering round the streets hoping to bump into Hank or Kit in a city now becoming as well known for its crime rate as for its beaches. She sighed as she pushed the papers around the table.

'Accept it,' she said to herself. 'Kit is pregnant. Hank is the father. You no longer are a part of his future. If you were, he would have left a message for you, or written. He and Kit have gone away together, probably to marry, so that the baby is not born a bastard.' She smashed her fist into the table scattering the papers and then sucked the pain from her knuckles. 'Who was the idiot who said, "It is better to have loved and lost / Than never to have loved at all'? He was obviously a masochist. Who needs this pain?' She put her head down on the table and the hair which Hank had delighted in covered the pages in a black satin cloth.

As she lay, her face hidden by the shroud of thick hair, Casey remembered the poignant story Hank had told her of a sudden snow squall which had iced up a lake where a pair of loons were nesting. As they cannot walk on land and need water to take off for flight, the female had paddled round ceaselessly and frantically in a large circle, trying to keep an area clear of ice so that the male could land with food for the chicks. Eventually the ice pressed in on the patch of clear water and they were forced to give up their efforts to save their young.

Casey felt as if she was a loon swimming in circles and doomed to failure in her efforts to find Hank. As the day faded, there were no tears left, only fear. The Inuit blood which still flowed in the veins of this modern-day Ticasuk taught her the fear that every Inuit lives with, the fear that an old shaman meant when he replied to a question by an Arctic researcher: 'We do not believe. We fear.'

For the Inuit it is the fear of the darkness and violence of nature. For Casey it was the fear that she would never see her lover again. The fear that a major part of her would always be lifeless and alone.

She remained lying across the table, defeated and dejected, until the ache in her neck and shoulder muscles forced her to sit up. She stretched and felt the shadow of a remembered pain in her ribs.

She crossed the room with the stiff, dragging steps of an old woman. She lifted the heavy telephone directory. It lay like a lodestone in her small hands.

The slip of paper marking the British Airways number fell to the floor as she opened the book. 'If they have a seat on the next flight to London, it'll mean that I must forget Hank and Alaska,' she said as she dialled the number. She listened to a disembodied voice asking her to wait her turn, as the lines were busy. The repetitive music which followed the announcement did little to soothe her.

A whale, one of the pod of Belukhas which wintered in Cook Inlet, surfaced to breathe. As the silver water shot high into the air, a dry sob escaped her lips.

'Hank,' she agonized, 'where are you? I don't want a life without you. Why have you not written?'

'May I help you, ma'am?'

Casey started and took a few seconds to gather her thoughts.

'Ma'am?'

'Yes, please. I want a seat to London.' She crossed her fingers as the airways computer spewed out the necessary information.

'Which class, ma'am?'

'First, please, and non-smoking.' She screwed up her eyes.

Let it be fully booked, she thought.

'Certainly, ma'am. Aisle or window seat?'

She felt like crying. Luck was not going to be with her.

'Window,' she said quietly.

She made a note of the departure and check-in times and listlessly dropped the receiver back onto the table, then moved around the room, dropping clothes into her suitcase carelessly. Usually she folded and packed everything very neatly.

Hank had teased her saying that it must be her Inuit genes which made her hoard and pack almost empty jars and tubes of cosmetics, piles of brochures and odd mementoes which she would never use or look at again. She had retaliated with typical Inuit logic saying that everything had a value and one never knew when these things would be useful.

Despondency hung heavy as an aura of deep mourning around her as she sat in the back of the rusted maroon taxi on the way to Anchorage Airport the following day. She barely glanced at the remaining gulls, geese and terns on the lakes around the international airport. She pulled the Quivuit scarf tighter around her neck. The wool from the Arctic musk ox warmed her and she closed her eyes.

The driver sighed. He enjoyed talking, it broke the boredom of his day, but this passenger was a silent one. He studied her surreptitiously in the mirror. Silent but good looking, he decided.

Chapter Twenty-seven

HANK SLUNG the green and black tote bag over his shoulder and hurried down the long walkway in Seattle Airport. He ignored the shops with their tempting duty-free items. He was on stand-by for the next flight to Anchorage. It seemed to him as if the whole population of Greater Seattle was in the airport, all intent on impeding him.

He moved as fast as his leg would allow. It was out of the brace, but running still reminded him of the injury.

'Watch it! Are you trying to catch a plane?' said an airport official as Hank bumped into him.

'Something like that,' grinned Hank.

As he approached the check-in counter his limp became more pronounced. The girl showed concern and by the time Hank had told her the story of the bear attack he was assured of a place on the flight.

The queue shuffled forward slowly to board the plane and Hank wondered whether Casey had received the letter he left to be posted in King Salmon.

He had decided to tell her the truth about how Kit managed to fall pregnant. He had written on into the night, covering page after page with the story of the abortion which was to be performed in a clinic in Florida. He explained that he was accompanying Kit to the clinic and then would leave her in Miami where she was planning to spend the winter with one of her sisters.

He tried to put onto paper all his guilt over Kit and his overwhelming love for Casey. Hank ended the letter by reminding her that he would be up in Barrow with Trapper Jack for the winter. He begged her to join him. He painted a world of dark polar beauty where they would not see the sun for seventy days. A time spent with Trapper Jack learning the old customs and culture of the northern Inuit.

He described how they would hunt and fish on the landfast ice. Hank tried to entice her to a world few outsiders knew. A place where eternity had meaning. *In Barrow, we will have time, time to be alone with our love*, he wrote.

The impassioned letter, unread and useless, now lay under a file on a desk. It would not be found until the following spring.

He disembarked from the Seattle flight and walked slowly into the international airport at Anchorage. There had been no reply at any of the addresses he had given Casey in his letter. He refused to believe that the silence meant she would not forgive or understand.

He knew that he would find her in Barrow. She would have booked into their room at the hotel and would be waiting for him. He had to cling to that idea. It was all the future that he had or wanted. A short while later he walked out of the airport shaking his head. The flight to Barrow was delayed.

In Alaska, airway schedules, like the life of the Arctic Inuit, is governed by the weather. Departure and arrival times of aircraft look good in schedule books, but coastal fogs, snow squalls and raging gales take little note of the neat dates and times. Flying in the Arctic means waiting.

Hank decided not to spend the time lounging around the airport. It was an aimless occupation which always left him feeling irritable and uneasy. The thought of booking a day room in the Captain Cook, having a work out in the downstairs gym and a hot shower, followed by sausages, eggs and sourdough in the Pantry, seemed far more attractive.

He slung his bag onto the back seat of the cab. Sitting sideways he stretched out his leg beside the bag and gave a sigh of relief.

'Accident?' asked the driver.

'Yeah, you could say so,' answered Hank. Soon they were deep in conversation on the habits of bears, which in turn led to moose and caribou.

'That guy is in a hurry,' remarked Hank as a rusted maroon taxi rocked past them.

'Probably has to catch the British Airways flight. It leaves about eleven-thirty, I think.'

Hank merely nodded and the driver continued with his story of a moose hunt where a grizzly stole the dead moose from the hunters. It only ended when they drew up outside the hotel.

'A single for the day?' said the girl at the check-in desk dubiously. 'I don't think we have one, sir.' She punched at a keyboard and the computer dutifully answered her questions.

A young man leaned over her shoulder. Hank watched her edge away from him.

One of the guys who can't keep his hands to himself, thought Hank.

It must be difficult for her, as he is obviously training her. If she wants her job then she has to learn to duck and dodge.

'There!' said the clerk. 'Give him this one. Ms Chargot has just booked out – or did she finally decide that she was the Countess of Edbury?' he asked the girl, running his fingers lightly across her back.

'She finally decided to book in as Ms Chargot,' she the girl, 'but the English often do that. They don't like the public to know who they are.' She shrugged his fingers away, feeling a little more secure with Hank standing in front of the desk watching.

Hank was dazed. Why would Casey call herself the Countess of Edbury? She must have bowed to family pressure and married Dursley. No! If she had, why was she here in Anchorage alone?

I swear that I will come back and marry you. He had to cling to her words. He must see her.

He had to force himself to stand still and smile ingratiatingly at the clerk. The man was his only hope of finding Casey.

'Chargot? Edbury?' he shouted. 'What does she look like?'

The clerk had noticed Casey and unsuccessfully tried to flirt with her as she paid her account. The memory of her rebuff still rankled. 'We are not allowed . . .'

'I'm her brother-in-law,' said Hank soothingly. He realized that if he antagonized this pimply faced man, with his hair greased back behind his ears, he would never be given a description of this 'Ms Chargot'.

'Then you know what she looks like,' retorted the young man triumphantly. 'You tell me.'

'Short, dark brown eyes, almost black thick straight hair.'

'That's her. Plus a great superstructure.'

As his hands described Casey's body in the air Hank clenched his fist, longing to drive it into the man's face.

'That's my sister-in-law. Have you any idea where the crazy woman was headed? She has left my brother,' he explained.

'She wasn't wearing any rings,' said the clerk.

'Then I'd better find her quickly and persuade her to go back to her kids, before she does anything stupid.'

'She wanted to make the BA flight to London.'

Hank looked at his watch. He would never make it back to the airport before they closed boarding for the flight.

'I need to get through to the departure lounge for British Airways,' he said. 'You obviously are the guy in charge here,' he flattered shamelessly. 'Could you?'

'Sure,' replied the check-in clerk, giving the young girl a squeeze as he moved her away from the computer and reached for the telephone. It seemed to ring for ever and Hank fought to stop himself from grabbing it.

'I do understand your regulations, but I have to speak to one of my guests before she boards the plane.' He watched the girl, certain that he was impressing her with his expertise. 'I am the manager of the Captain Cook Hotel. I must talk to Ms Chargot.' He held the phone from his ear and listened.

'I do understand, ma'am. Believe me I do. I run an hotel and the public drive me mad most of the time.'

Hank released his breath in an explosive hiss. He had not realized that he had been holding it.

'You will? Thank you, ma'am.' He held his hand over the receiver and turned to the girl. 'See. That's what you have to learn to do. Be firm.'

And lie, she thought to herself.

'Ms Chargot. The manager of the Captain Cook. I have your brother-in-law here.'

The girl at British Airways who had called Casey to the phone watched as a mask of total incomprehension pulled down tightly over her face. It was followed in quick succession by one of total disbelief and then one which lit her face with joy.

'Whatever she left behind or lost at the hotel has obviously been found,' said the one airline attendant to her friend. Her friend looked up for a brief moment from checking boarding passengers.

'With that grin she must have won the Irish Sweepstake,' she said and returned to her work.

'Thank you,' laughed Casey as she replaced the receiver. 'Could you tell me where I go to book a seat to Barrow?'

'Barrow!' the two women said incredulously. 'No one goes to Barrow.'

'Not unless they have to.'

'Do you know anything about the place?' asked the BA member who was still checking passes.

'Oh, yes. I love everything about it. It's a wonderful place.'

The airways staff looked at Casey in blank amazement. They had heard Barrow called many things, but never wonderful.

'Is she crazy or something?' asked the one, as they watched Casey swing down the aisle of uncomfortable plastic chairs and pick up her flight bag.

'Ma'am,' said the one girl, hastening down the aisle after Casey, 'you do realize that your baggage has already been checked onto this flight and we are due to leave in twenty minutes?'

'Keep the luggage,' laughed Casey, 'I don't want it.'

'You don't understand, ma'am. The flight will have to be delayed while your suitcase is located and taken off the plane. We cannot take off with unaccompanied baggage.'

Hank's words warm and deep still rang in her ears.

Your husband Hank loves you, Ticasuk. He wants to spend until eternity with you. He says I must tell you that he'll wait for you in Barrow until the sands of the desert blow over the Arctic.

It had taken Casey a few minutes to realize that for some reason Hank was phoning from the Captain Cook pretending to be her brother-in-law.

He did receive her message about the marriage and he did understand! her heart sang.

Once she heard his voice and understood that the message was from him, summer exploded in Alaska. Suddenly the grey skies were bold with sunlight. The much trampled airport carpet became a field of fuchsia Kamchatka rhododendrons and her feet danced through them as she ran to the door.

'Do you think we should call security?' said the one ground-staff girl.

'No. I've a feeling that the call from the Captain Cook manager was not because she left something, but someone.' She smiled at her assistant. 'She isn't crazy. She is just a woman in love.'